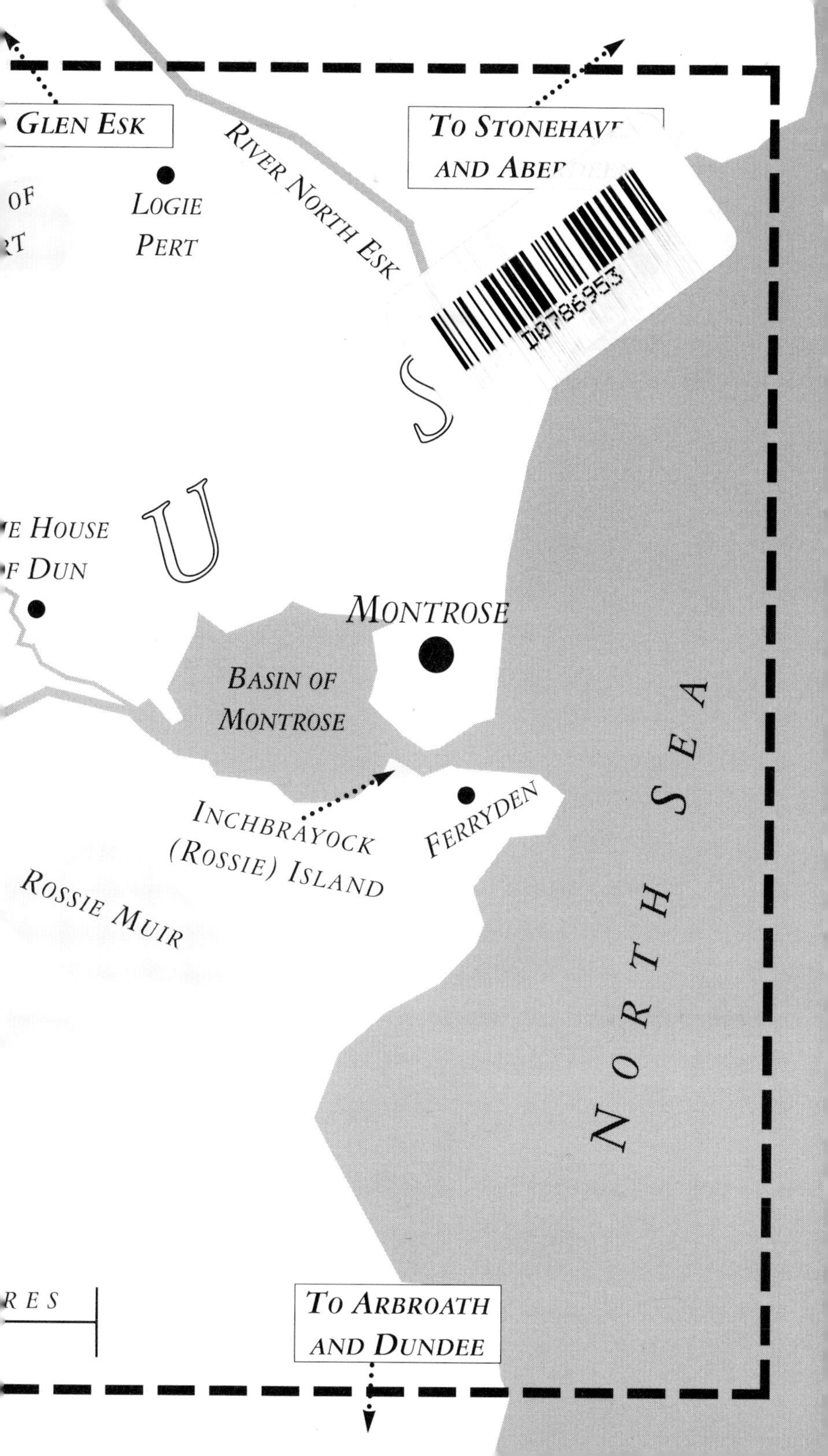

Glen Esk
To Stonehav
and Aber
River North Esk
of
rt
Logie
Pert
S
U
e House
f Dun
Montrose
Basin of
Montrose
Inchbrayock
(Rossie) Island
Ferryden
Rossie Muir
North Sea
res
To Arbroath
and Dundee

THE ASSOCIATION FOR SCOTTISH LITERARY STUDIES

NUMBER TWENTY-FOUR

FLEMINGTON

THE ASSOCIATION FOR SCOTTISH LITERARY STUDIES

The Association for Scottish Literary Studies aims to promote the study, teaching and writing of Scottish literature, and to further the study of the languages of Scotland.

To these ends, the ASLS publishes works of Scottish literature (of which this volume is an example), literary criticism in *Scottish Literary Journal*, scholarly studies of language in *Scottish Language*, and in-depth reviews of Scottish books in *SLJ Supplements*. And it publishes *New Writing Scotland*, an annual anthology of new poetry, drama and short fiction, in Scots, English and Gaelic, by Scottish writers.

All these publications are available as a single 'package', in return for an annual subscription. Enquiries should be sent to: ASLS, c/o Department of English, University of Aberdeen, Aberdeen AB9 2UB.

ANNUAL VOLUMES

1971 James Hogg, *The Three Perils of Man*, ed. Douglas Gifford.
1972 *The Poems of John Davidson*, vol. I, ed. Andrew Turnbull.
1973 *The Poems of John Davidson*, vol. II, ed. Andrew Turnbull.
1974 Allan Ramsay and Robert Fergusson, *Poems*, ed. Alexander M. Kinghorn and Alexander Law.
1975 John Galt, *The Member*, ed. Ian A. Gordon.
1976 William Drummond of Hawthornden, *Poems and Prose*, ed. Robert H. MacDonald.
1977 John G. Lockhart, *Peter's Letters to his Kinsfolk*, ed. William Ruddick.
1978 John Galt, *Selected Short Stories*, ed. Ian A. Gordon.
1979 Andrew Fletcher of Saltoun, *Selected Political Writings and Speeches*, ed. David Daiches.
1980 *Scott on Himself*, ed. David Hewitt.
1981 *The Party-Coloured Mind*, ed. David Reid.
1982 James Hogg, *Selected Stories and Sketches*, ed. Douglas S. Mack.
1983 Sir Thomas Urquhart of Cromarty, *The Jewel*, ed. R.D.S. Jack and R.J. Lyall.
1984 John Galt, *Ringan Gilhaize*, ed. Patricia J. Wilson.
1985 Margaret Oliphant, *Selected Short Stories of the Supernatural*, ed. Margaret K. Gray.
1986 James Hogg, *Selected Poems and Songs*, ed. David Groves.
1987 Hugh MacDiarmid, *A Drunk Man Looks at the Thistle*, ed. Kenneth Buthlay.
1988 *The Book of Sandy Stewart*, ed. Roger Leitch.
1989 *The Comic Poems of William Tennant*, ed. Alexander Scott and Maurice Lindsay.
1990 Thomas Hamilton, *The Youth and Manhood of Cyril Thornton*, ed. Maurice Lindsay.
1991 *The Complete Poems of Edwin Muir*, ed. Peter Butter.
1992 *The Tavern Sages: Selections from the 'Noctes Ambrosianae'*, ed. J.H. Alexander.
1993 *Gaelic Poetry in the Eighteenth Century*, ed. D.S. Thomson.
1994 Violet Jacob, *Flemington*, ed. Carol Anderson.

THE ASSOCIATION FOR SCOTTISH LITERARY STUDIES

GENERAL EDITOR – C.J.M. MACLACHLAN

Violet Jacob

Flemington

edited by

Carol Anderson

ABERDEEN

1994

First published in Great Britain, 1994
by The Association for Scottish Literary Studies
c/o Department of English
University of Aberdeen
Aberdeen AB9 2UB

ISBN 0 94887723 5

A catalogue record for this book is available from the British Library.

The Association for Scottish Literary Studies acknowledges subsidy from the Scottish Arts Council towards the publication of this volume.

Typeset by Roger Booth Associates, Newcastle upon Tyne
Printed by BPCAUP Aberdeen

Contents

Introduction

Violet Jacob's *Flemington*, first published in 1911, and long out of print, is a gripping historical novel; it is also a tragic drama, tightly written, poetic in its symbolic intensity, leavened by flashes of dry humour.

Flemington opens in 1727, giving us a glimpse of Archie Flemington's childhood. The larger part of the novel deals with Archie's young adulthood in the period around and following the Jacobite Rebellion of 1745, when Archie, ostensibly a humble portrait painter, is working as a spy for the Whig government. A commission to paint the portrait of a leading Jacobite leads Archie to a terrible inner conflict.

The plot components, commented a contemporary reviewer, are not fresh, but the treatment of them is:

> Many are the gallant romances which have been woven out of the grim tragedy of the rising under Bonnie Prince Charlie; the dilemma, too, of the secret service agent or, in the plain language of desperate men, the spy whose finer feelings are awakened by being trusted by those who were meant to be watched and betrayed by him is by no means original. These scenes and situations have been made familiar to us by great and favourite novelists alike, but even so, whosoever begins to read *Flemington* by Violet Jacob, in the expectation that he is about to traverse a well-worn path will surely be disappointed, and that very quickly… In truth, though the characters perform in an old theatre, there is nothing old about their play. There is an element of the unexpected and yet the inevitable running throughout the whole story which lifts it high above the ordinary level of the historical novel.[1]

Flemington, then, was well-received when it first appeared, and soon found some notable admirers. John Buchan wrote to Violet Jacob:

'My wife and I are overcome with admiration for it and we both agree that it is years since we read so satisfying a book. I think it the best Scots romance since *The Master of Ballantrae*. The art of it is outstanding'.[2] Violet Jacob also received letters from members of the public who were moved by her work. Madge Robertson of Paisley wrote to her about *Flemington* a few years after it first appeared: 'There were tears on my cheeks as I finished it – the emotion of it is so very genuine and it is expressed with so much restraint'.[3]

Violet Jacob was not a novice at the art of fiction. When *Flemington* appeared, its author was forty-four, and had already published four novels, and three volumes of short stories (two of these for children), as well as some volumes of poetry, both for adults and children. She had also written extensive diaries and letters while in India with her husband in the latter years of the nineteenth century.[4]

Flemington is therefore the work of a practised writer, although Violet Jacob's prose shows from the beginning considerable poise. Her first sustained work of fiction, *The Sheepstealers* (1902), is a vivid and entertaining work set against the so-called 'Rebecca riots' which took place in the 1830s and 1840s in south-west Wales.[5] The rioters in this protest movement, mainly the rural poor, outraged at having to pay tolls to travel along roads once free of passage, were led by men with blackened faces, dressed in women's clothing and claiming to act in the name of 'Rebecca'. Violet Jacob, who lived in the Anglo-Welsh borderlands for some years, and whose mother was Welsh, obviously had personal reasons for her concern with this episode in Welsh history, but the novel is interesting for its concern with social protest, and its exploration of character and psychology are striking too. Another early novel, *The Interloper* (1904), is a tautly-written, absorbing and moving romance, that also shows some engagement with themes Jacob would later develop. It has as its setting the scenes of her early life in Scotland, and it is to this world that *Flemington* returns.

A sense of place, and of the connections between people and place, seems to have been important to Violet Jacob, as they were to many writers in a period when 'regional' literature flourished, and not only in Scotland.[6] Before her marriage, Jacob had been Violet Kennedy-Erskine, belonging to a family that had held lands in the area of Dun, near Montrose, for many centuries. Violet herself lived furth of Scotland for much of her life, after her marriage to Arthur Jacob, an army officer of Irish origin, in 1894. Along with their son, Harry, who was born in 1895, they lived in, variously, India, Egypt, parts of England and the Anglo-Welsh borders. Violet Jacob's imagination, though, seems to have been most deeply stirred by the places she knew best. Chief among these was her 'Own Country'[7] – Scotland and especially Angus, which provides the landscapes of *Flemington*, and to which Violet Jacob returned for the last ten years of her life after Arthur's death. Unlike Willa Muir, for instance,[8] one of several writers who grew up in this area, Violet Jacob loved Montrose and the countryside around it. It would be wrong to limit her significance to the merely local; nevertheless, much of the matter of the novel draws on her experience and knowledge of this area.

Montrose was, in the eighteenth century, an important port, doing trade primarily with the Baltic countries, Holland, Flanders and France, all of which play a part either real or symbolic in Jacob's poetry and prose (her poetry, for instance, is full of references to the Baltic).[9] Like the north east of Scotland generally, Montrose and the area around the town were strongly Episcopalian and Jacobite; indeed, the 1715 Jacobite Rebellion ended here, when the defeated James (the 'Old Pretender') set sail for France from Montrose. Although traditionally a Presbyterian family (John Knox visited Dun), some of Jacob's ancestors, the Erskines of Dun, had played a part in the Jacobite movement. The House of Dun itself, the family home, now owned by the National Trust for Scotland and open to the public, was built to plans by William Adam, but original plans had been drawn up by 'Bobbing Johnnie' Erskine, the Earl of Mar, an ambiguous and changeable figure politically, and a leader of the 1715 rising. Another Erskine, David Erskine, Lord Dun (1670-1758), a judge in Edinburgh alongside such well-known figures as Lord Grange, was responsible for having the house built. He was an opponent of the Act of Union that linked Scotland and England politically in 1707, and a covert Jacobite.

Violet Jacob knew her family history well and wrote it up in *The Lairds of Dun*, which appeared in 1931; evidently, though, she knew the family stories long before this, for she puts them to good imaginative use in her novels, especially *Flemington*, just as Naomi Mitchison was to do in her later 'family history' novel, *The Bull Calves* (1947).[10] The character of David Logie of Balnillo in *Flemington* is obviously based on that of David Erskine, the Jacobite judge, and Dun is almost certainly the prototype for the House of Balnillo in the novel. The character of her real-life ancestor is described by John Ramsay of Ochtertyre, who knew the old judge, and comments that he was:

> ...accounted a man of honour and integrity, both on and off the bench. His piety and zeal for religion were conspicuous, even in times when all men prided themselves upon being decent in these matters. The pedantry of his talk and the starchiness of his manners made him the subject of ridicule among people who had neither his worth nor innocence of heart and life. He was likewise overrun with prejudice, which sometimes warps the judgment of able, well-intentioned men; but for that, one would be at a loss to account for his Toryism which approached very near to Jacobitism. How this could be reconciled to the oaths he had taken, is not the question here; but sometimes we see people wonderfully ingenious in grossly deceiving themselves.[11]

Violet Jacob herself remarks his apparently somewhat humourless, prim nature, but notes shrewdly: 'But under all this must have lain some sharp contradictory streak like the crack of light through a split panel which had made him the first Laird of Dun since the days of the Superintendant to venture to rebel against the overwhelming Presbyterian tradition that had held the family'.[12] There is here, perhaps, one clue as to the possible derivation of some of the numerous conflicts and dualities that haunt the novel.

The character of James Logie, David's brother in the novel, also seems inspired by the character of David Erskine's real-life elder brother, James (not younger as in the novel), a man of action, who fought all over Europe, not only with the Jacobites, but with Marlborough at Blenheim (and thus on different sides). Jacob had to use more imagination here than with David, for only a few bare facts are known of James, that suggest an adventurous, reckless character: he was always short of money and was disinherited by his family.[13] Portraits of both men hang in the House of Dun, and Violet Jacob must have grown up with these images. Perhaps it is from seeing these and other family portraits that she conceived also the idea of making Flemington himself a portrait painter; but then again, she herself was a gifted artist, and there is, arguably, much of Violet Jacob herself in the young protagonist of the novel.

Other elements in *Flemington* are based on historical events. The taking of the Government sloop in the novel, as Violet Jacob remarks in her prefatory note, is drawn from a true incident, which she recounts in *The Lairds of Dun*;[14] only a few details have been altered. The original vessel was called 'The Hazard', not 'The Venture', as it becomes in the novel, and although James Erskine was one of the protagonists along with a man called David Ferrier, the real-life James was at the time of the events actually seventy-four and not thirty-seven, illustrating how much imaginative transformation has taken place.

Violet Jacob denies that the novel is 'historical', 'none of the principal people in it being historic characters',[15] and it is true that she is not *primarily* interested in recreating past incidents or characters. Her *TLS* reviewer commented that *Flemington* is 'in fact little concerned with history, save as the background to the action'. In this sense she is unlike novelists such as Galt or Scott, who revelled, amongst other things, in the minutiae of the past for their own sake. But clearly the novel does make use of history, and it is perhaps Jacob's deep knowledge of, and involvement with, places, events and people that lends the novel some of its emotional power and air of veracity.

Yet if *Flemington* draws on the Scottish past, it is equally rooted in literature. Among the most important influences is that of Walter Scott, whose poetic works still line the shelves at the House of Dun. Several of the characters in Jacob's novels echo figures from Scott's fiction. A character called 'Mad Moll' in *The History of Aythan Waring* (1908), for example, recalls Madge Wildfire from *The Heart of Midlothian*, a novel which may also have fed into *The Sheepstealers*.

Grannie Stirk in *The Interloper* seems to draw on Scott's vigorous older peasant women characters, and the strong aristocratic women in Jacob's fiction are reminiscent of Scott too, though more sympathetically drawn. In *Flemington* itself, Skirling Wattie, the main speaker of Scots in the novel, whose lyrics form a significant part of the text, and whose sweet singing voice has in it 'the whole distinctive spirit of the national poetry of Scotland' (p.127), is a debased version of Scott's folk characters such as Wandering Willie in *Redgauntlet* and Edie Ochiltree in *The Antiquary*.[16] As in *Waverley*, the young protagonist gives the novel its title, and Flemington himself recalls Edward Waverley in certain respects:

> The youth and apparent frankness of Waverley stood in strong contrast to the shades of suspicion which darkened around him, and he had a sort of naivete and openness of demeanour that seemed to belong to one unhackneyed in the ways of intrigue, and which pleaded highly in his favour.[17]

Besides such local similarities, there are broad resemblances. Like Scott – and after him, Stevenson, another writer whose influence can be discerned in her work – Jacob takes a period in Scottish history in which warring factions clash, and the central conflict of the novel generates themes both specifically national (as Douglas Gifford, for instance, argues)[18] and also more general. The opening section of *Flemington* illustrates the way in which events and characters are rooted in, and formed by, the past, and the novel goes on to develop these themes and to show how the personal history of individuals is inseparable from larger events.

Focussed on two families, *Flemington* is based on a central structural opposition: that between Whig and Jacobite, opposing political and religious factions. On each side there is deeply-held conviction, indeed, dogmatism. Madam Flemington, one of the most ruthless characters in the novel, whose personal name, Christian, seems ironic, tells her grandson, 'I will have no half-measures as I have no half-sentiments' (p.80), and even more chillingly, when Archie protests that he cannot betray James Logie, 'We have to do with principles, not men' (p.80). Even James, a more sympathetic character, is nevertheless limited in vision; he has a 'generous and rather bigoted heart. For him, there were only two kinds of men, those who were for the Stuarts and those who were not' (p.60).

Thus, like Scott and Stevenson before her, Jacob explores such themes as the nature of loyalty, the effects of rigid devotion to political ends, and the allied concepts of treachery and betrayal. Madam Flemington has felt betrayed in the past at St Germain, and she in turn accuses Archie of betraying the Whig cause and herself. James, who is to feel betrayed by Archie too, has a stern view: 'when God calls us all to judgment, there will be no mercy for treachery' (p.65).

In the society of *Flemington*, it would seem, there is no room for humane compromise; and because of this, members of both the opposed families, which are themselves internally divided by differences of age and personality, face a series of dilemmas. *Flemington* explores the moral options for characters – and for readers – in a world where corruption co-exists with bigotry to destructive ends.

Between the warring factions, Archie, essentially principled but flexible, is caught. Like Scott's Edward Waverley, Jacob's hero comes from a politically divided background, his own parents being Jacobite; but unlike Waverley he is far from 'passive', and desperately embroiled in the situation. Although of firm Whig convictions like his grandmother, he can see beyond politics to common humanity and finds himself in an intolerable situation when required to betray James Logie, for the men are drawn to one another like brothers (p.67, p.73); the appalling alternative is to cut himself off from his grandmother.

Jacob explores the problems of choice elsewhere in her fiction: a difficult conflict is faced by Cecilia Raeburn in *The Interloper*, for instance, but the issues are more seriously developed here than in Jacob's earlier, lighter novel, with its more conventional 'happy ending', and the outcome of inflexible devotion to political ends and to moral stances is tragically illustrated. The boyish Archie has much in common with Stevenson's David Balfour, who faces a corrupt society and says near the end of *Catriona* 'till the end of time young folk (who are not yet used with the duplicity of life and men) will struggle as I did, and make heroical resolves… and the course of events will push them upon one side'.[19]

It should be noted, of course, that while Archie is by comparison with others in the novel a humane figure, he is in some ways an unlikely 'hero'; he not only belongs to the 'unromantic', unpopular Whig side, he is not straightforwardly 'in the right'. He is a government spy who sets out to betray a man offering him generous hospitality. Yet the reader is likely to be caught up in Archie's dilemma, and moved by it. Although the novel is related in the third person, the use of point of view establishes our sympathy for Archie; we share his perspective at key moments in the action, such as during the tense scenes at 'The Happy Land', and in the following chapter. With his 'feminine' refinement (p.37) he is vulnerable in a brutish society, although he appeals, paradoxically, to the soldier James (who has little time for 'this womanish trade' of painting, p.34), and to his betrayer, Skirling Wattie. Both, like the reader, respond to Archie's 'sensuous joy in the world, his love of life and its hazards and energies' (p.54), thus suggesting the problematic issues involved in forming judgments.

As in an earlier fictional tradition, appearance is shown to be no true guide to value in this morally treacherous universe. Of Archie, we read that 'his looks were the only really unreliable part of him' (p.83). James, too, is not altogether what he appears; he has a 'crooked mouth' (p.13), but he is an honest speaker, and his memories of the past, directly related by him, are touching for the reader as well as Archie. What is more, this man of war with his 'look of virility' (p.13) nevertheless reveals vulnerability 'like the defencelessness of a child looking upon the dark' (p.62). Strangely emblematic of many of the key concerns in the novel is the yellow dog. Outwardly the colour of cowardice, the ugly cur is nevertheless both brave and loyal.

Skirling Wattie, on the other hand, is described at one point as having a 'jovial face' (p.95), and yet, as the novel reveals, he is, at the same time, corrupt and unreliable. But then again, like other characters, Skirling Wattie is a complex figure. He may betray

Archie, but he fights for survival in a cruel world, and it is difficult not to respect his tenacious love of life and his spirit. David Balnillo, pompous and self-interested, both Jacobite and judge, treads the moral borderlands and survives where others more courageous are destroyed, but he is not, in the last analysis, evil.

Among the more challenging figures in the novel, Christian Flemington is a particularly interesting creation. Manipulative and in many ways destructive – her fan tellingly bears a picture of a bullfight (p.159), and she brings war into her personal relationships (p.79) – she is at the same time a passionate and spirited woman: like other Scottish women writers such as Margaret Oliphant before her, and Willa Muir later, Violet Jacob created some very powerful female characters.[20] Christian Flemington seems all the more remarkable when seen beside such weak men as the judge, or the minister in the opening scene, to whom she seems dangerously sexual and 'foreign'. Yet she is an isolated figure, one of the few female characters in the novel, and the reader may feel some pity for her errors, too, at the awful moment when she faces Cumberland and understands Archie's sure fate, especially when, after her exit the 'Butcher' cruelly remarks, 'Damn me, but I hate old women! They should have their tongues cut out' (p.225). His words suggest the nature of a society that despises women as well as 'feminine' qualities.

While Christian and other characters may not attract our fullest sympathy, the shifting perspective of the narrative voice, illuminating their experience and setting their attitudes in the context of this place and time, suggests they are not wholly to be condemned. In fact, with the exception of the Duke of Cumberland, there is no character one could describe as wholly bad or unsympathetic.

Flemington, then, sets out to undermine moral rigidity, and present a more complex vision than is held by many of the characters within its pages. Avoiding the 'moral certainties' of Scottish 'kailyard' fiction,[21] this novel offers a challenge to its readers, too; refusing to elicit clear or simple judgments, it implies that tolerance and compassion are qualities to be prized over all.

Morally challenging, this early twentieth century novel is, somewhat like Stevenson's fiction a little earlier, also both intensely realist and powerfully symbolic in its effects. Jacob presents Scotland at a deeply difficult period in its history. As James Logie tells Archie: 'I know how hard life can be and how anxious, nowadays. There is so much loss and trouble – God knows what may happen to this tormented country' (p.59). The troubled nature of the land and times is suggested in various ways. The name of the brothel, 'The Happy Land', is ironic, especially in the face of Jacob's descriptions of Scotland after Culloden.[22] Skirling Wattie, too, ironically seeming 'like the sovereign of some jovial and misgoverned kingdom' (p.88), may symbolically suggest the truncated and enfeebled state of Scottish culture, and its corruption; his soul is dark, his vanity about his singing 'the one piece of romance belonging to him; it hung over his muddy soul as a weaving of honeysuckle may hang over a dank pond' (p.148).

The 'muddy', barren nature of Scotland is suggested in the landscape, which is metaphorically suggestive throughout:

> [Archie] sat down on the scrubby waste land by a broom-bush, whose dry, burst pods hung like tattered black flags in the brush of green; their acrid smell was coming out as the sun mounted higher. Below him the marshy ground ran out to meet the water; and eastward the uncovered mud and wet sand, bared by the tide ebbing beyond Montrose, stretched along its shores to the town. (p.57)

The 'tattered black flags' seem to prefigure war; and the sea imagery that permeates the novel is disturbing. Archie is 'Adrift' (Chapter 10), a solitary figure in a sea of troubles (see p.124); the North Sea is 'a formless void in the night' (p.97), and James, on Inchbrayock, thinks how its only dwellers now are the dead

> ...those who were lying under his feet – seamen, for the most part, and fisher-folk, who had known the fury of the North Sea that was now beginning to crawl in and to surround them in their little township with its insidious arms, encircling in death the bodies that had escaped it in life. (p.109)

The people in this death-touched land are described as being like animals, emphasising the struggle for survival and, at times, the savagery of human nature. Logie's eyes 'shone in the dim room like the eyes of some animal watching in a cave' (p.47), Balnillo 'threw out his chest like a pouter pigeon' (p.163), Captain Hall is like a rabbit (p.99), Skirling Wattie a wild boar (p.126), Christian a cat (p.214). Some of these similes and metaphors are sustained and developed, such as the comparison of Archie with a dog; Christian Flemington 'had smiled at his devotion to her as she would have smiled with gratified comprehension at the fidelity of a favourite dog'(p.80). Archie 'was like a stray dog in a market place' (p.110); later, Lord Balnillo is like a dog in relation to Christian (p.177).

Many scenes take place in the darkness that is a creeping force 'drawing itself like an insidious net' (p.204), but light gleams through from time to time: 'the sun heaved up from beyond the bar' (p.110), so that the novel takes place 'In Darkness and in Light' (the title given to Chapter 6). There are flashes of brilliant colour: the crimson of tulips in Holland (p.64), the jewels that dangle from Christian Flemington's ears, 'the ruby earrings which shot blood-red sparks around her when she moved'(p.159), the 'rowan tree, whose berries were already beginning to colour for autumn' (p.204), and the 'red and gold' of the gean trees (p.21) on the Balnillo estate, which ' glowed carmine and orange, touches of quickening fire shot through the interstices of their branches' (p.55). It is a very visual book, a novel about a painter written with the eye of a painter.

The autumn scenes and colours and other seasonal references contribute to the creation of mood as well as the development of themes. Archie himself is associated, in James's mind, with Spring (p.39), but even the 'Prologue', set in the spring of Archie's life, takes place in autumn: Archie watches Mr Duthie depart 'between the yellowing leaves of the tree which autumn was turning into the clear-tinted ghost of itself' (p.10). Much of the action is set in a landscape of fallen leaves (p.25) and October light (p.54), and the 'Epilogue' closes with a sad autumnal scene. The chapter 'Winter' foreshadows the poem by Edwin Muir, 'Scotland's Winter',[23] that links that season with the times.

Flemington is not all dark: the narrative is compelling, with the qualities of a good adventure story, and there is a strain of wry humour, present in the narrative voice and suggested through the handling of David, for instance, and of Skirling Wattie and Christian Flemington. But unlike some of the many historical romances which appeared in this period, *Flemington* also has claims to be called a genuinely tragic novel.[24] Interesting, as its early *TLS* reviewer noted, for its sharp and effective depiction of character,[25] it works within a tight framework: events and characters move with seeming inevitability towards their fated ends.

The key figure is a young man with some of the characteristic qualities of the young Romantic hero. Archie is sensitive and artistic with a 'roving imagination' (p.16), one of those 'who live their lives with every nerve and fibre' (p.75), and pay the price for it. Like Archie Weir in *Weir of Hermiston*, Archie Flemington is a young idealist (see p.55, for instance), and like his namesake he has a Rousseauist perception of nature and of the essential goodness of creation; he longs to 'cast his body down upon the light-pervaded earth' (p.55), and to 'fling his soul' upwards into the sun. The reference to the sun here is significant later, as is the depiction of Archie's soul as a bird (p.55).

The choices and pressures that build up around Archie are finely explored; from the beginning when the roots of the tragedy are exposed, to the bitter end, the forces that drive individual personalities interact relentlessly with circumstance. Jacob was compared in her own time to Hardy,[26] and like him she alludes throughout the novel to the work of 'Fate': 'To most people who are haunted by a particular dread, Fate plays one of the tricks she loves so much. She is an expert boxer…' (p.181); but the references to 'Chance' and 'luck' leave the ultimate question – how much is really 'predestined'? – an open one.

The question of whether Archie's fate is a just one is, I think, more conclusively answered. There is little sense that justice has been done. Archie's death seems a tragic waste, and the reader's sense of injustice is heightened by the proximity of the scene in which Madam Flemington has her interview with Cumberland. The man's brutal inhumanity is in sharp contrast with the condemned youth's compassion and moral seriousness.

Tragic irony is omnipresent. It is ironic that Skirling Wattie should so misunderstand Archie's nature. It is ironic that Christian could have saved him in ways she did not understand. It is ironic that Archie is finally executed by one of the few men of honour, Callander, 'steadfast' (p.186) like the yellow cur, comparable to Archie himself in his integrity, yet 'the most repressed person' (p.184) Archie had met, inflexible in his devotion to duty. Although Archie understands and forgives, the reader may feel frustration.

There is some relief, however. Archie is, at least, released from an intolerable situation. The image, at his death, is of a solitary bird: 'this one was going into the sunrise' (p.232), recalling the scene when Archie longed for union with nature, with the sun; his bird-soul has finally been set free. His end in this way can be seen as modestly Christian, cathartic and affirmative. There is even, quite early on in the novel, an unusually explicit hint at an austere yet 'positive' view of suffering, foreshadowing later events:

> He did not think, any more than any of us think, that perhaps when we come to lie on our death-beds we shall know that, of all the privileges of the life behind us, the greatest has been the privilege of having suffered and fought. (p.94)

With his death the tormented Archie is released from suffering, and from the prison of the mere human flesh, having indeed 'suffered and fought', and the sunrise is a sign of hope for the future.

Nevertheless, the novel is shot through with events that reverberate long after they are over. This tragedy ends not with a death, but with those left behind. Early on in the novel, James remarks that 'the old beech tree by the stables wants a limb' (p.13), and this image recurs at the end, when we see him, alone in a dark autumnal room in Holland, with, outside, 'the jealous shadows of the beech-tree's mutilated arms' (p.233). James, in lonely exile, has returned to the scenes of his early love – and loss. It is significant that James has rescued the yellow dog, but the dead, mutilated beggar's bonnet is a reminder of what has gone before. We have been told 'love and loss are things that lay their shadows everywhere, and Madam Flemington had lost much' (p.149), and the sense of loss that has been frequently evoked is stronger here at the end than ever. We may remember James' words to Archie much earlier: 'We outlive trouble in time, Flemington; we outlive it, though we cannot outlive memory. We outlast it – that is a better word.' (p.67)

James has told Archie that fighting can be, for some soldiers like himself, a means of escaping private pain; James himself at one time turned to war 'for consolation as a man may turn to his religion' (p.62). By the end war surely offers little consolation; certainly, we have seen Archie's honourable sacrifice, and the compassionate gestures of James and Callander; but the way in which personal and public destruction and pain are interwoven is all the clearer.

Jacob's novel recreates the past in ways that seem, with hindsight, uncannily relevant not only to her own time, but her own life. *Flemington* was published in 1911: in Scotland it was the year of the big Glasgow Exhibition, when nationalism was on the agenda, a time of political uncertainty and growing industrial unrest. Above all, though, this was the period of build-up to war. Jacob's powerful images of wasteland and warfare, and of private grief, anticipate the outbreak of World War I in 1914 a mere three years after the publication of *Flemington.*

There is a grim irony in this, for Jacob's moving depiction of the young artist Archie Flemington surely owes much to her knowledge of, and love for, her own son, Harry Jacob, who died at the age of twenty in 1916, at the Battle of the Somme, five years after the novel appeared. This was the great, real tragedy of Violet Jacob's life, and according to Susan Tweedsmuir who knew her, it was a blow from which she never recovered:

> Violet Jacob had one son, whom she loved with all the depth of an imaginative and passionate nature. When he was killed in the 1914 War a spring in her broke. She never wrote a long book again, and turned to writing poems in the Scottish vernacular.[27]

NOTES

1 *Times Literary Supplement*, Thursday 30 November 1911, p.493, unsigned review of *Flemington* titled ' A Tale of the '45'.
2 Letter, 31 December 1911; National Library of Scotland, Acc. 6686.
3 Letter, 7 September 1915; National Library of Scotland, Acc. 6686.
4 Published for the first time in 1990. For full details of this and other publications by Violet Jacob see Bibliography.
5 This historical episode is documented by David J.V. Jones in *Rebecca's Children: A study of rural society, crime and protest* (Oxford: Clarendon Press, 1990).
6 Peter Keating discusses the 'new self-conscious regionalism' in British literature in chapter 6 of *The Haunted Study: A Social History of the English Novel 1875-1914* (first published London: Martin Secker and Warburg, 1989; reference here to the paperback edition, London: Fontana, 1991). He gives a good account of the Scottish dimension.
7 A reference to Jacob's volume of short stories, *Tales of my Own Country*, of 1922.
8 Muir's fictional town Calderwick is based on her experience of Montrose. In *Imagined Corners* (1935), for instance, the town is not flatteringly presented.
9 Jacob's poems include, for example, 'Baltic Street' (the name of a real street in Montrose) and 'The Wind Frae the Baltic', in the collection *Bonnie Joann*.
10 *The Bull Calves* (London: Jonathan Cape, 1947; reprinted Glasgow: Richard Drew Publishing, 1985).
11 *Scotland and Scotsmen in the Eighteenth Century* from the MSS of John Ramsay Esq of Ochtertyre, edited by Alexander Allardyce (Edinburgh and London: William Blackwood and Sons, 1888), 2 vols; vol 1, p.85.
12 *The Lairds of Dun* (London: John Murray, 1931), p.234.
13 For more details see *The Lairds of Dun*, pp.232-3.
14 *The Lairds of Dun*, pp.249-57.
15 'Author's Note to *Flemington*', p.xix. Further references to the novel are to this edition, and will be given in brackets after quotations.
16 Scott himself wrote in an Advertisement to the 1829 edition of *The Antiquary*: 'Many of the old Scottish mendicants were by no means to be confounded with the utterly degraded class of beings who now practise that wandering trade'.
17 Walter Scott, *Waverley* (first published 1814; see the recent edition ed. Claire Lamont (Oxford: Oxford University Press, 1986) Vol. II, Ch IX, p.161).
18 See 'Myth, Parody and Dissociation: Scottish Fiction 1814-1914', in Douglas Gifford (ed.) *The History of Scottish Literature, vol 3: Nineteenth Century* (Aberdeen: Aberdeen University Press, 1988), pp.217-259, esp. pp.242-3.
19 *Catriona*, first published 1893; see the recent edition ed. Emma Letley (Oxford: Oxford University Press, 1986), Ch. XX, p.382.

20 Among Oliphant's many novels, mention might be made of *Miss Marjoriebanks* (Edinburgh and London: Blackwood & Sons; reprinted London: Virago, 1988), *Hester* (London: Macmillan, 1883; reprinted London: Virago, 1984), *Kirsteen* (London: Macmillan, 1890; reprinted London: Dent, 1984). See also Willa Muir's *Mrs Ritchie* (London: Secker, 1933).

21 See Keating, *The Haunted Study*, p.338.

22 Apparently this was a real place, as suggested in *Montrose Standard and Mearns Register* 26 January 1912, p.12. See also note to p.42 of this novel.

23 First published in *One Foot in Eden* (London: Faber and Faber, 1956).

24 Keating (pp.348-56) discusses the great quantity and variety of historical fiction by British writers in this period, arguing that it was ultimately largely a 'literary disappointment' (p.351).

25 The reviewer comments that 'there is abundance of incident, vividly told, in the book, but the main interest is that of character. Every one who has any part to play, whether essential or supernumerary, is drawn with a sure and skilful hand, most powerful when it is most restrained; every one is given a definite individuality and no one is in any degree commonplace…' (p.493).

26 For instance by contemporary reviewers of *The Sheepstealers* (1902), as in *The Spectator*, 13 September 1902, p.368: 'it is free from the crushing pessimism of the novels of Mr Hardy, the writer to whom on his best and most poetic side Miss Jacob is more closely related'.

27 *The Lilac and the Rose* (London: Gerald Duckworth, 1952) p.55.

Bibliography of Books by Violet Jacob

The Baillie MacPhee (a poem), by Walter Douglas Campbell and Violet Kennedy-Erskine (William Blackwood, Edinburgh and London, 1888), with illustrations by Violet Kennedy-Erskine.

The Sheepstealers (William Heinemann, London, 1902), a novel.

The Infant Moralist (verses), by Lady Helena Carnegie and Mrs Arthur Jacob (R. Grant and Son, Edinburgh, and R.Brimley Johnson, London, 1903), with illustrations by Mrs Arthur Jacob.

The Interloper (William Heinemann, London, 1904), a novel.

The Golden Heart and Other Fairy Stories (William Heinemann, London, 1904).

Verses (William Heinemann, London, 1905).

Irresolute Catherine (John Murray, London, 1908), a novel.

The History of Aythan Waring (William Heinemann, London, 1908), a novel.

Stories Told by the Miller (John Murray, London, 1909), for children.

The Fortune Hunters and Other Stories (John Murray, London, 1910).

Flemington (John Murray, London, 1911), a novel.

Songs of Angus (John Murray, London, 1915), poems.

More Songs of Angus and Others (Country Life / George Newnes, London, and Charles Scribner's Sons, New York, 1918), poems.

Bonnie Joann and Other Poems (John Murray, London, 1921).

Tales of My Own Country (John Murray, London, 1922).
Two New Poems: 'Rohallion' and 'The Little Dragon' (Porpoise Press, Edinburgh, 1924).
The Northern Lights and Other Poems (John Murray, London, 1927).
The Good Child's Year Book (Foulis, London, 1928), with illustrations by Violet Jacob.
The Lairds of Dun (John Murray, London, 1931), a history of the Erskine family.
The Scottish Poems of Violet Jacob (Oliver & Boyd, Edinburgh, 1944).
The Lum Hat and Other Stories: Last Tales of Violet Jacob, edited by Ronald Garden (Aberdeen University Press, Aberdeen, 1982).
Diaries and Letters from India 1895-1900, edited by Carol Anderson (Canongate, Edinburgh, 1990).
'Thievie', a story from ***Tales of My Own Country*** is reprinted in Moira Burgess (ed.) *The Other Voice: Scottish Women's Writing Since 1808* (Polygon, Edinburgh, 1987), pp.123-39.

There are also stories and articles in journals.

Acknowledgements

I would like to thank the following people in particular for their interest, encouragement and generous help of various kinds: Margaret and Nigel Anderson, Sarah Bing, Tom Crawford, Joris and Jo Duytschaever, Emma Letley, Christopher MacLachlan, Douglas Mack and Isobel Murray. In addition I appreciate the assistance of librarians at Montrose Public Library and the National Library of Scotland, and representatives of the National Trust at the House of Dun. I am also indebted to numerous friends and colleagues in Scotland, especially in Glasgow, and in Italy and Japan, for their support.

Note on the Text

The text is based on the first edition of 1911. The following corrections have been made in the present edition.

Minor Corrections (page references are to the present edition, with references to the 1911 edition in brackets)

p.16, l.23: 'carrin' amended to 'carrying' (p.22).
p.22, l.17: space inserted between 'when you' (p.32).
p.41, l.31: word 'incessantly' split between lines has been restored (p.60).
p.76, l.11: 'over' corrected to 'ever' (p.111).
p.108, l.2: 'shiping' corrected to 'shipping' (p.157).
p.119, l.9: 'grapling' corrected to 'grappling' (p.175).
p.129, 2 lines from end: 'ruuning' corrected to 'running' (p.190).
p.155, l.20: 'seearch' corrected to 'search' (p.229).
p.190, l.7: 'began' corrected to 'begun' (p.280).
p.195, l.2: correct spacing inserted between 'which the' (p.288).
p.197, ll.2–3: correct spacing inserted between 'him the' (p.291).
p.200, 3 lines from end: word 'in' inserted (p.297).
p.209, 5 lines from end: letter 'c' lowered to usual level of case (p.311).
p.230, l.21: question mark removed (p.342).

Other Amendments

The Scots Brigade: pages 13, 63, 66, 71; 237 (note to p.13) (1911 edition pages 17–18, 92, 97, 104). This was printed both with and without an apostrophe. In the present edition the apostrophe has been dropped.

Bergen-op-Zoom: pages 66, 71, 109; 241 (note to p.66) (1911 edition pages 96, 104, 161). This name was spelled both with and without hyphens in the 1911 edition. In the present edition the hyphens have been used in all instances (following the majority of cases in Jacob's text, and given that both forms appear to be in modern usage).

p.14 (1911 edition, p.19). ' "He is cursin', ma lord" ': the 1911 edition omits 'is' (or 's). It is not clear whether this is deliberate or not.

p.87 (1991 edition, p.128) East Neuk. The 1911 edition spells the second word 'Nauk', a variant on the more usual 'Neuk', perhaps to suggest a particular pronunciation.

p.221 (1911 edition, p.327) Canongate. The 1911 edition uses the spelling 'Cannongate'.

Author's note

THIS book has no claim to be considered an historical novel, none of the principal people in it being historic characters; but the taking of the ship, as also the manner of its accomplishment, is true.

V.J.

BOOK I

CHAPTER I

PROLOGUE

Mr. Duthie walked up the hill with the gurgle of the burn he had just crossed purring in his ears. The road was narrow and muddy, and the house of Ardguys, for which he was making, stood a little way in front of him, looking across the dip threaded by the water. The tall white walls, discoloured by damp and crowned by their steep roof, glimmered through the ash-trees on the bank at his right hand. There was something distasteful to the reverend man's decent mind in this homely approach to the mansion inhabited by the lady he was on his way to visit, and he found the remoteness of this byway among the grazing lands of Angus oppressive.

The Kilpie burn, travelling to the river Isla, farther west, had pushed its way through the undulations of pasture that gave this particular tract, lying north of the Sidlaws, a definite character; and the formation of the land seemed to suggest that some vast ground-swell had taken place in the earth, to be arrested, suddenly, in its heaving, for all time. Thus it was that a stranger, wandering about, might come unwarily upon little outlying farms and cottages hidden in the trough of these terrestrial waves, and find himself, when he least awaited it, with his feet on a level with some humble roof, snug in a fold of the braes. It was in one of the largest of these miniature valleys that the house of Ardguys stood, with the Kilpie burn running at the bottom of its sloping garden.

Mr. Duthie was not a stranger, but he did not admire the unexpected; he disliked the approach to Ardguys, for his sense of suitability was great; indeed, it was its greatness which was driving him on his present errand. He had no gifts except the quality of decency, which is a gift like any other; and he was apt, in the company of Madam Flemington, to whose presence he was now hastening, to be made aware of the great inconvenience of his shortcomings, and the still greater inconvenience of his advantage. He crossed the piece of uneven turf dividing the house from the road, and ascended the short flight of stone steps, a spare, black figure in a three-cornered hat, to knock with no uncertain hand upon the door. His one great quality was staying him up.

Like the rest of his compeers in the first half of the seventeen hundreds, Mr. Duthie wore garments of rusty blue or grey during the week, but for this occasion he had plunged his ungainly arms and legs into the black which he generally kept for the Sabbath-day, though the change gave him little distinction. He was a homely and very uncultured person; and while the approaching middle of the century was bringing a marked improvement to country ministers as a class, mentally and socially, he had stood still.

He was ushered into a small panelled room in which he waited alone for a few minutes, his hat on his knee. Then there was a movement outside, and a lady came in, whose appearance let loose upon him all those devils of apprehension which had hovered about him as he made his way from his manse to the chair on which he sat. He rose, stricken yet resolute, with the cold forlorn courage which is the bravest thing in the world.

As Madam Flemington entered, she took possession of the room to the exclusion of everything else, and the minister felt as if he had no right to exist. Her eyes, meeting his, reflected the idea.

Christian Flemington carried with her that atmosphere which enwraps a woman who has been much courted by men, and, though she was just over forty-two, and a grandmother, the most inexperienced observer might know how strongly the fires of life were burning in her still. An experienced one would be led to think of all kinds of disturbing subjects by her mere presence; intrigue, love, power—a thousand abstract yet stirring things, far, far remote from the weather-beaten house which was the incongruous shell of this compelling personality. Dignity was hers in an almost appalling degree, but it was a quality unlike the vulgar conception of it; a dignity which could be all things besides distant; unscrupulous in its uses, at times rather brutal, outspoken, even jovial; born of absolute fearlessness, and conveying the certainty that its possessor would speak and act as she chose, because she regarded encroachment as impossible and had the power of cutting the bridge between herself and humanity at will. That power was hers to use and to abuse, and she was accustomed to do both. In speech she could have a plain coarseness which has nothing to do with vulgarity, and is, indeed, scarcely compatible with it; a coarseness which is disappearing from the world in company with many better and worse things.

She moved slowly, for she was a large woman and had never been an active one; but the bold and steady brilliance of her eyes, which the years had not faded, suggested swift and sudden action in a way that was disconcerting. She had the short, straight nose common to feline types, and time, which had spared her eyes, was duplicating her chin. Her eyebrows, even and black, accentuated the heavy silver of her abundant unpowdered hair, which had turned colour early, and an immense ruby hung from each of her tiny ears in a setting of small diamonds. Mr. Duthie, who noticed none of these things particularly, was, nevertheless, crushed by their general combination.

It was nine years before this story opens that Christian Flemington had left France to take up her abode on the small estate of Ardguys, which had been left to her by a distant relation. Whilst still almost a child, she had married a man much older than herself, and her whole wedded life had been spent at the Court of James II of England at St. Germain, whither her husband, a Scottish gentleman of good birth in the exiled King's suite, had followed his master, remaining after his death in attendance upon his widow, Mary Beatrice of Modena.

Flemington did not long survive the King. He left his wife with one son, who, on reaching manhood, estranged himself from his mother by an undesirable marriage; indeed, it was immediately after this latter event that Christian quitted her post at Court, retiring to Rouen, where she lived until the possession of Ardguys, which she inherited a few months later, gave her a home of her own.

Different stories were afloat concerning her departure. Many people said that she had gambled away the greater part of her small fortune and was forced to retrench in some quiet place; others, that she had quarrelled with, and been dismissed by, Mary Beatrice. Others, again, declared that she had been paid too much attention by the young Chevalier de St. George and had found it discreet to take herself out of his way; but the believers in this last theory were laughed to scorn; not because the world saw anything strange in the Chevalier's alleged infatuation, but because it was quite sure that Christian Flemington would have acted very differently in the circumstances. But no one could be certain of the truth: the one certain thing was that she was gone and that since her retreat to Rouen she had openly professed Whig sympathies. She had been settled at Ardguys, where she kept her political leanings strictly to herself, for some little time, when news came that smallpox had carried off her son and his undesirable wife, and, as a consequence, their little boy was sent home to the care of his Whig grandmother, much against the will of those Jacobites at the Court of St. Germain who were still interested in the family. But as nobody's objection was strong enough to affect his pocket, the child departed.

'Madam' Flemington, as she was called by her few neighbours, was in correspondence with none of her old friends, and none of these had the least idea what she felt about her loss or about the prospect of the child's arrival. She was his natural guardian, and, though so many shook their heads at the notion of his being brought up by a rank Whig, no one was prepared to relieve her of her responsibility. Only Mary Beatrice, mindful of the elder Flemington's faithful services to James, granted a small pension for the boy's upbringing from her meagre private purse; but as this was refused by Christian, the matter ended. And now, in the year of grace 1727, young Archie Flemington was a boy of eight, and the living cause of the Rev. William Duthie's present predicament.

Madam Flemington and the minister sat opposite to each other, silent. He was evidently trying to make a beginning of his business, but his companion was not in a mood to help him. He was a person who wearied her, and she hated red hair; besides which, she was an

Episcopalian and out of sympathy with himself and his community. She found him common and limited, and at the present moment, intrusive.

"It's sma' pleasure I have in coming to Ardguys the day," he began, and then stopped, because her eyes paralyzed his tongue.

"You are no flatterer," said she.

But the contempt in her voice braced him.

"Indeed, that I am not, madam," he replied; "neither shall it be said of me that I gang back from my duty. Nane shall assail nor make a mock of the Kirk while I am its minister."

"Who has made a mock of the Kirk, my good man?"

"Airchie."

The vision of her eight-year-old grandson going forth, like a young David, to war against the Presbyterian stronghold, brought back Madam Flemington's good-humour.

"Ye may smile, madam," said Duthie, plunged deeper into the vernacular by agitation, "ay, ye may lauch. But it ill beseems the grey hair on yer pow."

Irony always pleased her and she laughed outright, showing her strong white teeth. It was not only Archie and the Kirk that amused her, but the whimsical turn of her own fate which had made her hear such an argument from a man. It was not thus that men had approached her in the old days.

"You are no flatterer, Mr. Duthie, as I said before."

He looked at her with uncomprehending eyes.

A shout, as of a boy playing outside, came through the window, and a bunch of cattle upon the slope cantered by with their tails in the air. Evidently somebody was chasing them.

"Let me hear about Archie," said the lady, recalled to the main point by the sight.

"Madam, I would wish that ye could step west to the manse wi' me and see the evil abomination at my gate. It would gar ye blush."

"I am obliged to you, sir. I had not thought to be put to that necessity by one of your cloth."

"Madam——"

"Go on, Mr. Duthie. I can blush without going to the manse for it."

"An evil image has been set up upon my gate," he continued, raising his voice as though to cry down her levity, "an idolatrous picture. I think shame that the weans ganging by to the schule should see it. But I rejoice that there's mony o' them doesna' ken wha it is."

"Fie, Mr. Duthie! Is it Venus?"

"It has idolatrous garments," continued he, with the loud monotony of one shouting against a tempest, "and a muckle crown on its head——"

"Then it is not Venus," observed she. "Venus goes stripped."

"It is the Pope of Rome," went on Mr. Duthie; "I kent him when I saw the gaudy claes o' him and the heathen vanities on his pow. I kent it was himsel'! And it was written at the foot o' him, forbye that. Ay, madam, there was writing too. There was a muckle bag out frae his mou' wi' wicked words on it! 'Come awa' to Babylon wi' me, Mr. Duthie.' I gar'd the beadle run for water and a clout, for I could not thole that sic' a thing should be seen."

"And you left the Pope?" said Madam Flemington.

"I did," replied the minister. "I would wish to let ye see to whatlike misuse Airchie has put his talents."

"And how do you know it was Archie's work?"

"There's naebody hereabouts but Airchie could have made sic' a thing. The beadle tell't me that he saw him sitting ahint the whins wi' his box of paint as he gae'd down the manse road, and syne when he came back the image was there."

As he finished his sentence the door opened and a small figure was arrested on the threshold by the sight of him. The little boy paused, disconcerted and staring, and a faint colour rose in his olive face. Then his glum look changed to a smile in which roguery, misgiving, and an intense malicious joy were blended. He looked from one to the other.

"Archie, come in and make your reverence to Mr. Duthie," said Madam Flemington, who had all at once relapsed into punctiliousness.

Archie obeyed. His skin and his dark eyes hinted at his mother's French blood, but his bow made it a certainty.

The minister offered no acknowledgment.

If Archie had any doubt about the reason of Mr. Duthie's visit, it did not last long. The minister was not a very stern man in daily life, but now the Pope and Madam Flemington between them had goaded him off his normal peaceable path, and his expression bade the little boy prepare for the inevitable. Archie reflected that his grandmother was a disciplinarian, and his mind went to a cupboard in the attics where she kept a cane. But the strain of childish philosophy which ran through his volatile nature was of a practical kind, and it reminded him that he must pay for his pleasures, and that sometimes they were worth the expense. Even in the grip of Nemesis he was not altogether sorry that he had drawn that picture.

Madam Flemington said nothing, and Mr. Duthie beckoned to him to come nearer.

"Child," said he, "you have put an affront upon the whole o' the folk of this parish. You have raised up an image to be a scandal to the passers-by. You have set up a notorious thing in our midst, and you have caused words to issue from its mouth that the very kirk-officer, when he dichted it out wi' his clout, thought shame to look upon. I have jaloused it right to complain to your grandmother and to warn her, that she may check you before you bring disgrace and dismay upon her and upon her house."

Archie's eyes had grown rounder as he listened, for the pomp of the high-sounding words impressed him with a sense of importance, and he was rather astonished to find that any deed of his own could produce such an effect. He contemplated the minister with a curious detachment that belonged to himself. Then he turned to look at his grandmother, and, though her face betrayed no encouragement, the subtle smile he had worn when he stood at the door appeared for a moment upon his lips.

Mr. Duthie saw it. Madam Flemington had not urged one word in defence of the culprit, but, rightly or wrongly, he scented lack of sympathy with his errand. He turned upon her.

"I charge you—nay, I demand it of you," he exclaimed—"that you root out the evil in yon bairn's nature! Tak' awa' from him the foolish toy that he has put to sic' a vile use. I will require of you——"

"Sir," said Madam Flemington, rising, "I have need of nobody to teach me how to correct my grandson. I am obliged to you for your visit, but I will not detain you longer."

And almost before he realized what had happened, Mr. Duthie found himself once more upon the stone steps of Ardguys.

Archie and his grandmother were left together in the panelled room. Perhaps the boy's hopes were raised by the abrupt departure of his accuser. He glanced tentatively at her.

"You will not take away my box?" he inquired.

"No."

"Mr. Duthie has a face like this," he said airily, drawing his small features into a really brilliant imitation of the minister.

The answer was hardly what he expected.

"Go up to the cupboard and fetch me the cane," said Madam Flemington.

It was a short time later when Archie, rather sore, but still comforted by his philosophy, sat among the boughs of a tree farther up the hill. It was a favourite spot of his, for he could look down through the light foliage over the roof of Ardguys and the Kilpie burn to the rough road ascending beyond them. The figure of the retreating Mr. Duthie had almost reached the top and was about to be lost in the whin-patch across the strath. The little boy's eyes followed him between the yellowing leaves of the tree which autumn was turning into the clear-tinted ghost of itself. He had not escaped justice, and the marks of tears were on his face; but they were not rancorous tears, whose traces live in the heart long after the outward sign of their fall has gone. They were tears forced from him by passing stress, and their sources were shallow. Madam Flemington could deal out punishment thoroughly, but she was not one of those who burn its raw wounds with sour words, and her grandson had not that woeful sense of estrangement which is the lot of many children when disciplined by those they love. Archie adored his grandmother, and the gap of years between them was bridged for him by his instinctive and deep admiration. She was no companion to him, but she was a deity, and he had never dreamed of investing her with those dull attributes which the young will tack on to those who are much their seniors, whether they possess them or not. Mr. Duthie, who had just reached middle life, seemed a much older person to Archie.

He felt in his pocket for the dilapidated box which held his chief treasures—those dirty lumps of paint with which he could do such surprising things. No, there was not very much black left, and he must contrive to get some more, for the adornment of the other manse gatepost was in his mind. He would need a great deal of black, because this time his subject would be the devil; and there should be the same—or very nearly the same—invitation to the minister.

CHAPTER II

JETSAM

EIGHTEEN years after the last vestige of Archie's handiwork had vanished under the beadle's 'clout' two gentlemen were sitting in the library of a square stone mansion at the eastern end of the county of Angus. It was evening, and they had drawn their chairs up to a fireplace in which the flames danced between great hobs of polished brass, shooting the light from their thrusting tongues into a lofty room with drawn curtains and shelves of leather-bound books. Though the shutters were closed, the two men could hear, in the pauses of talk, a continuous distant roaring, which was the sound of surf breaking upon the bar outside the harbour of Montrose, three miles away. A small mahogany table with glasses and a decanter stood at Lord Balnillo's elbow, and he looked across at his brother James (whose life, as a soldier, had kept him much in foreign countries until the previous year) with an expression of mingled good-will and patronage.

David Logie was one of the many Scottish gentlemen of good birth who had made the law his profession, and he had just retired from the Edinburgh bench, on which, as Lord Balnillo, he had sat for hard upon a quarter of a century. His face was fresh-coloured and healthy, and, though he had not put on so much flesh as a man of sedentary ways who has reached the age of sixty-two might expect to carry, his main reason for retiring had been the long journeys on horseback over frightful roads, which a judge's duties forced him to take. Another reason was his estate of Balnillo, which was far enough from Edinburgh to make personal attention to it impossible. His wife Margaret, whose portrait hung in the dining-room, had done all the business for many years; but Margaret was dead, and perhaps David, who had been a devoted husband, felt the need of something besides the law to fill up his life. He was a lonely man, for he had no children, and his brother James, who sat opposite to him, was his junior by twenty-five years. For one who had attained to his position, he was slow and curiously dependent on others; there was a turn about the lines of his countenance which suggested fretfulness, and his eyes, which had looked upon so many criminals, could be anxious. He was a considerate landlord, and, in spite of the times in which he lived and the bottle at his elbow, a person of very sober habits.

James Logie, who had started his career in Lord Orkney's regiment of foot with the Scots Brigade in Holland, had the same fresh complexion as his brother and the same dark blue eyes; but they were eyes that had a different expression, and that seemed to see one thing at a time. He was a squarer, shorter man than Lord Balnillo, quicker of speech and movement. His mouth was a little crooked, for the centre of his lower lip did not come exactly under the centre of the upper one, and this slight mistake on the part of Nature had given his face a not unpleasant look of virility. Most people who passed James gave him a second glance. Both men were carefully dressed and wore fine cambric cravats and laced coats; and the shoes of the judge, which rested on the fender, were adorned by gilt buckles.

They had been silent for some time, as people are who have come to the same conclusion and find that there is no more to say, and in the quietness the heavy undercurrent of sound from the coast seemed to grow more insistent.

"The bar is very loud to-night, Jamie," said Lord Balnillo. "I doubt but there's bad weather coming, and I am loth to lose more trees."

"I see that the old beech by the stables wants a limb," observed the other. "That's the only change about the place that I notice."

"There'll be more yet," said the judge.

"You've grown weather-wise since you left Edinburgh, David."

"I had other matters to think upon there," answered Balnillo, with some pomp.

James smiled faintly, making the little twist in his lip more apparent.

"Come out to the steps and look at the night," said he, snatching, like most restless men, at the chance of movement.

They went out through the hall. James unbarred the front door and the two stood at the top of the flight of stone steps.

The entrance to Balnillo House faced northward, and a wet wind from the east, slight still, but rising, struck upon their right cheeks and carried the heavy muffled booming in through the trees. Balnillo looked frowning at their tops, which had begun to sway; but his brother's attention was fixed upon a man's figure, which was emerging from the darkness of the grass park in front of them.

"Who is that?" cried the judge, as the footsteps grew audible.

"It's a coach at the ford, ma lord—a muckle coach that's couped i' the water! Wully an' Tam an' Andrew Robieson are seekin' to ca' it oot, but it's fast, ma lord——"

"Is there anyone in it?" interrupted James.

"Ay, there was. But he's oot noo."

"Where is he?"

"He'll na' get forward the night," continued the man. "Ane of the horse is lame. He is cursin', ma lord, an' nae wonder—he can curse bonnie! Robieson's got his wee laddie wi' him, and he gar'd the loonie put his hands to his lugs. He's an elder, ye see."

The judge turned to his brother. It was not the first time that the ford in the Den of Balnillo had been the scene of disaster, for there was an unlucky hole in it, and the state of the roads made storm-bound and bedraggled visitors common apparitions in the lives of country gentlemen.

"If ye'll come wi' me, ma lord, ye'll hear him," said the labourer, to whom the profane victim of the ford was evidently an object of admiration.

Balnillo looked down at his silk stockings and buckled shoes.

"I should be telling the lasses to get a bed ready," he remarked hurriedly, as he re-entered the house.

James was already throwing his leg across the fence, though it was scarcely the cursing which attracted him, for he had heard oaths to suit every taste in his time. He hurried across the grass after the labourer. The night was not very dark, and they made straight for the ford.

The Den of Balnillo ran from north to south, not a quarter of a mile from the house, and the long chain of miry hollows and cart-ruts which did duty for a high road from Perth to Aberdeen plunged through it at the point for which the men were heading. It was a steep ravine filled with trees and stones, through which the Balnillo burn flowed and fell and scrambled at different levels on its way to join the Basin of Montrose, as the great estuary of the river Esk was called. The ford lay just above one of the falls by which the water leaped downwards, and the dense darkness of the surrounding trees made it difficult for Captain Logie to see what was happening as he descended into the black well of the Den. He could distinguish a confusion of objects by the light of the lantern which his brother's men had brought and set upon a stone; the ford itself reflected nothing, for it was churned up into a sea of mud, in which, as Logie approached, the outline of a good-sized carriage, lying upon its side, became visible.

"Yonder's the captain coming," said a voice.

Someone lifted the lantern, and he found himself confronted by a tall young man, whose features he could not see, but who was, no doubt, the expert in language.

"Sir," he said, "I fear you have had a bad accident. I am come from Lord Balnillo to find out what he can do for you."

"His lordship is mighty good," replied the young man, "and if he could force this mud-hole—which, I am told, belongs to him—to yield up my conveyance, I should be his servant for life."

There was a charm and softness in his voice which nullified the brisk impertinence of his words.

"I hope you are not hurt," said James.

"Not at all, sir. Providence has spared me. But He has had no mercy upon one of my poor nags, which has broken its knees, nor on my stock-in-trade, which is in the water. I am a travelling painter," he added quickly, "and had best introduce myself. My name is Archibald Flemington."

The stranger had a difficulty in pronouncing his *r*'s; he spoke them like a Frenchman, with a purring roll.

The other was rather taken aback. Painters in those days had not the standing in society that they have now, but the voice and manner were unmistakably those of a man of breeding. Even his freedom was not the upstart licence of one trying to assert himself, but the easy expression of a roving imagination.

"I should introduce myself too," said Logie. "I am Captain James Logie, Lord Balnillo's brother. But we must rescue your—your—baggage. Where is your postilion?"

Flemington held up the lantern again, and its rays fell upon a man holding the two horses which were standing together under a tree. James went towards them.

"Poor beast," said he, as he saw the knees of one of the pair, "he would be better in a stall. Andrew Robieson, send your boy to the house for a light, and then you can guide them to the stables."

Meanwhile, the two other men had almost succeeded in getting the carriage once more upon its wheels, and with the help of Flemington and Logie, it was soon righted. They decided to leave it where it was for the night, and it was dragged a little aside, lest it should prove a pitfall to any chance traveller who might pass before morning.

The two gentlemen went towards the house together, and the men followed, carrying Flemington's possessions and the great square package containing his canvases.

When they entered the Library Lord Balnillo was standing with his back to the fire.

"I have brought Mr. Flemington, brother," said Logie, "his coach has come to grief in the Den."

Archie stopped short, and putting his heels together, made much the same bow as he had made to Mr. Duthie eighteen years before.

A feeling of admiration went through James as the warm light of the house revealed the person of his companion, and something in the shrewd wrinkles round his brother's unimpressive eyes irritated him. He felt a vivid interest in the stranger, and the cautious old man's demeanour seemed to have raised the atmosphere of a lawcourt round himself. He was surveying the newcomer with stiff urbanity.

But Archie made small account of it.

"Sir," said Balnillo, with condescension, "if you will oblige me by making yourself at home until you can continue your road, I shall take myself for fortunate."

"My lord," replied Archie, "if you knew how like heaven this house appears to me after the bottomless pit in your den, you might take yourself for the Almighty."

Balnillo gave his guest a critical look, and was met by all the soft darkness of a pair of liquid brown eyes which drooped at the outer corners, and were set under thick brows following their downward lines. Gentleness, inquiry, appeal, were in them, and a quality which the judge, like other observers, could not define—a quality that sat far, far back from the surface. In spite of the eyes, there was no suggestion of weakness in the slight young man, and his long chin gave his olive face gravity. Speech and looks corresponded so little in him that Balnillo was bewildered; but he was a hospitable man, and he moved aside to make room for Archie on the hearth. The latter was a sorry sight, as far as mud went; for his coat was splashed, and his legs, from the knee down, were of the colour of clay. He held his hands out to the blaze, stretching his fingers as a cat stretches her claws under a caressing touch.

"Sit down and put your feet to the fire," said the judge, drawing forward one of the large armchairs, "and James, do you call for another glass. When did you dine, Mr. Flemington?"

"I did not dine at all, my lord. I was anxious to push on to Montrose, and I pushed on to destruction instead."

He looked up with such a whimsical smile at his own mishaps that Balnillo found his mouth widening in sympathy.

"I will go and tell them to make some food ready," said the captain, in answer to a sign from his brother.

Balnillo stood contemplating the young man; the lines round his eyes were relaxing a little; he was fundamentally inquisitive, and his companion matched no type he had ever seen. He was a little disturbed by his assurance, yet his instinct of patronage was tickled by the situation.

"I am infinitely grateful to you," said Archie. "I know all the inns in Brechin, and am very sensible how much better I am likely to dine here than there. You are too kind."

"Then you know these parts?"

"My home is at the other end of the county—at Ardguys."

"I am familiar with the name," said Balnillo, "but until lately, I have been so much in Edinburgh that I am out of touch with other places. I am not even aware to whom it belongs."

"It is a little property, my lord—nothing but a few fields and a battered old house. But it belongs to my grandmother Flemington, who brought me up. She lives very quietly."

"Indeed, indeed," said the judge, his mind making a cast for a clue as a hound does for the scent.

He was not successful.

"I had not taken you for a Scot," he said, after a moment.

"I have been told that," said Archie; "and that reminds me that it would be proper to tell your lordship what I am. I am a painter, and at this moment your hall is full of my paraphernalia."

Lord Balnillo did not usually show his feelings, but the look which, in spite of himself, flitted across his face, sent a gleam of entertainment through Archie.

"You are surprised," he observed, sighing. "But when a man has to mend his fortunes he must mend them with what tools he can. Nor am I ashamed of my trade."

"There is no need, Mr. Flemington," replied the other, with the measured benevolence he had sometimes used upon the bench; "what you tell me does you honour—much honour, sir."

"Then you did not take me for a painter any more than for a Scot?" said Archie, smiling at his host.

"I did not, sir," said the judge shortly. He was not accustomed to be questioned by his witnesses and he had the uncomfortable sensation of being impelled, in spite of a certain prejudice, to think moderately well of his guest.

"I have heard tell of your lordship very often," said the latter, suddenly, "and I know very well into what good hands I have fallen. I could wish that all the world was more like yourself."

He turned his head and stared wistfully at the coals.

Balnillo could not make out whether this young fellow's assurance or his humility was the real key-note to the man. But he liked some of his sentiments well enough. Archie wore his own hair, and the old man noticed how silky and fine the brown waves were in the firelight. They were so near his hand as their owner leaned forward that he could almost have stroked them.

"Are you going further than Montrose?" he inquired.

"I had hoped to cozen a little employment out of Aberdeen," replied Flemington; "but it is a mere speculation. I have a gallery of the most attractive canvases with me—women, divines, children, magistrates, provosts—all headless and all waiting to see what faces chance and I may fit on to their necks. I have one lady—an angel, I assure you, my lord!—a vision of green silk and white roses—shoulders like satin—the hands of Venus!"

Balnillo was further bewildered. He knew little about the arts and nothing about artists. He had looked at many a contemporary portrait without suspecting that the original had chosen, as sitters often did, an agreeable ready-made figure from a selection brought forward by a painter, on which to display his or her countenance. It was a custom which saved the trouble of many sittings and rectified much of the niggardliness or over-generosity of Nature.

"I puzzle you, I see," added Archie, laughing, "and no doubt the hair of Van Dyck would stand on end at some of our modern doings. But I am not Van Dyck, unhappily, and in common with some others I do half my business before my sitters ever see me. A client has only to choose a suitable body for his own head, and I can tell you that many are thankful to have the opportunity."

"I had no idea that portraits were done like that," said Lord Balnillo; "I never heard of such an arrangement before."

"But you do not think it wrong, I hope?" exclaimed Flemington, the gaiety dying out of his face. "There is no fraud about it! It is not as if a man deceived his sitter."

The half-petulant distress in his voice struck Balnillo, and almost touched him; there was something so simple and confiding in it.

"It might have entertained your lordship to see them," continued

Archie ruefully. "I should have liked to show you the strange company I travel with."

"So you shall, Mr. Flemington," said the old man. "It would entertain me very greatly. I only fear that the lady with the white roses may enslave me," he added, with rather obvious jocosity.

"Indeed, now is the time for that," replied Archie, his face lighting up again, "for I hope she may soon wear the head of some fat town councillor's wife of Aberdeen."

As he spoke Captain Logie returned with the news that dinner was prepared.

"I have been out to the stable to see what we could do for your horses," said he.

"Thank you a thousand times, sir," exclaimed Archie.

Lord Balnillo watched his brother as he led the painter to the door.

"I think I will come, too, and sit with Mr. Flemington while he eats," he said, after a moment's hesitation.

A couple of hours later Archie found himself in a comfortable bedroom. His valise had been soaked in the ford, and a nightshirt of Lord Balnillo's was warming at the fire. When he had put it on he went and looked at himself in an old-fashioned mirror which hung on the wall. He was a good deal taller than the judge, but it was not his own image that caused the indescribable expression on his face.

CHAPTER III

A COACH-AND-FIVE

ARCHIE sat in his bedroom at a table. The window was open, for it was a soft October afternoon, and he looked out meditatively at the prospect before him.

The wind that had howled in the night had spent itself towards morning, and by midday the tormented sky had cleared and the curtain of cloud rolled away, leaving a mellow sun smiling over the Basin of Montrose. He had never been within some miles of Balnillo, and the aspect of this piece of the country being new to him, his painter's eye rested appreciatively on what he saw.

Two avenues of ancient trees ran southward, one on either side of the house, and a succession of grass fields sloped away before him between these bands of timber to the tidal estuary, where the water lay blue and quiet with the ribbon of the South Esk winding into it from the west. Beyond it the low hills with their gentle rise touched the horizon; nearer at hand the beeches and gean-trees, so dear to Lord Balnillo's heart, were red and gold. Here and there, where the gale had thinned the leaves, the bareness of stem and bough let in glimpses of the distant purple which was the veil of the farther atmosphere. To the east, shut out from his sight by all this wood, was the town of Montrose, set, with its pointed steeple, like the blue silhouette of some Dutch town, between the Basin and the North Sea.

A pen was in Flemington's hand, and the very long letter he had just written was before him.

"BALNILLO HOUSE.

MADAM, MY DEAR GRANDMOTHER,

I beg you to look upon the address at the head of this letter, and to judge whether fortune has favoured your devoted grandson.

I am *on the very spot*, and, what is more, seem like to remain there indefinitely. Could anything in this untoward world have fallen out better? Montrose is a bare three miles from where I sit, and I can betake myself there on business when necessary, while I live as secluded as I please; cheek by jowl with the very persons whose acquaintance I had laid so many plots to compass. My dear grandmother, could you but have seen me last night, when I lay down after my labours, tricked out in my worshipful host's nightshirt! Though the honest man is something of a fop in his attire, his arms are not so long as mine, and the fine ruffles on the sleeves did little more than adorn my elbows, which made me feel like a lady till I looked at my skirts. Then I felt more like a highlandman. But I am telling you only effects when you are wanting causes.

I changed horses at Brechin, having got so far in safety just after dark, and went on towards Montrose, with the wind rising and never a star to look comfort at me through the coach window. Though I knew we must be on the right road, I asked my way at every hovel we passed, and was much interested when I was told that I was at the edge of my Lord Balnillo's estate, and not far from his house.

The road soon afterwards took a plunge into the very vilest place I ever saw—a steep way scarcely fit for a cattle-road, between a mass of trees. I put out my head and heard the rushing of water. Oh, what a fine thing memory is! I remembered having heard of the Den of Balnillo and being told that it was near Balnillo house and I judged we must be there. Another minute and we were clattering among stones; the water was up to the axle and we rocked like a ship. One wheel was higher than the other, and we leaned over so that I could scarcely sit. Then I was inspired. I threw myself with all my weight against the side, and dragged so much of my cargo of canvases as I could lay hold of with me. There was a great splash and over we went. It was mighty hard work getting out, for the devil caused the door to stick fast, and I had to crawl through the window at that side of the coach which was turned to the sky, like a roof. I hope I may never be colder. We turned to and got the horses out and on to dry ground, and the postilion, a very frog for slime and mud, began to shout, which soon produced a couple of men with a lantern. I shouted too, and did my poor best in the way of oaths to give the affair all the colour of reality I could, and I believe I was successful. The noise brought more people about us, and with them my lord's brother, Captain Logie, hurrying to the rescue with a fellow who had run to the house with news of our trouble. The result was that we ended our night, the coach with a cracked axle and a hole in the panel, the postilion in the servants' hall with half a bottle of good Scots whisky inside him, the horses—one with a broken knee—in the stable, and myself, as I tell you, in his lordship's nightshirt.

I promise you that I thought myself happy when I got inside the mansion—a solemn block, with a grand manner of its own and Corinthian pillars in the dining-room. His lordship was on the hearthrug, as solemn as his house, but with a pinched, precise look which it has not got. He was no easy nut to crack, and it took me a little time to establish myself with him, but the good James, his brother, left us a little while alone, and I made all the way I could in his favour. I may have trouble with the old man, and, at any rate, must be always at my best with him, for he seems to me to be silly, virtuous and cunning all at once. He is vain, too, and suspicious, and has seen so many wicked people in his judicial career that I must not let him confound me with them. I could see that he had difficulty in making my occupation and appearance match to his satisfaction. He wears a mouse-coloured velvet coat, and is very nice in the details of his dress. I should like you to see him—not because he would amuse you, but because it would entertain me so completely to see you together.

James, his brother, is cut to a very different pattern. He is many years younger than his lordship—not a dozen years older than myself, I imagine—and he has spent much of his life with Lord Orkney's regiment in Holland. There is something mighty attractive in his face, though I cannot make out what it is. It is strange that, though he seems to be a much simpler person than the old man, I feel less able to describe him. I have had much talk with him this morning, and I don't know when I have liked anyone better.

And now comes the triumph of well-doing—the climax to which all this faithful record leads. I am to paint his lordship's portrait (in his Judge's robes), and am installed here definitely for that purpose! I shall be grateful if you will send me my chestnut-brown suit and a couple of fine shirts, also the silk stockings which are in the top shelf of my cupboard, and all you can lay hands on in the matter of cravats. My valise was soaked through and through, and, though the clothes I am wearing were dried in the night, I am rather short of good coats, for I expected to end in an inn at Montrose rather than in a gentleman's house. Though I am within reach of Ardguys, and might ride to fetch them in person, I do not want to be absent unnecessarily. Any *important* letters that I may send you will go by a hand I know of. I shall go shortly to Montrose by way of procuring myself some small necessity, and shall search for that hand. Its owner should not be difficult to recognize, by all accounts. And now, my dear grandmother, I shall write myself

Your dutiful and devoted grandson,

ARCHIBALD FLEMINGTON."

Archie sealed his letter, and then rose and leaned far out of the window. The sun still bathed the land, but it was getting low; the treetops were thrusting their heads into a light which had already left the grass-parks slanting away from the house. The latter part of his morning had been taken up by his host's slow inspection of his canvases, and he longed for a sight of his surroundings. He knew that the brothers had gone out together, and he took his hat and stood irresolute, with his letter in his hand, before a humble-looking little locked case, which he had himself rescued the night before from among his submerged belongings in the coach, hesitating whether he should commit the paper to it or keep it upon his own person. It seemed to be a matter for some consideration. Finally, he put it into his pocket and went out.

He set forth down one of the avenues, walking on a gorgeous carpet of fallen leaves, and came out on a road running east and west, evidently another connecting Brechin with Montrose. He smiled as he considered it, realizing that, had he taken it last night, he would have escaped the Den of Balnillo and many more desirable things at the same time.

As he stood looking up and down, he heard a liquid rush, and saw to his right a mill-dam glimmering through the trees, evidently the goal of the waters which had soused him so lately. He strolled towards it, attracted by the forest of stems and golden foliage reflected in the pool, and by the slide down which the stream poured into a field, to wind, like a little serpent, through the grass. Just where it disappeared stood a stone mill-house abutting on the highway, from which came the clacking of a wheel. The miller was at his door. Archie could see that he was watching something with interest, for the man stood out, a distinct white figure, on the steps running up from the road to the gaping doorway in the mill-wall.

Flemington was one of those blessed people for whom common sights do not glide by, a mere meaningless procession of alien things. Humanity's smallest actions had an interest for him, for he had that love of seeing effect follow cause, which is at once priceless and childish—priceless because anything that lifts from us the irritating burden of ourselves for so much as a moment is priceless; and childish because it is a survival of the years when all the universe was new. Priceless yet again, because it will often lead us down unexpected side-tracks of knowledge in a world in which knowledge is power.

He sat down on the low wall bounding the mill-field, for he was determined to know what the miller was staring at. Whatever it was, it was on the farther side of a cottage built just across the road from the mill.

He was suddenly conscious that a bare-footed little girl with tow-coloured hair had appeared from nowhere, and was standing beside him. She also was staring at the house by the mill, but with occasional furtive glances at himself. All at once the heavy drone of a bagpipe came towards them, then the shrill notes of the chanter began to meander up and down on the blare of sonorous sound like a light pattern running over a dark background. The little girl removed her eyes from the stranger and cut a caper with her bare feet, as though she would like to dance.

It was evident that the sounds had affected Flemington, too, but not in the same way. He made a sharp exclamation under his breath, and turned to the child.

"Who is that playing?" he cried, putting out his hand.

She jumped back and stood staring.

"Who is that playing?" he repeated.

She was still dumb, scrubbing one foot against her bare ankle after the manner of the shoeless when embarrassed.

Archie was exasperated. He rose, without further noticing the child, and hurried towards the mill. When he had reached the place where the stream dived through a stone arch under the road he found she was following him. He heard the pad, pad, of her naked soles in the mud.

All at once she was moved to answer his question.

"Yon's Skirlin' Wattie!" she yelled after him.

But he strode on, taking no notice; fortune was playing into his hand so wonderfully that he was ceasing to be surprised. In the little yard of the cottage he found a small crowd of children, two women, and the miller's man, collected round the strangest assortment of living creatures he had ever seen. The name 'Skirlin' Wattie' had conveyed something to him, and he was prepared for the extraordinary, but his breath was almost taken away by the oddness of what he saw.

In the middle of the group was a stout wooden box, which, mounted on very low wheels, was transformed into the likeness of a rough go-cart, and to this were yoked five dogs of differing breeds and sizes. A half-bred mastiff in the wheel of the team was taking advantage of the halt and lay dozing, his jowl on his paws, undisturbed by the blast of sound which poured over his head, whilst his companion, a large, smooth-haired yellow cur, stood alert with an almost proprietary interest in what was going on awake in his amber eyes. The couple of collies in front of them sniffed furtively at the bystanders, and the wire-haired terrier, which, as leader, was harnessed singly in advance of the lot, was sharing a bannock with a newly-breeched man-child, the sinister nature of whose squint almost made the dog's confidence seem misplaced.

The occupant of the cart was an elderly man, whom accident had deprived of the lower part of his legs, both of which had been amputated just below the knee. He had the head of Falstaff, the shoulders of Hercules, and lack of exercise had made his thighs and back bulge out over the sides of his carriage, even as the bag of his pipes bulged under his elbow. He was dressed in tartan breeches and doublet, and he wore a huge Kilmarnock bonnet with a red knob on the top. The lower half of his face was distended by his occupation, and at the appearance of Flemington by the gate, he turned on him, above the billows of crimson cheek and grizzled whisker, the boldest pair of eyes that the young man had ever met. He was a masterly piper, and as the tune stopped a murmur of applause went through the audience.

"Man, ye're the most mountaineous player in Scotland!" said the miller's man, who was a coiner of words.

"Aye, dod, am I!" replied the piper.

"Hae?" continued the miller's man, holding out an apple.

The beggar took it with that silent wag of the back of the head which seems peculiar to the east coast of Scotland, and dropped it into the cart.

Archie handed him a sixpence.

"Ye'll hae to gie us mair noo!" cried the squinting child, whose eyes had seen straight enough, and who seemed to have a keen sense of values.

"Aye, a sang this time," added its mother.

"Ye'll get a pucklie meal an' a bawbee gin' ye sing 'The Tod'," * chimed in an old woman, who had suddenly put her head out of the upper story of the cottage.

The beggar laid down his pipes and spat on earth. Then he opened his mouth and gave forth a voice whose volume, flexibility, and extreme sweetness seemed incredible, considering the being from whom it emanated.

---

*Fox

"There's a tod aye blinkin' when the nicht comes doon,
Blinkin' wi' his lang een, and keekin' round an' roun',
Creepin' by the farm-yaird when gloamin' is to fa',
And syne there'll be a chicken or a deuk awa'.
Aye, when the guidwife rises there's a deuk awa'!

"There's a lass sits greetin' ben the hoose at hame,
For when the guidwife's cankered she gie's her aye the blame,
And sair the lassie's sabbin', and fast the tears fa',
For the guidwife's tynt a bonnie hen, and it's awa'.
Aye, she's no sae easy dealt wi' when her gear's awa'!

"There's a lad aye roamin' when the day gets late,
A lang-leggit deevil wi' his hand upon the gate
And aye the guidwife cries to him to gar the toddie fa',
For she canna thole to let her chicks an' deuks awa'.
Aye, the muckle bubbly-jock himsel' is ca'ed awa'!

"The laddie saw the tod gae by, an' killed him wi' a stane,
And the bonnie lass wha grat sae sair she sits nae mair her lane
But the guidwife's no contented yet—her like ye never saw,
Cries she, 'This time it is the lass, an' she's awa'!'
Aye, yon laddie's waur nor ony tod, for Jean's awa'!"

Archie beat the top rail of the paling with so much enthusiasm that the yellow cur began to bark. The beggar quieted him with a storm of abuse.

The beldame disappeared from the window, and her steps could be heard descending the wooden stair of the cottage. She approached the cart with a handful of meal on a platter which Skirling Wattie tilted into an old leather bag that hung on his carriage.

"Whaur's the bawbee?" cried the squinting child.

A shout of laughter went up, led by Archie.

"He kens there's nae muckle weicht o' meal, and wha' should ken it better?" said the beggar, balancing the bag on his palm and winking at the miller's man.

The latter, who happened to be the child's unacknowledged parent, disappeared behind the house.

"One more song, and I will supply the bawbee," said Archie,

throwing another coin into the cart. Skirling Wattie sent a considering glance at his patron; though he might not understand refinement, he could recognize it; and much of his local success had come from his nice appraisement of audiences.

"I'll gie ye Logie Kirk," said he.

"O Logie Kirk, among the braes
I'm thinkin' o' the merry days
Afore I trod the weary ways
That led me far frae Logie.

"Fine do I mind when I was young,
Abune thy graves the mavis sung,
And ilka birdie had a tongue
To ca' me back to Logie.

"O Logie Kirk, tho' aye the same,
The burn sings ae remembered name,
There's ne'er a voice to cry 'Come hame
To bonnie Bess at Logie!'

"Far, far awa' the years decline
That took the lassie wha was mine
And laid her sleepin' lang, lang syne
Among the braes at Logie."

His voice, and the wonderful pathos of his phrasing, fascinated Archie, but as the last cadences fell from his mouth, the beggar snatched up the long switch with which he drove his team and began to roar.

"A'm awa'!" he shouted, making every wall and corner echo. "Open the gate an' let me through, ye misbegotten bairns o' Auld Nick! Stand back, ye clortie-faced weans, an' let me out! Round about an' up the road! Just round about an' up the road, a' tell ye!"

The last sentences were addressed to the dogs who were now all on their legs and mindful of the stick whirling in the air above them.

Archie could see that he was not included in the beggar's general address, but, being nearest to the gate, he swung it open and the whole equipage dashed through, the dogs guided with amazing dexterity between the posts by their master's switch. The rapid circle they described on the road as they were turned up the hill towards Brechin seemed likely to upset the cart, but the beggar leaned outwards so adroitly that none of the four wheels left the ground. As they went up the incline he took up his pipes, and leaving the team to its own guidance, tuned up and disappeared round the next bend in a blast of sound.

Flemington would have given a great deal to run after him, and could easily have overtaken the cart, for its pace was not very formidable. But the whole community, including the tow-headed little girl, was watching Skirling Wattie out of sight and speculating, he knew, upon his own identity. So he walked leisurely on till the road turned at the top of the hill, and he was rewarded at the other side of its bend by the sight of the beggar halting his team by a pond at which the dogs were drinking. He threw a look around and behind him; then, as no human creature was to be seen, he gave a loud whistle, holding up his arm, and began to run.

Skirling Wattie awaited him at the pond-side, and as Archie approached, he could almost feel his bold eyes searching him from top to toe. He stopped by the cart.

"My name is Flemington," said he.

"A've heard worse," replied the other calmly.

"And I have a description of you in my pocket," continued Archie. "Perhaps you would like to see it."

The beggar looked up at him from under his bushy eyebrows, with a smile of the most robust and genial effrontery that he had ever seen on a human face.

"A'd need to," said he.

Archie took a folded paper from his pocket.

"You see that signature," he said, putting his forefinger on it.

The other reached up to take the paper.

"No, no," said Flemington, "this never goes out of my hand."

"That's you!" exclaimed the beggar, with some admiration. "Put it back. A' ken it."

He unhooked his leather bag, which hung inside the cart on its front board. This Archie perceived to be made, apparently for additional strength, of two thicknesses of wood. Skirling Wattie slid the inner plank upwards, and the young man saw a couple of sealed letters hidden behind it, one of which was addressed to himself

"Tak' yon," said the beggar, as the sound of a horse's tread was heard not far off, "tak' it quick an' syne awa' ye gang! Mind ye, a gang ilka twa days frae Montrose to Brechin, an a'm aye skirlin' as a gang."

"And do you take this one and have it sent on from Brechin," said Archie hurriedly, handing him the letter he had written to Madam Flemington.

The other wagged the back of his head, and laid a finger against the rim of his bonnet.

Archie struck into the fields by the pond, and had time to drop down behind a whin-bush before an inoffensive-looking farmer went by on his way between the two towns.

The beggar continued his progress, singing to himself, and Flemington, who did not care to face the mill and the curious eyes of the tow-headed little girl again, took a line across country back to Balnillo.

He hated the tow-headed little girl.

CHAPTER IV

BUSINESS

EVENTS seemed to Flemington to be moving fast.

Lord Balnillo dined soon after five, and during the meal the young man tried to detach his mind from the contents of the letter lying in his pocket and to listen to his host's talk, which ran on the portrait to be begun next morning,

The judge had ordered his robes to be taken out and aired carefully, and a little room with a north aspect had been prepared for the first sitting. The details of Archie's trade had excited the household below stairs, and the servant who waited appeared to look upon him with the curious mixture of awe and contempt accorded to charlatans and to those connected with the arts. Only James seemed to remain outside the circle of interest, like a wayfarer who pauses to watch the progress of some wayside bargain with which he has no concern. Yet, though Archie's occupations did not move Logie, the young man felt intuitively that he was anything but a hostile presence.

"With your permission I shall go early to bed to-night," said Flemington to his host, as the three sat over their wine by the dining-room fire and the clock's hands pointed to eight.

"Fie!" said the judge; "you are a young man to be thinking of such things at this hour."

"My bones have not forgotten yesterday——" began Archie.

"And what would you do if you had to ride the circuit, sir?" exclaimed Balnillo, looking sideways at him like a sly old crow. "Man, James, you and I have had other things to consider besides our bones! And here's Mr. Flemington, who might be your son and my grandson, havering about his bed!"

Archie laughed aloud.

"Captain Logie would need to have married young for that!" he cried. "And I cannot picture your lordship as anybody's grandfather."

"Come, Jamie, how old are you?" inquired his brother in a tone that had a light touch of gratification.

"I lose count nowadays," said James, sighing. "I must be near upon eight-and-thirty, I suppose. Life's a long business, after all."

"Yours has scarcely been long enough to have begotten me, unless you had done so at twelve years old," observed Archie.

"When I had to ride the circuit," began Balnillo, setting down his glass and joining his hands across his waistcoat, "I had many a time to stick fast in worse places than the Den yonder—ay, and to leave my horse where he was and get forward on my clerk's nag. I've been forced to sit the bench in another man's wig because my own had rolled in the water in my luggage, and was a plaster of dirt—maybe never fit to be seen again upon a Lord of Session's head."

Logie smiled with his crooked mouth. He remembered, though he did not mention, the vernacular rhyme written on that occasion by some impudent member of the junior bar:

"Auld David Balnillo gangs wantin' his wig,
And he's seekin' the loan of anither as big.
A modest request, an' there's naething agin' it,
But he'd better hae soucht a new head to put in it!"

"It was only last year," continued his brother, "that I gave up the saddle and the bench together."

"That was more from choice than from necessity—at least, so I have heard," said Archie.

"You heard that, Mr. Flemington?"

"My lord, do you think that we obscure country-folk know nothing? or that reputations don't fly farther than Edinburgh? The truth is that we of the younger generation are not made of the same stuff. That is what my grandmother tells me so often—so often that, from force of habit, I don't listen. But I have begun to believe it at last."

"She is a wise woman," said Balnillo.

"She has been a mighty attractive one," observed Archie meditatively; "at least, so she was thought at St. Germain."

"At St. Germain?" exclaimed the judge.

"My grandfather died in exile with his master, and my father too," replied Flemington quietly.

There was a silence, and then James Logie opened his mouth to speak, but Archie had risen.

"Let me go, Lord Balnillo," he said. "The truth is, my work needs a steady hand, and I mean to have it when I begin your portrait to-morrow."

When he had gone James took the empty seat by his brother.

"His grandfather with the King, and he following this womanish trade!" he exclaimed.

"I should like to have asked him more about his father," said Balnillo; "but——"

"He did not wish to speak; I could see that," said James. "I like the fellow, David, in spite of his paint-pots. I would like him much if I had time to like anything."

"I have been asking myself: am I a fool to be keeping him here?" said the other. "Was I right to let a strange man into the house at such a time? I am relieved, James. He is on the right side."

"He keeps his ears open, brother."

"He seems to know all about *me*," observed Balnillo. "He's a fine lad, Jamie—a lad of fine taste; and his free tongue hasn't interfered with his good sense. And I am relieved, as I said."

Logie smiled again. The affection he had for his brother was of that solid quality which accepts a character in the lump, and loves it for its best parts. David's little vanities and vacillations, his meticulous love of small things, were plain enough to the soldier, and he knew well that the bench and the bar alike had found plenty to make merry over in Balnillo. He had all the loyal feeling which the Scot of his time bore to the head of his family, and, as his sentiments towards him sprang from the heart rather than from the brain, it is possible that he undervalued the sudden fits of shrewdness which would attack his brother as headache or ague might attack another man. The fact that David's colleagues had never made this mistake was responsible for a career the success of which surprised many who knew the judge by hearsay alone. Drink, detail and indecision have probably ruined more characters than any three other influences in the world; but the two latter had not quite succeeded with Lord Balnillo, and the former had passed him over.

"I wonder——" said James—"I wonder is it a good chance that has sent him here? Could we make anything of him, David?"

"Whisht, James!" said the other, turning his face away quickly. "You go too fast. And, mind you, if a man has only one notion in his head, there are times when his skull is scarce thick enough to stand between his thoughts and the world."

"That is true. But I doubt Flemington's mind is too much taken up with his pictures to think what is in other men's heads."

"Maybe," replied Balnillo; "but we'll know that better a few days hence. I am not sorry he has gone to bed."

"I will give him an hour to get between his blankets," said Logie, drawing out his watch. "That should make him safe."

Meanwhile Flemington had reached his room and was pulling his great package of spare canvases from under his sombre four-poster. He undid the straps which secured them and drew from between two of them a long dark riding-coat, thrusting back the bundle into its place. He changed his clothes and threw those he had taken off on a chair. Then he took the little locked box he had saved so carefully from the catastrophe of the previous night, and, standing on the bed, he laid it on the top of the tester, which was near enough to the ceiling to prevent any object placed upon it from being seen. He gathered a couple of cushions from a couch, and, beating them up, arranged them between the bedclothes, patting them into a human-looking shape. Though he meant to lock his door and to keep the key in his pocket during the absence he contemplated, and though he had desired the servants not to disturb him until an hour before breakfast, he had the good habit of preparing for the worst.

He slipped out with the coat over his arm, turned the key and walked softly but boldly down into the hall. He paused outside the dining-room, listening to the hum of the brothers' voices, then disappeared down the back-stairs. If he found the door into the stable-yard secured he meant to call someone from the kitchen regions to open it and to announce that he was going out to look at his disabled horse. He would say that he intended to return through the front door, by which Captain Logie had promised to admit him.

Everything was quiet. The only sign of life was the shrill voice of a maid singing in the scullery as she washed the dishes, and the house was not shut up for the night. Through the yard he went and out unmolested, under the great arch which supported the stable clock, and then ran swiftly round to the front. He passed under the still lighted windows and plunged into a mass of trees and undergrowth which headed the eastern approach.

Once among the friendly shadows, he put on the coat, buttoning it closely about his neck, and took a small grey wig from one of its deep pockets. When he had adjusted this under his hat he emerged, crossed the avenue, dropped over the sunk wall dividing it from the fields, and made down them till he reached the Montrose road. Through the still darkness the sound of the Balnillo stable clock floated after him, striking nine.

There was not enough light to show him anything but his nearest surroundings. The wall which bounded the great Balnillo grassparks was at his left hand, and by it he guided his steps, keeping a perpetual look out to avoid stumbling over the inequalities and loose stones, for there were no side-paths to the roads in those days. He knew that the town was only three miles off, and that the dark stretch which extended on his right was the Basin of Montrose. A cold snap played in the air, reminding him that autumn, which in Scotland keeps its mellowness late, was some way forward, and this sting in the breath of night was indicated by a trembling of the stars in the dark vault overhead.

He hastened on, for time was precious. The paper which he had taken from Skirling Wattie's hands had bid him prepare to follow Logie into the town when dark set in, but it had been able to tell him neither at what hour the soldier would start nor whether he would walk or ride.

His chance in meeting the beggar so soon had put him in possession of James's usual movements immediately, but it had given him little time to think out many details, and the gaps in his plans had been filled in by guesswork. He did not think James would ride, for there had been no sound of preparation in the stable. His intention was to reach the town first, to conceal himself by its entrance, and when James should pass, to follow him to his destination. He had a rough map of Montrose in his possession, and with its help he had been able to locate the house for which he suspected him to be bound—a house known by the party he served to be one of the meeting-places of the adherents of Charles Edward Stuart.

Archie's buoyancy of spirit was sufficient to keep at arm's length a regret he could not quite banish; for he had the happy carelessness that carries a man easily on any errand which has possibilities of development, more from the cheerful love of chance than from responsible feeling. His light-hearted courage and tenacity were buried so deep under a luxuriance of effrontery, grace, and mother-wit, and the glamour of a manner difficult to resist, that hardly anyone but Madam Flemington, who had brought him up, suspected the toughness of their quality. He had the refinement of a woman, yet he had extorted the wonder of an east-coast Scotsman by his comprehensive profanity; the expression, at times, of a timid girl, yet he would plunge into a flood of difficulties, whose further shore he did not trouble to contemplate; but these contrasts in him spoke of no repression, no conscious effort. He merely rode every quality in his character with a loose rein, and while he attempted to puzzle nobody, he had the acuteness to know that his audience would puzzle itself by its own conception of him. The regret which he ignored was the regret that he was obliged to shadow a man who pleased him as much as did James Logie. He realized how much more satisfaction he would have got out of his present business had its object been Lord Balnillo. He liked James's voice, his bearing, his crooked mouth, and something intangible about him which he neither understood nor tried to understand. The iron hand of Madam Flemington had brought him up so consistently to his occupation that he accepted it as a part of life. His painting he used as a means, not as an end, and the changes and chances of his main employment were congenial to a temperament at once boyish and capable.

The Pleiades rode high above Taurus, and Orion's hands were coming up over the eastern horizon as he reached the narrow street which was the beginning of Montrose. The place was dark and ill-lit, like every country town of those days; and here, by the North Port, as it was called, the irregularities of the low houses, with their outside stairs, offered a choice of odd corners in which he might wait unseen.

He chose the narrowest part of the street, that he might see across it the more readily, and drew back into the cavity, roofed in by the 'stairhead' of a projecting flight of steps which ran sideways up a wall. Few people would leave the town at that hour, and those who were still abroad were likely to keep within its limits. A wretched lamp, stuck in a niche of an opposite building, made his position all the more desirable, for the flicker which it cast would be sufficient to throw up the figure of Logie should he pass beneath it. He watched a stealthy cat cross its shine with an air of suppressed melodrama that would have befitted a man-eating tiger, and the genial bellowing of a couple of drunken men came down the High Street as he settled his shoulders against the masonry at his back and resigned himself to a probable hour of tedium.

Not a mile distant, James Logie was coming along the Montrose road. He had trodden it many times in the darkness during the past weeks, and his mind was roving far from his steps, far even from the errand on which he was bent. He was thinking of Archie whom he believed to be snug in bed at Balnillo.

He had gone out last night and landed this fantastic piece of young humanity from the Den, as a man may land a salmon, and he had contemplated him ever since with a kind of fascination. Flemington was so much unlike any young man he had known that the difference half shocked him, and though he had told his brother that he liked the fellow, he had done so in spite of one side of himself. It was hard to believe that but a dozen years divided them, for he had imagined

Archie much younger, and the appeal of his boyishness was a strong one to Logie, who had had so little time for boyishness himself. His life since he was fifteen had been merged in his profession, and the restoration of the Stuarts had been for many years the thing nearest to his heart. There had been one exception to this, and that had long gone out of his life, taking his youth with it. He was scarcely a sad man, but he had the habit of sadness, which is as hard a one to combat as any other, and the burst of youth and buoyancy that had come in suddenly with Archie had blown on James like a spring wind. Archie's father and grandfather had died in exile, too, with Charles Edward's parents. And his eyes reminded him of other eyes.

The events that had taken place since the landing of the Prince in July had made themselves felt all up the east coast, and the country was Jacobite almost to a man. Charles Edward had raised his standard at Glenfinnan, had marched on Edinburgh in the early part of September, and had established himself in Holyrood on the surrender of the town. After his victory over Cope at Preston Pans, he had collected his forces on Portobello sands—thirteen regiments composed of the Highland clans, five regiments of Lowlanders, two troops of horse commanded by Lords Elcho and Balmerino, with two others under Lord Kilmarnock and Lord Pitsligo. The command of the latter consisted of Angus men armed with such weapons as they owned or could gather.

The insurgent army had entered England in two portions: one of these led by Lord George Murray, and one by the Prince himself, who marched at the head of his men, sharing the fatigues of the road with them, and fascinating the imagination of the Scots by his hopeful good-humour and his keen desire to identify himself with his soldiers. The two bodies had concentrated on Carlisle, investing the city, and after a few days of defiance, the mayor displayed the white flag on the ramparts and surrendered the town keys. After this, the Prince and his father had been proclaimed at the market cross, in presence of the municipality.

But in spite of this success the signs of the times were not consistently cheering to the Jacobite party. There had been many desertions during the march across the border, and no sooner had the Prince's troops left Edinburgh than the city had gone back to the Whig dominion. At Perth and Dundee the wind seemed to be changing too, and only the country places stuck steadily to the Prince and went on recruiting for the Stuarts.

Although he was aching to go south with the invaders, now that the English were advancing in force, Logie was kept in the neighbourhood of Montrose by the business he had undertaken. His own instincts and inclinations were ever those of a fighter, and he groaned in spirit over the fate which had made it his duty to remain in Angus, concerned with recruiting and the raising of money and arms. He had not yet openly joined the Stuarts, in spite of his ardent devotion to their cause, because it had been represented to him that he was, for the moment, a more valuable asset to his party whilst he worked secretly than he could be in the field. The question that perplexed the coast of Angus was the landing of those French supplies so sorely needed by the half-fed, half-clothed, half-paid troops, in the face of the English cruisers that haunted the coast; and it was these matters that kept Logie busy.

James knew the harbour of Montrose as men know the places which are the scenes of the forbidden exploits of their youth. This younger son, who was so far removed in years from the rest of his family as to be almost like an only child, was running wild in the town among the fisher-folk, and taking surreptitious trips across the bar when the staid David was pursuing his respectable career at a very different kind of bar in Edinburgh. He was the man that Montrose needed in this emergency, and to-night he was on his way to the town; for he would come there a couple of times in the week, as secretly as he could, to meet one David Ferrier, a country gentleman who had joined the regiment of six hundred men raised by Lord Ogilvie, and had been made deputy-governor of Brechin for the Prince.

Ferrier also was a man well calculated to serve the cause. He owned a small property and a farm not far from the village of Edzell, situated at the foot of a glen running up into the Grampians, and his perfect knowledge of the country and its inhabitants of all degrees gave him an insight into every turn of feeling that swept through it in those troubled days. The business of his farm had brought him continually into both Brechin and Montrose, and the shepherds, travelling incessantly with their flocks from hill to strath, formed one of his many chains of intelligence. He had joined Lord Ogilvie a couple of months earlier, and, though he was now stationed at Brechin with a hundred men of his corps, he would absent himself for a night at a time, staying quietly at Montrose in the house of a former dependent of his own, that he might keep an eye upon the movements of an English ship.

The Government sloop-of-war *Venture* had come into the harbour, carrying sixteen guns and about eighty men, and had anchored south of the town, in the strait made by the passage of the River Esk into the sea. Montrose, apparently, was to suffer for the work she had done as a port for Stuart supplies, for the *Venture*, lying at a convenient distance just under the fishing village of Ferryden, had fired heavily on the town, though no Jacobite troops were there. The commander had unrigged the shipping and burned two trading barques whose owners were townsmen, and he had landed a force at the fort, which had captured the town guns and had carried them on board a vessel lying at the quay.

Ferrier looked with complete trust to James Logie and his brother Balnillo. The old man, during his judicial career, had made some parade of keeping himself aloof from politics; and as his retirement had taken place previous to the landing of the Prince, he had sunk the public servant in the country gentleman before the world of politicians began to divide the sheep from the goats. For some time few troubled their heads about the peaceable and cautious old Lord of Session, whose inconspicuous talents were vegetating among the trees and grass-parks that the late Lady Balnillo had husbanded so carefully for him. As to his very much younger brother, who had been incessantly absent from his native land, his existence was practically forgotten. But because the Government's Secret Intelligence Department on the east coast had remembered it at last with some suspicion, Flemington had been sent to Montrose with directions to send his reports to its agent in Perth. And Flemington had bettered his orders in landing himself at Balnillo.

As Archie heard a steady tread approaching, he shrank farther back under the stair. He could only distinguish a middle-sized male figure which might belong to anyone, and he followed it with straining eyes to within a few feet of the lamp. Here it paused, and, skirting the light patch, stepped out into the middle of the way.

He scarcely breathed. He was not sure yet, though the man had come nearer by half the street; but the height matched his expectation, and the avoidance of the solitary light proved the desire for secrecy in the person before him. As the man moved on he slipped from his shelter and followed him, keeping just enough distance between them to allow him to see the way he went.

The two figures passed up the High Street, one behind the other, Flemington shrinking close to the walls and drawing a little nearer. Before they had gone a hundred yards, his unconscious guide turned suddenly into one of those narrow covered-in alleys, or closes, as they are called, which started at right angles from the main street.

Archie dived in after him as unconcernedly as he would have dived into the mouth of hell, had his interests taken him that way. These closes, characteristic of Scottish towns to this day, were so long, and burrowed under so many sightless-looking windows and doors, to emerge in unexpected places, that he admired James's knowledge of the short cuts of Montrose, though it seemed to him no more than natural. The place for which he conceived him to be making was a house in the New Wynd nicknamed the 'Happy Land', and kept by a well-known widow for purposes which made its insignificance an advantage. It was used, as he had heard, by the Jacobite community, because the frequent visitors who entered after dusk passed in without more comment from the townspeople than could be expressed in a lifted eyebrow or a sly nudge. It was a disconcerting moment, even to him, when the man in front of him stopped, and what he had taken for the distant glimmer of an open space revealed itself as a patch of whitewash with a door in it. The close was a cul-de-sac.

Flemington stood motionless as the other knocked at the door. Flight was undesirable, for James might give chase, and capture would mean the end of a piece of work of which he was justly proud. He guessed himself to be the fleeter-footed of the two, but he knew nothing of the town's byways, and other night-birds besides Logie might join in. But his bold wit did not desert him, for he gave a loud drunken shout, as like those he had heard at the North Port as he could make it, and lurched across the close. Its other inmate turned towards him, and as he did so Archie shouted again, and, stumbling against him, subsided upon the paved floor.

The door beyond them opened a little, showing a portion of a scared face and a hand which held a light.

"Guid sakes! what'll be wrang?" inquired a tremulous female voice.

The man was standing over Archie, pushing him with his foot. His answer may have reassured the questioner, but it had a different effect upon the heap on the ground.

"Hoot, woman! don't be a fool! It's me—Ferrier!"

CHAPTER V

"THE HAPPY LAND"

THE door opened a little further.

"Here," said Ferrier to the woman, "go up and bring me the roll of unwritten paper from the table."

"You'll no be coming in?"

"Not now. Maybe in another hour or more."

"But wha's yon?" said she.

"Lord! woman, have you lived all these years in Montrose and never seen a drunken man?" exclaimed he impatiently. "Shut the door, I'm telling you, and get what I want. He will not trouble you. He's past troubling anybody."

She obeyed, and Archie heard a bolt shot on the inside.

Though he had been startled on discovering his mistake, he now felt comforted by it, for, being unknown to Ferrier, he was much safer with him than he would have been with James. He raised his head and tried to get an idea of his companion's face, but the darkness of the close was too great to let him distinguish his features. He had discovered where he lived by accident, but though a description of the man was in the little box now reposing on the tester of his bed at Balnillo, he did not know him by sight. These things were going through his mind as the woman returned from her lodger's errand, and the door had just been made fast again when there was a step at the close's mouth and another man came quickly in, stopping short as he found it occupied.

Ferrier coughed.

"Ferrier?" said James's voice softly. "What is this?" he asked as his foot came in contact with Archie.

"It's a drunken brute who came roaring in here a minute syne and fell head over heels at my door," replied the other. "The town is full of them to-night."

He stooped down and took Flemington by the shoulder.

"Up you get!" he cried, shaking him.

Archie breathed heavily and let his whole weight hang on Ferrier's hand.

"Haud awa' frae me, lassie!" he expostulated thickly.

Logie laughed.

"He must be far gone indeed to take you for a lass," he observed.

Ferrier gave Archie a stronger shake.

"A'll no gang hame wantin' Annie!" continued Flemington, whose humour was beginning to find some pleasure in the situation.

The raw vernacular that he had mastered with absolute success in childhood was at his tongue's end still.

"Come, come," said James.

Ferrier moved forward, but Archie had reached out a limp hand and taken him by the ankle.

"Annie!" he muttered, "ma bonnie, bonnie Annie!"

Ferrier, who had nearly fallen forward, tried to strike out with his foot, but Archie's grip, nerveless yet clinging as a limpet, held him fast.

"A' tell ye, a'll nae gang hame wantin' Annie!" he repeated more loudly.

"He has me by the foot, damn him!" said Ferrier.

James swore quietly but distinctly.

"Annie! *Annie!*" roared Archie, making the silent close echo again.

"Great heavens!" exclaimed the exasperated James, "we shall have the whole town out of bed if this goes on! Shake him off, man, and let us be going."

He bent down as he spoke and groping in the darkness, found Flemington's heels. He seized them and began to drag him backwards as a man drags a fighting dog. He had a grip of iron.

The effect of the sudden pull on Ferrier was to make him lose his balance. He staggered against the side of the close, calling to Logie to desist.

Archie still held on with back-boneless tenacity; but as the scrape of flint and steel cut the darkness he knew that he had carried his superfluous pleasantries too far. He dared not loose Ferrier's ankle and roll to the wall, lest the action should prove him to be more wideawake and less intoxicated than he seemed. He could only bury his face in his sleeve.

His next sensation was a violent stab of burning pain in his wrist that made him draw it back with a groan.

"I knew that would mend matters," said James grimly, as he blew out the tiny twist of ignited tow and replaced it and the steel box in his pocket. "Come away—this sot has wasted our time long enough. He can sleep off his liquor as well here as anywhere else."

"You've helped to sober him," said Ferrier, as the two men went out of the close.

Flemington sat up. The burn stung him dreadfully, for the saltpetre in which the tow had been dipped added to the smart. But there was no time to be lost, so he rose and followed again.

Ferrier and Logie went off up the High Street, and turned down an offshoot of it which Archie guessed to be the New Wynd, because it answered to its position in his map of the town. He dashed to the corner and watched them by the one light which illuminated the narrow street till he could see them no longer. Then he flitted after them, a soft-footed shadow, and withdrew under a friendly 'stairhead,' as he had done at the North Port. A little farther on he could distinguish the two ascending an outside stair to a squat building, and he heard the sound of their knuckles on wood. Another minute and they were admitted.

The two captains were let into a small room in the back premises of 'The Happy Land' by a slatternly-looking woman, who disappeared when she had given them a light. Pens and ink lay upon the table and the smoke of lamps had blackened the ceiling. It was a wretched place, and the sound of rough voices came now and again from other parts of the house. James drew up a chair, and Ferrier also sat down, tossing the roll of paper to his companion.

"A young man called Flemington is at Balnillo painting my brother's portrait," said Logie. "It's a pity that I have not something of his gift for drawing."

"Flemington——?" said the other. "There is a widow Flemington who lives a mile or so this side of the Perthshire border; but that is the only part of the country I do not know."

"This is her grandson. She lived at St. Germain, and her husband was with King James. He is a strange lad—a fine lad too. My brother seems mightily taken up with him."

"Where is your plan?" asked Ferrier.

James took out a small pocket-book and laid it on the table; then he smoothed out the roll of paper, drew the points of the compass on it, and began to copy from the rough sketches and signs which covered the leaf of his little book.

Ferrier watched him in silence,

"I could not do that were it to save my life," he said at last.

"I learned something, campaigning by the walls of Dantzig," replied James.

Ferrier watched the growing of the hasty map with admiration. His own talents for organization and tactics had given this obscure landowner the position he held in the Prince's haphazard army, but the professional soldier was invaluable to him. He sat wondering how he could have got on without James.

"See," said Logie, pushing the paper to him, "here lies the *Venture* off Ferryden, at the south side of the river, and here is Inchbrayock Island. That English captain is a fool, or he would have landed some men there. You and I will land on it, Ferrier. And now," he went on, "the man is twice a fool, for, though he has taken the guns from the fort and put them on board one of the unrigged ships, he has left her beside the quay. This point that I have marked with a cross is where she is moored. It would be idle not to make use of such folly! Why, man, if we can carry through the work I have in my mind, we shall blow the *Venture* out of the water! Three nights I have skulked round the harbour, and now I think that every close and every kennel that opens its mouth upon it is in my head. And the island is the key to everything."

Logie's eyes shone in the dim room like the eyes of some animal watching in a cave.

"We must get possession of the ship at the quay-side," continued he. "Then we will take a couple of the town guns and land them on Inchbrayock. A hundred men from Brechin should be sufficient."

"It must be done at night," said the other.

"At night," said James, getting up and putting his hands on the back of his chair. "And now, as soon as possible, we must go down to the harbour and look carefully at the position of everything."

Ferrier stood up and stretched himself, as men so often will when they are turning over some unacknowledged intention.

James took up the roll of paper, glanced at it and threw it down again.

"I see it as though it had come by inspiration!" he cried. "I see that we have a blockhead to deal with, and when heaven sends such an advantage to His Highness, it is not you nor I, Ferrier, who will balk its design. You will not hang back?"

He looked at his friend as though he were ready to spring at him. But Ferrier went on with his own train of thought. He was a slower man than Logie, but if he lacked his fire, he lacked none of his resolution.

"You are right," he said. "A man is a fool who leaves what he has captured on the farther side of the river, who thinks, having taken his enemy's guns from a fort, that he can let it stand empty. He has done these follies because he knows that there are no troops in Montrose."

"Ay, but there are troops in Brechin!" burst out James.

"There are troops in Brechin," repeated Ferrier slowly, "and they must be got quietly into the town. I wish there were not eight miles of road between the two."

"I have not forgotten that," said James, "and to-night I mean to remain here till daylight and then return home by the side of the Basin. I will make my way along its shore and judge whether it be possible for you to bring your men by that route. If you can get them out of Brechin by the river-bank and so on along the side of the Esk, you will avoid the road and I will be waiting for you at the fort."

Logie had come round the little table and stood by his friend, waiting for him to speak.

"I will go with you," said Ferrier. "We can part below Balnillo, and I, too, will go back to Brechin by the river. I must know every step before I attempt to bring them in the dark. There must be no delays when the time comes."

James drew a long sigh of relief. He had never doubted his companion's zeal, but his heart had been on fire with the project he carried in it, and Ferrier's complete acceptance of it was balm to his spirit. He was a man who spared himself nothing, mentally or physically.

He folded the roll of paper and gave it to Ferrier.

"Keep it," said he. "Now we must go to the harbour."

CHAPTER VI

IN DARKNESS AND IN LIGHT

WHEN the men had disappeared into the house, Archie remained under his stairhead considering. He had been told in his instructions to discover two things—whether Logie was in touch with Ferrier, and whether 'The Happy Land' was frequented by the pair. Though Ferrier was in command of the small Jacobite force in Brechin, it was suspected that he spent an unknown quantity of his time in Montrose.

To the first of these questions he had already mastered the answer; it only remained for him to be absolutely certain that the house in front of him was 'The Happy Land.' He could not swear that he was in the New Wynd, though he was morally certain of it, but there were marks upon the house which would be proof of its identity. There would be a little hole, covered by an inside sliding panel, in the door of 'The Happy Land,' through which its inmates could see anyone who ascended the stair without being seen themselves, and there would be the remains of an ancient 'risp,' or tirling-pin, at one side of it.

Archie ran lightly across the street, crept up the staircase, and passed his palm over the wood. Yes, there was the hole, two inches deep in the solid door. He put in his finger and felt the panel in the farther side. Then he searched along the wall till his hand came in contact with the jagged edge of the ancient risp. There was no ring on it, for it had long been disused, but it hung there still—a useless and maimed veteran, put out of action.

He returned to his post satisfied. His discoveries had earned him the right to go home, but he did not mean to do so. How he was going to get back into Balnillo House, unseen, he did not know, and had not, so far, troubled himself to imagine. Perhaps he might have to stop out all night. He hoped not, but he was not going to meet trouble half-way. The house would be locked, the household—with the exception of the errant James—abed, and his own room was not upon the ground-floor. However, these were matters for later consideration, and he would remain where he was for a time. For all he knew, Ferrier and Logie might combine business with pleasure by staying in 'The Happy Land' till morning; but they were just as likely to come out within measurable time, and then he could see where they went. He was quite happy, as he was everywhere.

He fell to thinking of other things: of his host; with his thin, neat legs and velvet coat; of that 'riding the circuit' upon which the old man valued himself so much. In his mind's eye he figured him astride of his floundering nag at the edge of some uninviting bog in an access of precise dismay. That was how he would have wished to paint him. His powers of detachment were such that he became fascinated by the idea, and awoke from it with a start to hear the footsteps of Logie and Ferrier coming down the stairway opposite.

They did not retrace their way up the Wynd, but went on to its end and turned into a street leading southwards, whilst Archie slipped along in their wake. At last they reached a wilderness of sheds and lumber, above which stood a windmill on a little eminence, and the strong smell of sea and tar proclaimed the region of the harbour. A light shone clear and large across the dark space of water, touching the moving ripples, and this Archie guessed to be the riding-light of the *Venture*, which lay like a sullen watch-dog under Ferryden village.

He had to go very warily, for the pair in front stopped often and stood talking in low voices, but the bales and coils of rope and heaps of timber with which the quays were strewn gave him cover. He could not get close enough to them to hear what they said, but their figures were much plainer against the background of water than they had been in the streets, and he noted how often Logie would stretch out his arm, pointing to the solidary light across the straight.

There was scarcely any illumination on this side of it, and the unrigged shipping lay in darkness as Ferrier and his friend went along the quay and seated themselves on a windlass. Archie, drawing closer, could hear the rustle as the former unrolled James's map. The soldier took out his flint and steel and struck a light, covering it with his hand, and both men bent their heads over the paper. Archie's wrist smarted afresh as he saw it; his sleeve had rubbed the burn, and he could feel the oozing blood.

He crouched behind them, peering through the medley of ropes and tackle which hung on the windlass. By standing up he could have touched the two men. He had no idea what it was that they were studying, but his sharp wits told him that it must be a map of some kind, something which might concern the English ship across the waterway. He longed to get it. His confidence in his own luck was one of the qualities that had served him best, and his confidence in his own speed was great and, moreover, well-placed. He knew that he had twelve years of advantage over James, and, from the sound of Ferrier's voice, he judged that he had the same, or more, over him.

The temptation of chance overmastered him. He raised himself noiselessly, leaned over the intervening tackle, and made a bold snatch at the map, which Ferrier held whilst James was occupied with the lighted twist of tow.

But his luck was to fail him this time. Logie moved his hand, knocking it against Flemington's, and the light caught the paper's edge. A soft puff of sea-wind was coming in from over the strait, and in one moment the sheet was ablaze. Archie snatched back his hand and fled; but the glare of the burning paper had been bright enough to show Logie a man's wrist, on which there was a fresh, bleeding mark.

The bright flare of the paper only intensified the darkness for the two astounded men, and though each was instantly on his feet and running in the direction of the retreating footsteps, Archie had threaded the maze of amphibious obstacles and was plunging between the sheds into the street before either of them could get clear of the pitfalls of the quay.

He tore on, not knowing whither he went. His start had been a good one, but as he paused to listen, which he did when he had gone some way, he could hear them following. The town was so quiet that he met nobody, and he pressed on, trusting to luck for his direction.

Through the empty streets he went at the top of his speed, launched on the flood of chance, and steering as best he could for the north end of the town. Finally, an unexpected turning brought him within a few yards of the North Port. He waited close to the spot where he had first taken shelter, and listened; then, hearing nothing, he struck out at a brisk walk for the country, and was soon clear of Montrose.

He sat down by the wayside to rest. He had had a more sensational night than he expected, and though his spirits were still good, his ill-luck in missing the paper he had risked so much to obtain had cooled them a little, and by the light of this disappointment he looked rather ruefully on his poor prospects of getting to bed. It was past midnight, and there seemed nothing to do but to return to Balnillo and to make himself as comfortable as he could in one of the many out-buildings which the yard by its back-door contained. The household rose early, and at the unlocking of that door he must manage to slip in and gain his bedroom.

He rose, plodded home, and stole into the courtyard, where, searching in an outhouse, he found an endurable couch on a heap of straw. On this he spread his coat like a blanket, crawling under it, and, with a calmness born of perfect health and perfect nerves, was soon asleep.

When dawn broke it found him wakeful. He had not rested well, for his burnt wrist was very sore, and the straw seemed to find it out and to prick the wound, no matter how he might dispose his hand. He propped himself against the wall by the open outhouse-window, whence he could see the back door of Balnillo and watch for the moment of its first opening. It would be neck or nothing then, for he must enter boldly, trusting to hit on a lucky moment.

At last the growing light began to define details of the house, tracing them out on its great mass with an invisible pencil, and he thought he heard a movement within. The stable-clock struck six, and high above he could see the sun touching the slates and the stone angles of the chimney-stacks with the first fresh ethereal beam of a pure October morning. He inhaled its breath lovingly, and with it there fell from him the heaviness of his uneasy night. All was well, he told himself. His sensuous joy in the world, his love of life and its hazards and energies came back upon him, strong, clean, and ecstatic, and the sounds of a bolt withdrawn made him rise to his feet.

A maidservant came out carrying a lantern, whose beam burned with feeble pretentiousness in the coming sunlight. She set it down by the threshold and went past his retreat to the stable. No doubt she was going to call the men. When she had gone by he slipped out, and in a dozen paces was inside the house.

Another minute and he was in his room.

He looked with some amusement at the rough effigy of himself which he had made in the bed overnight, and when he had flung the cushion back to its place he got out of his clothes and lay down, sinking into the cool luxury of the sheets with a sigh of pleasure. But he had no desire to sleep, and when a servant came to wake him half an hour later he was ready to get up. He rose, dressed, wrote out the detailed description of his night's discoveries, and put the document in his pocket to await its chance of transmission.

A message was brought to him from Lord Balnillo as he left his room, which begged his guest to excuse his company at breakfast. He had been long astir, and busy with his correspondence; at eleven o'clock he would be ready for his sitting, if that were agreeable to Mr. Flemington.

As Mr. Flemington realized how easily he might have met the judge as he ran through the shuttered passage, his belief in the luck that had used him so scurvily last night returned.

There was no sign of James as Archie sat down to his meal, though a second place was set at the table, and as he did not want to ask embarrassing questions, he made no inquiry about him. Besides which, being immoderately hungry, he was too well occupied to trouble about anyone.

He went out upon the terrace when he had finished. The warm

greyness of the autumn morning was lifting from the earth and it was still early enough for long shadows to lie cool on the westward side of the timber. As they shortened, the crystal of the dew was catching shafts from the sun, and the parks seemed to lie waiting till the energy of the young day should let loose the forces of life from under the mystery of its spangled veil. Where the gean-trees glowed carmine and orange, touches of quickening fire shot through the interstices of their branches, and coloured like a tress of trailing forget-me-not, the South Esk wound into the Basin of Montrose, where the tide, ebbing beyond the town, was leaving its wet sands as a feasting-ground for all sorts of roving birds whose crying voices came faintly to Archie, mellowed by distance.

Truly this was a fascinating place, with its changing element of distant water, its great plain lines of pasture, its ordered vistas of foliage! The passion for beauty lay deep below the tossing, driving impulses of Flemington's nature, and it rose up now as he stood on the yew-edged terraces of Balnillo and gazed before him. For the moment everything in his mind was swallowed up but the abstract, fundamental desire for perfection, which is, when all is said and done, humanity's mainspring, its incessant though often erring guide, whose perverted behests we call sin, whose legitimate ones we call virtue; whose very existence is a guarantee of immortality.

The world, this crystalline morning, was so beautiful to Archie that he ached with the uncomprehended longing to identify himself with perfection; to cast his body down upon the light-pervaded earth and to be one with it, to fling his soul into the heights and depths of the limitless encompassing ether, to be drawn into the heart of God's material manifestation on earth—the sun. He understood nothing of what he felt, neither the discomfort of his imprisonment of flesh, nor the rapturous, tentative, wing-sweeps of the spirit within it. He left the garden terrace and went off towards the Basin, with the touch of that elemental flood of truth into which he had been plunged for a moment fresh on his soul. The whole universe and its contents seemed to him good—and not only good, but of consummate interest—humanity was fascinating. His failure to snatch the map from Ferrier's hand last night only made him smile. In the perfection of this transcendent creation all was, and must be, well!

His thoughts, woven of the same radiant appreciation, flew to James, whose personality appealed to him so strongly. The gentle blood which ran in the veins of the pair of brothers ran closer to the surface in the younger one; and a steadfast, unostentatious gallantry of heart seemed to be the atmosphere in which he breathed. He was one of those whose presence in a room would always be the strongest force in it, whether he spoke or was silent, and his voice had the tone of something sounding over great and hidden depths. It was not necessary to talk to him to know that he had lived a life of vicissitude, and Archie, all unsuspected, in the watches of last night had seen a side of him which did not show at Balnillo. His grim resourcefulness in small things was illustrated by the raw spot on the young man's wrist. That episode pleased Flemington's imagination —though it might have pleased him even better had the victim been someone else; but he bore James no malice for it, and the picture of the man haunting the dark quays, strewn with romantic, sea-going lumber, and scheming for the cause at his heart, whilst the light from the hostile ship trailed the water beside him, charmed his active fancy.

But it was not only his fancy that was at work. He knew that the compelling atmosphere of Logie had not been created by mere fancy, because there was something larger than himself, and larger than anything he could understand, about the soldier. And feeling, as he was apt to do, every little change in the mental climate surrounding him he had guessed that Logie liked him. The thought added to the exultation produced in him by the glory of the pure morning; and he suddenly fell from his height as he remembered afresh that he was here to cheat him.

It was with a shock that he heard Skirling Wattie's pipes as he reached the Montrose road, and saw the beggar's outlandish cart approaching, evidently on its return journey to Montrose. His heart beat against the report that lay in his pocket awaiting the opportunity that Fate was bringing nearer every moment. There was nobody to be seen as the beggar drew up beside him. The insolent joviality that pervaded the man, his almost indecent oddness—things which had pleased Archie yesterday struck cold on him now. He had no wish to stay talking to him, and he gave him the paper without a word more than the injunction to have it despatched.

He left him, hurrying across the Montrose road and making for the place where the ground began to fall away to the Basin. He sat down on the scrubby waste land by a broom-bush, whose dry, burst pods hung like tattered black flags in the brush of green; their acrid smell was coming out as the sun mounted higher. Below him the marshy ground ran out to meet the water; and eastward the uncovered mud and wet sand, bared by the tide ebbing beyond Montrose, stretched along its shores to the town.

The fall of the broom-covered bank was steep enough to hide anyone coming up from the lower levels, and he listened to the movements of somebody who was approaching, and to the crackling noise of the bushes as they were thrust apart.

The sound stopped; and Archie, leaning forward, saw James standing half-way up the ascent, with his back turned towards him, looking out across the flats. He knew what his thoughts were. He drew his right sleeve lower. So long as he did not stretch out his arm the mark could not be seen.

He did not want to appear as if he were watching Logie, so he made a slight sound, and the other turned quickly and faced him, hidden from the waist downwards in the broom. Then his crooked lip moved, and he came up the bank and threw himself down beside Flemington.

CHAPTER VII

TREACHERY

JAMES did not look as if he had been up all night, though he had spent the most part of it on foot with Ferrier. The refreshment of morning had bathed him too, but he was still harassed in mind by some of the occurrences of the last few hours. Last night he had seen the mark on the wrist stretched suddenly between himself and his friend, and had understood its significance. It was the mark that he had put there. As the two men listened to the flying footsteps that mystified them by their doublings in the darkness, it had dawned upon them that the intruder skulking behind the windlass and the tipsy reveller prone in the close were one and the same person. The drunkard was a very daring spy, as sober as themselves.

"You are out betimes," said Archie, with friendly innocence.

"I often am," replied James simply.

Archie pulled up a blade of grass and began to chew it meditatively.

"I see your long night has done you good," began Logie. "There were many things I should have liked to ask you, yesterday evening, but you went away so early that I could not."

Silence dropped upon the two: upon Logie, because his companion's manner last night had hinted at remembrances buried in regret and painful to dig up; on Flemington, because he knew the value of that impression, and because he would fain put off the moment when the more complete deception of the man whose sympathetic attitude he divined and whose generosity of soul was so obvious, must begin. He did not want to come to close quarters with James. He had hunted him and been hunted by him, but he had not yet been obliged to lie to him by word of mouth; and he had no desire to do so, here and now, in cold blood and in the face of all this beauty and peace.

"I could not but be interested in what you said," continued the other. "You did not tell us whether you had been at St. Germain yourself"

"Never!" replied Archie. "I was sent to Scotland at eight years old, and I have been here ever since."

He had taken the plunge now, for he had been backwards and forwards to France several times in the last few years, since he had begun to work for King George, employed in watching the movements of suspicious persons between one country and the other.

He looked down on the ground.

The more he hesitated to speak, the more he knew that he would impress James. He understood the delicacy of his companion's feeling by instinct. It was not only dissimulation which bade him act thus, it was the real embarrassment and discomfort which were creeping on him under the eyes of the honourable soldier; all the same, he hoped that his reluctant silence would save him.

"You think me impertinent," said Logie, "but do not be afraid that I mean to pry. I know how hard life can be and how anxious, nowadays. There is so much loss and trouble—God knows what may happen to this tormented country! But trouble does not seem natural when a man is young and light-hearted, as you are."

Archie was collecting materials wherewith to screen himself from his companion's sympathy. It would be easy to tell him some rigmarole of early suffering, of want endured for the cause which had lain dormant, yet living, since the unsuccessful rising of the '15, of the devotion to it of the parents he had scarcely known, of the bitterness of their exile, but somehow he could not force himself to do it. He remembered those parents principally as vague people who were ceaselessly playing cards, and whose quarrels had terrified him when he was small. His real interest in life had begun when he arrived at Ardguys and made the acquaintance of his grandmother, whose fascination he had felt, in common with most other male creatures. He had had a joyous youth, and he knew it. He had run the pastures, climbed the trees, fished the Kilpie burn, and known every country pleasure dear to boyhood. If he had been solitary, he had yet been perfectly happy. He had gone to Edinburgh at seventeen, at his own ardent wish, to learn painting, not as a profession, but as a pastime. His prospects were comfortable, for Madam Flemington had made him her heir, and she had relations settled in England who were always ready to bid him welcome when he crossed the border. Life had been consistently pleasant, and had grown exciting since the beginning of his work for Government. He wished to Heaven he had not met James this morning.

But to Logie, Archie was merely a youth of undoubted good breeding struggling bravely for his bread in an almost menial profession, and he honoured him for what he deemed his courage. There was no need to seek a reason for his poverty after hearing his words last night. His voice, when he spoke of his father's death in exile had implied all that was necessary to establish a claim on James's generous and rather bigoted heart. For him, there were only two kinds of men, those who were for the Stuarts and those who were not. People were very reticent about their political feelings in those days; some from pure caution and some because these lay so deep under mountains of personal loss and misfortune.

"I dare not look back," said Archie, at last, "I have to live by my trade and fight the world with my brush. You live by sticking your sword into its entrails and I by painting its face a better colour than Nature chose for it, and I think yours is the pleasanter calling of the two. But I am grateful to mine, all the same, and now it has procured me the acquaintance of his lordship and the pleasure of being where I am. I need not tell you that I find myself in clover."

"I am heartily glad of it," said James.

"Indeed, so am I," rejoined Archie, pleased at having turned the conversation so deftly, "for you cannot think what strange things happen to a man who has no recognized place in the minds of respectable people."

James rolled over on his chest, leaning on his elbows, and looked up at his companion sitting just above him with his dark, silky head clear cut against the background of green bush. The young man's words seemed to trip out and pirouette with impudent jauntiness in their hearer's face. Logie did not know that Archie's management of these puppets was a part of his charm. His detached points of view were restful to a man like James, one continually preoccupied by large issues. It was difficult to think of responsibilities in Archie's presence.

"You might never imagine how much I am admired below stairs!" said the latter. "While I painted a lady in the south, I was expected to eat with the servants, and the attentions of a kitchen-girl all but cost me my life. I found a challenge, offering me the choice of weapons in the most approved manner, under my dish of porridge. It came from a groom."

"What did you do?" asked James, astounded.

"I chose warming-pans," said Archie, "and that ended the matter."

James laughed aloud, but there was bitterness in his mirth. And this was a man born at St. Germain!

"We laugh," said he, "but such a life could have been no laughing matter to you."

"But I assure you it was! What else could I do?"

"You could have left the place——" began James. Then he stopped short, remembering that beggars cannot be choosers.

His expression was not lost on Archie, who saw that the boat he had steered so carefully into the shallows was drawing out to deep water again, and that he had used his luxuriant imagination to small purpose. He had so little self-consciousness that to keep James's interest upon himself was no temptation to him, though it might have been to some men. He cast about for something wherewith to blot his own figure from the picture.

"And you," he said, gravely, "you who think so much of my discomforts, and who have actually wielded the sword while I have merely threatened to wield the warming-pan—you must have seen stranger things than the kitchen."

"I?" said James, looking fixedly out to where the town steeple threw its reflection on the wet sand—"yes. I have seen things that I hope you will never see. It is not for me to speak ill of war, I who have turned to it for consolation as a man may turn to his religion. But war is not waged against men alone in some countries. I have seen it when it is waged against women and little children, when it is slaughter, not war. I have seen mothers—young, beautiful women—fighting like wild beasts for the poor babes that cowered behind their skirts, and I have seen their bodies afterwards. It would be best to forget—but who can forget?"

Archie sat still, with eyes from which all levity had vanished. He had known vaguely that James had fought under Marshal Lacy in the War of the Polish Succession, in the bloody campaign against the Turks, and again in Finland. The ironic futility of things in general struck him, for it was absurd to think that this man, seared by war and wise in the realities of events whose rumours shook Europe, one who had looked upon death daily in company with men like Peter Lacy, should come home to be hunted down back streets by a travelling painter. He contemplated his companion with renewed interest; no wonder he was ruthless in small things. He was decidedly the most fascinating person he had known.

"And you went to these things *for consolation*—so you said?"

"For consolation. For a thing that does not exist," said the other slowly.

He paused and turned to his companion with an expression that horrified the young man and paralyzed his curiosity. The power in his face seemed to have given way, revealing, for a moment, a defencelessness like the defencelessness of a child looking upon the dark; and it told Archie that there was something that even Logie dreaded and that that something was memory.

The deep places he had guessed in James's soul were deep indeed, and again Flemington was struck with humility, for his own unimportance in contrast with this experienced man seemed little less than pitiful. The feeling closed his lips, and he looked round at the shortening shadows and into the stir of coming sunlight as a man looks round for a door through which to escape from impending stress. He, who was always ready to go forward, recoiled because of what he foresaw in himself. His self-confidence was ebbing, for he was afraid of how much he might be turned out of his way by the influence on him of Logie. He wished that he could force their talk into a different channel, but his ready wits for once would not answer the call.

Something not understood by him was moving James to expression, as reserved men are compelled towards it at times. Perhaps the bygone youth in him rose up in response to the youth at his side. The many years dividing him from his brother, the judge, had never consciously troubled him in their intercourse, but the tremendous divergence in their respective characters had thrown him back upon himself. Archie seemed to have the power of turning a key that Balnillo had never held.

"But I am putting you out of conceit with the world," cried James abruptly; "let no one do that. Take all you can, Flemington! I did—I took it all. Love, roystering, good company, good wine, good play—all came to me, and I had my bellyful! There were merry times in Holland with the Scots Brigade. It was the best part of my life, and I went to it young. I was sixteen the day I stood up on parade for the first time."

"I have often had a mind to invade Holland," observed Archie, grasping eagerly at the impersonal part of the subject; "it would be paradise to one of my trade. The very thought of a windmill weaves a picture for me, and those strange, striped flowers the Dutchmen raise—I cannot think of their names now—I would give much to see them growing. You must have seen them in every variety and hue."

"Ay, I saw the tulips," said James, in a strange voice.

"The Dutchmen can paint them too," said Archie hurriedly.

"What devil makes you talk of tulips?" cried James. "Fate painted the tulips for me. Oh, Flemington, Flemington! In every country, in every march, in every fight, among dead and dying, and among dancers and the music they danced to, I have seen nothing but those gaudy flowers—beds of them growing like a woven carpet, and Diane among them!"

No feminine figure had come into the background against which stood Archie's conception of Logie.

"Diane?" he exclaimed involuntarily.

James did not seem to hear him.

"Her eyes were like yours," he went on. "When I saw you come into the light of the house two evenings since, I thought of her."

Neither spoke for a few moments; then James went on again:

"Fourteen years since the day I saw her last! She looked out at me from the window with her eyes full of tears. The window was filled with flowers—she loved them. The tulips were there again—crimson tulips—with her white face behind them."

Flemington listened with parted lips. His personal feelings, his shrinking dread of being drawn into the confidence of the man whom it was his business to betray, were swallowed by a wave of interest.

"I was no more than a boy, with my head full of cards and women and horses, and every devilry under heaven, when I went to the house among the canals. The Conte de Montdelys had built it, for he lived in Holland a part of the year to grow his tulips. He was a rich man—a hard, old, pinched Frenchman—but his passion was tulip-growing, and their cultivation was a new thing. It was a great sight to see the gardens he had planned at the water's edge, with every colour reflected from the beds, and the green-shuttered house in the middle. Even the young men of the Brigade were glad to spend an afternoon looking upon the show, and the Conte would invite now one, now another. He loved to strut about exhibiting his gardens. Diane was his daughter—my poor Diane! Flemington, do I weary you?"

"No, no, indeed!" cried Archie, who had been lost, wandering in an enchanted labyrinth of bloom and colour as he listened. The image of the house rising from among its waterways was as vivid to him as if he had seen it with bodily eyes.

"She was so young," said the soldier, "so gentle, so little suited to such as I. But she loved me—God knows why—and she was brave—brave to the end, as she lay dying by the roadside… and sending me her love…."

He stopped and turned away; Archie could say nothing, for his throat had grown thick. Logie's unconscious gift of filling his words with drama—a gift which is most often given to those who suspect it least—wrought on him.

James looked round, staring steadily and blindly over his companion's shoulder.

"I took her away," he went on, as though describing another man's experiences; "there was no choice, for the Conte would not tolerate me. I was a Protestant, and I was poor, and there was a rich Spaniard whom he favoured. So we went. We were married in Breda, and for a year we lived in peace. Such days—such days! The Conte made no sign, and I thought, in my folly, he would let us alone. It seemed as though we had gained paradise at last; but I did not know him—Montdelys."

"Then the boy was born. When he was two months old I was obliged to come back to Scotland; it was a matter concerning money which could not be delayed, for my little fortune had to be made doubly secure now, and I got leave from my regiment. I could not take Diane and the child, and I left them at Breda—safe, as I thought. At twenty-three we do not know men, not the endless treachery of them. Flemington, when God calls us all to judgment, there will be no mercy for treachery."

Archie's eyes, fixed on the other pair, whose keen grey light was blurred with pain, dropped. He breathed hard, and his nostrils quivered. "You seem to me as young as I was then. May God preserve you from man's treachery. He did not preserve me," said James.

"I do not know how Montdelys knew that she was defenceless," continued he, "but I think there must have been some spy of his watching us. As soon as I had left Holland he sent to her to say he was ill, probably dying, and that he had forgiven all. He longed for the sight of the boy, and he asked her to bring him that he might see his grandchild; she was to make her home with him while I was absent, and he would send word to me to join them on my return. Diane sent me the good news and went, fearing nothing, to find herself a prisoner.

"And all this time he had been working—he and the Spaniard—to get the Pope to annul our marriage, and they had succeeded.

What they said to her, what they did, I know not, and never shall know, but they could not shake Diane. I was on my way back to Holland when she managed to escape with the boy. Storms in the North Sea delayed me, but I was not disturbed, knowing her to be safe. I did not know when I landed at last that she was dead.... She swam the canal, Flemington, with the child tied on her shoulders, and the brother-officer of mine—a man in my own company, whom she had contrived to communicate with—was waiting for her with a carriage. My regiment had moved to Bergen-op-Zoom, and he meant to take her there. He had arranged it with the wife of my colonel, who was to give her shelter till I arrived, and could protect her myself. They had gone more than half-way to Bergen when they were overtaken, early in the morning. She was shot, Flemington. The bullet was meant for Carmichael, the man who was with her, but it struck Diane.... They laid her on the grass at the roadside and she died, holding Carmichael's hand, and sending—sending——"

He stopped.

"And the child?" said Archie at last.

"Carmichael brought him to Bergen, with his mother. He did not live. The bullet had grazed his poor little body as he lay in her arms, and the exposure did the rest. They are buried at Bergen."

Again Archie was speechless.

"I killed the Spaniard," said James. "I could not reach Montdelys; he was too old to be able to settle his differences in the world of men."

Archie did not know what to do. He longed with a bitter longing to show his companion something of what he felt, to give him some sign of the passion of sympathy which had shaken him as he listened; but his tongue was tied fast by the blighting knowledge of his true position, and to approach, by so much as a step, seemed only to blacken his soul and to load it yet more heavily with a treachery as vile as that which had undone James.

"I could not endure Holland afterwards," continued Logie; "once I had looked on that Spanish hound's dead body my work was done. I left the Scots Brigade and took service with Russia, and I joined

Peter Lacy, who was on his way to fight in Poland. Fighting was all I wanted, and God knows I had it. I did not want to be killed, but to kill. Then I grew weary of that, but I still stayed with Lacy, and followed him to fight the Turks. We outlive trouble in time, Flemington; we outlive it, though we cannot outlive memory. We outlast it—that is a better word. I have outlasted, perhaps outlived. I can turn and look back upon myself as though I were another being. It is only when some chance word or circumstance brings my youth back in detail that I can scarce bear it. You have brought it back, Flemington, and this morning I am face to face with it again."

"It does not sound as if you had outlived it," said the young man.

"Life is made of many things," said James; "whether we have lost our all or not, we have to plough on to the end, and it is best to plough on merrily. Lacy never complained of me as a companion in the long time we were together, for I was on his staff, and I took all that came to me, as I have done always. There were some mad fellows among us, and I was no saner than they! But life is quiet enough here in the year since I came home to my good brother."

The mention of Lord Balnillo made Flemington start.

"Gad!" he exclaimed, rising, thankful for escape, "and I am to begin the portrait this morning, and have set out none of my colours!"

"And I have gone breakfastless," said Logie with a smile, "and worse than that, I have spoilt the sunshine for you with my tongue, that should have been silent."

"No, no!" burst out Flemington rather hoarsely. "Don't think of that! If you only knew——"

He stood, unable to finish his sentence or to utter one word of comfort without plunging deeper into self-abhorrence.

"I must go," he stammered. "I must leave you and run."

James laid a detaining hand on him.

"Listen, Flemington," he said. "Listen before you go. We have learnt something of each other, you and I. Promise me that if ever you should find yourself in such a position as the one you spoke of—if you should come to such a strait as that—if a little help could make you free, you will come to me as if I were your brother. Your eyes are so like Diane's—you might well be hers."

Archie stood before him, dumb, as James held out his hand.

He grasped it for a moment, and then turned from him in a tumult of horror and despair.

CHAPTER VIII

THE HEAVY HAND

It was on the following day that Lord Balnillo stood in front of a three-quarter length canvas in the improvised studio; Archie had begun to put on the colour that morning, and the judge had come quietly upstairs to study the first dawnings of his own countenance alone. From the midst of a chaos of paint his features were beginning to appear, like the sun through a fog. He had brought a small hand-glass with him, tucked away under his velvet coat where it could not be seen, and he now produced it and began to compare his face with the one before him. Flemington was a quick worker, and though he had been given only two sittings, there was enough on the canvas to prompt the gratified smile on the old man's lips. He looked alternately at his reflection and at the judicial figure on the easel; Archie had a tactful brush. But though Balnillo was pleased, he could not help sighing, for he wished fervently that his ankles had been included in the picture. He stooped and ran his hand lovingly down his silk stockings. Then he took up the glass again and began to compose his expression into the rather more lofty one with which Flemington had supplied him.

In the full swing of his occupation he turned round to find the painter standing in the doorway, but he was just too late to catch the sudden flash of amusement that played across Archie's face as he saw what the judge was doing. Balnillo thrust the glass out of sight and confronted his guest.

"I thought you had gone for a stroll, sir," he said rather stiffly.

"My lord," exclaimed Flemington, "I have been searching for you everywhere. I've come, with infinite regret, to tell you that I must return to Ardguys at once."

Balnillo's jaw dropped.

"I have just met a messenger on the road," said the other; "he has brought news that my grandmother is taken ill, and I must hurry home. It is most unfortunate, most disappointing; but go I must."

"Tut, tut, tut!" exclaimed the old man, clicking his tongue against his teeth and forgetting to hope, as politeness decreed he should, that the matter was not serious.

"It is a heart-attack," said Archie.

"Tut, tut," said Balnillo again. "I am most distressed to hear it; I am indeed."

"I *may* be able to come back and finish the picture later."

"I hope so. I sincerely hope so. I was just studying the admirable likeness when you came in," said Balnillo, who would have given a great deal to know how much of his posturing Flemington had seen.

"Ah, my lord!" cried Archie, "a poor devil like me has no chance with you! I saw the mirror in your hand. We painters use a piece of looking-glass to correct our drawing, but it is few of our sitters who know that trick."

Guilty dismay was chased by relief across Balnillo's countenance.

"You are too clever for me!" laughed Flemington. "How did you learn it, may I ask?"

But Balnillo had got his presence of mind back.

"Casually, Mr. Flemington, casually—as one learns many things, if one keeps one's ears open," said he.

A couple of hours later Archie was on his way home. He had left one horse, still disabled, in the judge's stable, and he was riding the other into Brechin, where he would get a fresh one to take him on. Balnillo had persuaded him to leave his belongings where they were until he knew what chance there was of an early return. He had parted from Archie with reluctance. Although the portrait was the old man's principal interest, its maker counted for much with him; for it was some time since his ideas had been made to move as they always moved in Flemington's presence. The judge got much pleasure out of his own curiosity; and the element of the unexpected—that fascinating factor which had been introduced into domestic life—was a continual joy. Balnillo had missed it more than he knew since he had become a completely rural character.

Archie saw the Basin of Montrose drop behind him as he rode away with a stir of mixed feelings. The net that Logie had, in all ignorance, spread for him had entangled his feet. He had never conceived a like situation, and it startled him to discover that a difficulty, nowhere touching the tangible, could be so potent, so disastrous. He felt like a man who has been tripped up and who suddenly finds himself on the ground. He had risen and fled.

The position had become intolerable. He told himself in his impetuous way that it was more than he could bear; and now, every bit of luck he had turned to account, every precaution he had taken, all the ingenuity he had used to land himself in the hostile camp, were to go for nothing, because some look in his face, some droop of the eyes, had reminded another man of his own past, and had let loose in him an overwhelming impulse to expression.

"Remember what I told you yesterday," had been James's last words as Flemington put his foot in the stirrup. "There must be no more challenges."

It was that high-coloured flower of his own imagination, the picture of himself in the servants' hall, that had finally accomplished his defeat. How could he betray the man who was ready to share his purse with him?

And, putting the matter of the purse aside, his painter's imagination was set alight. The glow of the tulips and the strange house by the winding water, the slim vision of Diane de Montdelys, the gallant background of the Scots Brigade, the grave at Bergen-op-Zoom—these things were like a mirage behind the figure of James. The power of seeing things picturesquely is a gift that can turn into a curse, and that power worked on his emotional and imaginative side now. And furthermore, beyond what might be called the ornamental part of his difficulty, he realized that friendship with James, had he been free to offer or to accept it, would have been a lifelong prize.

They had spent the preceding day together after the sitting was over, and though Logie had opened his heart no more, and their talk had been of the common interests of men's lives, it had strengthened Archie's resolve to end the situation and to save himself while there was yet time. There was nothing for it but flight. He had told the judge that he would try to return, but he did not mean to enter the gates of Balnillo again, not while the country was seething with Prince Charlie's plots; perhaps never. He would remember James all his life, but he hoped that their ways might never cross again. And, behind that, there was regret; regret for the friend who might have been his, who, in his secret heart, would be his always.

He could, even now, hardly realize that he had been actually turned from his purpose. It seemed to him incredible. But there was one thing more incredible still, and that was that he could raise his hand to strike again at the man who had been stricken so terribly, and with the same weapon of betrayal. It would be as if James lay wounded on a battle-field and he should come by to stab him anew. The blow he should deal him would have nothing to do with the past, but Archie felt that James had so connected him in mind with the memory of the woman he resembled—had, by that one burst of confidence, given him so much part in the sacred kingdom of remembrance wherein she dwelt—that it would be almost as if something from out of the past had struck at him across her grave.

Archie sighed, weary and sick with Fate's ironic jests. There were some things he could not do.

The two men had avoided politics. Though Flemington's insinuations had conveyed to the brothers that he was like-minded with themselves, the Prince's name was not mentioned. There was so much brewing in James's brain that the very birds of the air must not hear. Sorry as he was when Flemington met him with the news of his unexpected recall, he had decided that it was well the young man should go. When this time of stress was over, when—and if—the cause he served should prevail, he would seek out Archie. The "if" was very clear to James, for he had seen enough of men and causes, of troops and campaigns and the practical difficulties of great movements, to know that he was spending himself in what might well be a forlorn hope. But none the less was he determined to see it through, for his heart was deep in it, and besides that, he had the temperament that is attracted by forlorn hopes.

He was a reticent man, in spite of the opening of that page in his life which he had laid before Flemington; and reticent characters are often those most prone to rare and unexpected bouts of self-revelation. But when the impulse is past, and the load ever present with them has been lightened for a moment, they will thrust it yet farther back behind the door of their lips, and give the key a double turn. He had enjoined Flemington to come to him as he would come to a brother for assistance, and it had seemed to Archie that life would have little more to offer had it only given him a brother like James. A cloud was on his spirit as he neared Brechin.

When he left the inn and would have paid the landlord, he thrust his hand into his pocket to discover a thin sealed packet at the bottom of it; he drew it out, and found to his surprise that, though his name was on it, it was unopened, and that he had never seen it before. While he turned it over something told him that the unknown handwriting it bore was that of James Logie. The coat he wore had hung in the hall at Balnillo since the preceding night, and the packet must have been slipped into it before he started.

As he rode along he broke the seal. The paper it contained had neither beginning nor signature, yet he knew that his guess was right.

"You will be surprised at finding this," he read, "but I wish you to read it when there are some miles between us. In these disturbed days it is not possible to tell when we may meet again. Should you return, I may be here or I may be gone God knows where, and for reasons of which I need not speak, my brother may be the last man to know where I am. But for the sake of all I spoke of yesterday, I ask you to believe that I am your friend. Do not forget that, in any strait, I am at your back. Because it is true, I give you these two directions: a message carried to Rob Smith's Tavern in the Castle Wynd at Stirling will reach me eventually, wheresoever I am. Nearer home you may hear of me also. There is a little house on the Muir of Pert, the only house on the north side of the Muir, a mile west of the fir-wood. The man who lives there is in constant touch with me. If you should find yourself in urgent need, I will send you the sum of one hundred pounds through him.

"Flemington, you will make no hesitation in the matter. You will take it for the sake of one I have spoken of to none but you, these years and years past."

And now he had to go home and to tell Madam Flemington that he had wantonly thrown away all the advantages gained in the last three days, that he had tossed them to the wind for a mere sentimental scruple! So far he had never quarrelled with his occupation; but now, because it had brought him up against a soldier of fortune whose existence he had been unaware of a few weeks ago, he had sacrificed it and played a sorry trick on his own prospects at the same time. He was trusted and valued by his own party, and, in spite of his youth, had given it excellent service again and again. He could hardly expect the determined woman who had made him what he was to see eye to eye with him.

Christian Flemington had kept her supremacy over her grandson. Parental authority was a much stronger thing in the mid-eighteenth century than it is now, and she stood in the position of a parent to him. His French blood and her long residence in France had made their relationship something like that of a French mother and son, and she had all his confidence in his young man's scrapes, for she recognized phases of life that are apt to be ignored by English parents in dealing with their children. She had cut him loose from her apron-strings early, but she had moulded him with infinite care before she let him go. There was a touch of genius in Archie, a flicker of what she called the *feu sacré*, and she had kept it burning before her own shrine. The fine unscrupulousness that was her main characteristic, her manner of breasting the tide of circumstance full sail, awed and charmed him. For all his boldness and initiative, his devil-may-care independence of will, and his originality in the conduct of his affairs, he had never freed his inner self from her thrall, and she held him by the strong impression she had made on his imagination years and years ago. She had set her mark upon the plastic character of the little boy whom she had beaten for painting Mr. Duthie's gate-post. That was an episode which he had never forgotten, which he always thought of with a smile; and while he remembered the sting of her cane, he also remembered her masterly routing of his enemy before she applied it. She had punished him with the thoroughness that was hers, but she had never allowed the minister to know what she had done. Technically she had been on the side of the angels, but in reality she had stood by the culprit. In spirit they had resented Mr. Duthie together.

He slept at Forfar that night, and pushed on again next morning; and as he saw the old house across the dip, and heard the purl of the burn at the end of his journey, something in his heart failed him. The liquid whisper of the water through the fine, rushlike grass spoke to him of childhood and of the time when there was no world but Ardguys, no monarch but Madam Flemington. He seemed to feel her influence coming out to meet him at every step his horse took. How could he tell his news? How could he explain what he had done? They had never touched on ethical questions, he and she.

As he came up the muddy road between the ash-trees he felt the chilly throe, the intense spiritual discomfort, that attends our plunges from one atmosphere into another. It is the penalty of those who live their lives with every nerve and fibre, who take fervent part in the lives of other people, to suffer acutely in the struggle to loose themselves from an environment they have just quitted, and to meet an impending one without distress. But it is no disproportionate price to pay for learning life as a whole. Also, it is the only price accepted.

He put his horse into the stable and went to the garden, being told that Madam Flemington was there. The day was warm and bright, and as he swung the gate to behind him he saw her sitting on a seat at the angle of the farther wall. She rose at the click of the latch, and came up the grass path to meet him between a line of espalier apple-trees and a row of phlox on which October had still left a few red and white blossoms.

The eighteen years that had gone by since the episode of the manse gate-post had not done much to change her appearance. The shrinking and obliterating of personality which comes with the passing of middle life had not begun its work on her, and at sixty-one she was more imposing than ever. She had grown a great deal stouter, but the distribution of flesh had been even, and she carried her bulk with a kind of self-conscious triumph, as a ship carries her canvas. A brown silk mantle woven with a pattern of flower-bouquets was round her shoulders, and she held its thick folds together with one hand; in the other she carried the book she had been reading. Her hair was as abundant as ever, and had grown no whiter. The sun struck on its silver, and red flashes came from the rubies in her ears.

She said nothing as Archie approached, but her eyes spoke inquiry and a shadow of softness flickered ever so slightly round her broad lips. She was pleased to see him, but the shadow was caused less by her affection for him than by her appreciation of the charming figure he presented, seen thus suddenly and advancing with so much grace of movement in the sunlight. She stopped short when he was within a few steps of her, and, dropping her book upon the ground without troubling to see where it fell, held out her hand for him to kiss. He touched it with his lips, and then, thrusting his arm into the phlox-bushes, drew out the volume that had landed among them. From between the leaves dropped a folded paper, on which he recognized his own handwriting.

"This is a surprise," said Madam Flemington, looking her grandson up and down.

"I have ridden. My baggage is left at Balnillo."

The moment of explanation would have to come, but his desire was to put it off as long as possible.

"There is your letter between the pages of my book,"said she. "It came to me this morning, and I was reading it again. It gave me immense pleasure, Archie. I suppose you have come to search for the clothes you mentioned. I am glad to see you, my dear; but it is a long ride to take for a few pairs of stockings."

"You should see Balnillo's hose!" exclaimed Flemington hurriedly. "I'll be bound the old buck's spindle-shanks cost him as much as his estate. If he had as many legs as a centipede he would have them all in silk."

"And not a petticoat about the place?"

"None nearer than the kitchen."

"He should have stayed in Edinburgh," said Madam Flemington, laughing.

She loved Archie's society.

"I hear that this Captain Logie is one of the most dangerous rebels in Scotland," she went on. "If you can lay him by the heels it is a service that will not be forgotten. So far you have done mighty well, Archie."

They had reached the gate, and she laid her hand on his arm.

"Turn back," she said. "I must consult you. I suppose that now you will be kept for some time at Balnillo? That nest of treason, Montrose, will give you occupation, and you must stretch out the portrait to match your convenience. I am going to take advantage of it too. I shall go to Edinburgh while you are away."

"To Edinburgh?" exclaimed Flemington.

"Why not, pray?"

"But you leave Ardguys so seldom. It is years——"

"The more reason I should go now," interrupted she. "Among other things, I must see my man of business, and I have decided to do it now. I shall be more useful to you in Edinburgh, too. I have been too long out of personal touch with those who can advance your interests. I had a letter from Edinburgh yesterday; you are better thought of there than you suspect, Archie. I did not realize how important a scoundrel this man Logie is, nor what your despatch to Montrose implied."

He was silent, looking on the ground.

She knew every turn of Archie's manner, every inflection of his voice. There was a gathering sign of opposition on his face—the phantom of some mood that must not be allowed to gain an instant's strength. It flashed on her that he had not returned merely to fetch his clothes. There was something wrong. She knew that at this moment he was afraid of her, he who was afraid of nothing else.

She stopped in the path and drew herself up, considering where she should strike. Never, never had she failed to bring him to his bearings. There was only one fitting place for him, and that was in the hollow of her hand.

"Grandmother, I shall not go back to Balnillo," said he vehemently.

If the earth had risen up under her feet Madam Flemington could not have been more astonished. She stood immovable, looking at him, whilst an inward voice, flying through her mind like a snatch of broken sound, told her that she must keep her head. She made no feeble mistake in that moment, for she saw the vital importance of the conflict impending between them with clear eyes. She knew her back to be nearer the wall than it had been yet. Her mind was as agile as her body was by nature indolent, and it was always ready to turn in any direction and look any foe squarely in the face. She was startled, but she could not be shaken.

"I've left Balnillo for good," said he again. "I cannot go back—I will not!"

"You—*will not?*" said Christian, half closing her eyes. The pupils had contracted, and looked like tiny black beads set in a narrow glitter of grey. "Is that what you have come home to say to *me?*"

"It is impossible!" he cried, turning away and flinging out his arms. "It is more than I can do! I will not go man-hunting after Logie. I will go anywhere else, do anything else, but not that!"

"There is nothing else for you to do."

"Then I will come back here."

"That you will not," said Christian.

He drew in his breath as if he had been struck.

"What are you that you should betray me, and yet think to force yourself on me without my resenting it? What do you think I am that I should suffer it?"

She laughed.

"I have not betrayed you," said he in a husky voice.

The loyal worship he had given her unquestioning through the long dependence and the small but poignant vicissitudes of childhood came back on him like a returning tide and doubled the cruelty of her words. She was the one person against whom he felt unable to defend himself. He loved her truly, and the thought of absolute separation from her came over him like a chill.

"I did not think you could speak to me in this way. It is terrible!"

he said. His dark eyes were full of pain. He spoke as simply as a little boy.

Satisfaction stole back to her. She had not lost her hold on him, would not lose it. Another woman might have flung an affectionate word into the balance to give the final dip to the scale, but she never thought of doing that; neither impulse nor calculation suggested it, because affection was not the weapon she was accustomed to trust. Her faith was in the heavy hand. Her generalship was good enough to tell her the exact moment of wavering in the enemy in front, the magic instant for a fresh attack.

"You are a bitter disappointment," she said. "Life has brought me many, but you are the greatest. I have had to go without some necessities in my time, and I now shall have to go without you. But I can do it, and I will."

"You mean that you will turn from me altogether?"

"Am I not plain enough? I can be plainer if you like. You shall go out of this house and go where you will. I do not care where you go. But you are forgetting that I have some curiosity. I wish to understand what has happened to you since you wrote your letter. That is excusable, surely."

"It is Logie," said he. "He has made it impossible for me. I cannot cheat a man who has given me all his confidence."

"He gave you his confidence?" cried Madam Flemington. "Heavens! He is well served, that stage-puppet Prince, when his servants confide in the first stranger they meet! Captain Logie must be a man of honour!"

"He is," said Archie. "It was his own private confidence he gave me. I heard his own history from his own lips, and, knowing it, I cannot go on deceiving him. I like him too much."

Madam Flemington was confounded. The difficulty seemed so strangely puerile. A whim, a fancy, was to ruin the work of years and turn everything upside down. On the top, she was exasperated with Archie, but underneath, it was worse. She found her influence and her power at stake, and her slave was being wrested from her, in spite of every interest which had bound them together. She loved him with a jealous, untender love that was dependent on outward circumstances, and she was proud of him. She had smiled at his devotion to her as she would have smiled with gratified comprehension at the fidelity of a favourite dog, understanding the creature's justifiable feeling, and knowing how creditable it was to its intelligence.

"What has all this to do with your duty?"she demanded.

"My duty is too hard," he cried. "I cannot do it, grandmother!"

"*Too hard!*" she exclaimed. "Pah! you weary me—you disgust me. I am sick of you, Archie!"

His lip quivered, and he met her eyes with a mist of dazed trouble in his own. A black curtain seemed to be falling between them.

"I told him every absurdity I could imagine," said he. "I made him believe that I was dependent upon my work for my daily bread. I did not think he would take my lies as he did. His kindness was so great—so generous! Grandmother, he would have had me promise to go to him for help. How can I spy upon him and cheat him after that?"

He stopped. He could not tell her more, for he knew that the mention of the hundred pounds would but make her more angry; the details of what Logie had written could be given to no one. He was only waiting for an opportunity to destroy the paper he carried.

"We have to do with principles, not men," said Madam Flemington. "He is a rebel to his King. If I thought you were so much as dreaming of going over to those worthless Stuarts, I would never see you nor speak to you again. I would sooner see you dead. Is *that* what is in your mind?"

"There is nothing farther from my thoughts," said he. "I can have no part with rebels. I am a Whig, and I shall always be a Whig. I have told you the plain truth."

"And now *I* will tell you the plain truth," said Madam Flemington. "While I am alive you will not enter Ardguys. When you cut yourself off from me you will do so finally. I will have no half-measures as I have no half-sentiments. I have bred you up to support King George's interests against the whole band of paupers at St. Germain, that you may pay a part of the debt of injury they laid upon me and mine. Mary Beatrice took my son from me. You do not know what you have to thank her for, Archie, but I will tell you now! You have to thank her that your mother was a girl of the people—of the streets—a slut taken into the palace out of charity. She was forced on my son by the Queen and her favourite, Lady Despard. That was how they rewarded us, my husband and me, for our fidelity! He was in his grave, and knew nothing, but I was there. I am here still, and I remember still!"

The little muscles round her strong lips were quivering.

Archie had never seen Madam Flemington so much disturbed, and it was something of a shock to him to find that the power he had known always as self-dependent, aloof, unruffled, could be at the mercy of so much feeling.

"Lady Despard was one of that Irish rabble that followed King James along with better people, a woman given over to prayers and confessions and priests. She is dead, thank God! It was she who took your mother out of the gutter, where she sang from door to door, meaning to make a nun of her, for her voice was remarkable, and she and her priests would have trained her for a convent choir. But the girl had no stomach for a nunnery; the backstairs of the palace pleased her better, and the Queen took her into her household, and would have her sing to her in her own chamber. She was handsome, too, and she hid the devil that was in her from the women. The men knew her better, and the Chevalier and your father knew her best of all. But at last Lady Despard got wind of it. They dared not turn her into the streets for fear of the priests, and to save her own son the Queen sacrificed mine."

She stopped, looking to see the effect of her words. Archie was very pale.

"Is my true name Flemington?" he asked abruptly.

"You are my own flesh and blood," said she, "or you would not be standing here. Their fear was that the Chevalier would marry her privately, but they got him out of the way, and your father seduced the girl. Then, to make the Chevalier doubly safe, they forced him to make her his wife—he who was only nineteen! They did it secretly, but when the marriage was known, I would not receive her, and I left the court and went to Rouen. I have lived ever since in the hope of seeing the Stuarts swept from the earth. Your father is gone, and you are all I have left, but you shall go too if you join yourself to them."

"I shall not do that," said he.

"Do you understand now what it costs me to see you turn back?" said Madam Flemington.

The mantle had slipped from her shoulders, and her white hands, crossed at the wrists, lay with the fingers along her arms. She stood trying to dissect the component parts of his trouble and to fashion something out of them on which she might make a new attack. Forces outside her own understanding were at work in him which were strong enough to take the fine edge of humiliation off the history she had just told him; she guessed their presence, unseen though they were, and her acute practical mind was searching for them. She was like an astronomer whose telescope is turned on the tract of sky in which, as his science tells him, some unknown body will arise.

She had always taken his pride of race for granted, as she took her own. The influx of the base blood of the "slut" had been a mortification unspeakable, but to Madam Flemington, the actual treachery practised on her had not been the crowning insult. The thing was bad, but the manner of its doing was worse, for the Queen and Lady Despard had used young Flemington as though he had been of no account. The Flemingtons had served James Stuart wholeheartedly, taking his evil fortunes as though they had been their own; they had done it of their own free will, high-handedly. But Mary Beatrice and her favourite had treated Christian and her son as slaves, chattels to be sacrificed to the needs of their owner. There was enough nobility in Christian to see that part of the business as its blackest spot.

She had kept the knowledge of it from Archie, because she had the instinct common to all savage creatures (and Christian's affinity with savage creatures was a close one) for the concealment of desperate wounds. Her silks, her ruby earrings, her physical indolence, her white hands, all the refinements that had accrued to her in her world-loving life, all that went to make the outward presentment of the woman, was the mere ornamental covering of the savage in her.

That savage watched Archie now.

Madam Flemington was removed by two generations from Archie, and there was a gulf of evolution between them, unrealized by either. Their conscious ideals might be identical; but their unconscious ideals, those that count with nations and with individuals, were different. And the same trouble, one that might be accepted and acknowledged by each, must affect each differently. The old regard a tragedy through its influences on the past, and the young through its influences on the future. To Archie, Madam Flemington's revelation was an insignificant thing compared to the horror that was upon him now. It was done and it could not be undone, and he was himself, with his life before him, in spite of it. It was like the withered leaf of a poisonous plant, a thing rendered innocuous by the processes of nature. What process of nature could make his agony innocuous? The word 'treachery' had become a nightmare to him, and on every side he was fated to hear it.

Its full meaning had only been brought home to him two days ago, and now the hateful thing was being pressed on him by one who had suffered from it bitterly. What could he say to her? How was he to make her see as he saw? His difficulty was a sentimental one, and one that she would not recognize.

Archie was not logical. He had still not much feeling about having deceived Lord Balnillo, whose hospitality he had accepted and enjoyed, but, as he had said, he could not go "man-hunting" after James, who had offered him a brother's help, whose heart he had seen, whose life had already been cut in two by the baneful thing. There was little room in Archie's soul for anything but the shadow of that nightmare of treachery, and the shadow was creeping towards him. Had his mother been a grand-duchess of spotless reputation, what could her virtue or her blue blood avail him in his present distress? She was nothing to him, that "slut" who had brought him forth; he owed her no allegiance, bore her no grudge. The living woman to whom he owed all stood before him beloved, admired, cutting him to the heart.

He assented silently; but Christian understood that, though he looked as if she had carried her point, his looks were the only really unreliable part of him. She knew that he was that curious thing—a man who could keep his true self separate from his moods. It had taken her years to learn that, but she had learnt it at last.

For once she was, like other people, baffled by his naturalness. It was plain that he suffered, yet she could not tell how she was to mould the hard stuff hidden below his suffering. But she must work with the heavy hand.

"You will leave here to-morrow," she said; "you shall not stay here to shirk your duty"; and again the pupils of her eyes contracted as she said it.

"I will go now," said he.

CHAPTER IX

"TOUJOURS DE L'AUDACE"

"DOAG," said the beggar, addressing the yellow cur, "you an' me'll need to be speerin' aboot this. Whiles, it's no sae easy tellin' havers frae truth."

Though Skirling Wattie was on good terms with the whole of his team, the member of it whom he singled out for complete confidence, whom he regarded as an employer might regard the foreman of a working gang, was the yellow cur. The abuse he poured over the heads of his servants was meant more as incentive than as rebuke, and he fed them well, sharing his substance honestly with them, and looking to them for arduous service in return. They were a faithful, intelligent lot, good-tempered, but for one of the collies, and the accepted predominance of the yellow cur was merely one more illustration of the triumph of personality. His golden eyes, clear, like unclouded amber, contrasted with the thick and vulgar yellow of his close coat, and the contrast was like that between spirit and flesh. He was a strong, untiring creature, with blunt jaws and legs that seemed to be made of steel, and it was characteristic of him that he seldom laid down but at night, and would stand turned in his traces as though waiting for orders, looking towards his master as the latter sang or piped, whilst his comrades, extended in the dust, took advantage of the halt.

The party was drawn up under the lee of a low wall by the grassy side of the Brechin road, and its grotesqueness seemed greater than ever because of its entirely unsuitable background.

The wall encircled the site of an ancient building called Magdalen Chapel, which had long been ruined, and now only survived in one detached fragment and in the half-obliterated traces of its foundations. Round it the tangled grass rose, and a forest of withered hemlock that had nearly choked out the nettles, stood up, traced like lacework against the line of hills beyond the Basin. In summer its powdery white threw an evanescent grace over the spot. The place was a haunt of Skirling Wattie's, for it was a convenient half-way house between Montrose and Brechin, and the trees about it gave a comforting shelter from both sun and rain.

The tailboard of the cart was turned to the wall so that the piper could lean his broad back against it, and there being not a dozen inches between the bottom of his cart and the ground, he was hidden from anyone who might chance to be in the chapel precincts. The projecting stone which made a stile for those who entered the enclosure was just level with his shoulder, and he had laid his pipes on it while he sat with folded arms and considered the situation. He had just been begging at a farm, and he had heard a rumour there that Archie Flemington was gone from Balnillo, and had been seen in Brechin, riding westwards, on the preceding morning. The beggar had got a letter for him behind his sliding boards which had to be delivered without delay.

"Doag," said he again, "we'll awa' to auld Davie's."

Skirling Wattie distrusted rumour, for the inexactitudes of human observation and human tongues are better known to a man who lives by his wits than to anybody else. He was not going to accept this news without sifting it. To Balnillo he would go to find out whether the report was true. The only drawback was that "auld Davie," as he called the judge, abhorred and disapproved of beggars, and he did not know how he might stay in the place long enough to find out what he wanted. He was a privileged person at most houses, from the sea on the east to Forfar on the west, but Lord Balnillo would none of him. Nevertheless, he turned the wheels of his chariot in his direction.

He wondered, as he went along, why he had not seen Archie by the way; but Archie had not left Balnillo by the Brechin road, being anxious to avoid him. What was the use of receiving instructions that he could not bring himself to carry out? The last person he wished to meet was the beggar.

Wattie turned into the Balnillo gates and went up the avenue towards the stable. His pipes were silent, and the fallen leaves muffled the sound of his wheels. He knew about the mishap that had brought Flemington as a guest to the judge, and about the portrait he was painting, for tidings of all the happenings in the house reached the mill sooner or later. That source of gossip was invaluable to him. But, though the miller had confirmed the report that Flemington had gone, he had been unable to tell him his exact destination.

He drove into the stable yard and found it empty but for a man who was chopping wood. The latter paused between his strokes as he saw who had arrived.

"A'm seekin' his lordship," began Wattie, by way of discovering how the land lay.

"Then ye'll no find him," replied the woodman, who was none other than the elder, Andrew Robieson, and who, like his master, disapproved consistently of the beggar. He was a sly old man, and he did not think it necessary to tell the intruder that the judge, though not in the house, was within hearing of the pipes. It was his boast that he "left a' to Providence," but he was not above an occasional shaping of events to suit himself

The beggar rolled up to the back-door at the brisk pace he reserved for public occasions. A shriek of delight came from the kitchen window as the blast of his pipes buzzed and droned across the yard. The tune of the 'East Neuk of Fife' filled the place. A couple of maidservants came out and stood giggling as Wattie acknowledged their presence by a wag of the head that spoke gallantry, patronage, ribaldry—anything that a privileged old rogue can convey to young womanhood blooming near the soil. A groom came out of the stable and joined the group.

The feet of the girls were tapping the ground. The beggar's expression grew more genially provocative, and his eyeballs rolled more recklessly as he blew and blew; his time was perfect. The groom, who was dancing, began to compose steps on his own account. Suddenly there was a whirl of petticoats, and he had seized one of the girls round the middle.

They spun and counter-spun; now loosing each other for the more serious business of each one's individual steps, now enlacing again, seeming flung together by some resistless elemental wind. The man's gaze, while he danced alone, was fixed on his own feet as though he were chiding them, admiring them, directing them through niceties which only himself could appreciate. His partner's hair came down and fell in a loop of dull copper-colour over her back. She was a finely-made girl, and each curve of her body seemed to be surging against the agitated sheath of her clothes. The odd-woman-out circled round the pair like a fragment thrown off by the spin of some travelling meteor. The passion for dancing that is even now part of the life of Angus had caught all three, let loose upon them by the piper's handling of sound and rhythm.

In the full tide of their intoxication, a door in the high wall of the yard opened and Lord Balnillo came through it. The fragment broke from its erratic orbit and fled into the house with a scream; the meteor, a whirling twin-star, rushed on, unseeing. The piper, who saw well enough, played strong and loud; not the king himself could have stopped him in the middle of a strathspey. The yellow dog, on his feet among his reposing companions, showed a narrow white line between his lips, and the hackles rose upon his plebeian neck.

"Silence!" cried Lord Balnillo. But the rest of his words were drowned by the yell of the pipes.

As the dancers drew asunder again, they saw him and stopped. His wrath was centred on the beggar, and man and maid slunk away unrebuked.

Wattie finished his tune conscientiously. To Balnillo, impotent in the hurricane of braying reeds, each note that kept him dumb was a new insult, and he could see the knowledge of that fact in the piper's face. As the music ceased, the beggar swept off his bonnet, displaying his disreputable bald head, and bowed like the sovereign of some jovial and misgoverned kingdom. The yellow dog's attitude forbade Balnillo's nearer approach.

"Go!" shouted the judge, pointing a shaking forefinger into space. "Out with you instantly! Is my house to be turned into a house of call for every thief and vagabond in Scotland? Have I not forbidden you my gates? Begone from here immediately, or I will send for my men to cudgel you out!"

But he leaped back, for he had taken a step forward in his excitement, and the yellow cur's teeth were bare.

"A'm seekin' the painter-laddie," said the beggar, giving the dog a good-humoured cuff.

"Away with you!" cried the other, unheeding. "You are a plague to the neighbourhood. I will have you put in Montrose jail! Tomorrow, I promise you, you will find yourself where you cannot make gentlemen's houses into pandemoniums with your noise."

"A'd like Brechin better," rejoined the beggar; "it's couthier in there."

Balnillo was a humane man, and he prided himself, as all the world knew, on some improvements he had suggested in the Montrose prison. He was speechless.

"Ay," continued Wattie, "a'm thinkin' you've sent mony a better man than mysel' to the tolbooth. But, dod! a'm no mindin' that. A'm asking ye, *whaur's the painter-lad?*"

One of Balnillo's fatal qualities was his power of turning in mid-career of wrath or eloquence to dally with side-issues.

He swallowed the fury rising to his lips,

"What! Mr. Flemington?" he stammered. "What do you want of Mr. Flemington?"

"Is yon what they ca' him? Well, a'm no seekin' onything o' him. It's him that's seekin' me."

Astonishment put everything else out of Balnillo's mind. He glared at the intruder, his lips pursed, his fingers working.

"He tell't me to come in-by to the muckle hoose and speer for him," said the other. "There was a sang he was needin'. He was seekin' to lairn it, for he liket it fine, an' he tell't me to come awa' to the hoose and lairn him. Dod! maybe he's forgotten. Callants like him's whiles sweer to mind what they say, but auld stocks like you an' me's got mair sense."

"I do not believe a word of it," protested Balnillo.

"Hoots! ye'll hae to try, or the puir lad'll no get his sang," exclaimed Skirling Wattie, smiling broadly. "Just you cry on him to come down the stair, an' we'll awa' ahint the back o' yon wa', an' a'll lairn him the music! It's this way."

He unscrewed the chanter and blew a few piercing notes. The sound flew into the judge's face like the impact of a shower of pebbles. He clapped his hands to his ears.

"I tell you Mr. Flemington is not here!" he bawled, raising his voice above the din. "He is gone. He is at Ardguys by this time."

"Man, is yon true? Ye're no leein'?" exclaimed Wattie, dropping his weapon.

"Is yon the way to speak to his lordship?" said the deep voice of Andrew Robieson, who had come up silently, his arms full of wood, behind the beggar's cart.

"Turn this vagabond away!" exclaimed Balnillo, almost beside himself. "Send for the men; bring a horsewhip from the stable! Impudent rogue! Go, Robieson—quick, man!"

But Wattie's switch was in his hand, and the dogs were already turning; before the elder had time to reach the stables, he had passed out under the clock and was disappearing between the trees of the avenue. He had learned what he wished to know, and the farther side of Brechin would be the best place for him for the next few days. He reflected that fortune had favoured him in keeping Captain Logie out of the way. There would have been no parleying with Captain Logie.

BOOK II

CHAPTER X

ADRIFT

ARCHIE rode along in a dream. He had gone straight out of the garden, taken his horse from the stable, and ridden back to Forfar, following the blind resolution to escape from Ardguys before he should have time to realize what it was costing him. He had changed horses at the posting-house, and turned his face along the way he had come. Through his pain and perplexity the only thing that stood fast was his determination not to return to Balnillo. "I will go now," he had said to Madam Flemington, and he had gone without another word, keeping his very thoughts within the walled circle of his resolution, lest they should turn to look at familiar things that might thrust out hands full of old memories to hold him back.

In the middle of his careless life he found himself cut adrift without warning from those associations that he now began to feel he had valued too little, taken for granted too much.

Balnillo was impossible for him, and in consequence he was to be a stranger in his own home. Madam Flemington had made no concession and had put no term to his banishment, and though he could not believe that such a state of things could last, and that one sudden impulse of hers could hurl him out of her life for ever, she, who had lived for him, had told him that she would "do without him." Then, as he assured himself of this, from that dim recess wherein a latent truth hides until some outside light flashes upon its lair, came the realization that she had not lived for him alone. She had lived for him that she might make him into the instrument she desired, a weapon fashioned to her hand, wherewith she might return blow for blow.

All at once the thought made him spiritually sick, and the glory and desirableness of life seemed to fade. He could not see through its dark places, dark where all had been sunshine. He had been a boy yesterday, a man only by virtue of his astounding courage and resource, but he was awakening from boyhood, and manhood was hard. His education had begun, and he could not value the education of pain—the soundest, the most costly one there is—any more than any of us do whilst it lasts. He did not think, any more than any of us think, that perhaps when we come to lie on our death-beds we shall know that, of all the privileges of the life behind us, the greatest has been the privilege of having suffered and fought.

All he knew was that his heart ached, that he had disappointed and estranged the person he loved best, and had lost, at any rate temporarily, the home that had been so dear. But hope would not desert him, in spite of everything. Madam Flemington had gone very wide of the mark in suspecting him of any leaning towards the Stuarts, and she would soon understand how little intention he had of turning rebel. There was still work for him to do. He had been given a free hand in details, and he would go to Brechin for the night; to-morrow he must decide what to do. Possibly he would ask to be transferred to some other place. But nothing that heaven or earth could offer him should make him betray Logie.

Madam Flemington had seen him go, in ignorance of whether he had gone in obedience or in revolt. Perhaps she imagined that her arguments and the hateful story she had laid bare to him had prevailed, and that he was returning to his unfinished portrait. In the excitement of his interview with her, he had not told her anything but that he refused definitely to spy upon James any more.

He had started for Ardguys so early, and had been there such a short time, that he was back in Forfar by noon. There he left his horse, and, mounting another, set off for Brechin. He was within sight of its ancient round tower, grey among the yellowing trees above the South Esk, when close to his left hand there rose the shrill screech of a pipe, cutting into his abstraction of mind like a sharp stab of pain. It was so loud and sudden that the horse leaped to the farther side of the road, snorting, and Flemington, sitting loosely, nearly lost his seat. He pulled up the astonished animal, and peered into a thicket of alder growing by the wayside. The ground was marshy, and the stunted trees were set close, but, dividing their branches, he saw behind their screen an open patch in the midst of which was Skirling Wattie's cart. His jovial face seemed to illuminate the spot.

"Dod!" exclaimed the piper, "ye was near doon! A'd no seek to change wi' you. A'm safer wi' ma' doags than you wi' yon horse. What ailed ye that ye gae'd awa' frae Balnillo?"

"Private matters," said Archie shortly.

"Aweel, they private matters was no far frae putting me i' the tolbooth. What gar'd ye no tell me ye was gaein'?"

"Have you got a letter for me?" said Flemington, as Wattie began to draw up his sliding-board.

"Ay, there's ane. But just wait you, ma lad, till a tell ye what a was sayin' to auld Davie——"

"Never mind what you said to Lord Balnillo," broke in Flemington; "I want my letter."

He slipped from the saddle and looped the rein over his arm.

"Dinna bring yon brute near me!" cried Wattie, as horse and man began to crush through the alders. "A'm fell feared o' they unchancy cattle."

Archie made an impatient sound and threw the rein over a stump. He approached the cart, and the yellow dog, who was for once lying down, opened his wary golden eyes, watching each movement that brought the intruder nearer to his master without raising his head.

"You are not often on this side of Brechin," said Archie, as the beggar handed him the packet.

"Fegs, na!" returned Wattie, "but auld Davie an' his tolbooth's on the ither side o't an' it's no safe yonder. It's yersel' I hae to thank for that, Mr. Flemington. A didna ken whaur ye was, sae a gae'd up to the muckle hoose to speer for ye. The auld stock came doon himsel'. Dod! the doag gar'd him loup an' the pipes gar'd him skelloch. But he tell't me whaur ye was."

"Plague take you! did you go there asking for me?" cried Archie.

"What was a to dae? A tell't Davie ye was needin' me to lairn ye a sang! 'The painter-lad was seekin' me,' says I, 'an' he tell't me to come in-by.'"

Flemington's annoyance deepened. He did not know what the zeal of this insufferable rascal had led him to say or do in his name, and he had the rueful sense that the tangle he had paid such a heavy price to escape from was complicating round him. The officious familiarity of the piper exasperated him, and he resented Government's choice of such a tool. He put the letter in his pocket, and began to back out of the thicket. He would read his instructions by himself.

"Hey! ye're no awa', man?" cried Wattie.

"I have no time to waste," said Flemington, his foot in the stirrup.

"But ye've no tell't me whaur ye're gaein'!"

"Brechin!"

Archie called the word over his shoulder, and started off at a trot, which he kept up until he had left the alder-bushes some way behind him.

Then he broke the seal of his letter, and found that he was to convey the substance of each report that he sent in, not only to His Majesty's intelligence officer at Perth, but to Captain Hall, of the English ship *Venture*, that was lying under Ferryden. He was to proceed at once to the vessel, to which further instructions for him would be sent in a couple of days' time.

He pocketed the letter and drew a breath of relief, blessing the encounter that he had just cursed, for a road of escape from his present difficulty began to open before him. He must take to his own feet on the other side of Brechin, and go straight to the *Venture*. He would be close to Montrose, in communication with it, though not within the precincts of the town, and safe from the chance of running against Logie. Balnillo and his brother would not know what had become of him, and Christian Flemington would be cured of her suspicions by the simple testimony of his whereabouts.

He would treat the two days that he had spent at the judge's house as if they had dropped out of his life, and merely report his late presence in Montrose to the captain of the sloop. He would describe his watching of the two men who came out of 'The Happy Land,' and how he had followed them to the harbour through the darkness; how he had seen them stop opposite the ship's light as they discussed their plans; how he had tried to secure the paper they held. He would tell the captain that he believed some design against the ship to be on foot, but he would not let Logie's name pass his lips; and he would deny any knowledge of the identity of either man, lest the mention of Ferrier should confirm the suspicions of those who guessed he was working with James. When he had reported himself to Perth from the ship, he would no longer be brought into contact with Skirling Wattie, which at that moment struck him as an advantage.

The evenings had begun to close in early. As he crossed the Esk bridge and walked out of Brechin, the dusk was enwrapping its parapet like a veil. He hurried on, and struck out along the road that would lead him to Ferryden by the southern shore of the Basin. His way ran up a long ascent, and when he stood at the top of the hill the outline of the moon's disc was rising, faint behind the thin cloudy bank that rested on the sea beyond Montrose. There was just enough daylight left to show him the Basin lying between him and the broken line of the town's twinkling lights under the muffled moon.

It was quite dark when he stood at last within hail of the *Venture*. As he went along the bank at the Esk's mouth, he could see before him the cluster of houses that formed Ferryden village, and the North Sea beyond it, a formless void in the night, with the tide far out. Though the moon was well up, the cloud-bank had risen with her, and taken all sharpness out of the atmosphere.

At his left hand the water crawled slithering at the foot of the sloping bank, like a dark, full-fed snake, and not thirty yards out, just where it broadened, stretching to the quays of Montrose, the vessel lay at anchor, a stationary blot on the slow movement. Upstream, between her and the Basin, the wedge-shaped island of

Inchbrayock split the mass of water into two portions.

Flemington halted, taking in the dark scene, which he had contemplated from its reverse side only a few nights ago. Then he went down to the water and put his hands round his mouth.

"*Venture* ahoy!" he shouted.

There was no movement on the ship. He waited, and then called again, with the same result. Through an open porthole came a man's laugh, sudden, as though provoked by some unexpected jest. The water was deep here, and the ship lay so near that every word was carried across it to the shore.

The laugh exasperated him. He threw all the power of his lungs into another shout.

"Who goes there?" said a voice.

"Friend," replied Archie; and, fearing to be asked for a countersign, he called quickly, "Despatches for Captain Hall."

"Captain Hall is ashore," announced a second voice, "and no one boards us till he returns."

The *Venture* was near enough to the bank for Archie to hear some derisive comment, the words of which he could not completely distinguish. A suppressed laugh followed.

"Damn it!" he cried, "am I to be kept here all night?"

"Like enough, if you mean to wait for the captain."

This reply came from the open porthole, in which the light was obliterated by the head of the man who spoke.

There was a sound as of someone pulling him back by the heels, and the port was an eye of light again.

Flemington turned and went up the bank, and as he reached the top and sprang on to the path he ran into a short, stoutish figure which was beginning to descend. An impatient expletive burst from it.

"You needn't hurry, sir," said Archie, as the other hailed the vessel querulously; "you are not likely to get on board!"

"What? what? Not board my own ship?"

Flemington was a good deal taken aback. He could not see much in the clouded night, but no impression of authority seemed to emanate from the indistinguishable person beside him.

"Ten thousand pardons, sir!" exclaimed the young man. "You are Captain Hall? I have information for you, and am sent by His Majesty's intelligence officer in Perth to report myself to you. Flemington is my name."

For a minute the little man said nothing, and Archie felt rather than saw his fidgety movements. He seemed to be hesitating.

A boat was being put off from the ship. She lay so near to them that a mere push from her side brought the craft almost into the bank.

"It is so dark that I must show you my credentials on board," said Archie, taking Captain Hall's acquiescence for granted.

He heard his companion drawing in his breath nervously through his teeth. No opposition was made as he stepped into the boat.

When he stood on deck beside Hall the ship was quiet and the sounds of laughter were silent. He had the feeling that everyone on board had got out of the way on purpose as he followed the captain down the companion to his cabin. As the latter opened the door the light within revealed him plainly for the first time.

He was a small ginger-haired man, whose furtive eyes were set very close to a thin-bridged, aquiline nose; his gait was remarkable because he trotted rather than walked; his restless fingers rubbed one another as he spoke. He looked peevish and a little dissipated, and his manner conveyed the idea that he felt himself to have no business where he was. As Archie remarked that, he told himself that it was a characteristic he had never yet seen in a seaman. His dress was careless, and a winestain on his cravat caught his companion's eye. He had the personality of a rabbit.

Hall did not sit down, but stood at the farther side of the table looking with a kind of grudging intentness at his guest, and Flemington was inclined to laugh, in spite of the heavy heart he had carried all day. The other moved about with undecided steps. When at last he sat down, just under the swinging lamp, Archie was certain that, though he could be called sober, he had been drinking.

"Your business, sir," he began, in a husky voice. "I must tell you that I am fatigued. I had hoped to go to bed in peace."

He paused, leaning back, and surveyed Flemington with injured distaste.

"There is no reason that you should not," replied Archie boldly. "I have had a devilish hard day myself. Give me a corner to lie in to-night, and I will give you the details of my report quickly."

He saw that he would meet with no opposition from Hall, whose one idea was to spare himself effort, and that his own quarters on board the *Venture* were sure. No doubt long practice had enabled the man to look less muddled than he felt. He sat down opposite to him.

The other put out his hand, as though to ward him off.

"I have no leisure for business to-night," he said. "This is not the time for it."

"All the same, I have orders from Perth to report myself to you, as I have told you already," said Archie. "If you will listen, I will try to make myself clear without troubling you to read anything. I have information to give which you should hear at once."

"I tell you that I cannot attend to you," said Hall.

"I shall not keep you long. You do not realize that it is important, sir."

"Am I to be dictated to?" exclaimed the other, raising his voice. "This is my own ship, Mr. Flem—Fling—Fl ——"

The name presented so much difficulty to Hall that it died away in a tangled murmur, and Archie saw that to try to make him understand anything important in his present state would be labour lost.

"Well, sir," said he, "I will tell you at once that I suspect an attack on you is brewing in Montrose. I believe that it may happen at any moment. Having delivered myself of that, I had best leave you."

The word "attack" found its way to the captain's brain.

"It's impossible!" he exclaimed crossly. "Why, plague on't, I've got all the town guns! Nonsense, sir—no'sense! Come, I will call for a bottle of wine, 'n you can go. There's an empty bunk, I s'pose."

The order was given and the wine was brought. Archie noticed that the man who set the bottle and the two glasses on the table threw a casual look at Hall's hand, which shook as he helped his guest. He had eaten little since morning, and drunk less. Now that he had attained his object, and found himself in temporary shelter and temporary peace, he realized how glad he was of the wine. When, after a single glassful, he rose to follow the sailor who came to show him his bunk, he turned to bid good-night to Hall. The light hanging above the captain's head revealed every line, every contour of his face with merciless candour; and Flemington could see that no lover, counting the minutes till he should be left with his mistress, had ever longed more eagerly to be alone with her than this man longed to be alone with the bottle before him.

Archie threw himself thankfully into his bunk. There was evidently room for him on the ship, for there was no trace of another occupant in the little cabin; nevertheless, it looked untidy and unswept. The port close to which he lay was on the starboard side of the vessel, and looked across the strait towards the town. The lamps were nearly all extinguished on the quays, and only here and there a yellow spot of light made a faint ladder in the water. The pleasant trickling sound outside was soothing, with its impersonal, monotonous whisper. He wondered how long Hall would sit bemusing himself at the table, and what the discipline of a ship commanded by this curiously ineffective personality could be. To-morrow he must make out his story to the little man. He could not reproach himself with having postponed his report, for he knew that Hall's brain, which might possibly be clearer in the morning, was incapable of taking in any but the simplest impressions to-night.

Tired as he was, he did not sleep for a long time. The scenes of the past few days ran through his head one after another—now they appeared unreal, now almost visible to his eyes. Sometimes the space of time they covered seemed age-long, sometimes a passing flash. This was Saturday night, and all the events that had culminated in the disjointing of his life had been crowded into it since Monday. On Monday he had not suspected what lay in himself. He would have gibed had he been told that another man's personality, a page out of another man's history, could play such havoc with his own interests.

He wondered what James was doing. Was he—now—over there in the darkness, looking across the rolling, sea-bound water straight to the spot on which he lay? Would he—-could space be obliterated and night illumined—look up to find his steady eyes upon him? He lay quiet, marvelling, speculating. Then Logie, the shadowy town, the burning autumn-trees of Balnillo, the tulips round the house in far-away Holland, fell away from his mind, and in their place was the familiar background of Ardguys, the Ardguys of his childhood, with the silver-haired figure of Madam Flemington confronting him; that terrible, unsparing presence wrapped about with something greater and more arresting than mere beauty; the quality that had wrought on him since he was a little lad. He turned about with a convulsive breath that was almost a sob.

Then, at last, he slept soundly, to be awakened just at dawn by the roar of a gun, followed by a rattle of small shot, and the frantic hurrying of feet overhead.

CHAPTER XI

THE GUNS OF MONTROSE

WHEN Archie lay and pictured James on the other side of the water his vision was a true one, but, while he saw him on the quay among the sheds and windlasses, he had set him in the wrong place.

James stood at the point of the bay formed by the Basin of Montrose, at the inner and landward side of the town, not far from the empty fort from which Hall had taken the guns. The sands at his feet were bare, for the tide was out, and the salt, wet smell of the oozing weed blew round him on the faint wind. He was waiting for Ferrier.

They had chosen this night, as at this hour the ebbing water would make it possible for the hundred men of Ferrier's regiment to keep clear of the roads, and to make their way from Brechin on the secluded shore of the Basin. Logie had not been there long when he heard the soft sound of coming feet, and the occasional knocking of shoes against stone. As an increasing shadow took shape, he struck his hand twice against his thigh, and the shadow grew still. He struck again and in another minute Ferrier was beside him; the soldiers who followed halted behind their leader. The two men said little to each other, but moved on side by side, and the small company wound up the rising slope of the shore to the deserted fort and gathered at its foot.

James and his friend went on a little way and stood looking east down the townward shore of the strait past the huddled houses massed together at this end of Montrose. The water slid to the sea, and halfway down the long quay in front of them was moored the unrigged barque that held the town guns—the four-pounders and six-pounders that had pointed their muzzles for so many years from the fort walls towards the thundering bar.

Hall had not concerned himself to bring the vessel into his own immediate neighbourhood, nor even to put a few dozen yards of water between her and the shore. He knew that no organized rebel force existed within nine miles of where she lay, and that the Jacobites among the townsmen could not attempt any hostile movement unaided. He had eighty men on board the *Venture* with him, and from them he had taken a small guard which was left in charge of the barque. Every two or three days he would send a party from the sloop to patrol the streets of Montrose, and to impress disloyally inclined people. His own investigations of the place had not been great, for, though he went ashore a good deal, it cannot be said that King George's interests were much furthered by his doings when he got there.

When Logie and Ferrier had posted a handful of men in the empty fort, they went on towards the barque's moorings followed by the rest, and leaving a few to guard the mouth of each street that opened on the quay. The whole world was abed behind the darkened windows and the grim stone walls that brooded like blind faces over the stealthy band passing below. When they reached the spot where the ferry-boat lay that plied between Montrose and the south shore of the strait, two men went down to the landing-stage, and, detaching her chains, got her ready to push off. Then, with no more delay, the friends pressed on to the main business of their expedition. As they neared the barque, a faint shine forward where her bows pointed seaward suggested that someone on board was waking, so, judging it best to make the attack before an alarm could be given, the two captains ran on with their men, and were climbing over the bulwarks and tumbling on to her deck before Captain Hall's guard, who were playing cards round a lantern, had time to collect their senses.

The three players sprang to their feet, and one of them sent a loud cry ringing into the darkness before he sprawled senseless, with his head laid open by the butt-end of Ferrier's pistol. In this unlooked-for onslaught, that had come upon them as suddenly as the swoop of a squall in a treacherous sea, they struck blindly about, stumbling into the arms of the swarming, unrecognized figures that had poured in on their security out of the peaceful night. James had kicked over the lantern, and the cards lay scattered about under foot, white spots in the dimness. The bank of cloud was thinning a little round the moon, and the angles of the objects on deck began to be more clearly blocked out. One of the three, who had contrived to wrench himself from his assailant's hold, sprang away and raced towards the after-part of the ship, where, with the carelessness of security, he had left his musket. Three successive shots was the signal for help from the *Venture* in case of emergency, and he made a gallant effort to get free to send this sign of distress across the strait. But he was headed back and overpowered before he could carry out his intention. One of his companions was lying as if dead on the deck, and the other, who had been cajoled to silence by the suggestive caress of a pistol at the back of his ear, was having his arms bound behind him with his own belt.

Not a shot had been fired. Except for that one cry from the man who lay so still at their feet, no sound but the scuffling and cursing on the barque disturbed the quiet. Ferrier's men hustled their prisoners below into the cabin, where they were gagged and secured and left under the charge of a couple of soldiers. No roving citizen troubled the neighbourhood at this hour, for the fly-by-nights of Montrose looked farther inland for their entertainment, and the fisher-folk, who were the principal dwellers in the poor houses skirting the quays, slept sound, and recked little of who might be quarrelling out of doors so long as they lay warm within them. The barque was some way upstream from the general throng of shipping—apart, and, as Hall had thought, the more safe for that, for his calculations had taken no count of an enemy who might come from anywhere but the town. He had never dreamed of the silent band which had been yielded up by the misty stretches of the Basin.

James leaned over the vessel's side towards the *Venture*, and thought of Captain Hall. He had seen him in a tavern of the town, and had been as little impressed by his looks as was Flemington. He had noticed the uncertain eye, the restless fingers, the trotting gait, and had held him lightly as a force; for he knew as well as most men know who have knocked about this world that character—none other—is the hammer that drives home every nail into the framework of achievement.

But he had no time to spend in speculations, for his interest was centred in the ferry-boat that was now slipping noiselessly towards them on the current, guided down-stream by the couple of soldiers who had unmoored her. As she reached the barque a rope was tossed down to her, and she was made fast. The stolen guns were hauled from their storage, and a six-pounder lowered, with its ammunition, into the great tub that scarcely heaved on the slow swirl of the river; and whilst the work was going on, Ferrier and James stepped ashore to the quay, and walked each a short way along it, watching for any movement or for the chance of surprise. There was nothing: only, from far out beyond the shipping, a soft rush, so low that it seemed to be part of the atmosphere itself, told that the tide was on the turn.

In the enshrouding night the boat was loaded, and a dozen or so of the little company pushed off with their spoil. Ferrier went with them, and Logie, who was to follow with the second gun, watched the craft making her way into obscurity, like some slow black river monster pushing blindly out into space.

The scheme he had been putting together since the arrival of the *Venture* was taking reality at last, and though he could stand with folded arms on the bulwark looking calmly at the departing boat, the fire in his heart burned hot. Custom had inured him to risks of every kind, and if his keenness of enterprise was the same as it had been in youth, the excitement of youth had evaporated. It was the depths that stirred in Logie, seldom the surface. Like Archie Flemington, he loved life, but he loved it differently. Flemington loved it consciously, joyously, pictorially; James loved it desperately—so desperately that his spirit had survived the shock which had robbed it of its glory, for him. He was like a faithful lover whose mistress has been scarred by smallpox.

He could throw himself heart and soul into the Stuart cause, its details and necessities—all that his support of it entailed upon him, because it had, so to speak, given him his second wind in the race of life. Though he was an adventurer by nature, he differed from the average adventurer in that he sought nothing for himself. He did not conform to the average adventuring type. He was too overwhelmingly masculine to be a dangler about women, though since the shipwreck of his youth he had more than once followed in the train of some complaisant goddess, and had reaped all the benefits of her notice; he was no snatcher at casual advantages, but a man to whom service in any interest meant solid effort and unsparing sacrifice. Also he was one who seldom looked back. He had done so once lately, and the act had shaken him to the heart. Perhaps he would do so oftener when he had wrought out the permanent need of action that lay at the foundation of his nature.

When the boat had come back, silent on the outflowing river, and had taken her second load, he lowered himself into the stern as her head was pulled round again towards Inchbrayock.

The scheme fashioned by the two men for the capture of the vessel depended for its success on their possession of this island. As soon as they should land on it, they were to entrench the two guns, one on its south-eastern side, as near to the *Venture* as possible, and the other on its northern shore, facing the quays. By this means the small party would command, not only the ship, but the whole breadth of the river and its landing-places, and would be able to stop communication between Captain Hall and the town. Heavy undergrowth covered a fair portion of Inchbrayock, and the only buildings upon it—if buildings they could be called—were the walls of an old graveyard and the stones and crosses they encircled. Though the island lay at a convenient part of the strait, no bridge connected it with Montrose, and those who wished to cross the Esk at that point were obliged to use the ferry. The channel dividing its southern shore from the mainland being comparatively narrow, a row of gigantic stepping-stones carried wayfarers dry-shod across its bed, for at low tide there was a mere streak of water curling serpent-wise through the mud.

When the guns were got safely into position on the island it was decided that Ferrier was to return to the barque and take the remaining four-pounders with all despatch to a piece of rising ground called Dial Hill, that overlooked the mass of shipping opposite Ferryden.

He did not expect to meet with much opposition, should news of his action be carried to the town, for its main sympathies were with his side, and the force on the Government vessel would be prevented from coming over the strait to oppose him until he was settled on his eminence by the powerful dissuaders he had left behind him on Inchbrayock. He was to begin firing from Dial Hill at dawn, and James, who was near enough to the *Venture* to see any movement that might take place on her, was to be ready with his fire and with his small party of marksmen to check any offensive force despatched from the ship to the quays. Hall would thus be cut off from the town by the fire from Inchbrayock, on the one hand, and, should he attempt a landing nearer to the watermouth, by the guns on Dial Hill, on the other.

James had placed himself advantageously. The thicket of elder and thorn which had engulfed one end of the burial-ground made excellent concealment, and in front of him was the solid wall, through a gap in which he had turned the muzzle of his six-pounder. He sat on the stump of a thorn-tree, his head in his hands, waiting, as he knew he would have to wait, for some time yet, till the first round from Dial Hill should be the signal for his own attack. The moon had made her journey by this hour, and while she had been caught in her course through the zenith in the web of cloud and mist that thickened the sky, she was now descending towards her rest through a clear stretch; she swung, as though suspended above the Basin, tilted on her back, and a little yellower as she neared the earth; a dying, witch-like thing, halfway through her second quarter. James, looking up, could see her between the arms of the crosses and the leaning stones.

The strangeness of the place arrested his thoughts and turned them into unusual tracks, for, though far from being an unimaginative man, he was little given to deliberate contemplation. The distant inland water under the lighted half disc was pale, and a faintness seemed to lie upon the earth in this hour between night and morning. His thoughts went to the only dwellers on Inchbrayock, those who were lying under his feet—seamen, for the most part, and fisher folk, who had known the fury of the North Sea that was now beginning to crawl in and to surround them in their little township with its insidious arms, encircling in death the bodies that had escaped it in life. Some of them had been far afield, farther than he had ever been, in spite of all his campaigns, but they had come in over the bar to lie here in the jaws of the outflowing river by their native town. He wondered whether he should do the same; times were so uncertain now that he might well take the road into the world again. The question of where his bones should lie was a matter of no great interest to him, and though there was a vague restfulness in the notion of coming at last to the slopes and shadows of Balnillo, he knew that the wideness of the world was his natural home. Then he thought of Bergen-op-Zoom....

After a while he raised his head again, roused, not by the streak of light that was growing upon the east, but by a shot that shattered the silence and sent the echoes rolling out from Dial Hill.

CHAPTER XII

INCHBRAYOCK

ARCHIE sprang up, unable, for a moment, to remember where he was. He was almost in darkness, for the port looked northward, and the pale light barely glimmered through it, but he could just see a spurt of white leap into the air midway across the channel, where a second shot had struck the water. As he rushed on deck a puff of smoke was dispersing above Dial Hill. Then another cloud rolled from the bushes on the nearest point of Inchbrayock Island, and he felt the *Venture* shiver and move in her moorings. Captain Hall's voice was rising above the scuffling and running that was going on all over the ship, and the dragging about of heavy objects was making the decks shake.

He went below and begun to hustle on his clothes, for the morning air struck chill and he felt the need of being ready for action of some kind. In a few minutes he came up warily and crept round to the port side, taking what cover he could. Then a roar burst from the side of the *Venture* as she opened fire.

He stood, not knowing what to do with himself. It was dreadful to him to have to be inactive whilst his blood rose with the excitement round him. No one on the vessel remembered his existence; he was like a stray dog in a marketplace, thrust aside by every passer brushing by on the business of life.

It was soon evident that, though the guns on the hill commanded the *Venture*, their shot was falling short of her. As the sun heaved up from beyond the bar, the quays over the water could be seen filling with people, and the town bells began to ring. An increasing crowd swarmed upon the landing-stage of the ferry, but the boat herself had been brought by James to the shore of Inchbrayock, and nobody was likely to cross the water whilst the island and the high ground seaward of the town was held by the invisible enemy which had come upon them from heaven knew where. Captain Hall was turning his attention exclusively on Inchbrayock, and Flemington, who had got nearer to the place where he stood, gathered from what he could hear that the man on Dial Hill was wasting his ammunition on a target that was out of range. A shot from the vessel had torn up a shower of earth in the bank that sloped from the thicket to the river-mud, and another had struck one of the gravestones on the island, splitting it in two; but the fire went on steadily from the dense tangle where the churchyard wall no doubt concealed earthworks that had risen behind it in the dark hours. This, then, was the outcome of James's night-wanderings with Ferrier.

Archie contemplated Captain Hall where he stood in a little group of men. He looked even less of a personage in the morning light than he had done in the cabin, and the young man suspected that he had gone to bed in his clothes. This reminded him that he himself was unwashed, unshaven, and very hungry. Whatsoever the issue of the attack might be, there was no use in remaining starved and dirty, and he determined to go below to forage and to find some means of washing. There was no one to gainsay him at this time of stress, and he walked into Hall's cabin reflecting that he might safely steal anything he could carry from the ship, if he were so minded, and slip overboard across the narrow arm to the bank with nothing worse than a wetting.

Whilst he was attending to his own necessities, the booming went on overhead, and at last a shout from above sent him racing up from the welcome food he had contrived to secure. The wall on Inchbrayock was shattered in two or three places and the unseen gun was silent. The cannonade from Dial Hill had stopped, but a train of figures was hurrying across from the northern shore of the island, taking shelter among the bushes and stones. A boat was being lowered from the *Venture*, for the tide, now sweeping in, had covered the mud, making a landing possible. Men were crowding into her, and as Flemington got round to his former place of observation she was being pushed off.

Hall, who was standing alone, caught sight of him and came towards him; his face looked swollen and puffy, and his eyes were bloodshot.

"We have been attacked," he began—"attacked most unexpectedly!"

"I had the honour to report that possibility to you last night, sir," replied Flemington, with a trifle of insolence in his manner.

An angry look shot out of Hall's rabbit eyes. "What could you possibly have known about such a thing?" he cried. "What reason had you for making such a statement?"

"I had a great many," said Archie, "but you informed me that you had no leisure to listen to any of them until this morning. Perhaps you are at leisure now?"

"You are a damned impudent scoundrel!" cried the other, noticing Flemington's expression, which amply justified these words, "but you had better take care! There is nothing to prevent me from putting you under arrest."

"Nothing but the orders I carry in my pocket," replied Archie. "They are likely enough to deter you."

The other opened his mouth to speak, but before he could do so a shot crashed into the fore part of the ship, and a hail of bullets ripped out from the thicket on the island; the boat, which was half-way between the *Venture* and Inchbrayock, spun round, and two of the rowers fell forward over their oars. Hall left Archie standing where he was.

The gun that the ship's gunners believed themselves to have disabled had opened fire again, after a silence that had been, perhaps, but a lure to draw a sortie from her; and as it was mere destruction for the boat to attempt a landing in the face of the shot, she had orders to put back.

The position in which he was placed was now becoming clear to Hall. He was cut off from communication with the quays by the guns safely entrenched on the island, and those on Dial Hill, though out of range for the moment, would prevent him from moving nearer to the water-mouth or making an attempt to get out to sea. He could not tell what was happening in the town opposite, and he had no means of finding out, for the whole of the cannon that he had been mad enough to leave by the shore was in the enemy's possession, and would remain so unless the townspeople should rise in the Government interest for their recapture. This he was well aware they would not do.

His resentment against his luck, and the tale-bearing voice within, which told him that he had nothing to thank for it but his own carelessness, grew more insistent as his head grew clearer. He had been jerked out of sleep, heavy-headed, and with a brain still dulled by drink, but the morning freshness worked on him, and the sun warmed his senses into activity. The sight of Flemington, clean, impertinent, and entirely comprehensive of the circumstances, drove him mad; and it drove him still madder to know that Archie understood why he had been unwilling to see his report last night.

Hall's abilities were a little superior to his looks. So far he had served his country, not conspicuously, but without disaster, and had he been able to keep himself as sober as most people contrived to be in those intemperate days, he might have gone on his course with the same tepid success. He was one who liked the distractions of towns, and he bemoaned the fate that had sent him to anchor in a dull creek of the East Coast, where the taverns held nothing but faces whose unconcealed dislike forbade conviviality, and where even the light women looked upon his uniform askance. He was not a lively comrade at the best of times, and here, where he was thrown upon the sole society of his officers, with whom he was not popular, he was growing more morose and more careless as his habits of stealthy excess grew upon him. Archie, with his quick judgment of his fellow-men, had measured him accurately, and he knew it. In the midst of the morning's disaster the presence of the interloper, his flippant civility of word and insolence of manner, made his sluggish blood boil.

It was plain that the party on the island must be dislodged before anything could be done to save the situation, and Hall now decided to land as large a force as he could spare upon the mainland. By marching it along the road to Ferryden he would give the impression that some attempt was to be made to cross the strait nearer to the coast, and to land it between Dial Hill and the sea. Behind Ferryden village a rough track turned sharply southward up the bank, and this they were to take; they would be completely hidden from Inchbrayock once they had got over the crest of the land, and they were to double back with all speed along the mainland under shelter of the ridge, and to go for about a mile parallel with the Basin. When they had got well to the westward side of the island, they were to wheel down to the Basin's shore at a spot where a grove of trees edged the brink; for here, in a sheltering turn of backwater among the trunks and roots, a few boats were moored for the convenience of those who wished to cross straight to Montrose by water instead of taking the usual path by the stepping-stones over Inchbrayock Island.

They were to embark at this place, and, hugging the shore, under cover of its irregularities, to approach Inchbrayock from the west. If they should succeed in landing unseen, they would surprise the enemy at the further side of the graveyard whilst his attention was turned on the *Venture.* The officer to be sent in command of the party believed it could be done, because the length of the island would intervene to hide their manoeuvres from the town, where the citizens, crowding on the quays, would be only too ready to direct the notice of the rebels to their approach.

As the boat put off from the ship Archie slipped into it; he seemed to have lost his definite place in the scheme of things during the last twenty-four hours; he was nobody's servant, nobody's master, nobody's concern; and in spite of his bold reply to Hall's threat of arrest, he knew quite well that though the captain would stop short of such a measure, he might order him below at any moment; the only wonder was that he had not done so already. He did not know into what hands he might fall, should Hall be obliged to surrender, and this contingency appeared to be growing likely. By tacking himself on to the landing-party he would at least have the chance of action, and though, having been careful to keep out of Hall's sight, he had not been able to discover their destination, he had determined to land with the men.

After they had disembarked, he went boldly up to the officer in charge of the party and asked for permission to go with it, and when this was accorded with some surprise, he fell into step. As they tramped along towards Ferryden, he managed to pick up something of the work in hand from the man next to him. His only fear was of the chance of running against Logie; nevertheless, he made up his mind to trust to luck to save him from that, because he believed that Logie, as a professional soldier, would be in command of the guns on the hill. It was from Dial Hill that the tactical details of the attack could best be directed, and if either of the conspirators were upon the island, Archie was convinced it would be Ferrier.

They soon reached Ferryden. The sun was clear and brave in the salt air over the sea, and a flock of gulls was screaming out beyond the bar, dipping, hovering, swinging sideways against the light breeze, now this way, now that way, their wanton voices full of mockery, as though the derisive spirits imprisoned in the ocean had become articulate, and were crying out on the land. The village looked distrustfully at the approach of the small company, and some of the fisher-wives dragged their children indoors as if they thought to see them kidnapped. Such men as were hanging about watched them with sullen eyes as they turned in between the houses and made for the higher ground.

The boom of the *Venture's* guns came to them from time to time, and once they heard a great shout rise from the quays, but they could see nothing because of the intervening swell of the land. They passed a farm and a few scattered cottages; but these were empty, for their inmates had gone to the likeliest places they could find for a view of what was happening in the harbour.

Presently they went down to the Basin, straggling by twos and threes. At the water's edge a colony of beeches stood naked and leafless, their heads listed over westward by the winds that swept up the river's mouth. They were crowded thick about the creek down which Flemington and his companions came, and at their feet, tied to the gnarled elbows of the great roots beneath which the water had eaten deep into the bank, lay three or four boats with their oars piled inside them. The beech-mast of years had sunk into the soil, giving a curious mixture of heaviness and elasticity to the earth as it was trodden; a water-rat drew a lead-coloured ripple along the transparency, below which the undulations of the bottom lay like a bird's-eye view of some miniature world. The quiet of this hidden landing-place echoed to the clank of the rowlocks as the heavy oars were shipped, and two boatloads slid out between the stems.

Archie, who was unarmed, had borrowed one of the officer's pistols, not so much with the intention of using it as from the wish for a plausible pretext for joining the party. At any time his love of adventure would welcome such an opportunity, and at this moment he did not care what might happen to him. He seemed to have no chance of being true to anybody, and it was being revealed to him that, in these circumstances, life was scarcely endurable. He had never thought about it before, and he could think of nothing else now. It was some small comfort to know that, should his last half-hour of life be spent on Inchbrayock, Madam Flemington would at least understand that she had wronged him in suspecting him of being a turncoat. If only James could know that he had not betrayed him—or, rather, that his report was in the hands of that accursed beggar before they met among the broom-bushes! Yet, what if he did know it? Would his loathing of the spy under the roof-tree of his brother's house be any the less? He would never understand—never know. And yet he had been true to him in his heart, and the fact that he had now no roof-tree of his own proved it.

They slipped in under the bank of the island and disembarked silently. The higher ground in the middle of it crossed their front like the line of an incoming wave, hiding all that was going on on its farther side. They were to advance straight over it, and to rush down upon the thicket where the gun was entrenched with its muzzle towards the *Venture*. There was to be no working round the north shore, lest the hundreds of eyes on the quays should catch sight of them, and a hundred tongues give the alarm to the rebels. They were to attack at once, only waiting for the sound of another shot to locate the exact place for which they were to make. They stood drawn up, waiting for the order.

Archie dropped behind the others. His heart had begun to sink.

He had assured himself over and over again that Logie must be on Dial Hill; yet as each moment brought him nearer to contact with the enemy, he felt cold misgiving stealing on him. What if his guesses had been wrong? He knew that he had been a fool to run the risk he had taken. Chance is such a smiling, happy-go-lucky deity when we see her afar off; but when we are well on our steady plod towards her, and the distance lessens between us, it is often all that we can do to meet her eyes—their expression has changed. Archie's willingness to take risks was unfailing and temperamental, and he had taken this one in the usual spirit, but so much had happened lately to shake his confidence in life and in himself that his high heart was beating slower. Never had he dreaded anything as much as he dreaded James's knowledge of the truth; yet the most agonizing part of it all was that James could not know the whole truth, nor understand it, even if he knew it. Archie's reading of the other man's character was accurate enough to tell him that no knowledge of facts could make Logie understand the part he had played.

Sick at heart, he stood back from the party, watching it gather before the officer. He did not belong to it; no one troubled his head about him, and the men's backs were towards him. He stole away, sheltered by a little hillock, and ran, bent almost double, to the southern shore of the island. He would creep round it and get as near as possible to the thicket. If he could conceal himself, he might be able to see the enemy and the enemy's commander, and to discover the truth while there was yet time for flight. He glanced over his shoulder to see if the officer had noticed his absence, and being reassured, he pressed on. He knew that anyone who thought about him at all would take him for a coward, but he did not reckon that. The dread of meeting James possessed him.

Sheep were often brought over to graze the island, and their tracks ran like network among the bushes. He trod softly in and out, anxious to get forward before the next sound of the gun should let loose the invading-party upon the rebels. He passed the end of the stepping-stones which crossed the Esk's bed to the mainland; they were now nearly submerged by the tide rising in the river. He had not known of their existence, and as he noticed them with surprise, a shot shook the air, and though the thicket, now not far before him, blocked his view of the *Venture*'s hull, he saw the tops of her masts tremble, and knew that she had been struck.

Before him, the track took a sharp turn round a bend of the shore, which cut the path like a little promontory, so that he could see nothing beyond it, and here he paused. In another few minutes the island would be in confusion from the attack, and he might discover nothing. He set his teeth and stepped round the corner.

The track widened out and then plunged into the fringe of the thicket. A man was kneeling on one knee with his back to Flemington; his hands were shading his eyes, and he was peering along a tunnel-shaped gap in the branches, through which could be seen a patch of river and the damaged bows of the *Venture*.

Archie's instinct was to retreat, but before he could do so, the man jumped up and faced him. His heart leaped to his mouth, for it was James.

* * * *

Logie stood staring at him. Then he made a great effort to pick up the connecting-link of recollection that he felt sure he must have dropped. He had been so much absorbed in the business in hand that he found it impossible for a moment to estimate the significance of any outside matter. Though he was confounded and disturbed by the unlooked-for apparition of the painter, the idea of hostility never entered his mind.

"Flemington?" he exclaimed, stepping towards him.

But the other man's expression was so strange that he stopped, conscious of vague disaster. What had the intruder come to tell him? As he stood, Flemington murmured something he could not distinguish, then turned quickly in his tracks.

Logie leaped after him, and seized him by the shoulder before he had time to double round the bend.

"Let me go!" cried Archie, his chest heaving; "let me go, man!"

But James's grip tightened; he was a strong man, and he almost dragged him over. As he held him, he caught sight of the Government pistol in his belt. It was one that the officer who had lent it to Flemington had taken from the ship.

He jerked Archie violently round and made a snatch at the weapon, and the younger man, all but thrown off his balance, thrust his arm convulsively into the air. His sleeve shot back, laying bare a round, red spot outside the brown, sinewy wrist.

Then there flashed retrospectively before James's eye that same wound, bright in the blaze of the flaming paper; and with it there flashed comprehension.

His impulse was to draw his own pistol, and to shoot the spy dead, but Archie recovered his balance, and was grappling with him so that he could not get his arm free. The strength of the slim, light young man astonished him. He was as agile as a weasel, but James found in him, added to his activity, a force that nearly matched his own.

There was no possible doubt of Logie's complete enlightenment, though he kept his crooked mouth shut and uttered no word. His eyes wore an expression not solely due to the violent struggle going on; they were terrible, and they woke the frantic instinct of self-preservation in Flemington. He knew that James was straining to get out his own pistol, and he hung on him and gripped him for dear life. As they swayed and swung to and fro, trampling the bents, there rose from behind the graveyard a yell that gathered and broke over the sound of their own quick breaths like a submerging flood, and the bullets began to whistle over the rising ground.

Archie saw a change come into James's eyes; then he found himself staggering, hurled with swift and tremendous force from his antagonist. He was flung headlong against the jutting bend round which he had come, and his forehead struck it heavily; then, rolling down to the track at its foot, he lay stunned and still.

CHAPTER XIII

THE INTERESTED SPECTATOR

As James Logie dashed back to his men to meet this unexpected attack, he left Flemington lying with his face to the bank and his back towards the river; he was so close to the edge of the island that his hair rested on the wet sand permeated by the returning tide coming up the Esk. James's whole mind had gone back like a released spring to its natural preoccupation, and he almost forgot him before he had time to join the brisk affray that was going on.

But though Archie lay where he fell, and was as still as a heap of driftwood, it was only a few minutes before he came to himself. Perhaps the chill of the damp sand under his head helped to revive him; perhaps the violence of the blow had been broken by the sod against which he had been hurled. He stirred and raised himself, dazed, but listening to the confused sounds of fighting that rang over Inchbrayock. His head hurt him, and instinctively he grubbed up a handful of the cold, wet sand and held it to his brow. His wits had not gone far, for there had been no long break in his consciousness, and he got on his feet and looked round for the best means of escape.

James knew all. That was plain enough; and on the issue of the skirmish his own liberty would depend if he did not get clear of the island at once. He went back round the bend, and looking up the shore he saw a couple of the stepping-stones which were only half covered by the tide. In the middle of the channel they had disappeared already, but at either edge they lay visible, like the two ends of a partly submerged chain. Blood was trickling down his face, but he washed it off, and made hastily for the crossing, wading in.

The Esk was not wide just there, though it was far deeper than he had fancied it, and he stumbled along, churning up the mud into an opaque swirl through which he could not see the bottom. He climbed the further bank, wasting no time in looking behind him, and never stopped until he stood, panting and dizzy, on the high ridge of land from which he could overlook Inchbrayock and the harbour and town. He was a good deal exhausted, for his head throbbed like a boiling pot, and his hands were shaking. He lay down in a patch of whins, remembering that he was on the sky-line. He meant to see which way the fortunes of war were going to turn before deciding what to do with himself. Thanks to chance, his business with Captain Hall was not finished, nor even begun; but as things seemed at present, Captain Hall might be a prisoner before the leisure which had been the subject of his own gibes that morning should arrive. The vessel's guns had roared out again as he struggled up the steep, but there had been silence on the island, and even the rattle of musketry had now stopped. Something decisive must have taken place, though he could not guess what it was, and he was too far away to distinguish more than the moving figures in the graveyard.

He was high enough to see the curve of the watery horizon, for Ferryden village was some way below him. His view was only interrupted by a group of firs that stood like an outpost between him and the land's end. He lay among his friendly whin-bushes, staring down on the strait. If James were victorious he knew that there would soon be a hue and cry on his own tracks; but though alive to the desirableness of a good start in these circumstances, he felt that he could not run while there remained any chance of laying the whole of his report before Captain Hall. He thought, from what he had seen of the man, that the less he was reckoned with by his superiors the better, but it was not his business to consider that. As he turned these things over in his mind his eyes were attracted to Dial Hill, upon which the sudden sign of a new turn of events could be read.

He could see the group of men with the guns below the flagstaff which crowned its summit, and what now attracted his attention was a dark object that had been run up the ropes, its irregular outline flapping and flying against the sky as it was drawn frantically up and down.

Flemington was blessed with long sight, and he was certain that the two sharp-cut ends that waved like streamers as the dark object dipped and rose, were the sleeves of a man's coat. He saw a figure detach itself from the rest and run towards the seaward edge of the eminence. Ferrier—for he supposed now that Ferrier was on the hill—must be signalling out to sea with this makeshift flag.

He half raised himself from his lair. The cold grey-green of the ocean spread along the world's edge, broken by tiny streaks of foam as the wind began to freshen, and beyond the fir-trees, seen through their stems, the reason of the activity on Dial Hill slid into sight.

A ship was coming up the coast not a couple of miles out, and as Flemington watched her she stood in landward, as though attracted out of her course by the signals and the sound of firing in Montrose harbour. She was too far off for him to distinguish her colours, but he knew enough about shipping to be certain that she was a French frigate.

He dropped back into his place; whilst these sensational matters were going forward he did not suppose that anyone would think of pursuing him. The fact that the rebels were signalling her in suggested that the stranger might not be unexpected, and in all probability she carried French supplies and Jacobite troops. The likelihood of an interview with Captain Hall grew more remote.

The frigate drew closer; soon she was hidden from him by the jutting out of the land. Another shot broke from the *Venture*, but the quick reply from the island took all doubt of the issue of the conflict from Archie's mind. James was in full possession of the place, and the surprise must have been a failure.

Archie watched eagerly to see the ship arrive in the river-mouth. It was evident that Hall, from his position under the south shore of the strait, had not seen her yet. Presently she rounded the land and appeared to the hundreds of eyes on the quays, a gallant, silent, winged creature, a vivid apparition against the band of sea beyond the opening channel of the Esk, swept towards the town as though by some unseen impulse of fate. The shout that went up as she came into view rose to where Archie lay on the hillside.

The tide was now running high, and she passed in under Dial Hill. Her deck was covered with troops, and the waving of hats and the cheers of the townspeople, who were pouring along the further side of the harbour, made the truth plain to the solitary watcher among the whins. The *Venture* sent a shot to meet her that fell just in front of her bows, but although it was followed by a second, that cut her rigging, no great harm was done, and she answered with a broadside that echoed off the walls of the town till the strait was in a roar. It had no time to subside before James's gun on Inchbrayock began again.

Flemington could see that Hall's surrender could only be a matter of time; the new-comer would soon be landing her troops out of his range, and, having done so, would be certain to attack the *Venture* from the Ferryden side of the river. Half of Hall's men were on the island, which was in possession of the rebels, his vessel was damaged and in no condition to escape to sea, even had there been no hostile craft in his way and no Dial Hill to stand threatening between him and the ocean.

The time had come for Archie to think of his own plight and of his own prospects. He was adrift again, cut off even from the disorderly ship that had sheltered him last night, and from the unlucky sot who commanded her. His best plan would be to take the news of Hall's capture to Edinburgh, for it would be madness for him to think of going to Perth, whilst his identity as a Government agent would be published by Ferrier and Logie all over that part of the country. He was cast down as he sat with his hand to his aching head, and now that it had resulted in that fatal meeting, his own folly in going to the island seemed incredible.

His luck had been so good all his life, and after the many years that he had trusted her, the jade had turned on him! He had been too high-handed with her, that was the explanation of it! He had asked too much. He had been over-confident in her, over-confident in himself. Flemington was neither vain nor conceited, being too heartily interested in outside things to take very personal points of view; he merely went straight on, with the joy of life lighting his progress. But now he had put the crown on his foolhardiness. He had had so many good things—strength, health, wits, charm; the stage of his stirring life whereon to use them, and behind that stage the peaceful background of the home he loved, filled with the presence of the being he most admired and revered on earth.

But new lights had broken in on him of late. Troublous lights, playing from behind a curtain that hid unknown things. Suddenly he had turned and followed them, impelled by uncomprehended forces in himself, and it seemed that in consequence all around him had shifted, disintegrated, leaving him stranded. Once more as he watched, his anxious eyes on the scene below him, his heart full of his own perplexities, a last roar of shot filled the harbour, and then, on the *Venture*, he saw the flag hauled down.

He rose and looked about him, telling himself that he must get as far from the neighbourhood of Montrose as he could in the shortest possible time. Sixty miles of land stretched between him and Edinburgh, and the only thing for him to do was to start by way of the nearest seaport from which he could sail for Leith. He was a very different figure from the well-appointed young man who had ridden away from Ardguys only yesterday, for he was soaked to above the knees from wading in the Esk; blood had dripped on his coat from the cut on his forehead, and his hair at the back was clogged with sand. Excitement had kept him from thinking how cold he was, and he had not known that he was shivering; but he knew it as he stood in the teeth of the fresh wind. He laughed in spite of his plight; it was so odd to think of starting for Edinburgh from a whin-bush.

He turned southwards, determining to go forward till he should strike the road leading to the seaport of Aberbrothock; by sticking to the high ground he would soon come to it at the inland end of the Basin, and by it he might reach Aberbrothock by nightfall, and thence take sail in the morning. This was the best plan he could devise, though he did not care to contemplate the miles he would have to trudge. He knew that the broken coast took a great inward curve, and that by this means he would be avoiding its ins and outs, and he wished that he did not feel so giddy and so little able to face his difficulties. He remembered that the money he had on him made a respectable sum, and realized that the less worth robbing he looked, the more likely he would be to get to his journey's end in safety. He stepped out with an effort; southward he must go, and for some time to come Angus must know him no more.

CHAPTER XIV

IN SEARCH OF SENSATION

WHEN Skirling Wattie had delivered his letter to Flemington on the foregoing day, he watched the young man out of sight with disgust, and cursed him for a high-handed jackanapes. He was not used to be treated in such a fashion. There was that about Archie which took his fancy, for the suggestion of stir and movement that went everywhere with Flemington pleased him, and roused his unfailing curiosity. The beggar's most pleasant characteristic was his interest in everybody and everything; his worst, the unseasonable brutality with which he gratified it.

A livelihood gained by his own powers of cajolery and persistence had left him without a spark of respect for his kind. He would have been a man of prowess had his limbs been intact—and destiny, in robbing his body of activity, had transferred that quality to his brains. His huge shoulders and broad fists, the arrogant male glare of his roving eye, might well hint at the wisdom of providence in keeping his sphere of action to the narrow limits of a go-cart. Those who look for likenesses between people and animals would be reminded by him of a wild boar; and it was almost shocking to anyone with a sense of fitness to hear the mellow and touching voice, rich with the indescribable quiver of pathos and tragedy, that proceeded from his bristly jaws when he sang. The world that it conjured up before imaginative listeners was a world of twilight; of stars that drew a trail of tear-dimmed lustre about the ancient haunted places of the country; stars that had shone on battlefields and on the partings of lovers; that had looked on the raids of the border, and had stood over the dark border-towers among the peat.

It was a strange truth that, in the voice of this coarse and humble vagabond, lay the whole distinctive spirit of the national poetry of Scotland.

In the last few months his employment had added new zest to his life, for it was not only the pay he received for his occasional carrying of letters that was welcome to him; his bold and guileful soul delighted in the occupation for its own sake. He was something of a student of human nature, as all those who live by their wits must be of necessity; and the small services he was called upon to give brought him into contact with new varieties of men. Archie was new to him, and, in the beggar's opinion, immeasurably more amusing than anyone he had seen yet. In modern parlance he would be called 'a sportsman', this low-bred old ruffian who had lost his legs, and who was left to the mercy of his own ingenuity and to the efforts of the five dumb animals which supplemented his loss. He had—all honour to him—kept his love of life and its chances through his misfortune; and though he did not know it himself, it was his recognition of the same spirit in Flemington that made him appreciate the young man.

His services to the state had not been important up to the present time. A few letters carried, a little information collected, had been the extent of his usefulness. But, though he was not in their regular employ, the authorities were keeping a favourable eye on him, for he had so far proved himself capable, close-mouthed, and a very miracle of local knowledge.

He sat in his cart looking resentfully after Flemington between the stems of the alders and the lattice of their golden-brown leaves, and, though the one word tossed over the rider's shoulders did not tell him much, he determined he would not lose sight of Archie if he could help it. "Brechin" might mean anything from a night's lodging to a lengthened stay, but he would follow him as far as he dared and set about discovering his movements. Skirling Wattie had friends in Brechin, as he had in most places round about, and certain bolt-holes of his own wherein he could always find shelter for himself and his dogs; but he did not mean to trust himself nearer than these refuges to Lord Balnillo, at any rate, not for a few days. Chance had relieved him of the letter for which he was responsible sooner than he expected, and at present he was a free man. He roused his team, tucked his pipes into their corner of the cart, and, guiding himself carefully between the trees, issued from the thicket like some ribald vision of goblinry escaped from the world of folk-lore.

He turned towards Brechin, and set off for the town at a brisk trot, the yellow dog straining at his harness, and his comrades taking their pace from him. Every inch of the road was known to Wattie, every tree and tuft, every rut and hole; and as there were plenty of these last, he bumped and swung along in a way that would have dislocated the bones of a lighter person. The violent roughness of his progress was what served him for exercise and kept him in health. There were not many houses near the highway, but the children playing round the doors of the few he passed hailed him with shouts, and he answered them, as he answered everyone, with his familiar wag of the head.

When he entered Brechin and rolled past the high, circular shaft of its round tower, the world made way for him with a grin, and when it was not agile enough to please him, he heralded himself with a shrill note from the chanter, which he had unscrewed from his pipes. Business was business with him. He meant to lie in the town to-night, but he was anxious to get on to Flemington's tracks before the scent was cold.

He drove to the Swan inn and entered the yard, and there he had the satisfaction of seeing Archie's horse being rubbed down with a wisp of straw. Its rider, he made out, had left the inn on foot half an hour earlier, so, with this meagre clue, he sought the streets and the company of the idlers haunting their thievish corners, to whom the passing stranger and what might be made out of him were the best interests of the day. By the time the light was failing he had traced Flemington down to the river, where he had been last seen crossing the bridge. The beggar was a good deal surprised; he could not imagine what was carrying Archie away from the place.

In the dusk he descended the steep streets running down to the Esk, and, slackening his pace, took out a short, stout pair of crutches that he kept beside him, using them as brakes on either side of the cart. People who saw Wattie for the first time would stand, spell-bound, to watch the incredible spectacle of his passage through a town, but, to the inhabitants of Brechin, he was too familiar a sight for anything but the natural widening of the mouth that his advent would produce from pure force of habit.

The lights lit here and there were beginning to repeat themselves in the water, and men were returning to their houses after the day's work as he stopped his cart and sent out that surest of all attractions, the first notes of 'The Tod', into the gathering mists of the river-side. By ones and twos, the details of a sympathetic audience drew together round him as his voice rose over the sliding rush of the Esk. Idlers on the bridge leaned over the grey arches as the sound came to them above the tongue of the little rapid that babbled as it lost itself in the shadow of the woods downstream.

Then the pipes took up their tune. Jests and roars of laughter oiled the springs of generosity, and the good prospects of supper and a bed began to smile upon the beggar. When darkness set in, he turned his wheels towards a shed that a publican had put at his disposal for the night, and he and his dogs laid themselves down to rest in its comfortable straw. The yellow cur, relieved from his harness, stole closer and closer to his master and lay with his jowl against the pipes. Presently Wattie's dirty hand went out and sought the coarse head of his servant.

"Doag," he was muttering, as he went to sleep.

Perhaps in all the grim, grey little Scottish town, no living creature closed its eyes more contentedly than the poor cur whose head was pillowed in paradise because of the touch that was on it.

Morning found man and dogs out betimes and migrating to the heart of the town. Wattie was one who liked to get an early draught from the fountain-head of news, to be beforehand, so to speak, with his day. The Swan inn was his goal, and he had not got up the hill towards it when his practised eye, wise in other men's movements, saw that the world was hurrying along, drawn by some magnet stronger than its legitimate work. The women were running out of their houses too. As he toiled up the steep incline, a figure burst from the mouth of a wynd and came flying down the middle of the narrow way.

"Hey! what ails ye, man? What's 'ahind ye?" he cried, stopping his cart and spreading out his arms as though to embrace the approaching man.

The other paused. He was a pale, foolish-looking youth, whose progress seemed as little responsible as that of a discharged missile.

"There's fechtin!" he yelled, apparently addressing the air in general.

"Fechtin?"

"Ay, there's fechtin at Montrose this hour syne! Div ye no hear them, ye deef muckle swine?" continued the youth, rendered abusive by excitement.

The two stared in each other's faces as those do who listen. Dull and distant, a muffled boom drove in from the coast. A second throb followed it.

The youth dropped his raised hands and fled on.

Wattie turned his dogs, and set off down the hill without more delay. Here was the reason that Archie had left the town! It was in expectation of this present disturbance on the coast that he had slipped out of Brechin by the less frequented road round the Basin.

He scurried down the hill, scattering the children playing in the kennel with loud imprecations and threats. He sped over the bridge, and was soon climbing the rise on the farther side of the Esk. If there was fighting going on, he would make shift to see it, and Montrose would be visible from most of his road. Soon he would get a view of the distant harbour, and would see the smoke of the guns whose throats continued to trouble the air. Also, he would get forward unmolested, for there would be the width of the Basin between himself and Lord Balnillo.

He breathed his team when he reached the top of the hill; for he was a scientific driver, and he had some way to go. He cast a glance down at the place he had left, rejoicing that no one had followed him out of it. When he was on his own errands he did not like company, preferring, like most independent characters, to develop his intentions in the perfect freedom of silence.

When he drew near enough to distinguish the *Venture*, a dark spot under the lee of Ferryden, he saw the white puffs of smoke bursting from her, and the answering clouds rising from the island. There had been no time to hear the rumours of the morning before he met the pale young man, or he would have learned that a body of Prince Charles's men under Ferrier had left Brechin last night whilst he lay sound asleep in the straw among his dogs. He could not imagine where the assailants had come from who were pounding at the ship from Inchbrayock.

The fields sloped away from him to the water, leaving an uninterrupted view. He pressed on to the cross-roads at which he must turn along the Basin's shore. From there on, the conformation of the land, and the frequent clumps of trees, would shut out both town and harbour from his sight until he came parallel with the island.

He halted at the turning for a last look at the town. The firing had ceased, which reconciled him a little to the eclipse of the distant spectacle; then he drove on again, unconscious of the sight he was to miss. For, unsuspected by him, as by the crowd thronging the quays of Montrose, the French frigate was creeping up the coast, and she made her appearance in the river-mouth just as Wattie began the tamer stage of his journey.

The yellow cur and his companions toiled along at their steady trot, their red tongues hanging. The broadside from the French ship rang inland, and the beggar groaned, urging them with curses and chosen abuse. His intimate knowledge of the neighbourhood led him to steer for the identical spot on which Flemington, crouched in his whin-bush, had looked down on the affray, and he hoped devoutly that he might reach that point of vantage while there was still something to be seen from it. Silence had settled on the strait once more.

Not far in front a man was coming into sight, the first creature Wattie had seen since leaving Brechin, whose face was turned from the coast. He seemed a person of irresolute mind, as well as of vacillating feet, for every few yards he would stop, hesitating, before resuming his way. The beggar cursed him heartily for a drunkard, for, though he had a lively sympathy with backsliders of that kind, he knew that accurate information was the last thing to be expected from them. Before the wayfarers had halved the distance between them the man stopped, and sitting down by the tumbledown stone dyke at the roadside, dropped his head in his hands. As the cart passed him a few minutes later, he raised a ghastly face, and Skirling Wattie pulled up astounded, with a loud and profane exclamation, as he recognized Flemington.

Though Archie had been glad to escape from the beggar yesterday, he was now thankful to see anyone who might pass for a friend. He tried to smile, but his eyes closed again, and he put out his hand towards the dyke.

"I'm so devilish giddy," he said.

Wattie looked at the cut on his head and the stains of blood on his coat.

"Ye've gotten a rare dunt," he observed.

Archie, who seemed to himself to be slipping off the rounded edge of the world, made no reply.

The other sat eyeing him with perplexity and some impatience. He did not know what he wanted most—to get to Montrose, or to get news out of Flemington. The dogs lay down in the mud. Flemington kept his hand to his eyes for a minute, and then lifted his head again.

"The ship has surrendered," he said, speaking with difficulty; "I have been on the high ground watching. She struck her flag. A French frigate——"

He stopped again. The road on which he sat was whirling down into illimitable space.

The other took in his plight. His coat, torn in his struggle with Logie, was full of whin-prickles, and the wet mud was caked on his legs. His soft, silky hair was flattened on his forehead.

"Ye've been fechtin' yersel', ma lad," said Wattie. "Whaur hae ye been?"

"There's a rebel force on Inchbrayock," said Archie, with another effort; "I have been on the island. Yes, I've been fighting. A man recognized me—a man I saw at—on the road by Balnillo. They will be hunting me soon, and I have papers on me they must not find, and money—all the money I have. God knows how I am to get away! I must get to Aberbrothock."

"What was ye sayin' aboot the French?"

In broken sentences, and between his fits of giddiness, Archie explained the situation in the harbour, and the beggar listened, his bristly brows knit, his bonnet thrust back on his bald head; and his own best course of action grew clear to him. Montrose would soon be full of rebel soldiers, and though these might be generous audiences when merry with wine and loose upon the streets, their presence would make him no safer from Lord Balnillo. Wattie knew that the judge's loyalty was beginning to be suspected, and that he might well have friends among the Prince's officers, whose arrival might attract him to the town. And to serve Archie would be a good recommendation for himself with his employers, to say nothing of any private gratitude that the young man might feel.

"Bide you whaur ye are!" he exclaimed, rousing his dogs. "Lad, a'll hae to ca' ye oot o' this, an' dod! we'll need a' our time!"

Not far from them a spring was trickling from the fields, dropping in a spurt through the damp mosses between the unpointed stones of the dyke. The obedient dogs drew their master close to it, and he filled a battered pannikin that he took from among his small collection of necessities in the bottom of the cart. He returned with the water, and when Archie had bathed his head in its icy coldness, he drew a whisky-bottle from its snug lair under the bagpipes, and forced him to drink. It was half full, for the friendly publican had replenished his store before they parted on the foregoing night. As the liquid warmed his stomach, Archie raised his head slowly.

"I believe I can walk now," he said at last.

"Ye'll need to try," observed Wattie dryly. "Ye'll no can ride wi' me. Come awa', Maister Flemington. Will a gi' ye a skelloch o' the pipes to help ye alang?"

"In God's name, no!" cried Archie, whose head was splitting.

He struggled on to his feet. The whisky was beginning to overcome the giddiness, and he knew that every minute spent on the highroad was a risk.

The beggar was determined to go to Aberbrothock with Archie; he did not consider him in a fit state to be left alone, and he counselled him to leave the road at once, and to cut diagonally across the high ground, whilst he himself, debarred by his wheels from going across country, drove back to the cross roads, and took the one to the coast. By doing this the pair would meet, Flemington having taken one side of the triangle, while Wattie had traversed the other two. They were to await each other at a spot indicated by the latter, where a bit of moor encroached on the way.

As Wattie turned again to retrace his road, he watched his friend toiling painfully up the slanting ground among the uneven tussocks of grass with some anxiety. Archie laboured along, pausing now and again to rest, but he managed to gain the summit of the ridge. Wattie saw his figure shorten from the feet up as he crossed the sky-line, till his head and shoulders dropped out of sight like the topsails of a ship over a clear horizon; he was disappointed at having missed the sight of so much good fighting. Archie's account had been rather incoherent, but he gathered that the rebels were in possession of the harbour, and that a French ship had come in in the middle of the affray full of rebel troops. He shouted the information to the few people he met.

He turned southward at the cross roads. Behind him lay the panorama of the Basin and the spread of the rolling country; Brechin, the Esk, the woods of Monrummon Moor, stretching out to Forfar, and, northward, the Grampians, lying with their long shoulders in the autumn light. His beat for begging was down there across the water and round about the country between town and town; but though his activities were in that direction, he knew Aberbrothock and the coast well, for he had been born in a fishing-village in one of its creeks, and had spent his early years at sea. He would be able to put Archie in the way of a passage to Leith without much trouble and without unnecessary explanations; Archie had money on him, and could be trusted to pay his way.

He was the first to reach the trysting-place, and he drew up, glad to give his team a rest; at last he saw Archie coming along with the slow, careful gait of a man who is obliged to consider each step of his way separately in order to get on at all.

"Sit ye doon," he exclaimed, as they met.

"If once I sit down I am lost," said Archie. "Come on."

He started along the road with the same dogged step, the beggar keeping alongside. They had gone about half a mile when Flemington clutched at a wayside bush and then slid to the ground in a heap.

Wattie pulled up, dismayed, and scanned their surroundings. To let him lie there by the road was out of the question. He could not tell how much his head had been injured, but he knew enough to be sure that exposure and cold might bring a serious illness on a man in his state; he did not understand that the whisky he had given Archie was the worst possible thing for him. To the beggar, it was the sovereign remedy for all trouble of mind or body.

He cursed his own circumscribed energies; there was no one in sight. The nearest habitation was a little farmhouse on the skirts of the moor with one tiny window in its gable-end making a dark spot, high under the roof

Wattie turned his wheels reluctantly towards it. Unwilling though he was to draw attention to his companion, there was no choice.

CHAPTER XV

WATTIE HAS THEORIES

THOUGH Skirling Wattie seldom occupied the same bed on many consecutive nights, his various resting-places had so great a family likeness that he could not always remember where he was when he chanced to wake in the small hours. Sheds, barns, stables harboured him in the cold months when luck was good; loanings, old quarries, whin-patches, the alder clump beyond Brechin, or the wall-side at Magdalen Chapel, in the summer.

To-night he lay in the barn abutting on the tiny farmhouse at which he had sought shelter for Archie. He had met with a half-hearted reception from the woman who came to the door. Her man was away, she told him, and she was unwilling to admit strangers in his absence. She had never seen Wattie before, and it was plain that she did not like his looks. He induced her at last, with the greatest difficulty, to give shelter in her barn to the comrade whom he described as lying in extremity at the roadside. Finally, she despatched her son, a youth of fifteen, to accompany the beggar, and to help to bring the sufferer back.

Cold water revived Archie again, and he reached the barn with the assistance of the lad, who, better disposed than his mother, cut a bundle of dry heather, which he spread in a corner for his comfort. The woman looked with silent surprise at her undesired guest; she had thought to see a fellow-traveller of different condition in company with the masterful old blackguard in the cart. Her glances and her expressive silence made Wattie uneasy, but there was no help for their plight whilst Flemington could scarcely stand.

The beggar had spent the rest of that day in the barn. He was not suffered to enter the farm, nor was he offered any food; but he had enough store by him from what he had collected in Brechin for his own needs and those of his team. Archie's only requirement was the bowl of water that his companion had obtained from the boy. He lay alternately dozing and tossing on his pile of heather. His body was chilled, for his high boots had been full of the Esk water, and Wattie had hesitated to draw them off, lest he should be unable to get them on again after their soaking.

Night fell on the barn at last. Wattie slept sound, with the yellow cur's muzzle against his shoulder; but he awoke towards midnight, for Archie's feverish voice was coming from the corner in which he lay. He inclined his ear, attracted by the recurrent name of Logie which ran through the disconnected babblings, rising again and again like some half-drowned object carried along a swift stream. The darkness made every word seem more distinct.

"Listen to me!" cried Flemington. "Logie! Logie! you do not understand... it is safe... it is burnt! Nobody shall know it from me.... I cannot take your money, Logie... I will tell you everything, but you will not understand...."

The beggar was holding his breath.

"I did not guess it was Inchbrayock... I thought it would not be Inchbrayock! Logie, I will say nothing... but I will tell you all. For God's sake, Logie,... I swear it is true!... Listen...."

Skirling Wattie could hear him struggling as though he were fighting for his life.

"Not to Ardguys... I cannot go back to Ardguys! I shall never tell... never, never tell... but I shall know where you are! They shall never know. *Ah!*" cried Archie, raising his voice like a man in distress calling for help, "it is you, Logie!... My God, let me go!"

The beggar dragged himself nearer. The fragment of moon did no more than turn the chinks and cracks of the barn to a dull grey, and he could hardly see the outline of his companion.

The nightmares that were tormenting Archie pointed to something that must have happened before he came by his hurt, and the injury and the chill had produced these light-headed wanderings; there were troubles boiling in his mind that he had kept behind his teeth so long as his tongue was under control. Wattie wondered what was all this talk of Lord Balnillo's brother. It seemed as if there were some secret between this man, suspected, as he well knew, of being an active rebel, and Flemington. Had it been light, Wattie would have tried to get at the papers that Archie had spoken of as being on him when they met, for these might give him some clue to the mystery. He sat in the dark leaning against the wall of the barn, his arms tightly folded across his great chest, his lips pursed, his gaze bent on the restless figure that he could just distinguish.

All at once Archie sat up.

"Where are you?" he asked in a high, strained voice.

"A'm here," replied the beggar.

"Is it you, Logie?" exclaimed Flemington.

"It's mysel'."

Wattie smoothed the roughness out of his accent as best he could. The other seemed to be hovering on the brink of consciousness. He sank back.

"It is not Logie," he said; "but you can tell him——"

Wattie leaned forward and laid his broad palm firmly and very gently on his shoulder.

"What'll a' tell him?" said he.

Flemington turned towards him and groped about with his hot hand.

"Tell him from me that he can trust me," he said in a hoarse, earnest whisper.

The beggar's touch seemed to quiet him. He lay still, murmuring indistinctly between snatches of silence. Once again he sat up, groping about.

"You will not forget?" he said.

"Na, na," replied Wattie.

He pushed him gently back, patting him now and again as a nurse might pat a restless child, and Archie grew calmer. The hand quieted him. Rough, dirty, guileful, profane as he was, without scruple or conscience or anything but the desire to do the best for himself, Skirling Wattie had got, lodged in body or spirit, or in whatsoever part of man the uncomprehended force dwells, that personal magnetism which is independent alike of grace and of virtue, which can exist in a soil that is barren of either. It may have been that which the yellow cur, with the clear vision belonging to some animals, recognized and adored; seeing not only the coarse and jovial reprobate who was his master, but the shadow of the mysterious power that had touched him.

The dog, awakened by Archie's cry, found that the beggar had moved, and drew closer to his side. Flemington dozed off again, and Wattie sat thinking; he longed to stir him up, that he might have the chance of hearing more of his rambling talk. But he refrained, not from humane feeling, but from the fear that the talker, if he were tampered with, might be too ill to be moved on the morrow. Sleep was his best chance, and Wattie had made up his mind that if it were possible to move him, he would prevail on the boy to get a beast from the nearest place that boasted anything which could carry him to Aberbrothock. He knew that Flemington could pay for it, and he would direct him to a small inn in that place whose landlord, besides being a retired smuggler, was a distant kinsman of his own. The matter of a passage to Leith could be arranged through the same source for a consideration. Archie should take his chance by himself.

He realized with some bitterness the bright opportunities that can be lost upon a being who has no legs to speak of; for he could easily have relieved him of what money he carried had he been an able-bodied man. It was not that he lacked the force for such deeds, but that honesty was wantonly thrust upon him because his comings and goings were so conspicuous. Notoriety takes heavy toll; and he had about the same chance as the king of being conveniently mislaid. He would have given a good deal for a sight of the papers that Archie carried, and though the darkness interfered with him now, he promised himself that he would see them if the morning light should find him still delirious. He could not make out how ill he was; and in spite of his curiosity, he was not prepared to befriend him with the chance of his growing worse. To have him dying upon his hands would be a burden too great to endure, even should it lead to no awkward questionings. He would get rid of him to-morrow, whether his curiosity were satisfied or not: he had heard enough to make him suspect very strongly that Flemington was in the pay of the rebels as well as in that of the King. It was a situation that he, personally, could very well understand. But the night turned, and Archie grew more peaceful as the hours went by. He had one or two bouts of talking, but they were incoherent and fitful, and his mind appeared now to be straying among different phantoms. There was no more about Logie, and Wattie could only make out the word 'Ardguys', which he knew as the name of a place beyond Forfar; and as he had discovered in Brechin that Flemington lived somewhere in those parts, he guessed that his thoughts were roving about his home. His breathing grew less laboured, and the watcher could hear at last that he slept. The moon dropped, and with her going the crevices lost their greyness and the barn grew black. The beggar, who was a healthy sleeper, laid himself down again, and in the middle of his cogitations passed into oblivion.

When he awoke the place was light, and Archie was looking at him with intelligent eyes; they were hollow, and there were dark shadows below them, but they were the eyes of a man in full possession of his wits.

"We must get out of this place," he said. "I have been standing up, but my knees seem so heavy I can hardly walk. My bones ache, Wattie; I believe there is fever in me, but I must get on. Damn it, man, we are a sorry pair to be cast on the world like this! I fear I took terrible liberties with your whisky yesterday."

It was a still, misty morning when the beggar, having harnessed his dogs, went out to look for the boy. When he was gone, Flemington fumbled with his shaking fingers for the different packets that he carried. All were there safely—his letters, his money. He trusted nobody, and he did not like having to trust the beggar.

His feverish head and the ague in his bones told him that he could scarcely hope to get to Aberbrothock on foot. His boots were still wet, and a bruise on his hip that he had got in falling yesterday had begun to make itself felt. He propped himself against the wall and reached out for the water beside him.

Wattie had been some time away when the barn door opened and the farm-woman appeared on the threshold, considering him with suspicious disfavour.

He dragged himself to his feet and bowed as though he were standing upon an Aubusson carpet instead of upon a pallet of withered heather. The action seemed to confirm her distrust.

"Madam," said he, "I have to thank you for a night's shelter and for this excellent refreshment. You are too good. I drink to you."

He raised the broken delf bowl with the drain of water that remained in it. Being conscious of inhospitality, she was not sure how much irony lay in his words, and his face told her nothing.

"It's the last ye'll get here," said she.

The more she looked at Flemington the more she was impressed by his undesirability as a guest. She was one of those to whom anything uncommon seemed a menace.

"Madam, I notice that you dislike me—why?"

"Wha are ye?" she inquired after a pause, during which he faced her, smiling, his eyebrows raised.

"We are two noblemen, travelling for pleasure," said he.

She crossed her arms, snorting.

"Heuch!" she exclaimed contemptuously. "A' wish ma gudeman was hame. He'd sort the pair o' ye!"

"If you think we have any design on your virtue," he continued, "I beg you to dismiss the idea. I assure you, you are safe with us. We are persons of the greatest delicacy, and my friend is a musician of the first rank. I myself am what you see—your humble servant and admirer."

"Ye're a leear and a Frenchman!" cried she.

Her eyes blazed. A little more provocation, and she might have attacked him. At this moment Wattie's cart drove into the yard behind her, axle deep in the sea of mud and manure that filled the place. She turned upon the newcomer. She could not deal with Archie, but the beggar was a foe she could understand, and she advanced, a whirl of abuse, upon him. The yellow dog's growling rose, battling with her strident tones, and Archie, seeing the mischief his tongue had wrought, limped out, fearful of what might happen.

"Stand awa' frae the doag, wumman! He'll hae the legs o' ye roogit aff yer henches gin he get's a haud o' ye!" roared Wattie, as the yellow body leaped and bounded in the traces.

Amid a hurricane of snarling and shouts he contrived, by plying his stick, to turn the animals and to get them out of the yard.

Archie followed him, but before he did so he paused to turn to his enemy, who had taken shelter in the doorway of the barn. He could not take off his hat to her because he had no hat to take off, having lost it on Inchbrayock Island, but he blew a kiss from the points of his fingers with an air that almost made her choke. Wattie, looking back over his shoulder, called angrily to him. He could not understand what he had done to the woman to move her to such a tempest of wrath, but he told himself that, in undertaking to escort Archie, he had made a leap in the dark. He would direct him to his cousin's house of entertainment in Aberbrothock, and return to his own haunts without delay.

At the nearest point of road the boy was standing by a sorry-looking nag that he held by the ear.

A few minutes later they had parted, and the boy, made happy by the coin he had been given, was returning to the farm, while the beggar, who had also reaped some profit in the last twenty-four hours, watched his late companion disappearing down the road. When he was out of sight he turned his own wheels in the direction of Brechin, and set off at a sober pace for that friendly town. He was singing to himself as he went, first because he owned the price of another bottle of whisky; secondly, because he was delighted to be rid of Flemington; and thirdly, because an inspiring idea had come to him.

His dogs, by the time they drew him into Brechin, would have done two heavy days' work, and would deserve the comparative holiday he meant to give them. He would spend to-morrow in the town with his pipes in the company of that congenial circle always ready to spring from the gutter on his appearance. Then, after a good night's rest, and when he should have collected a trifle, he would go on to Forfar and learn for certain whether Archie lived at Ardguys and who might be found there in his absence.

His idea was to arrive at the house with the last tidings of the young man; to give an account of the attack on the *Venture*, its surrender, Flemington's injury, and his own part in befriending him. It took some time, in those days of slow communication, for public news to travel so much as across a county, but even should the tale of the ship have reached Ardguys, the news of Archie could scarcely have preceded him. He hoped to find someone—for preference an anxious mother, who would be sensible of how much he had done for her son. There would be fresh profit there.

And not only profit. There was something else for which the beggar hoped, though profit was his main object. He pictured some tender, emotional lady from whose unsuspicious heart he might draw scraps of information that would fit into his own theories. He would try the effect of Logie's name, and there would be no harm in taking a general survey of Flemington's surroundings and picking up any small facts about him that he could collect.

His own belief in Archie's double dealing grew stronger as he jogged along; no doubt that shrewd and unaccountable young man was driving a stiff trade. There was little question in his mind that the contents of the letter he had put into his hands by the alder-clump had been sold to Captain James Logie, and that its immediate result had been the taking of the ship. He had learned from Archie's ravings that there had been a question of money between himself and Logie. The part that he could make nothing of was the suggestion, conveyed by Archie in the night, that he and the judge's brother had been fighting. "Let me go, Logie!" he had cried out in the darkness, and the blow on his forehead, which was bleeding when he found him, proved recent violence.

But though he could not explain these puzzles, nor make them tally with his belief, his theory remained. Flemington was in league with Logie. For the present he determined to keep his suspicions to himself.

CHAPTER XVI

THE TWO ENDS OF THE LINE

THREE days afterwards Wattie sat at the gates of Ardguys and looked between the pale yellow ashtrees at the house. There was nobody about at the moment to forbid his entrance, and he drove quietly in at a foot's pace and approached the door. The sun shone with the clear lightness of autumn, and the leaves, which had almost finished the fitful process of falling, lay gathered in heaps by the gate, for Madam Flemington liked order. On the steep pitch of the ancient slate roof a few pigeons, white and grey, sat in pairs or walked about with spasmodic dignity. The whole made a picture, high in tone, like a water-colour, and the clean etched lines of the stripped branches gave it a sharp delicacy and threw up the tall, light walls. All these things were lost upon the beggar.

He had informed himself in Forfar. He knew that the place was owned and lived in by a lady of the name of Flemington, who was the grandmother of the young man from whom he had lately parted. He had learned nothing of her character and politics because of the seclusion in which she lived, and he stared about him on every side and scanned the house for any small sign that might give him a clue to the tastes or occupations of its inhabitant. Whilst he was so engaged the front-door opened and the sound sent all the pigeons whirling from the roof into the air in flashes of grey-blue and white. Madam Flemington stood on the top step.

The beggar's hand went instinctively to his bonnet. He was a little taken aback—why, he did not know—and he instantly abandoned his plan of an emotional description of Archie's plight. She stood quite still looking down at him.

Her luxuriant silver hair was covered by a three-cornered piece of black lace that was tied in a knot under her chin, and she wore the 'calash,' or hood, with which the ladies of those days protected their headdresses when they went out. A short furred cloak was round her.

She considered Wattie with astonishment. Then she beckoned to him to approach.

"Who and what are you?" she asked, laying her hand on the railing that encircled the landing of the steps.

That question was so seldom put to him that it struck him unawares, like a stone from behind a hedge. He hesitated.

"A've got news for yer leddyship," he began.

"I asked your name," said Madam Flemington.

"Wattie Caird," replied he. "Skirling Wattie, they ca' me."

The countryside and its inhabitants did not appeal to Christian, but this amazing intruder was like no one she had ever seen before. She guessed that he was a beggar, and she brushed aside his announcement of news as merely a method of attracting attention.

"You are one of the few persons in these parts who can afford to keep a coach," she remarked.

A broad smile overspread his ribald countenance, like the sun irradiating a public-house.

"Dod, ma leddy, a'd think shame to visit ye on fut," said he, with a wag of his head.

"You have better reasons than that," she replied rather grimly.

"Aye, aye, they're baith awa'," said he, looking at the place where his legs should have been. "A'm an ill sicht for the soutars!"

She threw back her head and laughed a little.

She had seen no one for months, with the exception of Archie, who was so quick in mind and speech, and the humour of this vagabond on wheels took her fancy. There was no whining servility about him, in spite of his obvious profession.

The horrified face of a maidservant appeared for one moment at a window, then vanished, struck back by the unblessed sight of her mistress, that paralyzing, unapproachable power, jesting, apparently, with Skirling Wattie, the lowest of the low. The girl was a native of Forfar, the westernmost point of the beggar's travels, and she had often seen him in the streets.

"You face life boldly," said Madam Flemington.

"An' what for no? Fegs, greetin' fills naebody's kyte."*

She laughed again.

"You shall fill yours handsomely," said she; "go to the other door and I will send orders to the women to attend to you."

"Aye, will I," he exclaimed, "but it wasna' just for a piece that a' cam' a' the way frae the muir o' Rossie."

"From where?" said she,

"The muir o' Rossie," repeated he. "Ma leddy, it was awa' yonder at the tail o' the muir that a' tell't Maister Flemington the road to Aberbrothock."

"Mr. Flemington?"

"Aye, yon lad Flemington—an' a deevil o' a lad he is to tak' the road wi'! Ma leddy, there's been a pucklie fechtin' aboot Montrose, an' the Prince's men hae gotten a haud o' King George's ship that's in by Ferryden. As a' gaed doon to the toon, a' kaipit† wi' Flemington i' the road. He'd gotten a clour on's heed. He was fechtin' doon aboot Inchbrayock, he tell't me."

"Fighting? With whom?" asked Madam Flemington, fixing her tiger's eyes on him.

The beggar had watched her face narrowly while he spoke for the slightest flicker of expression that might indicate the way her feelings were turning.

"He was fechtin' wi' Captain Logie," he continued boldly, "a fell man yon—ye'll ken him, yer leddyship?"

"By name," said Christian.

"A'm thinkin' it was frae him that he got the clour on 's heed. A' gie'd him ma guid whisky bottle, an' a' got water to him frae a well. A' ca'd him awa' frae the roadside—he didna ken wha would be aifter him ye see—an' a' gar'd a clatterin' auld wife at the muir side gie's a shelter yon nicht. A' didna' leave the callant, ma' leddy, till a' got a shelt to him. He's to Edinburgh. A' tell't him wha'd get him a passage to Leith—a'm an Aberbrothock man, mysel', ye ken."

* Stomach. † Met.

"And did he send you to me?"

"Aye, did he," said he, lying boldly.

There was no sign of emotion, none even of surprise, on her face. Her heart had beaten hard as the beggar talked, and the weight of wrath and pain that she had carried since she had parted with Archie began to lighten. He had listened to her—he had not gone against her. How deep her words had fallen into his heart she could not tell, but deep enough to bring him to grips with the man who had made the rift between them.

"Are you sure of what you say?" she asked quickly; "did you see them fight?"

"Na, na, but 'twas the lad himsel' that tell't me. He was on the ship."

"He was on the ship?"

"Aye, was he. And he gae'd oot wi' the sodgers to deave they rebels frae Inchbrayock. They got the ship, ma leddy, but they didna get him. He escapit."

"Did you say he was much hurt?" said Madam Flemington.

"Hoots! ye needna' fash yersel', ma leddy! A' was feared for him i' the nicht, but there wasna' muckle wrang wi' him when he gae'd awa', or, dod, a' wouldna' hae left him!"

He had no mind to spoil his presentment of himself as Good Samaritan.

So far he had learnt nothing. He had spoken of the Prince's men as rebels without a sign of displeasure showing on Madam Flemington's face. Archie might be playing a double game and she might be doing the same, but there was nothing to suggest it. She was magnificently impersonal. She had not even shown the natural concern that he expected with regard to her own flesh and blood.

"Go now," said she, waving her hand towards the back part of the house; "you shall feed well, you and your dogs; and when you have finished you can come to these steps again, and I will give you some money. You have done well by me."

She re-entered the house and he drove away to the kitchen-door, dismissed.

If Wattie hoped to discover anything more there about the lady and her household, he was disappointed. The servants raised their chins in refined disapproval of the vagrant upon whom their mistress had seen fit to waste words under the very front windows of Ardguys. They resolved that he should find the back-door, socially, a different place, and only the awe in which they stood of Christian compelled them to obey her to the letter. A crust or two would have interpreted her wishes, had they dared to please themselves. But Madam Flemington knew every resource of her larder and kitchen, for French housekeeping and the frugality of her exiled years had taught her thrift. She would measure precisely what had been given to her egregious guest, down to the bones laid, by her order, before his dogs.

The beggar ate in silence, amid the brisk cracking made by five pairs of busy jaws; the maids were in the stronghold of the kitchen, far from the ungenteel sight of his coarse enjoyment. When he had satisfied himself, he put the fragments into his leathern bag and went round once more to the front of the house.

A window was open on the ground-floor, and Madam Flemington's large white hand came over the sill holding a couple of crown pieces. She was sitting on the window-seat within. Her cloak and the calash had disappeared, and Wattie could see the fine poise of her head. She dropped the coin into the cart as he drove below.

As he looked up he thought that if she had been imposing in her outdoor garments she was a hundredfold more so without them. He was at his ease with her, but he wondered at it, though he was accustomed to being at his ease with everybody. A certain vanity rose in him, coarse remnant of humanity as he was, before this magnificent woman, and when he had received the silver, he turned about, facing her, and began to sing.

He was used to the plebeian admiration of his own public, but a touch of it from her would have a different flavour. He was vain of his singing, and that vanity was the one piece of romance belonging to him; it hung over his muddy soul as a weaving of honeysuckle may hang over a dank pond. Had he understood Madam Flemington perfectly, he might have sung 'The Tod', but as he only understood her superficially, he sang 'Logie Kirk'. He did not know how nearly the extremities of the social scale can draw together in the primitive humours of humanity. It is the ends of a line that can best be bent to meet, not one end and the middle.

Yet, as 'Logie Kirk' rang out among the spectral ash-trees, she sat still, astonished, her head erect, like some royal animal listening; it moved her, though its sentiment had naught to do with her mood at present, nor with her cast of mind at any time. But love and loss are things that lay their shadows everywhere, and Madam Flemington had lost much; moreover, she had been a woman framed for love, and she had not wasted her gifts.

As his voice ceased, she rose and threw the window up higher.

"Go on," she said.

He paused, taking breath, for a couple of minutes. He knew songs to suit all political creeds, but this time he would try one of the Jacobite lays that were floating round the country; if it should provoke some illuminating comment from her, he would have learned something more about her, and incidentally about Archie, though it struck him that he was not so sure of the unanimity of interest between the grandmother and grandson which he had taken for granted before seeing Madam Flemington.

His cunning eyes were rooted on her as he sang again.

"My love stood at the loanin' side
    And held me by the hand,
The bonniest lad that e'er did bide
    In a' this waefu' land;
There's but ae bonnier to be seen
    Frae Pentland to the sea,
And for his sake but yestereen
    I sent my love frae me.

"I gie'd my love the white, white rose
    That's at my feyther's wa',
It is the bonniest flower that grows
    Where ilka flower is braw.
There's but ae brawer that I ken
    Frae Perth unto the main,
And that's the flower o' Scotland's men
    That's fechtin' for his ain.

"If I had kept whate'er was mine,
As I had gie'd my best,
My hairt were licht by day, and syne
The nicht wad bring me rest;
There is nae heavier hairt to find
Frae Forfar toon to Ayr,
As aye I sit me doon to mind
On him I see nae mair.

"Lad, gin ye fa' by Chairlie's side,
To rid this land o' shame,
There will na be a prouder bride
Than her ye left at hame;
But I will see ye whaur ye sleep
Frae lowlands to the peat,
And ilka nicht at mirk I'll creep
To lay me at yer feet."

"You sing well," said Christian when he had stopped; "now go."

She inclined her head and turned from the window. As his broad back, so grotesque in its strange nearness to the ground, passed out between the gate-posts of Ardguys, she went over to the mantelpiece.

Her face was set, and she stood with clasped hands gazing into the fireplace. She was deeply moved, but not by the song, which only stirred her to bitterness, but by the searching tones of the beggar's voice, that had smitten a way through which her feelings surged to and from her heart. The thought that Archie had not utterly broken away from her unnerved her by the very relief it brought. She had not known till now how much she had suffered from what had passed between them. Her power was not all gone. She was not quite alone. She would have scorned to admit that she could not stand in complete isolation, and she admitted nothing, even to herself. She only stood still, her nerves quivering, making no outward sign.

Presently she rang a little hand-bell that was on the table.

The genteel-minded maid appeared.

"Mysie," said Madam Flemington, "in three days I shall go to Edinburgh."

CHAPTER XVII

SOCIETY

LORD BALNILLO looked out of his sedan chair as it emerged from the darkness of a close on the northern slope of the Old Town of Edinburgh. Far down in front of him, where the long alley stopped, a light or two was seen reflected in the black water of the Nor' Loch that lay between the ancient city and the ground on which the new one was so soon to rise. The shuffling footfalls of his chairmen, echoing off the sides of the covered entry, were drowned in the noise that was going on a little way farther forward, where the close widened out into a square courtyard. One side of this place was taken up by the house of Lady Anne Maxwell, for which the judge was bound.

It had been raining, and Edinburgh was most noisomely dirty under foot, so Balnillo's regard for his silk-clad legs and the buckled shoes on his slim feet, had made him decide to be carried to his kinswoman's party. He wore his favourite mouse colour, but the waistcoat under his velvet coat was of primrose satin, and the lace under his chin had cost him more than he liked to remember.

The courtyard sent up a glow of light into the atmosphere of the damp evening, for the high houses towering round it rose black into the sky, limiting the shine and concentrating it into one patch. From above, it must have looked like a dimly illuminated well. It was full of sedan chairs, footmen, lantern-carriers and caddies, and the chattering, pushing, jesting, and oaths were keeping the inhabitants of the neighbouring 'lands'—such of them as were awake, for Edinburgh kept early hours in those days—from going to sleep.

The sedan chairs were set down at the door, for they could seldom be carried into the low and narrow entrances of even the best town houses, and here, at Lady Anne's, the staircase wound up inside a circular tower projecting from the wall.

The caddies, or street-messengers of Edinburgh, that strange brotherhood of useful, omniscient rascals, without whose services nothing could prosper, ran in and out among the crowd in search of odd jobs. Their eyes were everywhere, their ears heard everything, their tongues carried news of every event. The caddies knew all that happened in society, on the bench, in shops, in wynds, in churches, and no traveller could be an hour in the town before they had made his name and business common property. In an hour and a half his character would have gone the same way. Their home by day was at the Market Cross in the High Street, where they stood in gossiping groups until a call let one of them loose upon somebody else's business. It was the perpetual pursuit of other people's business that had made them what they were.

A knot of caddies pressed round the door of Lady Anne Maxwell's house as Lord Balnillo, sitting erect in order not to crease his clothes and looking rather like an image carried in a procession, was kept at a standstill whilst another guest was set down. Through the open window of his chair there pressed a couple of inquisitive faces.

"Hey, lads!" cried a caddie, "it's Davie Balnillo back again!"

"Losh, it's himsel'! Aweel, ma lord, we're fine an' pleased to see ye! Grange is awa' in ben the hoose. I'se warrant he doesna' ken wha's ahint him!"

Balnillo nodded affably. The instant recognition pleased the old man, for he had only reached Edinburgh in time to dress for his cousin's party; also, Lord Grange was a friend of his, and he was glad to hear that he was in front. As he looked complacently upon the crowd, his chairmen suddenly stepped forward, almost throwing him out of his seat.

A cry rose round him.

"Canny! Canny! ye Hieland deevils! Ye'll hae the pouthered wiggie o' him swiggit aff his heed! Haud on, Davie; we'll no let ye cowp!"

Balnillo was rather annoyed, for he had been knocked smartly against the window-frame, and a little cloud of powder had been shaken on his velvet sleeve; but he knew that the one thing a man might not lose before the caddies was his temper, if he did not want his rage, his gestures, and all the humiliating details of his discomfiture to be the town talk next day. He looked as bland as he could while he resettled himself.

"It'll no be waur nor ridin' the circuit, ma lord?" inquired a voice.

A laugh went round the group, and the chair moved on and was set down at its destination. Though the caddies' knowledge of the judge went as far down as his foibles, the one thing that they did not happen to know was the motive that had brought him to Edinburgh.

The doings in the harbour had disturbed Balnillo mightily; for, though the success of Ferrier and James in taking the *Venture* rejoiced him, he was dismayed by what he had heard about Archie Flemington. His brother had told him everything. When Captain Hall and his men had been conveyed as prisoners to the town, and the ship had been taken possession of by Prince Charles' agent in Montrose, Logie had gone hastily to Balnillo to give the news to David, and to prepare for his own departure to join the Stuart army. There was no longer any need for secrecy on his part, and it had always been his intention to declare himself openly as soon as he had done his work in Montrose. The place was well protected, and, besides the town guns that he and Ferrier had taken from Hall, there were the two armed vessels—both now belonging to the Prince—lying in the harbour.

The arrival of the frigate with her supplies had turned Montrose from a rebelliously-inclined town into a declared Jacobite stronghold. The streets and taverns were full of Lord John Drummond's troops, the citizens had given vent to their feelings upon the town bells, bonfires blazed in the streets, and Prince Charlie's name was on every lip; girls wore white roses on their breasts, and dreamed at night of the fascinating young spark who had come to set Scotland alight. The intense Jacobitism of Angus seemed to have culminated in the quiet seaport.

In all this outburst of loyalty and excitement the cautious

Balnillo did not know what to do. The risk of announcing his leanings publicly was a greater one than he cared to take, for his stake in the country and the land was considerable, and he was neither sanguine enough to feel certain of the ultimate triumph of the Stuarts like the Montrose people, nor generous enough to disregard all results like James. As he told himself, after much deliberation, he was "best away."

He had heard from James of Archie's sudden appearance upon the island, armed with a Government weapon and in company with the attacking force from the ship, and had listened to James's grim denunciation of him as a spy, his passionate regrets that he had not blown his brains out there and then. James's bitterness had been so great that David told himself he could scarcely recognize his quiet brother.

There was abundant reason for it, but Logie had seemed to be beside himself. He had scarcely eaten or slept during the short time that he had been with him, and his face had kept the judge's tongue still. After his account of what had happened, Balnillo had not returned to the subject again.

Step by step the judge had gone over all the circumstances of Flemington's sudden emergence from the Den on that windy night, and had seen how he had himself been cozened and flattered into the business of the portrait which stood unfinished, in solitary and very marked dignity, in the room with the north light. He was a man who suspected some of his own weaknesses, though his knowledge did not prevent him from giving way to them when he thought he could do so safely, and he remembered the adroit bits of flattery that his guest had strewn in his path, and how obligingly he had picked them up. He was shrewd enough to see all that. He thought of the sudden departure when Madam Flemington's mysterious illness had spirited Archie out of the house at a moment's notice, and he saw how he had contrived to imbue both himself and James with the idea that he shared their political interests, without saying one definite word; he thought of his sigh and the change in his voice as he spoke of his father's death "in exile with his master."

These things stood up in a row before Balnillo, and ranged themselves into a sinister whole. The plain truth of it was that he had entertained a devil unawares.

There had been a great search for Flemington when the skirmish on Inchbrayock was over. It was only ceasing when the French frigate swam into the river-mouth like a huge water-bird, and James, plunged in the struggle, was unable to spare a thought to the antagonist he had flung from him at the first sound of the attack.

But when the firing had stopped, and the appearance of the foreign ship made the issue of the conflict certain, he returned to the spot where he had left Archie, and found him gone. He examined the sand for some trace of the vanished man's feet, but the tide was now high in the river, and his footprints had been swallowed by the incoming rush. The stepping-stones were completely covered, and he knew that these—great fragments of rock as they were—would now be lying under enough water to drown a man who should miss his footing while the tide surged through this narrow stretch of the Esk's bed. He guessed that the spy had escaped by them, though a short time later the attempt would have been impossible. He made a hasty search of the island, and, finding no sign of Flemington, he returned with his men and the prisoners they had taken, leaving the dead to be carried over later to the town for burial. The boats were on the Montrose side of Inchbrayock, and, their progress being hampered by the wounded, some time was lost before he could spare a handful of followers to begin the search for Flemington. He picked up a few volunteers upon the quays, and despatched them immediately to cross the strait and to search the southern shores of both the river and the Basin; but they had barely started when Flemington and the beggar were nearing the little farm on Rossie moor. Archie had spent so little time on the open road, thanks to his companion's advice, that none of those whom the pursuers met and questioned had seen him. Before dusk came on, their zeal had flagged; and though one, quicker-witted than his comrades, had suggested the moor as a likely goal for their quarry, he had been overborne by their determination that the fugitive, a man who had been described to them as coming from the other side of the county, would make in that direction.

When James had gone to join the Stuart army on its march to England, his brother, waiting until the Prince had left Holyrood, set forth for Edinburgh. It would have been difficult for him to remain at home within sound of the noisy rejoicings of Montrose without either joining in the general exultation or holding himself conspicuously aloof. Prudence and convenience pointed to the taking of a little holiday, and his own inclination did not gainsay them.

He had not been in Edinburgh since his retirement, and the notion of going there, once formed, grew more and more to his taste. A hundred things in his old haunts drew him: gossip, the liberal tables of his former colleagues, the latest modes in coats and cravats, the musical assemblies at which he had himself performed upon the flute, the scandals and anecdotes of the Parliament House and the society of elegant women. He loved all these, though his trees and parks had taken their places of late. He loved James too, and the year they had spent together had been agreeable to him; but politics and family affection—the latter of the general rather than the individual kind—strong as their bonds were, could not bring the brothers into true touch with each other. James was preoccupied, silent, restless, and David had sometimes felt him to be inhuman in his lack of interest in small things, and in his carelessness of all but the great events of life. And now, as Balnillo stepped forth at Lady Anne Maxwell's door, he was hugging himself at the prospect of his return to the trimmings and embroideries of existence. He walked up the circular staircase, and emerged into the candle-light of the long, low room in which his cousin's guests were assembled.

Lady Anne was a youngish widow, with a good fortune and a devouring passion for cards. She had all the means of indulging her taste, for not only did she know every living being who went to the making of Edinburgh society, but, unlike most of her neighbours, she owned the whole of the house in which she lived, and, consequently, had space wherein to entertain them. While nearly all the Edinburgh world dwelt in its flat, and while many greater ladies than herself were contented to receive their guests in their bedchambers, and to dance and drink tea in rooms not much bigger than the boudoirs of their descendants, Lady Anne could have received Prince Charles Edward himself in suitable circumstances had she been so minded. But she was very far from having any such aspiration, and had not set foot in Holyrood while the Prince was there, for she was a staunch Whig. As she greeted her cousin Balnillo, she was wondering how far certain rumours that she had heard about him were true, and whether he also had been privy to the taking of the sloop-of-war in Montrose harbour, for it was just a week since the news of Logie's exploit had reached Edinburgh. One of David's many reasons for coming to her party was his desire to make his reappearance in the polite world in a markedly Whig house.

He stood talking to Lord Grange in the oak-panelled room half full of people; through an open door another smaller appartment could be seen crowded with tables and card-players. Lady Anne, all of whose guests were arrived, had vanished into it, and the two judges stood side by side. Lord Grange, who valued his reputation for sanctity above rubies, did not play cards—at least, not openly—and Balnillo, discovering new faces, as those must who have been over a year absent from any community, was glad to have him at his elbow to answer questions. Silks rustled, fans clicked, and the medley of noises in the court below came up, though the windows were shut.

The candles, dim enough to our modern standards of lighting, shone against the darkness of polished wood, and laughter and talk were escaping, like running water out of a thicket, from a knot of people gathered round a small, plump, aquiline-nosed woman. The group was at the end of the room, and now and again an individual would detach himself from it, to return, drawn by some jest that reached him ere he had crossed the floor.

"Mrs. Cockburn's wit has not rusted this twelvemonth," observed Lord Grange.

"I marvel she has any left after nine years of housekeeping with her straitlaced father-in-law," replied Balnillo in a preoccupied voice.

His eyes were elsewhere.

"Ah!" said Grange, pulling a righteous face.

The group round Mrs. Cockburn opened, and she caught sight of him for the first time. She bowed and smiled civilly, showing her rather prominent teeth, then, noticing Balnillo, she came over to the two men. Her friends stepped apart to let her pass, watching her go with that touch of proprietary pride which a small intimate society feels in its more original members. It was evident that her least acts were deemed worthy of observation.

As she greeted David, he turned round with a low bow.

"My lord, I thought you were buried!" she exclaimed.

"Dead and buried," droned Grange, for the sake of saying something.

"Not dead," exclaimed she, "else I had been in mourning!"

Balnillo bowed again, bringing his attention back with a jerk from the direction in which it had been fixed.

"Come, my lord, what have you been doing all this long time?"

"I have been endeavouring to improve my estate, ma'am."

"And meanwhile you have left us to deteriorate. For shame, sir!"

"Edinburgh morals are safe in Lord Grange's hands," rejoined Balnillo, with a sudden flash of slyness.

Mrs. Cockburn smiled behind her fan. There were odd stories afloat about Grange. She looked appreciatively at Balnillo. He had not changed, in spite of his country life; he was as dapper, as ineffective, and as unexpected as ever. She preferred him infinitely to Grange.

"Fie, Davie!" broke in the latter, with a leer; "you are an ungallant dog! Here is Mrs. Cockburn wasting her words on you, and you do nothing but ogle the lady yonder by the window."

Three pairs of eyes—the bright ones of Mrs. Cockburn, the rather furtive ones of Balnillo, and the sanctimonious orbs of Lord Grange—turned in one direction.

"Mrs. Cockburn is all knowledge, as she is all goodness," observed the last named, pompously. "Pray, ma'am, tell us who is that lady?"

CHAPTER XVIII

BALNILLO FINDS PERFECTION

A SCONCE of candles beside a window-recess shed a collective illumination from the wall, and Christian Flemington stood full in their light, contemplating the company with superb detachment, and pervaded by that air, which never left her, of facing the world, unaided and unabashed, with such advantages as God had given her. Her neck, still white and firm, was bare, for she wore no jewels but the ruby earrings which shot blood-red sparks around her when she moved. Long necks were in fashion in those days, and hers was rather short, but the carriage of her head added enough to its length to do more than equalize the difference. Her hair was like massed silver, and her flesh—of which a good deal could be seen—rose like ivory above the wine-colour of her silk gown, which flowed in spreading folds from her waist to the ground. A Spanish fan with carved tortoiseshell sticks, a thing of mellow browns and golds, was half closed between her fingers. When she opened it, it displayed the picture of a bull-fight.

"That is Mrs. Flemington—Madam Flemington, as I am told many people call her—I presume, because she came to Scotland from France. You should know her, my lord," she added, addressing Balnillo; "you are from Angus."

But Balnillo was speechless.

Grange, who was transferring a pinch of snuff from his box to his nose, paused, his hand midway between the two.

"Is she the widow of Andrew Flemington, who was in France with King James?"

"The same," replied Mrs. Cockburn, tossing her head.

She had small sympathy with the Stuarts.

"I had not expected to see the lady here. Not that I know aught about her views. We have a bare acquaintance, and she is like yourself, Lord Balnillo—just arrived in Edinburgh when our young hero has left Holyrood."

"She has been a fine woman," said Lord Grange, his eye kindling.

"You may use the present tense, my lord," said Mrs. Cockburn.

"Aha!" sniggered Grange, who adhered to the time-honoured beliefs of his sex, "you dare to show yourself generous!"

"I dare to show myself what I am, and that is more than all the world can do," said she, looking at him very hard.

He shifted from foot to foot. At this moment the gallows, to which he had condemned a few people in his time, struck him as a personal inconvenience.

"Ma'am," said he, swallowing his rage, "you must present Davie, or he will lose what senses he has."

"Come, then, my lord, I will befriend you," said she, glad of the chance to be rid of Grange.

Balnillo followed her, unable to escape had he wished to do so.

Christian was a woman who stood very still. She turned her head without turning her body as Mrs. Cockburn approached with her request, and Balnillo saw her calm acquiescence.

His breath had been almost taken away as he learned the identity of the stranger. Here was the woman who knew everything about that astounding young man, his late guest, whose alarming illness had recalled him, who had lived at St. Germain with the exiled queen, yet who was the grandmother of a most audacious Whig spy! There was no trace of recent ill-health here. He had pictured some faint, feeble shred of old womanhood, not the commanding creature whose grey eyes were considering him as he advanced under cover of her leisurely consent. She seemed to measure him carelessly as he stood before her. He was torn asunder in mind, awestruck, dragged this way by his surprised admiration, that way by his intense desire to wring from her something about Flemington. Here was a chance, indeed! But Balnillo felt his courage drown in the rising fear of being unable to profit by that chance. Admiring bewilderment overcame every other feeling. He no longer regretted the price he had paid for the lace on his cravat.

His name had roused Madam Flemington, though she gave no sign of the thrill that went through her as it fell from Mrs. Cockburn's lips. As David stood before her in the correct yet sober foppery of his primrose and mouse-colour, she regretted that she was quite ignorant of the pretext on which Archie had left his picture unfinished, nor upon what terms he had parted with the judge. She had no reason for supposing Balnillo to be aware of the young man's real character. He had been fighting with James Logie, according to Skirling Wattie, yet there seemed to be no enmity in the business, for here was his brother, Lord Balnillo, assiduous in getting himself presented to her. Mrs. Cockburn had put her request with a smiling hint at the effect she had produced on his lordship. Christian glanced at David's meticulous person and smiled, arrogantly civil, secretly anxious, and remained silent, ready to follow his lead with caution.

The shrewd side of Balnillo was uppermost to-night, stimulated perhaps by the sight of society and by the exhilarating sound of its voice. He recovered his momentarily scattered wits and determined to approach his new acquaintance with such direct and simple questions as might seem to her to be the natural inquiries of a man interested in Flemington, and innocent of any mystery concerning him. It was quite possible—so he reasoned—that she was unaware of the details of what had happened on Inchbrayock Island. Archie had fled, and the search for him had produced no result; he was unlikely to have made for his own home if he did not wish to be found, and he and Madam Flemington might not have met since the affair of the *Venture*. It should be his—Balnillo's—task to convince her of his ignorance.

His intense curiosity about Archie was almost stronger than his wrath against him. Unlike James, whose bitterness was too deep for words, whose soul was driven before the fury of his own feelings like a restless ghost, David still looked back with a certain pleasant excitement to Flemington's meteoric flash through the even atmosphere of his daily life. He would dearly have liked to bring him to justice, but he was anxious to hear a little more of him first.

He had a curious mixture of feelings about him. There was no vainer man in Scotland than Balnillo, and if the mental half of his vanity had suffered from the deception practised on it, the physical half was yet preening itself in the sunny remembrance of the portrait at home—the portrait of David Balnillo as he would fain have had the world see him—the portrait, alas and alas! unfinished. He could not feel quite as James felt, who had opened his purse, and, more—far more than that—had laid open the most sacred page of his life before Flemington. He had placed his personal safety in his hands, too, though he counted that as a matter of less moment.

"Madam," said Balnillo, "to see you is to rejoice that you have recovered from your serious illness."

"You are very obliging, my lord. I am quite well," replied Christian, concealing a slight surprise at this remark.

"I am most happy in being presented to you," he continued. "What news have you of my charming friend Mr. Flemington, may I ask?"

"When I heard your name, my lord, I determined to be acquainted with you, if only to thank you for your kindness to my boy. He could not say enough of yourself and your brother. I hope Captain Logie is well. Is he with you this evening?"

The mention of James acted on David as he had designed that the mention of Archie should act on Madam Flemington. These two people who were playing at innocence were using the names of their relations to scare the enemy as savage tribes use the terrific faces painted on their shields. Balnillo, in beginning the attack, had forgotten his own weak point, and he remembered that he could give no satisfactory account of his brother at the present moment. But his cunning was always at hand.

"I had half expected to see him here," said he, peering round the room; "there was some talk of his coming. I arrived somewhat late, and I have hardly spoken to anyone but my Lord Grange and Mrs. Cockburn. The sight of yourself, ma'am, put other matters out of my head."

"Ah, sir," exclaimed Christian, "I fear that your ardour was all on behalf of Archie! But I am accustomed to that."

She cast a look of indolent raillery at him, drawing back her head and veiling her eyes, fiery and seductive still, with the momentary sweep of their thick lashes.

Balnillo threw out his chest like a pouter pigeon. He had not been so happy for a long time. As he did so, she remembered Archie's account of his silk legs, and his description of him as being "silly, virtuous, and cunning all at once." Silly she could well believe him to be; virtuous he might be; whether he was cunning or not, time would show her. She did not mean to let him go until she had at least attempted to hear more about James Logie.

"Madam," said he, "since seeing you I have forgotten Mr. Flemington. Can I say more?"

So far she was completely puzzled as to how much he knew about Archie, but it was beginning to enter her mind that her own illness, of which she had just learned from him, had been the young man's pretext for leaving his work when it was only begun. Why else had the judge mentioned it? And who but Flemington could have put the idea into his head?

She determined to make a bold attack on possibilities.

"Archie was distracted by my illness, poor boy, and I fear that your lordship's portrait suffered. But you will understand his anxiety when I tell you that I am the only living relation that he has, and that his devotion to me——"

"He needs no excuse!" cried David fervently.

She laid her hand upon his arm.

"I am still hardly myself," she said. "I cannot stand long. Fetch me a chair, my lord."

He skipped across the floor and laid hold upon one just in time, for a gentleman was on the point of claiming it. He carried it back with the air of a conqueror.

"Apart—by the curtain, if you please," said Christian, waving her hand. "We can speak more comfortably on the fringe of this rout of chattering people."

He set the chair down in a quiet place by the wall, and she settled herself upon it, leaning back, her shoulder turned from the company. Balnillo's delight deepened.

"And the portrait, my lord. He did not tell me what arrangement had been made for finishing it," said Christian, looking up at him as he stood beside her.

She seemed to be completely unconcerned, and she spoke with a leisurely dignity and ease that turned his ideas upside down. He could make nothing of it. She appeared to court the subject of Archie and the picture. He could only guess her to be innocent, and his warm admiration helped his belief. At no moment since he knew the truth from his brother's lips had Archie's character seemed so black as it did now. David's indignation waxed as he grew more certain that Flemington had deceived the noble woman to whom he owed so much, even as he had deceived him. He was becoming so sure of it that he had no desire to enlighten her. He longed to ask plainly where Archie was, but he hesitated. Even the all-wise Mrs. Cockburn was ignorant of this lady's political sympathies, and knew her only as the widow of a loyal exile. What might — what would be her feelings if she were to see her grandson in his real character?

Righteous anger smouldered under Balnillo's primrose waistcoat, and his spasmodic shrewdness began to doze in the increasing warmth of his chivalrous pity for this new and interesting victim of the engaging rogue.

"Mr. Flemington's concern was so great when he left my house that no arrangement was made," said he. "I had not the heart to trouble him with my unimportant affairs when so much was at stake."

Of the two cautious people who were feeling their way in the dark, it was the judge who was the more mystified, for he had laid hold of a definite idea, and it was the wrong one. Christian was merely putting a bold face on a hazardous matter, and hoping to hear something of Logie. She had not sought the introduction. David would have been the butt of her amused scorn had she been free enough from anxiety to be entertained. But she could not imagine on what footing matters really stood, and she was becoming inclined to suspect the beggar's statement that Flemington had been fighting with James. Her longing to see Archie was great.

She loved him in her own way, though she had driven him from her in her mortification and her furious pride. She had not believed that he would really go there and then; that he, who had served her purposes so gallantly all his life, would take her at her word. What was he doing? Why had he gone to Edinburgh? Her own reason for coming had been the hope of seeing him. She had been four days in the town now, and she dared not make open inquiries for him, not knowing how far his defection had gone. She had accused him of turning to the Stuarts, and he had denied the accusation, not angrily, but with quiet firmness. Two horrible possibilities had occurred to her: one, that he was with the Prince, and might be already known to the Government as a rebel; the other, that he had never reached Edinburgh—that his hurt had been worse than the beggar supposed, and that he might be ill or dying, perhaps dead. But it was only when she lay awake at night that she imagined these things. In saner moments and by daylight she put them from her. She was so well accustomed to being parted from him, and to the knowledge that he was on risky business, that she would not allow herself to be really disturbed. She assured herself that she must wait and watch; and now she was glad to find herself acquainted with Balnillo, who seemed to be the only clue in her hand. Mercifully, he had all the appearance of being an old fool.

"I see that you are too modest to tell me anything of the picture," she began. "I hope it promised well. You should make a fine portrait, and I believe that Archie could do you justice. He is at his best with high types. Describe it to me."

David espied a vacant chair, and, drawing it towards him, sat down to the subject with the same gusto that most men bring to their dinners. He cleared his throat.

"I should have wished it to be full length," said he, "but Mr. Flemington had no suitable canvas with him. I wore my robes, and he was good enough to say that the crimson was appropriate and becoming to me. Personally, I favour quiet colours, as you see, ma'am."

"I see that you have excellent taste."

He bowed, delighted.

"I remarked you as you came in," continued she, "and I asked myself why these gentlemen looked so garish. Observe that one beside the door of the card-room, my lord. I am sure that he chose his finery with some care, yet he reminds me of a clown at a merrymaking."

"True, true—excellently true!"

"In my youth it was the man of the world who set the fashions; now it is the tailor and the young sir fresh from his studies. What should these persons know of the subject?"

Balnillo was in heaven; from force of habit he ran his hand down the leg crossed upon his knee. The familiar inward curve of the slim silk ankle between his fingers was like the touch of a tried and creditable friend; it might almost be said that he turned to it for sympathy. He would have liked to tell his ankle that to-night he had found a perfection almost as great as its own.

Lord Grange, who had taken leave of his hostess and was departing, paused to look at him.

"See," said he, taking an acquaintance by the elbow, "look yonder at that doited Davie Balnillo."

"He is telling her about his riding of the circuit," said the other, grinning.

"The circuit never made him smile like that," replied Grange sardonically.

An hour later Christian Flemington stood at the top of the circular staircase. Below it, Balnillo was at the entrance-door, sending everyone within reach of his voice in search of her sedan chair. When it was discovered, he escorted her down and handed her into it, then, according to the custom of the time, he prepared to attend its progress to her lodgings in Hyndford's Close. The streets were even dirtier and damper than before, but he was as anxious to walk from Lady Anne's party as he had been determined to be carried to it. He stepped along at the side of the chair, turning, when they passed a light, to see the dignified silhouette of Madam Flemington's head as it appeared in shadow against the farther window.

Speech was impossible as they went, for avoidance of the kennel and the worse obstacles that strewed the city at that hour, before the scavengers had gone their rounds, kept David busy. The only profit that a man got by seeing his admired one home in Edinburgh in 1745 was the honour and glory of it.

When she emerged from the chair in Hyndford's Close he insisted upon mounting the staircase with her, though its narrowness compelled them to go in single file; and when they stopped halfway up at the door in the towering 'land,' he bade her goodnight and descended again, consoled for the parting by her permission that he should wait upon her on the following day.

Christian was admitted and sailed into her little room. A light was in it and Archie was standing at the foot of the bed.

Surprises had been rolling up round Madam Flemington all the evening; surprise at meeting Balnillo, surprise at his attitude; and this crowning surprise of all. She was bewildered, but the blessing of unexpected relief fell on her. She went towards him, her hands outstretched, and Flemington, who was looking at her with a wistfulness she had never seen in him before, took them and held them fast.

"Oh, Archie!" she exclaimed.

She could say no more.

They sat down at the wide hearth together, the shadow of the great carved bed sprawling over the crowded space between the walls and over Christian's swelling silks. Then he told her the history of the time since they parted in Ardguys garden; of his boarding of the *Venture*; of the fight with the rebels at Inchbrayock; of his meeting with Wattie; of how he had reached Aberbrothock half dead, and had lain sick for two days in an obscure tavern by the shore; how he had finally sailed for Leith and had reached Edinburgh.

Christian heard him, her gaze fixed upon the fire. She had elicited nothing about James Logie from Balnillo, and there was no word of him in Archie's story. She longed to speak of him, but would not; she longed to know if the beggar had told the truth in saying that the two men had actually fought, but she asked nothing, for she knew that her wisest part was to accept the essentials, considering them as the whole. She would ask no questions.

Archie had come back. She had forbidden Ardguys to him and he had evaded her ban by coming here. Yet he came, having proved himself loyal, and she would ignore the rest.

BOOK III

CHAPTER XIX

THE WINTER

APRIL is slow in Scotland, distrustful of her own identity, timid of her own powers. Half dazed from the long winter sleep, she is often bewildered, and cannot remember whether she belongs to winter or to spring.

After the struggles and perplexities of the months that had elapsed since Balnillo and Christian Flemington met in Edinburgh, she had come slowly to herself amid storms of sleet. Beyond the Grampians, in the North, her awakened eyes looked on a country whose heart had been broken at Culloden. The ragged company that gathered round its Prince on that Wednesday morning was dispersed among the fastnesses of the hills, or lying dead and dying among the rushes and heather, whilst Cumberland's soldiers finished their bloody business; the April snow that had blown in the faces of the clansmen as they hurled their unavailing valour on the Whig army had melted upon mounds of slain, and in the struggle of an hour the hopes of half a century had perished. Superior numbers, superior artillery, and superior generalship, had done their work; when the English dragoons had recovered themselves after the Highland charge, they pursued almost to the gates of Inverness, returning again to the battlefield before night should darken upon the carnage, to despatch the wounded wretches who still breathed among their dead comrades.

The country smelt of blood; reeked of it. For miles and miles round Inverness, where the search for fugitives was hottest, burnt hovels and blackened walls made blots upon the tardy green of spring. Women went about, white-faced and silent, trying to keep from their eyes the self-betraying consciousness of hidden terrors; each striving to forget the peat-stack on the moor where some hunted creature was lying, the scrub in the hollow that sheltered some wounded body, the cranny in the hill to which she must journey painfully after dark with the crusts in her apron.

The shot still rattled out over the countryside where the search was going on, and where, when it had been successful, a few maimed and haggard men stood along some shieling wall in front of a platoon of Cumberland's musketry. All down the shores of Loch Ness and among the hills above the Nairn water south-west of Culloden, the dark rocks raised their broken heads to the sky over God knows what agonies of suffering and hunger. The carrion-crow was busy in the land. One-fifth of Prince Charles's army was dead upon the battle-field, and the church and tolbooth of Inverness were full of wounded prisoners, to whom none—not even the surgeons of their own party—were suffered to attend.

And so April passed, and May was near her passing. Cumberland lay at Fort Augustus, to which place he had retired with Kingston's Horse and eleven battalions of foot. The victorious army was the richer by much spoil, and money was free; the Duke's camp was merry with festivities and races, and in the midst of it he enjoyed a well-earned leisure, enlivened by women and dice. He had performed his task of stamping out the danger that threatened his family with admirable thoroughness, and he had, besides, the comfortable prospect of a glorious return to London, where he would be the hero of the general rejoicing that was to follow. He was rooted at Fort Augustus, a rock of success and convivial self-satisfaction in the flood of tears and anguish and broken aspiration that had drowned half Scotland.

The Prince had begun his wanderings in the West, hiding among the hills and corries of the islands, followed by a few faithful souls, and with a price of thirty thousand pounds on his head, whilst Cumberland's emissaries, chief among whom was John Campbell of Mamore, Commandant of the West Highland garrisons, searched the country in every direction. The rank and file of his army—such of his men as were not dead or in prison—were scattered to the four winds; and those officers who had escaped after Culloden were in hiding, too, some despairing, some holding yet to the forlorn hope of raising his standard anew when the evil day should be over. Among these last was James Logie.

He had come unhurt through the battle. Complete indifference about personal issues had wrapped him round in a protecting atmosphere, as it seems to enwrap and protect the unconcerned among men. He had left the field in company with the Prince and a few friends, with whom he reached the Ford of Falie on the Nairn River. They had held a rapid council at this place, Prince Charles desiring that the remnant of his army should rendezvous at Ruthven, in Badenoch, whilst he made his way to France; for his hopes were living still, and he still looked for support and supplies from the French king. He had taken leave of his companions at the ford, and had set off with half a dozen followers for the coast.

Logie turned his face towards Angus. He had been a conspicuous figure in the Prince's immediate circle, and he knew that he had no time to lose if he was to cross the Grampians alive. He thirsted to get back, and to test the temper of the east coast after the news of the reverse; like his master, he was not beaten yet. He did not know what had become of Ferrier and the Angus men, for he had been on the Prince's staff; but the friends had met on the night before the battle, and it was a compact between them, that, should the day go against them, and should either or both survive the fight, they were to make for the neighbourhood of Forfar, where they would be ready, in case of necessity, to begin on their task of raising new levies for the cause.

He had reached the Spey, and had gained Deeside in safety by the shores of the Avon, crossing the Grampians near the sources of the Isla.

In the long winter that had passed since he joined the Prince in the field, James had not forgotten Flemington. His own labours in Angus and at the taking of the *Venture*, completely as they had filled his mind in the autumn, had sunk back into the limbo of insignificant things, but Archie was often in his thoughts, and some time before the advance on Inverness he had heard with indescribable feelings that he was intelligence officer to the Duke of Cumberland. The terrible thing to Logie was that Archie's treachery seemed to have poisoned the sacred places in his own past; when he turned back to it now, it was as though the figure of the young man stood blocking his view, looking at him with those eyes that were so like the eyes of Diane, and were yet the eyes of a traitor.

He could not bear to think of that October morning by the Basin of Montrose. Perhaps the story that a fatal impulse had made him lay bare to his companion had been tossed about—a subject of ridicule on Flemington's lips, its telling but one more proof to him of the folly of men. He could scarcely believe that Archie would treat the record of his anguish in such a way; but then, neither could he have believed that the sympathy in Archie's face, the break in his voice, the tension of his listening attitude, were only the stock-in-trade of a practised spy. And yet this horror had been true. In spite of the unhealed wound that he carried, in spite of the batterings of his thirty-eight years, Logie had continued to love life, but now he had begun to tell himself that he was sick of it.

And for another very practical reason his generous impulses and his belief in Flemington had undone him. Perhaps if the young painter had come to Balnillo announcing an ostentatious adherence to the Stuarts, he might have hesitated before taking him at his own value; but his apparent caution and his unwillingness to speak, and the words about his father at St. Germain, which he had let fall with all the quiet dignity of a man too upright to pass under false colours, had done more to put the brothers on the wrong track than the most violent protestations. Balnillo had been careful, in spite of his confidence in his guest; but in the sympathy of his soul James had given Flemington the means of future access to himself. Now the tavern in the Castle Wynd at Stirling could be of use to him no longer, and he knew that only the last extremity must find him in any of the secret haunts known to him in the Muir of Pert.

Madam Flemington had never reopened the subject of James Logie with Archie. In her wisdom she had left well alone. Installed in her little lodging in Hyndford's Close, with her woman Mysie, she had made up her mind to remain where she was. There was much to keep her in Edinburgh, and she could not bring herself to leave the centre of information and to bury herself again in the old white house among the ash-trees, whilst every post and every horseman brought word of some new turn in the country's fortunes.

News of the Highland army's retreat to Scotland, of the Battle of Falkirk, of the despatch of the Duke of Cumberland to the North, followed one another as the year went by, and still she stayed on. With her emergence from the seclusion of the country came her emergence from the seclusion she had made for herself; and on the Duke's thirty hours' occupation of Holyrood, she threw off all pretence of neutrality, and repaired with other Whig ladies to the palace to pay her respects to the stout, ill-mannered young General whose unbeguiling person followed so awkwardly upon the attractive figure of his predecessor.

Now that Archie was restored to her, Christian found herself with plenty of occupation. The contempt she had hitherto professed for Edinburgh society seemed to have melted away, and every card-party, every assembly and rout, knew her chair at its door, her arresting presence in its midst. Madam Flemington's name was on a good many tongues that winter. Many feared her, some maligned her, but no one overlooked her. The fact that she was the widow of an exiled Jacobite lent her an additional interest; and as the polite world set itself to invent a motley choice of reasons for her adherence to the House of Hanover—which it discovered before her reception by the Duke at Holyrood made it public—it ended by stumbling on the old story of a bygone liaison with Prince Charles's father. The idea was so much to its taste that it was generally accepted; and Christian, unknown to herself, became the cast-off and alienated mistress of that Prince whom her party had begun to call 'The Old Pretender.' It was scarcely a legend that would have conciliated her had it come to her ears, but, as rumour is seldom on speaking terms with its victims, she was ignorant of the interested whispers which followed her through the wynds and up the staircases of the Old Town.

But the reflected halo of royalty, while it casts deep shadows, reaches far. The character of royal light of love stood her in good stead, even among those to whom her supposed former lover was an abhorred spectre of Popery and political danger. The path that her own personality would surely open for her in any community was illumined and made smooth by the baleful interest that hangs about all kingly irregularities, and there was that in her bearing which made people think more of the royal and less of the irregular part of the business. Also, among the Whigs, she was a brand plucked from the burning, one who had turned from the wrong party to embrace the right. Edinburgh, Whig at heart, in spite of its backslidings, admired Madam Flemington.

And not only Edinburgh, but that curious fraction of it, David Balnillo.

The impression that Christian had made upon the judge had deepened as the weeks went by. By the time he discovered her true principles, and realized that she was no dupe of Archie's, but his partisan, he had advanced so far in his acquaintance with her, had become so much her servant, that he could not bring himself to draw back. She had dazzled his wits and played on his vanity, and that vanity was not only warmed and cosseted by her manner to him, not only was he delighted with herself and her notice, but he had begun to find in his position of favoured cavalier to one of the most prominent figures in society a distinction that it would go hard with him to miss.

He had begun their conversation at Lady Anne Maxwell's party by the mention of Archie Flemington, but his name had not come up between them again, and when his enlightenment about her was complete, and the talk which he heard in every house that he frequented revealed her in her real colours, he had no further wish to discuss the man into whose trap he had fallen.

David Balnillo's discoveries were extremely unpalatable to him. If Christian had cherished his vanity, she had made it smart, too. No man, least of all one like the self-appreciative judge, can find without resentment that he has been, even indirectly, the dupe of a person to whom he has attached himself; but when that person is a woman, determined not to let him escape from her influence, the case is not always desperate. For three unblessed days it was wellnigh desperate with Balnillo, and he avoided her completely, but at the end of that time a summons from her was brought to him that his inclination for her company and the chance sight of Lord Grange holding open the door of her chair forbade him to disobey. She had worded her command as though she were conferring a favour; nevertheless, after an hour's hesitation, David had taken his hat and repaired to Hyndford's Close, dragging his dignity after him like a dog on a leash.

If she guessed the reason of his absence from her side she made no remark, receiving him as if she had just parted from him, with that omission of greeting which implies so much. She had sent for him, she said, because her man of business had given her a legal paper that she would not sign without his advice. She looked him in the face as fearlessly as ever, and her glance sparkled with its wonted fire. For some tormented minutes he could not decide whether or no to charge her with knowledge of the fraud that had been carried on under his roof, but he had not the courage to do so. Also, he was acute enough to see that she might well reply to his reproaches by reminding him that he had only himself to thank for their acquaintance. She had not made the advances; his own zeal had brought about their situation. He felt like a fool, but he saw that in speaking he might look like one, which some consider worse.

He left her, assuring himself that all was fair in love and politics; that he could not, in common good breeding, withhold his help from her in her legal difficulty; that, should wind of Archie's dealings with him get abroad in the town, he would be saving appearances in avoiding a rupture with the lady whose shadow he had been since he arrived in Edinburgh, and that it was his duty as a well-wisher of Prince Charles to keep open any channel that might yield information about Flemington's movements. Whatsoever may have been the quality of his reasons, their quantity was remarkable. He did not like the little voice that whispered to him that he would not have dared to offer them to James.

There was no further risk of a meeting with Archie, for within a few days of the latter's appearance in Hyndford's Close he had been sent to the Border with instructions to watch Jedburgh and the neighbourhood of Liddesdale, through which the Prince's army had passed on its march to England. Madam Flemington knew that the coast was clear, and David had no suspicion that it had been otherwise. Very few people in Edinburgh were aware of Flemington's visit to it; it was an event of which even the caddies were ignorant.

And so Balnillo lingered on, putting off his return to Angus from week to week. His mouse-coloured velvet began to show signs of wear and was replaced by a suit of dark purple; his funds were dwindling a little, for he was not a rich man, and a new set of verses about him was going the round of the town. Then, with January, came the battle of Falkirk and the siege of Stirling Castle, and the end of the month brought Cumberland and the mustering of loyal Whigs to wait upon him at Holyrood Palace.

David departed quietly. He had come to Edinburgh to avoid playing a marked part in Angus, and he now returned to Angus to avoid playing a marked part in Edinburgh. He was behaving like the last remaining king in a game of draughts when he skips from square to square in the safe corner of the board; but he did not know that Government had kept its eye on all his doings during the time of his stay. Perhaps it was on account of her usefulness in this and in other delicate matters that Madam Flemington augured well for her grandson, for when the Whig army crossed the Forth, Archie went with it as intelligence officer to the Duke of Cumberland.

CHAPTER XX

THE PARTING OF THE WAYS

JULY spread a mantle of heather over the Grampians. In Glen Esk, the rough road into the Lowlands, little better than a sheep-track, ran down the shore of Loch Lee, to come out at last into the large spaces at the foot of the hills. The greyness of the summer haze lay over everything, and the short grass and the roots of bog-myrtle and thyme smelt warm and heady, for the wind was still. The sun seemed to have sucked up some of the heather-colour out of the earth; the lower atmosphere was suffused with a dusty lilac where, high overhead, it softened the contours of the scattered rocks. Amongst carpets of rush and deep moss, dappled with wet patches, the ruddy stems of the bog-asphodel raised slim, golden heads that drooped a little, as though for faintness, in the scented warmth. An occasional bumble-bee passed down wind, purposeful and ostentatious, like a respectable citizen zealous on the business of life.

No one looking along the windings of the Glen, and drawing in the ardent quietness of the summer warmth, would have supposed that fire and sword had been through it so lately. Its vastness of outline hid the ruined huts and black fragments of skeleton gable-ends that had smoked up into the mountain stillness. Homeless women and children had fled down its secret tracks; hunted men had given up their souls under its heights. The rich plainland of Angus had sent its sons to fight for the Prince in the North, and of those who survived to make their way back to their homes, many had been overtaken by the pursuit that had swept down behind them through the hills. No place had a darker record than Glen Esk.

Archie Flemington rode down the Glen with his companion some little way in front of the corporal and the three men who followed them. His left arm was in a sling, for he had received a sabre-cut at Culloden; also, he had been rolled on by his horse, which was killed under him, and had broken a rib. His wound, though not serious, had taken a long time to heal, for the steel had cut into the arm bone; he looked thin, too, for the winter had been a time of strenuous work.

One of the three private soldiers, the last of the small string of horsemen, had a rope knotted into his reins, the other end of which was secured round the middle of a short, thickset man who paced sullenly along beside the horse. The prisoner's arms were bound at his back, his reddish beard was unkempt, and his clothes ragged; he made a sorry figure in the surrounding beauty.

Nearly two months had gone by since the Battle of Culloden, and the search for fugitives was still going on in remote places. Cumberland, who was on the point of leaving Fort Augustus for Edinburgh on his way to London, had given orders for a last scouring of Glen Esk. The party had almost reached its mouth, and its efforts had resulted only in the capture of this one rebel; but, as there was some slight doubt of his identity, and as the officer who rode beside Archie was one whose conscience ranked a great way above his convenience, the red-bearded man had fared better than many of those taken by Cumberland's man-hunters. If he were the person they supposed him to be, he was an Angus farmer distantly related to David Ferrier, and he was now being brought to his own country for identification.

Captain Callandar, the officer in command, was a long, lean, bony man with a dark face, a silent, hard-bitten fellow from Ligonier's regiment. He and Archie had met very little before they started south together, and they had scarcely progressed in acquaintance in the few days during which they had ridden side by side. They had shared their food on the bare turf by day, lain down within a few yards of each other at night; they had gone through many of the same experiences in the North, and they belonged to the same victorious army, yet they knew little more of each other than when they started. But there was no dislike between them, certainly none on Archie's side, and if the other was a little critical of the foreign roll of his companion's *r's*, he did not show it.

Archie's tongue had been quiet enough. He was riding listlessly along, and, though he looked from side to side, taking in the details of what he saw from force of habit, they seemed to give him no interest. He puzzled Callandar a good deal, for he had proved to be totally different from anything that he had expected. The soldier was apt to study his fellow-men, when not entirely swallowed up by his duty, and he had been rather pleased when he found that Cumberland's brilliant intelligence officer was to accompany him down Glen Esk. He had heard much about him. Archie's quick answers and racy talk had amused the Duke, who, uncompanionable himself, felt the awkward man's amazement at the readiness of others, and scraps of Flemington's sayings had gone from lip to lip, hall-marked by his approval. Callandar was taciturn and grave, but he was not stupid, and he had begun to wonder what was amiss with his companion. He decided that his own society must be uncongenial to him, and, being a very modest man, he did not marvel at it.

But the sources of Archie's discomfort lay far, far deeper than any passing irritation. It seemed to him now, as he reached the mouth of the Glen, that there was nothing left in life to fear, because the worst that could come upon him was looming ahead, waiting for him, counting his horse's steps as he left the hills behind.

An apprehension, a mere suggestion of what might be remotely possible, a skeleton that had shown its face to him in sleepless or overwrought moments since Cumberland's victory, had become real. To most people who are haunted by a particular dread, Fate plays one of the tricks she loves so much. She is an expert boxer, and whilst each man stands up to her in his long, defensive fight, his eye upon hers, guarding himself from the blow he expects to receive in the face, she hits him in the wind and he finds himself knocked out.

But she had dealt otherwise with Archie; for a week ago he had been specially detailed to proceed to Angus to hunt for that important rebel, Captain James Logie, who was believed to have made his way southward to his native parts.

At Fort Augustus it was felt that Flemington was exactly the right man to be entrusted with the business. He was familiar with the country he had to search, he was a man of infinite resource and infinite intelligence; and Cumberland meant to be pleasant in his harsh, ungraceful manner, when he gave him his commission in person, with a hint that he expected more from Mr. Flemington than he did from anybody else. He was to accompany Captain Callandar and his three men. The officer, having made a last sweep of Glen Esk, was to go on by Brechin to Forfar, where he would be joined by another and larger party of troops that was on its way down Glen Clova from Braemar, for Cumberland was drafting small forces into Angus by way of the Grampians, and the country was filling with them.

He had dealt drastically with Montrose. The rebellion in the town had been suppressed, and the neighbourhood put under military law. This bit of the east coast had played a part that was not forgotten by the little German general, and he was determined that the hornet's nest he had smoked out should not re-collect. Whilst James Logie was at large there could be no security.

Of all the rebels in Scotland, Logie was the man whom Cumberland was most desirous to get. The great nobles who had taken part in the rising were large quarry indeed, but this commoner who had worked so quietly in the eastern end of Angus, who had been on the Prince's staff, who had the experience of many campaigns at his back, whose ally was the notorious Ferrier, who had seized the harbour of Montrose under the very guns of a Government sloop of war, was as dangerous as any Highland chieftain, and the news that he had been allowed to get back to his own haunts made the Whig generals curse. Though he might be quiet for the moment, he would be ready to stir up the same mischief on the first recrudescence of Stuart energy. It was not known what had happened to Ferrier, for although he was a marked man and would be a rich haul for anybody who could deliver him up to Cumberland, he was considered a less important influence than James; and Government had scarcely estimated his valuable services to the Jacobites, which were every whit as great as those of his friend.

Lord Balnillo was a puzzle to the intelligence department. His name had gone in to headquarters as that of a strongly suspected rebel; he was James's brother; yet, while Archie had included him in the report he had entrusted to the beggar, he had been able to say little that was definite about him. The very definite information he had given about James and Ferrier, the details of his pursuit of the two men and his warning of the attack on the *Venture*, had mattered more to the authorities than the politics of the peaceable old judge, and Balnillo's subsequent conduct had been so little in accordance with that of his brother that he was felt to be a source of small danger. He had been no great power on the bench, where his character was so easy that prisoners were known to think themselves lucky in appearing before him. No one could quite account for his success in the law, and the mention of his name in the legal circles of Edinburgh raised nothing worse than a smile. He had taken no part in the rejoicing that followed James's feat at Montrose, but had taken the opportunity of leaving the neighbourhood, and during his long stay in Edinburgh he had frequented Whig houses and had been the satellite of a conspicuous Whig lady, one who had been received by Cumberland with some distinction, the grandmother of the man who had denounced Logie. The authorities decided to leave him alone.

When the hills were behind the riders and the levels of the country had sunk and widened out on either hand, they crossed the North Esk, which made a shallow curve by the village of Edzell. The bank rose on its western side, and the shade of the trees was delightful to the travellers, and particularly to the prisoner they carried with them. As the horses snuffed at the water they could hardly be urged through it, and Callandar and Archie dismounted on the farther shore and sat on a boulder whilst they drank. They watched them as they drew the draught up their long throats and raised their heads when satisfied, to stare, with dripping muzzles, at distant nothings, after the fashion of their kind. The prisoner's aching arms were unbound that he might drink too.

"Egad, I have pitied that poor devil these last miles," said Archie, as the man knelt at the brink and extended his stiffened arms into a pool.

The other nodded. Theoretically he pitied him, but a rebel was a rebel.

"You have no bowels of compassion. They are not in your instructions, Callandar. They should be served out, like ammunition."

Callandar turned his grave eyes on him.

"The idea displeases you?" said Archie.

"It would complicate our duty."

He spoke like a humourless man, but one side of his mouth twitched downwards a little, and Flemington, who had the eye of a lynx for another man's face, decided that the mere accident of habit had prevented it from twitching up. He struck him as the most repressed person he had ever seen.

"There would not be enough at headquarters to go round," observed Archie.

Callandar's mouth straightened, and, like the horses, he looked at nothing. Criticism was another thing not in his instructions.

"They have drunk well," he said at last. "An hour will bring us to the foot of Huntly Hill. We can halt and feed them at the top before we turn off towards Brechin. You know this country better than I do."

"Wait a little," said Archie. "I am no rebel, and you may have mercy on me with a clear conscience."

He had slipped his arm out of the sling and was resting it on his knee.

"You are in pain?" exclaimed Callandar, astonished.

Archie laughed.

"Why, man, do you think I ride for pleasure with the top half of a bone working east and the bottom half working west?"

"I thought——" began Callandar.

"You thought me churlish company, and maybe I have been so. But this ride has been no holiday for me."

"I did not mean that. I would have said that I thought your wound was mended."

"My flesh-wound is mended and so is my rib," said Flemington, "but there are two handsome splinters hobnobbing above my elbow, and I can tell you that they dance to the tune of my horse's jog."

Callandar's opinion of him rose. He had found him disappointing as a companion, but Archie had hid his pain, and he understood people who did that.

The Edzell villagers turned out to stare at them as they passed a short time later, when they took the road again. After the riders left its row of houses their way ran from the river-level through fields that had begun to oust the moor, rising to the crest of Huntly Hill, on the farther side of which the southern part of Angus spread its partial cultivation down to the Basin of Montrose. Archie's discomfort seemed to grow; he shifted his sling again and again, and Callandar could see his mouth set in a hard line. Now and then an impatient sound of pain broke from him. They rode on, silent, the long rise of the hill barring their road like a wall, and the stems of the fir-strip that crowned it beginning to turn to a dusky black against the sky, which was cooling off for evening. Flemington's horse was a slow walker, and he had begun to jog persistently. His rider, holding him back, had fallen behind. Callandar rode on, preoccupied, and when, roused from his thoughts, he turned his head, Archie waved him on, shouting that he would follow more slowly, for the troopers moved at a foot's pace because of their prisoner, and he stayed abreast of them.

As Callandar passed a green sea of invading bracken that had struggled on to the road his jaw dropped and he pulled up. Behind the feathering waves an individual was sitting in a wooden box on wheels, and four dogs, harnessed to the rude vehicle, were lying on the ground in their leathern traces. He noticed with astonishment that the man had lost the lower parts of his legs.

"You'll be Captain Callandar," said Wattie, his twinkling eyes on the others uniform; "you're terrible late."

"What do you want?" said the officer, amazed.

The beggar peered through the fern and saw the knot of riders and their prisoner coming along the road some little way behind.

"Whaur's yon lad Flemington?" he demanded.

"What do you want?" exclaimed Callandar again. "If you are a beggar you have chosen a strange place to beg in."

For answer Wattie pulled up his sliding panel and took out two sealed letters, holding them low in the shelter of the fern, as if the midges, dancing their evening dance above the bracken-tops, should not look upon them. Callandar saw that one of the letters bore his own name.

"Whisht," said the beggar, thrusting them back quickly, "come doon here an' hae a crack wi' me."

As Callandar had been concerned exclusively with troops and fighting, he knew little about the channels of information working in the country, and it took him a moment to explain the situation to himself. He dismounted under the fixed glare of the yellow dog. He was a man to whom small obstacles were invisible when he had a purpose, and he almost trod on the animal, without noticing the suppressed hostility gathering about his heels. But, so long as his master's voice was friendly, the cur was still, for his unwavering mind answered to its every tone. Probably no spot in all Angus contained two such steadfast living creatures as did this green place by the bracken when Callandar and the yellow dog stood side by side.

The soldier tethered his horse and sat down on the moss. Wattie laid the letters before him; the second was addressed to Archie. Callandar broke the seal of the first and read it slowly through; then he sat silent, examining the signature, which was the same that Flemington had showed to the beggar on the day when he met him for the first time, months ago, by the mill of Balnillo.

He was directed to advance no farther towards Brechin, but to keep himself out of sight among the woods round Huntly Hill, and to watch the Muir of Pert, for it was known that the rebel, James Logie, was concealed somewhere between Brechin and the river. He was not upon the Balnillo estate, which, with Balnillo House, had been searched from end to end, but he was believed to be in the neighbourhood of the Muir.

"You know the contents of this?" asked Callandar, as he put away the paper inside the breast of his coat.

"Dod, a ken it'll be aboot Logie. He's a fell man, yon. Have ye na got Flemington wi' ye?"

Callandar looked upon his companion with disapproval. He had never seen him, never heard of him before, and he felt his manner and his way of speaking of his superiors to be an outrage upon discipline and order, which were two things very near his heart.

He did not reply.

"Whaur's Flemington?" demanded the beggar again.

"You make very free with Mr. Flemington's name."

"Tuts!" exclaimed Wattie, ignoring the rebuke, "a've got ma orders the same as yersel', an' a'm to gie yon thing to him an' to nae ither body. Foo will a dae that if a dinna ken whaur he is?"

His argument was indisputable.

"Mr. Flemington will be with me in a moment," said Callandar stiffly. "He is following."

The sound of horses' feet was nearing them upon the road, and Callandar rose and beckoned to Archie to come on.

"Go to the top of the hill and halt until I join you," he told the corporal as the men passed.

As Archie dismounted and saw who was behind the bracken, he recoiled. It was to him as if all that he most loathed in the past came to meet him in the beggar's face. Here, at the confines of the Lowland country, the same hateful influences were waiting to engulf him. His soul was weary within him.

He barely replied to Wattie's familiar greeting.

"Do you know this person?" inquired Callandar.

He assented.

"Ay, does he. Him and me's weel acquaint," said Wattie, closing an eye. "Hae, tak' yon."

He held out the letter to Flemington.

The young man opened it slowly, turning his back to the cart, and his brows drew together as he read.

His destiny did not mean him to escape. Logie had been marked down, and the circle of his enemies was narrowing round him. Flemington was to go no farther, and he was to remain with Callandar to await another message that would be brought to their bivouac on Huntly Hill, before approaching nearer to Brechin.

He stood aside, the paper in his hand. Here was the turning-point; he was face to face with it at last. He could not take part in

Logie's capture; on that he was completely, unalterably determined. What would be the end of it all for himself he could not think. Nothing was clear, nothing plain, but the settled strength of his determination. He looked into the mellowing light round him, and saw everything as though it were unreal; the only reality was that he had chosen his way. Heaven was pitiless, but it should not shake him. Far above him a solitary bird was winging its way into the spaces beyond the hills; the measured beat of its wings growing invisible as it grew smaller and smaller and was finally lost to sight. He watched it, fascinated, with the strange detachment of those whose senses and consciousness are numbed by some crisis. What was it carrying away, that tiny thing that was being swallowed by the vastness? His mind could only grasp the idea of distance... of space....

Callandar was at his elbow, and his voice broke on him as the voice of someone awakening him from sleep.

"These are my orders," he was saying, as he held out his own letter; "you know them, for I am informed here that they are the duplicate of yours."

There was no escape. Callandar knew the exact contents of both papers. Archie might have kept his own orders to himself, and have given him to suppose that he was summoned to Forfar or Perth, and must leave him; but that was impossible. He must either join in hunting Logie, or leave the party on this side of Huntly Hill.

"We had better get on," said Callandar.

They mounted, and as they did so, Wattie also got under way. His team was now reduced to four, for the terrier which had formerly run alone in the lead had died about the new year.

He took up his switch, and the yellow cur and his companions whirled him with a mighty tug on to the road. He had been waiting for some time in the bracken for the expected horseman, and as the dogs had enjoyed a long rest, they followed the horses at a steady trot. Callandar and Flemington trotted too, and the cart soon fell behind. Beyond the crest of Huntly Hill the Muir of Pert sloped eastwards towards the coast, its edges resting upon the Esk, but before the road began to ascend it forked in two, one part running upwards, and the other breaking away west towards Brechin.

"Callandar, I am going to leave you," said Archie, pulling up his horse.

"To leave?" exclaimed the other blankly. "In God's name, where are you going?"

"Here is the shortest way to Brechin, and I shall take it. I must find a surgeon to attend to this arm. There is no use for me to go on with you when I can hardly sit in my saddle for pain."

"But your orders?" gasped Callandar.

"I will make that right. You must go on alone. Probably I shall join you in a few days, but that will depend on what instructions I get later. If you hear nothing from me you will understand that I am busy out of sight. My hands may be full—that is, if the surgeon leaves me with both of them. Good-bye, Callandar."

He turned his horse and left him. The other opened his mouth to shout after him, ordering him to come back, but remembered that he had no authority to do so. Flemington was independent of him; he belonged to a different branch of the King's service, and although he had fought at Culloden he was under different orders. He had merely accompanied his party, and Callandar knew very well that, though his junior in years, he was a much more important person than himself. The nature of Archie's duties demanded that he should be given a free hand in his movements, and no doubt he knew what he was about. But had he been Callandar's subordinate, and had there been a surgeon round the nearest corner, his arm might have dropped from his shoulder before the officer would have permitted him to fall out of the little troop. Callandar had never in all his service seen a man receive definite orders only to disobey them openly.

He watched him go, petrified. His brain was a good one, but it worked slowly, and Archie's decision and departure had been as sudden as a thunderbolt. Also, there was contempt in his heart for his softness, and he was sorry.

Archie turned round and saw him still looking after him. He sent back a gibe to him.

"If you don't go on I will report you for neglect of duty!" he shouted, laughing.

CHAPTER XXI

HUNTLY HILL

CALLANDAR rode up Huntly Hill. The rose-red of the blossoming briar that decks all Angus with its rubies glowed in the failing sunlight, and the scent of its leaf came in puffs from the wayside ditches; the blurred heads of the meadow-sweet were being turned into clouds of gold as the sun grew lower and the road climbed higher. In front the trees began to mantle Huntly Hill.

He had just begun the ascent at a foot's pace when he heard the whirr of the beggar's chariot-wheels behind him, then at his side, and he turned in his saddle and looked down on his pursuer's bald crown. Wattie had cast off his bonnet, and the light breeze springing up lifted the fringe of his grizzled hair.

"Whaur awa's Flemington?" he cried, as he came up.

The other answered by another question; his thoughts had come back to the red-haired prisoner at the top of the hill, and it struck him that the man in the cart might recognize him.

"What's your name?" he asked abruptly.

"Wattie Caird."

"You belong to these parts?"

He nodded.

"Then come on; I have not done with you yet."

"A'm asking ye whaur's Flemington?"

If Callandar had pleased himself he would have driven Wattie down the hill at the point of the sword, his persistence and his pestilent, unashamed curiosity were so distasteful to him. But he had a second use for him now. He was that uncommon thing, a disciplinarian with tact, and by virtue of the combination in himself he understood that the troopers in front of him, who had been looking forward eagerly to getting their heads once more under a roof that night, would be disgusted by the orders he was bringing. He had noticed the chanter sticking out from under Wattie's leathern bag, and he thought that a stirring tune or two might ease matters for them. He did not see his way to dispensing with him at present, so he tolerated his company.

"Mr. Flemington has a bad wound," he answered. "He has gone to Brechin to have it attended to."

"Whaur did he get it?"

"At Culloden Moor."

"They didna tell me onything aboot that."

"Who tells you anything about Mr. Flemington? What do you know about him?"

"Heuch!" exclaimed Wattie, with contempt, "it's mysel' that should tell them! A ken mair aboot Flemington than ony ither body—a ken fine what's brocht yon lad here. He's seeking Logie, like a'body else, but he kens fine he'll na get him—ay, does he!"

Callandar looked down from his tall horse upon the grotesque figure so close to the ground. He was furious at the creature's assumption of knowledge.

"You are a piper?" said he.

"The best in Scotland."

"Then keep your breath for piping and let other people's business be," he said sternly.

"Man, dinna fash. It's King Geordie's business and syne it's mine. Him and me's billies. Ay, he's awa', is he, Flemington?"

Callandar quickened his horse's pace; he was not going to endure this offensive talk. But Wattie urged on his dogs too, and followed hard on his heels.

All through the winter, whilst the fortunes of Scotland were deciding themselves in the North, he had been idle but for his piping and singing, and he had had little to do with the higher matters on which he had been engaged in the autumn, whilst the forces of the coming storm were seething south of the Grampians. He had not set eyes on Flemington since their parting by the farm on Rossie Moor, but many a night, lying among his dogs, he had thought of Archie's voice calling to Logie as he tossed and babbled in his broken dreams.

He had long since drawn his conclusion and made up his mind that he admired Archie as a mighty clever fellow, but he was convinced that he was more astute than anybody supposed, and it gave him great delight to think that, probably, no one but himself had a notion of the part Flemington was playing. Wattie was well aware of his advancement, for his name was in everybody's mouth. He knew that he was on Cumberland's staff just as Logie was on the staff of the Prince, and he wagged his head as he thought how Archie must have enriched himself at the expense of both Whig and Jacobite. It was his opinion that, knowledge being marketable, it was time that somebody else should enrich himself too. He would have given a great deal to know whether Flemington, as a well-known man, had continued his traffic with the other side, and as he went up the hill beside the dark Whig officer he was turning the question over in his mind.

He had kept his suspicions jealously to himself. Whilst Flemington was far away in the North, and all men's eyes were looking across the Grampians, he knew that he could command no attention, and he had cursed because he believed his chance of profit to be lost. Archie had gone out of range, and he could not reach him; yet he kept his knowledge close, like a prudent man, in case the time should come when he might use it. And now Flemington had returned, and he had been sent out to meet him.

The way had grown steep, and as Callandar's horse began to stumble, the soldier swung himself off the tired beast and walked beside him, his hand on the mane.

Wattie was considering whether he should speak. If his information were believed, it would be especially valuable at this time, when the authorities were agog to catch Logie, and the reward for his services must be considerable if there was any justice in the world. They would never catch Logie, because Flemington was in league with him. Wattie knew what many knew—that the rebel was believed to be somewhere about the great Muir of Pert, now just in front of them, but so far as he could make out, the only person who was aware of how the wind set with Archie was himself.

What he had seen at the foot of Huntly Hill had astonished him till he had read its meaning by the light of his own suspicions. Though he had not been close enough to the two men to hear exactly what passed between them when they parted, he had seen them part. He had seen Callandar standing to look after the other as though uncertain how to act, and he had heard Archie's derisive shout. There was no sign of a quarrel between them, yet Callandar's face suggested they had disagreed; there was perplexity in it and underlying disapproval. He had seen his gesture of astonishment, and the way in which he had sat looking after Flemington at the cross roads, reining back his horse, which would have followed its companion, was eloquent to the beggar. Callandar had not expected the young man to go.

Wattie did not know the nature of the orders he had brought, but he knew that they referred to Logie. He understood that those who received them were hastening to meet those who had despatched them, and would be with them that night; and this proved to him how important it was that the letters should be in the hand of the riders before they advanced farther on their way. He had been directed to wait on the northern side of Huntly Hill, and had been specially charged to deliver them before Callandar crossed it. He told himself that only a fool would fail to guess that they referred to this particular place. But the illuminating part to Wattie was the speech he had heard by the bracken: it was all that was needed to explain the officer's stormy looks.

"These are my orders," Callandar had said, "but you know them, for I am informed that they are the duplicate of yours."

Archie had disobeyed them, and Wattie was sure that he had gone, because the risk of meeting Logie was too great to be run. Now was the time for him to speak.

He had no nicety, but he had shrewdness in plenty. He was sudden and persistent in his address, and divining the obstacles in Callandar's mind, he charged them like a bull.

"Flemington'll na let ye get Logie," said he.

He made his announcement with so much emphasis that the

man walking beside him was impressed in spite of his prejudices. He was annoyed too. He turned on him angrily.

"Once and for all, what do you mean by this infernal talk about Mr. Flemington?" he cried, stopping short. "You will either speak out, or I will take it upon myself to make you. I have three men in the wood up yonder who will be very willing to help me. I believe you to be a meddlesome liar, and if I find that I am right you shall smart for it."

But the beggar needed no urging, and he was not in the least afraid of Callandar.

"It's no me that's sweer to speak, it's yersel' that's sweer to listen," said he, with some truth. "Dod, a've tell't ye afore an' a'm telling ye again—*Flemington'll no let ye get him!* He's dancin' wi' George, but he's takin' the tune frae Chairlie. Heuch! dinna tell me! There's mony hae done the same afore an' 'll dae it yet!"

The officer was standing in the middle of the road, a picture of perplexity.

"It's no the oxter of him that gars him gang," said Wattie, breaking into the broad smile of one who is successfully letting the light of reason into another's mind. "It's no his airm. Maybe it gies him a pucklie twist, whiles, and maybe it doesna, but it's no that that gars the like o' him greet. *He wouldna come up Huntly Hill wi you, for he ken't he was ower near Logie.* It's that, an' nae mair!"

Callandar began to think back. He had not heard one complaint from Archie since the day they rode out of Fort Augustus together, and he remembered his own astonishment at hearing he was in pain from his wound. It seemed only to have become painful in the last couple of hours.

"It is easy to make accusations," he said grimly, "but you will have to prove them. What proof have you?"

"Is it pruifs ye're needin'? Fegs, a dinna gang aboot wi' them in ma poke! A can tell ye ma pruifs fine, but maybe ye'll no listen."

He made as though to drive on.

Callandar stepped in front of the dogs, and stood in his path.

"You will speak out before I take another step," said he. "I will have no shuffling. Come, out with what you know! I will stay here till I get it."

CHAPTER XXII

HUNTLY HILL (*continued*)

CALLANDAR sat a little apart from his men on the fringe of the fir-wood; on the other side of the clearing on which the party had bivouacked Wattie formed the centre of a group. It was past sunset, and the troop-horses, having been watered and fed, were picketed together. Callandar's own horse snatched at the straggling bramble-shoots behind a tree.

The officer sat on a log, his chin in his hand, pondering on the amazing story that the beggar had divulged. It was impossible to know what to make of it, but, in spite of himself, he was inclined to believe it. He had questioned and cross-questioned him, but he had been able to form no definite opinion. Wattie had described his meeting with Archie on the day of the taking of the ship; he had told him how he had accompanied him on his way, how he had been forced to ask shelter for him at the farm, how he had lain and listened in the darkness to his feverish wanderings and his appeals to Logie. If the beggar's tale had been true, there seemed to be no doubt that the intelligence officer whose services were so much valued by Cumberland, had taken money from the rebels, though it seemed that he had hesitated over the business. His conscience must have smitten him even in his dreams. "I will say nothing, but I will tell you all!" he had cried to Logie. "I shall know where you are, but they shall never know!" In his delirium, he had taken the beggar for the man whose fellow-conspirator he was proving himself to be, and when consciousness was fighting to return, and he had sense enough to know that he was not speaking to Logie, it was his companion's promise to deliver a message of reassurance that had given him peace and sleep. "Tell him that he can trust me," he had said. What puzzled Callandar was the same thing that had puzzled Wattie: why had these two men, linked together by a hidden understanding, fought? Perhaps Flemington had repented of the part he was playing, and had tried to cut himself adrift. "Let me go!" he had exclaimed. It was all past Callandar's comprehension. At one moment he was inclined to look on Wattie as an understudy for the father of lies; at another, he asked himself how he could have had courage to invent such a calumny—how he had dared to choose a man for his victim who had reached the position that Archie had gained. But he realized that, had Wattie been inventing, he would hardly have invented the idea of a fight between Flemington and Captain Logie. That little incongruous touch seemed to Callandar's reasonable mind to support the truth of his companion's tongue.

And then there was Flemington's sudden departure. It did not look so strange since he had heard what the beggar had to say. He began to think of his own surprise at finding Archie in pain from a wound which seemed to have troubled him little, so far, and to suspect that his reliable wits had been stimulated to find a new use for his injured arm by the sight of Huntly Hill combined with the news in his pocket. His gorge rose at the thought that he had been riding all these days side by side with a very prince among traitors. His face hardened. His own duty was not plain to him, and that perturbed him so much that his habitual outward self-repression gave way. He could not sit still while he was driven by his perplexities. He sprang up, walking up and down between the trees. Ought he to send a man straight off to Brechin with a summary of the beggar's statement? He could not vouch for the truth of his information, and there was every chance of it being disregarded, and himself marked as the discoverer of a mare's nest. There was scarcely anything more repugnant to Callandar than the thought of himself in this character, and for that reason, if for no other, he inclined to the risk; for he had the overwhelmingly conscientious man's instinct for martyrdom.

His mind was made up. He took out his pocket-book and wrote what he had to say in the fewest and shortest words. Then he called the corporal, and, to his extreme astonishment, ordered him to ride to Brechin. When the man had saddled his horse, he gave him the slip of paper. He had no means of sealing it, here in the fir-wood, but the messenger was a trusted man, one to whom he would have committed anything with absolute conviction. He was sorry that he had to lose him, for he could not tell how long he might be kept on the edge of the Muir, nor how much country he would have to search with his tiny force; but there was no help for it, and he trusted that the corporal would be sent back to him before the morrow. He was the only person to whom he could give the open letter. When the soldier had mounted, Callandar accompanied him to the confines of the wood, giving him instructions from the map he carried.

Wattie sat on the ground beside his cart; his back was against a little raised bank. Where his feet should have been, the yellow dog was stretched, asleep. As Callandar and his corporal disappeared among the trees, he began to sing 'The Tod' in his rich voice, throwing an atmosphere of dramatic slyness into the words that made his hearers shout with delight at the end of each verse.

When he had finished the song, he was barely suffered to take breath before being compelled to begin again; even the prisoner, who lay resting, still bound, within sight of the soldiers, listened, laughing into his red beard. But suddenly he stopped, rising to his feet:

> "A lang-leggit deevil wi' his hand upon the gate,
> An' aye the Guidwife cries to him——"

Wattie's voice fell, cutting the line short, for a rush of steps was bursting through the trees—was close on them, dulled by the pine-needles underfoot—sweeping over the stumps and the naked roots. The beggar stared, clutching at the bank. His three companions sprang up.

The wood rang with shots, and one of the soldiers rolled over on his face, gasping as he tried to rise, struggling and snatching at the ground with convulsed fingers. The remaining two ran, one towards the prisoner, and one towards the horses which were plunging against each other in terror; the latter man dropped midway, with a bullet through his head.

The swiftness of the undreamed-of misfortune struck panic into Wattie, as he sat alone, helpless, incapable either of flight or of resistance. One of his dogs was caught by the leaden hail and lay fighting its life out a couple of paces from where he was left, a defenceless thing in this sudden storm of death. Two of the remaining three went rushing through the trees, yelping as the stampeding horses added their share to the danger and riot. These had torn up their heel-pegs, which, wrenched easily from a resistance made for the most part of moss and pine-needles, swung and whipped at the ends of the flying ropes behind the crazy animals as they dashed about. The surviving trooper had contrived to catch his own horse, and was riding for his life towards the road by which they had come from Edzell. The only quiet thing besides the beggar was the yellow cur who stood at his master's side, stiff and stubborn and ugly, the coarse hair rising on his back.

Wattie's panic grew as the drumming of hoofs increased and the horses dashed hither and thither. He was more afraid of them than of the ragged enemy that had descended on the wood. The dead troopers lay huddled, one on his face and the other on his side; the wounded dog's last struggles had ceased. Half a dozen men were pursuing the horses with outstretched arms, and Callandar's charger had broken loose with its comrades, and was thundering this way and that, snorting and leaping, with cocked ears and flying mane.

The beggar watched them with a horror which his dislike and fear of horses made agonizing, the menace of these irresponsible creatures, mad with excitement and terror, so heavy, so colossal when seen from his own helpless nearness to the earth that was shaking under their tread, paralyzed him. His impotence enwrapped him, tragic, horrible, a nightmare woven of death's terrors; he could not escape; there was no shelter from the thrashing hoofs, the gleaming iron of the shoes. The cumbrous perspective of the great animals blocked out the sky with its bulk as their rocking bodies went by, plunging, slipping, recovering themselves within the cramped circle of the open space. He knew nothing of what was happening, nor did he see that the prisoner stood freed from his bonds. He knew James Logie by sight, and he knew Ferrier, but, though both were standing by the red-bearded man, he recognized neither. He had just enough wits left to understand that Callandar's bivouac had been attacked, but he recked of nothing but the thundering horses that were being chased to and fro as the circle of men closed in. He felt sick as it narrowed and he could only flatten himself, stupefied, against the bank. The last thing he saw was the yellow coat of his dog, as the beast cowered and snapped, keeping his post with desperate tenacity in the din.

The bank against which he crouched cut the clearing diagonally, and as the men pressed in nearer round the horses, Callandar's charger broke out of the circle followed by the two others. A cry from the direction in which they galloped, and the sound of frantic nearing hoofs, told that they had been headed back once more. The bank was high enough to hide Wattie from them, as they returned, but he could feel the earth shake with their approach, which rang in his ears like the roar of some dread, implacable fate. He could see nothing now, as he lay half-blind with fear, but he was aware that his dog had leaped upon the bank behind him, and he heard the well-known voice, hoarse and brutal with defiant agony, just above his head. All the qualities that have gone to make the dog the outcast of the East seemed to show in the cur's attitude as he raised himself, an insignificant, common beast, in the path of the great, noble, stampeding creatures. It was the curse of his curship that in this moment of his life, when he hurled all that was his in the world—his low-bred body—against the danger that swooped on his master, he should take on no nobility of aspect, nothing to picture forth the heart that smote against his panting ribs. Another moment and the charger had leaped at the bank, just above the spot where Skirling Wattie's grizzled head lay against the sod.

The cur sprang up against the overwhelming hulk, the smiting hoofs, the whirl of heel-ropes, and struck in mid-air by the horse's knee, was sent rolling down the slope. As he fell there was a thud of dislodged earth, and the charger, startled by the sudden apparition of the prostrate figure below him, slipped on the bank, stumbled, sprang, and checked by the flying rope, crashed forward, burying the beggar under his weight.

James and Ferrier ran forward as the animal struggled to its feet, unhurt; it tore past the men, who had broken their line as they watched the fall. The three horses made off between the trees, and Logie approached the beggar. He lay crushed and mangled, as quiet as the dead troopers on the ground.

There was no mistaking Wattie's rigid stillness, and as James and Ferrier, with the red-bearded man, approached him, they knew that he would never rise to blow his pipes nor to fill the air with his voice again. The yellow dog was stretched, panting, a couple of paces from the grotesque body, which had now, for the first time, taken on dignity. As Logie bent to examine him, and would have lifted him, the cur dragged himself up; one of his hind-legs was broken, but he crawled snarling to the beggar's side, and turned his maimed body to face the men who should dare to lay a hand on Wattie. The drops poured from his hanging tongue and his eye was alight with the dull flame of pain. He would have torn Logie to bits if he could, as he trailed himself up to shelter the dead man from his touch. He made a great effort to get upon his legs and his jaws closed within an inch of James's arm.

One of the men drew the pistol from his belt.

"Ay, shoot the brute," said another.

James held up his hand.

"The man is dead," said he, looking over his shoulder at his comrades.

"And you would be the same if yon dog could reach you," rejoined Ferrier. "Let me shoot him. He will only die lying here."

"Let him be. His leg is broken, that is all."

The cur made another attempt to get his teeth into Logie, and almost succeeded.

Ferrier raised his pistol again, but James thrust it back.

"The world needs a few such creatures as that in it," said he. "Lord! Ferrier, what a heart there is in the poor brute!"

"Stand away from him, Logie, he is half mad."

"We must get away from this place," said James, unheeding, "or that man who has ridden away will bring the whole country about our ears. It has been a narrow escape for you, Gourlay," he said to the released prisoner. "We must leave the old vagabond lying where he is."

"There is no burying him with that devil left alive!" cried Ferrier. "I promise you I will not venture to touch him."

"My poor fellow," said James, turning to the dog, "it is of no use; you cannot save him. God help you for the truest friend that a man ever had!"

He pulled off his coat and approached him. The men stood round, looking on in amazement as he flung it over the yellow body. The dog yelled as Logie grasped and lifted him, holding him fast in his arms; but his jaws were muffled in the coat, and the pain of the broken limb was weakening his struggles.

Ferrier looked on with his hands on his hips. He admired the dog, but did not always understand James.

"You are going to hamper yourself with him now?" he exclaimed.

"Give me the piper's bonnet," said the other. "There! push it into the crook of my arm between the poor brute and me. It will make him go the easier. You will need to scatter now. Leave the piper where he is. A few inches of earth will do him no good. Ferrier, I am going. You and I will have to lie low for awhile after this."

The cur had grown exhausted, and ceased to fight; he shivered and snuffled feebly at the Kilmarnock bonnet, the knob of which made a red spot against the shirt on James's broad breast. Ferrier and Gourlay glanced after him as he went off between the trees. But as they had no time to waste on the sight of his eccentricities, they disappeared in different directions.

Dusk was beginning to fall on the wood and on the dead beggar as he lay with his two silent comrades, looking towards the Grampians from the top of Huntly Hill.

CHAPTER XXIII

THE MUIR OF PERT

CALLANDAR watched his corporal riding away from the confines of the wood. His eyes followed the horse as it disappeared into hollows and threaded its way among lumps of rock. He stood for some time looking out over the landscape, now growing cold with the loss of the sun, his mind full of Flemington. Then he turned back with a sigh to retrace his way. His original intention in bringing Wattie up the hill came back to him, and he remembered that he had yet to discover whether he could identify the red-bearded man. It was at this moment that the fusillade from his halting-place burst upon him. He stopped, listening, then ran forward into the wood, the map from which he had been directing the corporal clutched in his hand.

He had gone some distance with the soldier, so he only reached the place when the quick disaster was over to hear the hoof-beats of the escaping horses dying out as they galloped down Huntly Hill. The smoke of the firearms hung below the branches like a grey canopy, giving the unreality of a vision to the spectacle before him. He could not see the beggar's body, but the overturned cart was in full view, a ridiculous object, with its wooden wheels raised, as though in protest, to the sky. He looked in vain for a sign of his third man, and at the sight of the uniform upon the two dead figures lying on the ground he understood that he was alone. Of the three private soldiers who had followed him down Glen Esk there was not one left with him. Archie, the traitor, was gone, and only the red-bearded man remained. He could see him in the group that was watching James Logie as he captured the struggling dog.

Callandar ground his teeth; then he dropped on one knee and contemplated the sight from behind the great circle of roots and earth that a fallen tree had torn from the sod. Of all men living he was one of the last who might be called a coward, but neither was he one of those hot-heads who will plunge, to their own undoing and to that of other people, into needless disaster. He would have gone grimly into the hornet's nest before him, pistol in hand, leaving heaven to take care of the result, had the smallest advantage to his king and country been attainable thereby. His own death or capture would do no more than prevent him from carrying news of what had happened to headquarters, and he decided, with the promptness hidden behind his taciturn demeanour, that his nearest duty was to identify James Logie, if he were present. Callandar's duty was the only thing that he always saw quickly.

From his shelter he marked the two Jacobite officers, and, as he knew Ferrier very well from description, he soon made out the man he wanted. James was changed since the time when he had first come across Archie's path. His clothes were worn and stained, and the life of wandering and concealment that he had led since he parted from the Prince had set its mark on him. He had slept in as many strange places of late as had the dead beggar at his feet; anxious watching and lack of food and rest were levelling the outward man to something more primitive and haggard than the gallant-looking gentleman of the days before Culloden, yet there remained to him the atmosphere that could never be obliterated, the personality that he could never lose until the earth should lie on him. He was no better clothed than those who surrounded him, but his pre-eminence was plain. The watcher devoured him with his eyes as he turned from his comrades, carrying the dog.

As soon as he was out of sight, the rebels scattered quietly, and Callandar crouched lower, praying fortune to prevent anyone from passing his retreat. None approached him, and he was left with the three dead men in possession of the wood.

He rose and looked at his silent comrades. It would be useless to follow Logie, because, with so many of his companions dispersing at this moment about the fringes of the Muir of Pert, he could hardly hope to do so unobserved. There would be no chance of getting to close quarters with him, which was Callandar's chief desire, for the mere suspicion of a hostile presence would only make James shift his hiding-place before the gathering troops could draw their cordon round him. He abandoned the idea with regret, telling himself that he must make a great effort to get to Brechin and to return with a mounted force in time to take action in the morning. The success of his ambush and his ignorance that he had been watched would keep Logie quiet for the night.

He decided to take the only road that he knew, the one by which Flemington had left him. The upper one entangled itself in the Muir, and might lead him into some conclave of the enemy. He began to descend in the shadows of the coming darkness that was drawing itself like an insidious net over the spacious land. He had almost reached the road, when a moving object not far from him made him stop. A man was hurrying up the hill some little way to his right, treading swiftly along, and, though his head was turned from Callandar, and he was not near enough for him to distinguish his features, the sling across his shoulder told him that it was Flemington.

Callandar stood still, staring after him. Archie's boldness took away his breath. Here he was, returning on his tracks, and if he kept his direction, he would have to pass within a few hundred yards of the spot on which he knew that the companions he had left would be halted; Callandar had pointed out the place to him as they approached the hill together.

Archie took a wider sweep as he neared the wood, and the soldier, standing in the shadow of a rowan-tree, whose berries were already beginning to colour for autumn, saw that he was making for the Muir, and knew that the beggar was justified. One thing only could be bringing him back. He had come, as Wattie had predicted, to warn Logie.

He had spoken wisdom, that dead vagabond, lying silent for ever among the trees; he had assured him that Flemington would not suffer him to take Logie. He knew him, and he had laughed at the idea of his wounded arm turning him out of his road. "It's no the like o' that that gars the like o' him greet," he had said; and he was right. Callandar, watching the definite course of the figure through the dusk, was sure that he was taking the simplest line to a retreat whose exact position he knew. He turned and followed, running from cover to cover, his former errand abandoned. It was strange that, in spite of all, a vague gladness was in his heart, as he thought that Archie was not the soft creature that he had pretended to be. There were generous things in Callandar. Then his generous impulse turned back on him in bitterness, for it occurred to him that Archie had been aware of what lay waiting for them, and had saved himself from possible accident in time.

They went on till they reached the border of the Muir, Flemington going as unconcernedly as if he were walking in the streets of Brechin, though he kept wide of the spot on which he believed the riders to have disposed themselves for the night. There was no one who knew him in that part of the country, and he wore no uniform to make him conspicuous in the eyes of any chance passer in this lonely neighbourhood. As Callandar emerged from the straggling growth at the Muir's edge, he saw him still in front going through the deep thickness of the heather.

Callandar wished that he knew how far the Muir extended, and exactly what lay on its farther side. His map was thrust into his coat, but it was now far too dark for him to make use of it; the tall figure was only just visible, and he redoubled his pace, gaining a little on it. A small stationary light shone ahead, evidently the window of some muirland hovel. There is nothing so difficult to decide as the distance of a light at night, but he guessed that it was the goal towards which Archie was leading. He went forward, till the young man's voice hailing someone and the sound of knocking made him stop and throw himself down in the heather. He thought he heard a door shut. When all had been quiet for a minute he rose up, and, approaching the house, took up his stand not a dozen yards from the walls.

Perplexity came on him. He had been surprisingly successful in pursuing Flemington unnoticed as far as this hovel, but he had yet to find out who was inside it. Perhaps the person he had heard speaking was Logie, but equally perhaps not. There was no sound of voices within, though he heard movements; he dared not approach the uncurtained window to look in, for the person whose step he heard was evidently standing close to it. He would wait, listening for that person to move away, and then would try his luck. He had spent perhaps ten minutes thus occupied when, without a warning sound, the door opened and Archie stood on the threshold, as still as though he were made of marble. It was too dark for either man to see more than the other's blurred outline.

Flemington looked out into the night.

"Come in, Callandar!" he called. "You are the very man I want!"

The soldier's astonishment was such that his feet seemed frozen to the ground. He did not stir.

"Come!" cried Archie. "You have followed me so far that you surely will not turn back at the last step. I need you urgently, man. Come in!"

He held the door open.

Callandar entered, pushing past him, and found himself in a low, small room, wretchedly furnished, with another at the back opening out of it. Both were empty, and the light he had seen was standing on the table.

"There is no one here!" he exclaimed.

"No," said Flemington.

"Where is the man you were speaking to?"

"He is gone. The ill-mannered rogue would not wait to receive you."

"It was that rebel! It was Captain Logie!" cried Callandar.

"It was not Logie; you may take my word for that," replied Archie. He sat down on the edge of the table and crossed his legs. "Try again, Callandar," he said lightly.

Callandar's lips were drawn into an even line, but they were shaking. The mortification of finding that Archie had been aware of his presence, had pursued his way unconcerned, knowing that he followed, had called him in as a man calls the serving-man he has left outside, was hot in him. No wonder his own concealment had seemed so easy.

"You have sent him to warn Logie—that is what you have done!" he cried. "You are a scoundrel—I know that!"

He stepped up to him, and would have laid hold of his collar, but the sling stopped him.

"I have. Callandar, you are a genius."

As the other stood before him, speechless, Flemington rose up.

"You have got to arrest me," he said; "that is why I called you in. I might have run out by the back of the house, like the man who is gone, who went with my message almost before the door was shut. Look! I have only one serviceable arm and no sword. I left it where I left my horse. And here is my pistol; I will lay it on the table, so you will have no trouble in taking me prisoner. You have not had your stalking for nothing, after all, you mighty hunter before the Lord!"

"You mean to give yourself up—you, who have taken so much care to save yourself?"

"I have meant to ever since I saw you under the rowan-tree watching me, flattened against the trunk like a squirrel. I would as soon be your prisoner as anyone else's—sooner, I think."

"I cannot understand you!" exclaimed Callandar, taking possession of the weapon Archie had laid down.

"It is hard enough to understand oneself but I do at last," said the other. "Once I thought life easy, but mine has been mighty difficult lately. From here on it will be quite simple. And there will not be much more of it, I fancy."

"You are right there," said Callandar grimly.

"I can see straight before me now. I tell you life has grown simple."

"You lied at the cross roads."

"I did. How you looked after me as I went! Well, I have done what I suppose no one has ever done before: I have threatened to report you for neglecting your duty." He threw back his head and laughed. "And I am obliged to tell you to arrest me now. O Callandar, who will correct your backslidings when there is an end of me?"

The other did not smile as he looked at Flemington's laughing eyes, soft and sparkling under the downward curve of his brows.

Through his anger, the pity of it all was smiting him, though he was so little given to sentiment. Perhaps Archie's charm had told on him all the time they had been together, though he had never decided whether he liked him or not. And he looked so young when he laughed.

"What have you done?" he cried, pacing suddenly up and down the little room. "You have run on destruction, Flemington; you have thrown your life away. Why have you done this —you?"

"If a thing is worthless, there is nothing to do but throw it away."

Callandar watched him with pain in his eyes.

"What made you suspect me?" asked Archie. "You can tell me anything now. There is only one end to this business. It will be the making of you."

"Pshaw!" exclaimed the other, turning away.

"Why did you follow me?" continued Archie.

Callandar was silent.

"Tell me this," he said at last: "What makes you give yourself up now, without a struggle or a protest, when little more than two hours ago you ran from what you knew was to come, there, at the foot of the hill? Surely your friends would have spared *you!*"

"Now it is I who do not understand you," said Archie.

His companion stood in front of him, searching his face.

"Flemington, are you lying? On your soul, are you lying?"

"Of what use are lies to me now?" exclaimed Archie impatiently. "Truth is a great luxury; believe me, I enjoy it."

"You knew nothing of what was waiting for us at the top of Huntly Hill?"

"Nothing, as I live," said Archie.

"The beggar betrayed you," said Callandar. "When you were gone he told me that you were in Logie's pay—that you would warn him. He was right, Flemington."

"I am not in Logie's pay—I never was," broke in Archie.

"I did not know what to think," the soldier went on; "but I took him up Huntly Hill with me, and when we had unsaddled, and the men were lying under the trees, I sent the corporal to Brechin with the information. I went with him to the edge of the wood, and when I came back there was not a man left alive. Logie and Ferrier were there with a horde of their rebels. They had come to rescue the prisoner, and he was loose."

"Then he *was* Ferrier's cousin!" exclaimed Flemington. "We were right."

"One of my men escaped," continued Callandar, "or I suppose so, for he was gone. The beggar and the other two were killed, and the horses had stampeded."

"So Wattie is dead," mused Flemington. "Gad, what a voice has gone with him!"

"They did not see me, but I watched them; I saw him—Logie—he went off quickly, and he took one of the beggar's dogs with him, snarling and struggling, with his head smothered in his coat. Then I went down the hill, meaning to make for Brechin, and I saw you coming back. I knew what you were about, thanks to that beggar."

Neither spoke for a minute. Archie was still sitting on the table. He had been looking on the ground, and he raised his eyes to his companion's face.

Something stirred in him, perhaps at the thought of how he stood with fate. He was not given to thinking about himself, but he might well do so now.

"Callandar," he said, "I dare say you don't like me——" Then he broke off, laughing. "How absurd!" he exclaimed. "Of course you hate me; it is only right you should. But perhaps you will understand—I think you will, if you will listen. I was thrown against Logie—no matter how—but, unknowing what he did, he put his safety in my hands. He did more. I had played upon his sympathy, and in the generosity of his heart he came to my help as one true man might do to another. I was not a true man, but he did not know that; he knew nothing of me but that I stood in need, and he believed I was as honest as himself. He thought I was with his own cause. That was what I wished him to believe—had almost told him."

Callander listened, the lines of his long face set.

"I had watched him and hunted him," continued Archie, "and my information against him was already in the beggar's hands, on its way to its mark. I could not bring myself to do more against him then. What I did afterwards was done without mention of his name. You see, Callander, I have been true to nobody."

He paused, waiting for comment, but the other made none.

"After that I went to Edinburgh," he continued, "and he joined the Prince. Then I went north with Cumberland. I was freed from my difficulty until they sent me here to take him. The Duke gave me my orders himself, and I had to go. That ride with you was hell, Callandar, and when we met the beggar to-day I had to make my choice. That was the turning-point for me. I could not go on."

"He said it was not your wound that turned you aside."

"He was a shrewd rascal," said Flemington. "I wish I could tell how he knew so much about me."

"It was your own tongue: once you spent the night in a barn together when you were lightheaded from a blow, and you spoke all night of Logie. You said enough to put him on your track. That is what he told me as we went up Huntly Hill."

Archie shrugged his shoulders and rose up.

"Now, what are you going to do?" he said.

"I am going to take you to Brechin."

"Come, then," said Archie, "we shall finish our journey together after all. It has been a hard day. I am glad it is over."

They went out together. As Callandar drew the door to behind them Archie stood still.

"If I have dealt double with Logie, I will not do so with the king," said he. "This is the way out of my difficulty. Do you understand me, Callandar?"

The darkness hid the soldier's face.

Perhaps of all the people who had played their part in the tangle of destiny, character, circumstance, or whatsoever influences had brought Flemington to the point at which he stood, he was the one who understood him best.

CHAPTER XXIV

THE VANITY OF MEN

THE last months had been a time of great anxiety to Lord Balnillo. In spite of his fine steering and though he had escaped from molestation, he was not comfortable as he saw the imprisonments and confiscations that were going on; and the precariousness of all that had been secure disturbed him and made him restless. He was unsettled, too, by his long stay in Edinburgh, and he hankered afresh after the town life in which he had spent so many of his years. His trees and parks interested him still, but he looked on them, wondering how long he would be allowed to keep them. He was lonely, and he missed James, whom he had not seen since long before Culloden, the star of whose destiny had led him out again into the world of chance.

He had the most upsetting scheme under consideration that a man of his age can entertain. At sixty-four it is few people who think seriously of changing their state, yet this was what David Balnillo had in mind; for he had found so many good reasons for offering his hand to Christian Flemington that he had decided at last to take that portentous step. The greatest of these was the effect that a alliance with the Whig lady would produce in the quarters from which he feared trouble. His estate would be pretty safe if Madam Flemington reigned over it.

It was pleasant to picture her magnificent presence at his table; her company would rid country life of its dulness, and on the visits to Edinburgh, which he was sure she would wish to make, the new Lady Balnillo would turn their lodging into a bright spot in society. He smoothed his silk stockings as he imagined the stir that his belated romance would make. He would be the hero of it, and its heroine, besides being a safeguard to his property, would be a credit to himself.

There were some obstacles to his plan, and one of them was Archie; but he believed that, with a little diplomacy, that particular difficulty might be overcome. He would attack that side of the business in a very straightforward manner. He would make Madam Flemington understand that he was large-minded enough to look upon the episode in which he had borne the part of victim in a reasonable yet airy spirit. In the game in which their political differences had brought them face to face the honours had been with the young man; he would admit that with a smile and with the respect that one noble enemy accords to another. He would assure her that bygones should be bygones, and that when he claimed Archie as his grandson-in-law, he would do so without one grudging backward glance at the circumstances in which they had first met. His magnanimity seemed to him an almost touching thing, and he played with the idea of his own apposite grace when, in some sly but genial moment, he would suggest that the portrait upstairs should be finished.

What had given the final touch to his determination was a message that James had contrived to send him, which removed the last scruple from his heart. His brother's danger had weighed upon David, and it was not only its convenience to himself at this juncture which made him receive it with relief. Logie was leaving the country for Holland, and the next tidings of him would come from there, should he be lucky enough to reach its shores alive.

Since the rescue of Gourlay the neighbourhood of the Muir of Pert—the last of his haunts in which Logie could trust himself—had become impossible for him, and he was now striving to get to a creek on the coast below Peterhead. It was some time since a roof had been over him, and the little cottage from which Flemington had despatched his urgent warning stood empty. Its inmate had been his unsuspected connection with the world since his time of wandering had begun; for though his fatal mistake in discovering this link in his chain of communication to Flemington had made him abjure its shelter, he had had no choice for some time between the Muir and any other place.

The western end of the county swarmed with troops. Montrose was subdued; the passes of the Grampians were watched; there remained only this barren tract west of the river; and the warning brought to him from a nameless source had implored him to abandon it before the soldiery, which his informant assured him was collecting to sweep it from end to end, should range itself on its borders.

Archie had withheld his name when he sent the dweller in the little hovel speeding into the night. He was certain that in making it known to James he would defeat his own ends, for Logie would scarcely be disposed to trust his good faith, and might well look on the message as a trick to drive him into some trap waiting for him between the Muir and the sea.

James did not give his brother any details of his projected flight; he merely bade him an indefinite good-bye. The game was up—even he was obliged to admit that—and Ferrier, whose ardent spirit had been one with his own since the beginning of all things, was already making for a fishing village, from which he hoped to be smuggled out upon the high seas. Nothing further could be gained in Angus for the Stuart cause. The friends had spent themselves since April in their endeavours to resuscitate the feeling in the country, but there was no more money to be raised, no more men to be collected. They told themselves that all they could do now was to wait in the hope of a day when their services might be needed again. That day would find them both ready, if they were above ground.

David knew that, had James been in Scotland, he would not have dared to think of bringing Christian Flemington to Balnillo.

He had a feeling of adventure when he started from his own door for Ardguys. The slight awe with which Christian still inspired him, even when she was most gracious, was beginning to foreshadow itself, and he knew that his bones would be mighty stiff on the morrow; there was no riding of the circuit now to keep him in practice in the saddle. But he was not going to give way to silly apprehensions, unsuited to his age and position; he would give himself every chance in the way of effect. The servant who rode after him carried a handsome riding-suit for his master to don at Forfar before making the last stage of his road. It grieved Balnillo to think how much of the elegance of his well-turned legs must be unrevealed by his high boots. He was a personable old gentleman, and his grey cob was worthy of carrying an eligible wooer. He reached Ardguys, and dismounted under its walls on the following afternoon.

He had sent no word in front of him. Christian rose when he was ushered into her presence, and laid down the book in her hand, surprised.

"You are as unexpected as an earthquake," she exclaimed, as she saw who was her visitor.

"But not as unwelcome?" said David.

"Far from it. Sit down, my lord. I had begun to forget that civilization existed, and now I am reminded of it."

He bowed, delighted.

A few messages and compliments, a letter or two despatched by hand, had been their only communications since the judge left Edinburgh, and his spirits rose as he found that she seemed really pleased to see him.

"And what has brought you?" asked Christian, settling herself with the luxurious deliberation of a cat into the large chair from which she had risen. "Something good, certainly."

"The simple desire to see you, ma'am. Could anything be better?"

It was an excellent opening; but he had never, even in his youth, been a man who ran full tilt upon anything. He had scarcely ever before made so direct a speech.

She smiled, amused. There had been plenty of time for thought in her solitude; but, though she had thought a good deal about him, she had not a suspicion of his errand. She saw people purely in relation to the uses she had for them, and, officially, she had pronounced him harmless to the party in whose interests she had kept him at her side. The circumstances were not those which further sentiment.

"I have spent this quiet time in remembering your kindnesses to me," he began, inspired by her smile.

"You call it a quiet time?" she interrupted. "I had not looked on it in that way. Quiet for us, perhaps, but not for the country."

"True, true," said he, in the far away tone in which some people seek to let unprofitable subjects melt.

Now that the active part of the rebellion had become history, she had no hesitation in speaking out from her solid place on the winning side.

"This wretched struggle is over, and we may be plain with one another, Lord Balnillo," she continued. "You, at least, have had much to alarm you."

"I have been a peaceful servant of law and order all my life," said he, "and as such I have conceived it my place to stand aloof. It has been my duty to restrain violence of all kinds."

"But you have not restrained your belongings," she observed boldly.

He was so much taken aback that he said nothing.

"Well, my lord, it is one of my regrets that I have never seen Captain Logie. At least you have to be proud of a gallant man," she went on, with the same impulse that makes all humanity set a fallen child upon its legs.

But Balnillo had a genius for scrambling to his feet.

"My brother has left the country in safety," he rejoined, with one of those random flashes of sharpness that had stood him in such good stead. His cunning was his guardian angel; for he did not know what she knew—namely, that Archie had left Fort Augustus in pursuit of James.

"Indeed?" she said, silenced.

She was terribly disappointed, but she hid her feelings in barefaced composure.

The judge drew his chair closer. Here was another opening, and his very nervousness pushed him towards it.

"Ma'am," he began, clearing his throat, "I shall not despair of presenting James to you. When the country is settled—if—in short——"

"I imagine that Captain Logie will hardly trust himself in Scotland either in my lifetime or in yours. We are old, you and I," she added, the bitterness of her disappointment surging through her words.

She watched him to see whether this barbed truth pierced him; it pierced herself as she hurled it.

"Maybe," said he; "but age has not kept me from the business I have come upon. I have come to put a very particular matter before you."

She was still unsuspicious, but she grew impatient. He had wearied her often in Edinburgh with tedious histories of himself, and she had endured them then for reasons of policy; but she felt no need of doing so here. It was borne in upon her, as it has been borne in upon many of us, that a person who is acceptable in town may be unendurable in the country. She had not thought of that as she welcomed him.

"Ma'am," he went on, intent on nothing but his affair, "I may surprise you—I trust I shall not offend you. At least you will approve the feelings of devotion, of respect, of admiration which have brought me here. I have an ancient name, I have sufficient means—I am not ill-looking, I believe——"

"Are you making me a proposal, my lord?"

She spoke with an accent of derision; the sting of it was sharp in her tone.

"There is no place for ridicule, ma'am. I see nothing unsuitable in my great regard for you."

He spoke with real dignity.

She had not suspected him of having any, personally, and she had forgotten that an inherited stock of it was behind him. The rebuke astonished her so much that she scarcely knew what reply to make.

"As I said, I believe I am not ill-looking," he repeated, with an air that lost him his advantage. "I can offer you such a position as you have a right to expect."

"You also offer me a brother-in-law whose destination may be the scaffold," she said brutally; "do not forget that."

This was not to be denied, and for a moment he was put out. But it was on these occasions that he shone.

"Let us dismiss family matters from our minds and think only of ourselves," said he; "my brother is an outlaw, and as such is unacceptable to you, and your grandson has every reason to be ashamed to meet me. We can set these disadvantages, one against the other, and agree to ignore them."

"I am not disposed to ignore Archie," said she.

"Well, ma'am, neither am I. I hope I am a large-minded man—indeed, no one can sit on the bench for the time that I have sat on it and not realize the frailty of all creatures——"

"My lord—-" began Christian.

But it is something to have learned continuance of speech professionally, and Balnillo was launched; also his own magnanimous attitude had taken his fancy.

"I will remember nothing against him," said he. "I will forget his treatment of my hospitality, and the discreditable uses to which he put my roof."

"Sir!" broke in Christian.

"I will remember that, according to his lights, he was in the exercise of his duty. Whatsoever may be my opinion of the profession to which he was compelled, I will thrust it behind me with the things best forgotten."

"That is enough, Lord Balnillo," cried Madam Flemington, rising.

"Sit, madam, sit. Do not disturb yourself! Understand me, that I will allow every leniency. I will make every excuse! I will dwell, not on the fact that he was a spy, but on his enviable relationship to yourself."

She stood in the middle of the room, threatening him with her eyes. Some people tremble when roused to the pitch of anger that she had reached; some gesticulate; Christian was still.

He had risen too.

"If you suppose that I could connect myself with a disloyal house you are much mistaken," she said, controlling herself with an effort. "I have no quarrel with your name, Lord Balnillo; it is old enough.

My quarrel is with the treason in which it has been dipped. But I am very well content with my own. Since I have borne it, I have kept it clean from any taint of rebellion."

"But I have been a peaceful man," he protested. "As I told you, the law has been my profession. I have raised a hand against no one."

"Do you think I do not know you?" exclaimed she. "Do you suppose that my ears were shut in the winter, and that I heard nothing in all the months I spent in Edinburgh? What of that, Lord Balnillo?"

"You made no objection to me then, ma'am, I was made happy by being of service to you."

She laughed scornfully.

"Let us be done with this," she said. "You have offered yourself to me and I refuse the offer. I will add my thanks."

The last words were a masterpiece of insolent civility.

A gilt-framed glass hung on the wall, one of the possessions that she had brought with her from France. David suddenly caught sight of his own head reflected in it above the lace cravat for which he had paid so much ; the spectacle gathered up his recollections and his present mortification, and fused them into one stab of hurt vanity.

"I see that you can make no further use of me," he said.

"None."

He walked out of the room. At the door he turned and bowed.

"If you will allow me, I will call for my horse myself," said he.

He went out of the house and she stood where she was, thinking of what he had told her about his brother; she had set her heart upon Archie's success in taking Logie, and now the man had left the country and his chance was gone. The proposal to which she had just listened did not matter to her one way or the other, though he had offended her by the attitude he took up when making it. He was unimportant. It was of Archie that she thought as she watched the judge and his servant ride away between the ash-trees. They were crossing the Kilpie burn when her maid came in, bringing a letter. The writing on it was strange to Christian.

"Who has brought this?" she asked as she opened it.

"Just a callant," replied the girl.

She read the letter, which was short. It was signed 'R. Callandar, Captain,' and was written at Archie Flemington's request to tell her that he was under arrest at Brechin on a charge of conspiring with the king's enemies.

The writer added a sentence, unknown, as he explained, to Flemington.

"The matter is serious," he wrote, "the Duke of Cumberland is still in Edinburgh. It might be well if you could see him. Make no delay, as we await his orders."

She stood, turning cold, her eyes fixed on the maid.

"Eh—losh, mem!" whimpered Mysie, approaching her with her hands raised.

Madam Flemington felt as though her brain refused to work. There seemed to be nothing to drive it forward. The world stood still. The walls, an imprisoning horror, shut her in from all movement, all action, when action was needed. She had never felt Ardguys to be so desperately far from the reach of humanity, herself so much cut off from it, as now. And yet she must act. Her nearest channel of communication was the judge, riding away.

"Fool!" she cried, seizing Mysie, "run—run! Send the boy after Lord Balnillo. Tell him to run!"

The maid hesitated, staring at the pallor of her mistress's face.

"Eh, but, mem—sit you down!" she wailed.

Christian thrust her from her path as though she had been a piece of furniture, and swept into the hall. A barefooted youth was outside by the door. He stared at her, as Mysie had done. She took him by the shoulder.

"Run! Go instantly after those horses! That is Lord Balnillo!" she cried, pointing to the riders, who were mounting the rise beyond the burn. "Tell him to return at once. Tell him he must come back!"

He shook off her grip and ran. He was a corner-boy from Brechin and he had a taste for sensation.

Madam Flemington went back into her room. Mysie followed her, whimpering still, and she pushed her outside and sank down in her large chair. She could not watch the window, for fear of going mad.

She sat still and steady until she heard the thud of bare feet on the stone steps, and then she hurried out.

"He tell't me he wadna bide," said the corner-boy breathlessly. "He was vera well obliged to ye, he bad' me say, but he wadna bide."

Christian left him and shut herself into the room, alone. Callandar's bald lines had overpowered her completely, leaving no place in her brain for anything else. But now she saw her message from Lord Balnillo's point of view, and anger and contempt flamed up again, even in the midst of her trouble.

"The vanity of men! Ah, God, the vanity of men!" she cried, throwing out her hands, as though to put the whole race of them from her.

CHAPTER XXV

A ROYAL DUKE

THE Duke of Cumberland was at Holyrood House. He had come down from the North by way of Stirling, and having spent some days in Edinburgh, he was making his final arrangements to set out for England. He was returning in the enviable character of conquering hero, and he knew that a great reception awaited him in London, where every preparation was being made to do him honour; he was thinking of these things as he sat in one of the grim rooms of the ancient palace. There was not much luxury here; and looking across the table at which he sat and out of the window, he could see the dirty roofs of the Canongate—a very different prospect from the one that would soon meet his eyes. He was sick of Scotland.

Papers were littered on the table, and his secretary had just carried away a bundle with him. He was alone, because he expected a lady to whom he had promised an audience, but he was not awaiting her with the feelings that he generally brought to such occasions. Cumberland had received the visits of many women alone since leaving England, but his guests were younger than the one whose approach he could now hear in the anteroom outside. He drew his brows together, for he expected no profit and some annoyance from the interview.

He rose as she was ushered in and went to the open fireplace, where he stood awaiting her, drawn up to his full height, which was not great. The huge iron dogs behind him and the high mantelpiece above his head dwarfed him with their large lines. He was not an ill-looking young man, though his hair, pulled back and tied after the fashion of the day, showed off the receding contours that fell away from his temples, and made his blue eyes look more prominent than they were.

He moved forward clumsily as Christian curtsied.

"Come in, madam, come in. Be seated. I have a few minutes only to give you," he said, pointing to a chair on the farther side of the table.

She sat down opposite to him.

"I had the honour of being presented to your Royal Highness last year," she said.

"I remember you well, ma'am," replied he shortly.

"It is in the hope of being remembered that I have come," said she. "It is to ask you, Sir, to remember the services of my house to yours."

"I remember them, ma'am; I forget nothing."

"I am asking you, in remembering, to forget one thing," said she. "I shall not waste your Royal Highness's time and mine in beating about bushes. I have travelled here from my home without resting, and it is not for me to delay now."

He took up a pen that lay beside him, and put the quill between his teeth.

"Your Royal Highness knows why I have come," continued she, her eyes falling from his own and fixing themselves on the pen in his mouth. He removed it with his fat hand, and tossed it aside.

"There is absolute proof against Flemington," said he. "He accuses himself. I presume you know that."

"I do. This man—Captain Logie—has some strange attraction for him that I cannot understand, and did him some kindness that seems to have turned his head. His regard for him was a purely personal one. It was personal friendship that led him to—to the madness he has wrought. His hands are clean of conspiracy. I have come all this way to assure your Highness of that."

"It is possible," said Cumberland. "The result is the same. We have lost the man whose existence above ground is a danger to the kingdom."

"I have come to ask you to take that difference of motive into consideration," she went on. "Were the faintest shadow of conspiracy proved, I should not dare to approach you; my request should not pass my lips. I have been in correspondence with him during the whole of the campaign, and I know that he served the king loyally. I beg your Highness to remember that now. I speak of his motive because I know it."

"You are fortunate, then," he interrupted.

"Captain Callandar, to whom he gave himself up, wrote me two letters at his request, one in which he announced his arrest, and one which I received as I entered my coach to leave my door. Archie knows what is before him," she added; "he has no hope of life and no knowledge of my action in coming to your Highness. But he wished me to know the truth—that he had conspired with no one. He is ready to suffer for what he has done, but he will not have me ashamed of him. Look, Sir——"

She pushed the letter over to him.

"His motives may go hang, madam," said Cumberland.

"Your Highness, if you have any regard for us who have served you, read this!"

He rose and went back to the fireplace.

"There is no need, madam. I am not interested in the correspondence of others."

He was becoming impatient; he had spent enough time on this lady. She was not young enough to give him any desire to detain her. She was an uncommon-looking woman, certainly, but at her age that fact could matter to nobody. He wondered, casually, whether the old stories about her and Charles Edward's father were true. Women struck him only in one light.

"You will not read this, your Royal Highness?" said Christian; with a little tremor of voice.

"No, ma'am. I may tell you that my decision has not altered. The case is not one that admits of any question."

"Your Highness," said Christian, rising, "I have never made an abject appeal to anyone yet, and even now, though I make it to the son of my king, I can hardly bring myself to utter it. I deplore my—my boy's action from the bottom of my soul. I sent him from me—I parted from him nearly a year ago because of this man Logie."

He faced round upon her and put his hands behind his back.

"What!" he exclaimed, "you knew of this? You have been keeping this affair secret between you?"

"He went to Montrose on the track of Logie in November," said she; "he was sent there to watch his movements before Prince Charles marched to England, and he did so well that he contrived to settle himself under Lord Balnillo's roof. In three days he returned to me. He had reported on Logie's movements—I know that—your Highness's agents can produce his report. But he returned to my house to tell me that, for some fool's reason, some private question of sentiment, he would follow Logie no longer. 'I will not go man-hunting after Logie'—those were his words."

"Madam——" began Cumberland.

She put out her hand, and her gesture seemed to reverse their positions.

"I told him to go—I told him that I would sooner see him dead than that he should side with the Stuarts! He answered me that he could have no part with rebels, and that his act concerned Logie alone. Then he left me, and on his way to Brechin he received orders to go to the Government ship in Montrose Harbour. Then the ship was attacked and taken."

"It was Flemington's friend, Logie, who was at the bottom of that business," said Cumberland.

"He met Logie and they fought," said Madam Flemington. "I know none of the details, but I know that they fought. Then he went to Edinburgh."

"It is time that we finished with this!" exclaimed Cumberland. "No good is served by it."

"I am near the end, your Highness," said Christian, and then paused, unnerved by the too great suggestiveness of her words.

"These things are no concern of mine," he observed in the pause; "his movements do not matter. And I may tell you, ma'am, that my leisure is not unlimited."

It was nearing the close of the afternoon, and the sun stood like a red ball over the mists of the Edinburgh smoke. Cumberland's business was over for the day, and he was looking forward to dining that evening with a carefully chosen handful of friends, male and female.

Her nerve was giving way against the stubborn detachment of the man. She felt herself helpless, and her force ineffective. Life was breaking up round her. The last man she had confronted had spurned her in the end—through a mistake, it was true—but the opportunity had been given him by her own loss of grip in the bewilderment of a crisis. This one was spurning her too. But she went on.

"He performed his work faithfully from that day forward, as your Royal Highness knew when you took him to the North. His services are better known to you, Sir, than to anyone else. He gave himself up to Captain Callandar as the last proof that he could take no part with the rebels. He threw away his life."

"*That*, at least, is true," said the Duke, with a sneer. He was becoming exasperated, and the emphasis which he put on the word 'that' brought the slow blood to her face. She looked at him as though she saw him across some mud-befouled stream. Even now her pride rose above the despair in her heart. He was not sensitive, but her expression stung him.

"I am accustomed to truth," she replied.

He turned his back. There was a silence.

"I came to ask for Archie's life," she said, in a toneless, steady voice, "but I will go, asking nothing. Your Royal Highness has nothing to give that he or I would stoop to take at your hands."

He stood doggedly, without turning, and he did not move until the sound of her sweeping skirts had died away in the anteroom. Then he went out, a short, stoutish figure passing along the dusty corridors of Holyrood, and entered a room from which came the ring of men's voices.

A party of officers in uniform got up as he came in. Some were playing cards. He went up to one of the players and took those he held from between his fingers.

"Give me your hand, Walden," said he, "and for God's sake get us a bottle of wine. Damn me, but I hate old women! They should have their tongues cut out."

CHAPTER XXVI

THE VANISHING BIRD

THE houses of Brechin climb from the river up the slope, and a little camp was spread upon the crest of ground above them, looking down over the uneven pattern of walls, the rising smoke, and the woods that cradled the Esk. Such of Cumberland's soldiery as had collected in Angus was drawn together here, and as the country was settling down, the camp was increased by detachments of horse and foot that arrived daily from various directions. The Muir of Pert was bare, left to the company of the roe-deer and the birds, for James had been traced to the coast, and the hungry North Sea had swallowed his tracks.

The spot occupied by the tents of Callandar's troop was in the highest corner of the camp, the one farthest from the town, and the long northern light that lingered over the hill enveloped the camp sounds and sights in a still, greenish clearness. There would be a bare few hours of darkness.

Callandar was now in command of a small force consisting of a troop of his own regiment which had lately marched in, and two of his men stood sentry outside the tent in which Archie Flemington was sitting at an improvised table writing a letter.

He had been a close prisoner since his arrest on the Muir of Pert, and during the week that had elapsed, whilst correspondence about him and orders concerning him had gone to and fro between Brechin and Edinburgh, he had been exclusively under Callandar's charge. That arrangement was the one concession made on his behalf among the many that had been asked for by his friends. At his own request he was to remain Callandar's prisoner till the end, and it was to be Callandar's voice that would give the order for his release at sunrise to-morrow, and Callandar's troopers whose hands would set him free.

The two men had spent much time together. Though the officer's responsibility did not include the necessity of seeing much of his prisoner, he had chosen to spend nearly all his leisure in Archie's tent. They had drawn very near together, this incongruous pair, though the chasm that lay between their respective temperaments had not been bridged by words. They had sat together on many evenings, almost in silence, playing cards until one of them grew drowsy, or some officious cock crowed on the outskirts of the town. Of the incident which had brought them into their present relationship, they spoke not at all; but sometimes Archie had broken out into snatches of talk, and Callandar had listened, with his grim smile playing about his mouth, to his descriptions of the men and things amongst which his short life had thrown him. As he looked across at his companion, who sat, his eyes sparkling in the light of the lantern, his expression changing with the shades of humour that ran over his words, like shadows over growing corn, he would be brought up short against the thought of the terrible incongruity to come—death. He could not think of Archie and death. At times he would have given a great deal to pass on his responsibility to some other man, and to turn his back on the place that was to witness such a tragedy. In furthering Archie's wishes by his own application for custody of him he had given him a great proof of friendship—how great he was only to learn as the days went by. Would to God it were over—so he would say to himself each night as he left the tent. He had thought Archie soft when they parted at the cross-roads, and he had been sorry. There was no need for sorrow on that score; never had been. The sorrow to him now was that so gallant, so brilliant a creature was to be cut off from the life of the world, to go down into the darkness, leaving so many of its inhabitants half-hearted, half-spirited, half alive, to crawl on in an existence which only interested them inasmuch as it supplied their common needs.

His hostility against Logie ran above the level of the just antagonism that a man feels for his country's enemy, and he questioned whether his life were worth the price that Flemington was paying for it. The hurried words that Archie had spoken about Logie as they left the hovel together had told him little, and that little seemed to him inadequate to explain the tremendous consequences that had followed. What had Logie said or done that had power to turn him out of his way? A man may meet many admirable characters among his enemies without having his efforts paralyzed by the encounter. Flemington was not new to his trade, and had been long enough in the secret service to know its requirements. A certain unscrupulousness was necessarily among them, yet why had his gorge only risen against it now? Callandar could find no signs in him of the overwrought sensibility that seemed to have prompted his revolt against his task. Logie had placed his safety in Archie's hands, and it was in order to end that safety that the young man had gone out; he had laid the trap and the quarry had fallen into it. What else had he expected? It was not that Callandar could not understand the scruple; what he could not understand was why a man of Archie's occupation should suddenly be undone by it. Having accepted his task, his duty had been plain. In theory, a rebel, to Callandar was a rebel, no more, and Archie, by his deed, had played a rebel's part; yet, in spite of that, the duty he must carry out on the morrow was making his heart sink within him. One thing about Archie stood out plain—he was not going to shirk his duty to his king and yet take Government money. Whatsoever his doings, the prisoner who sat in the tent over yonder would be lying under the earth to-morrow because he was prepared to pay the last price for his scruple. No, he was not soft.

Callandar would have died sooner than let him escape, yet his escape would have made him glad.

Callandar came across the camp and passed between the two sentries into Flemington's tent. The young man looked up from his writing.

"You are busy," said the officer.

"I have nearly done. There seems so much to do at the last," he added.

The other sat down on the bed and looked at him, filled with grief. The lantern stood by Archie's hand. His head was bent into the circle of light, and the yellow shine that fell upon it warmed his olive skin and brought out the brown shades in his brows and hair. The changing curves of his mouth were firm in the intensity of his occupation. He had so much expression as a rule that people seldom thought about his features but Callandar now noticed his long chin and the fine lines of his nostril.

His pen scratched on for a few minutes; then he laid it down and turned round.

"You have done me many kindnesses, Callandar," said he, "and now I am going to ask you for another—the greatest of all. It is everything to me that Captain Logie should get this letter. He is safe, I hope, over the water, but I do not know where. Will you take charge of it?"

"I will," said the other—"yes."

The very name of Logie went against him.

"You will have to keep it some little time, I fear," continued Archie, "but when the country has settled down you will be able to reach him through Lord Balnillo. Promise me that, if you can compass it, he shall get this."

"If it is to be done, I will do it."

"From you, that is enough," said Flemington, "I shall rest quietly."

He turned to his writing again.

Callandar sat still, looking round the tent vaguely for something to distract his heavy thoughts. A card lay on the ground and he picked it up. It was an ace, and the blank space of white round it was covered with drawing. His own consideration had procured pens and books—all that he could find to brighten the passing days for his prisoner. This was the result of some impulse that had taken Flemington's artistic fingers.

It was a sketch of one of the sentries outside the tent door. The figure was given in a few lines, dark against the light, and the outline of the man's homely features had gained some quality of suggestiveness and distinction by its passage through Archie's mind, and by the way he had placed the head against the clouded atmosphere made by the smoke rising from the camp. Through it, came a touched-in vision of the horizon beyond the tents. He looked at it, seeing something of its cleverness, and tossed it aside.

When Archie had ended his letter, he read it through:

"When this comes to your hands perhaps you will know what has become of me," he had written, "and you will understand the truth. I ask you to believe me, if only because these are the last words I shall ever write. A man speaks the truth when it is a matter of hours with him.

"You know what brought me to Balnillo, but you do not know what sent me from it. I went because I had no courage to stay. I was sent to find out how deep you were concerned in the Stuart cause and to watch your doings. I followed you that night in the town, and my wrist bears the mark you set on it still. That morning I despatched my confirmation of the Government's suspicions about you. Then I met you and we sat by the Basin of Montrose. God knows I have never forgotten the story you told me.

"Logie, I went because I could not strike you again. You had been struck too hard in the past, and I could not do it. What I told you about myself was untrue, but you believed it, and would have helped me. How could I go on?

"Then, as I stood between the devil and the deep sea, my orders took me to the *Venture*, and we met again on Inchbrayock. I had made sure you would be on the hill. When I would have escaped from you, you held me back, and as we struggled you knew me for what I was.

"You know the rest as well as I do, and you know where I was in the campaign that followed. Last of all I was sent out with those who were to take you on the Muir of Pert. I had no choice but to go—the choice came at the cross-roads below Huntly Hill. It was I who sent the warning to you from the little house on the Muir. You had directed me there for a different purpose. I sent no name with my message, knowing that if I did you might suspect me of a trick to entrap you again. That is all. There remained only the consequences, and I shall be face to face with them to-morrow.

"There is one thing more to say. Do not let yourself suppose that I am paying for your life with mine. I might have escaped had I tried to do so—it was my fault that I did not try. I had had enough of untruth, and I could no longer take the king's money; I had served his cause ill, and I could only pay for it. I have known two true men in my life—you and the man who has promised that you shall receive this letter. If you will think of me without bitterness, remember that I should have been glad.

ARCHIBALD FLEMINGTON."

He folded the paper and rose, holding it out to Callandar.

"I am contented," said he; "go now, Callandar. You look worn out. I believe this last night is trying you more than it tries me."

* * * *

It was some little time after daybreak that Callandar stood again at the door of the tent under the kindling skies. Archie was waiting for him and he came out. The eyes of the sentries never left them as they went away together, followed by the small armed guard that was at Callandar's heels.

The two walked a little apart, and when they reached the outskirts of the camp they came to a field, an insignificant rough enclosure, in which half a dozen soldiers were gathered, waiting. At the sight of Callandar the sergeant who was in charge of them began to form them in a line some paces from the wall.

Callandar and Flemington stopped. The light had grown clear, and the smoke that was beginning to rise from the town thickened the air over the roofs that could be seen from where they stood. The daily needs and the daily avocations were beginning again for those below the hill, while they were ceasing for ever for him who stood above in the cool morning. In a few minutes the sun would get up; already there was a sign of his coming in the eastward sky.

The two men turned to each other; they had nothing more to say. They had settled every detail of this last act of their short companionship, so that there should be no hesitation, no mistake, nothing to be a lengthening of agony for one, nor an evil memory for the other.

Archie held out his hand.

"When I look at you," he said.

"Yes," said Callandar.

"There are no words, Callandar. Words are nothing—but the last bit of my life has been the better for you."

For once speech came quickly to the soldier.

"The rest of mine will be the better for you," he answered. "You said once that you were not a true man. You lied."

Flemington was giving all to disprove the accusation of untruth, and it was one of the last things he was to hear.

So, with these rough words—more precious to him than any that could have been spoken—sounding in his ears, he walked away and stood before the wall. The men were lined in front of him.

His eyes roved for a moment over the slope of the country, the town roofs, the camp, then went to the distance. A solitary bird was crossing the sky, and his look followed it as it had followed the one he had seen when he made his choice at the foot of Huntly Hill. The first had flown away, a vanishing speck, towards the shadows gathering about the hills. This one was going into the sunrise. It was lost in the light....

"Fire!" said Callandar.

For Archie was looking at him with a smile.

CHAPTER XXVII

EPILOGUE

JAMES LOGIE stood at the window of a house in a Dutch town. The pollarded beech, whose boughs were trimmed in a close screen before the walls, had shed its golden leaves and the canal waters were grey under a cloudy sky. The long room was rather dark, and was growing darker. By the chair that he had left lay a yellow cur.

He had been standing for some minutes reading a letter by the fading light, and his back was towards the man who had brought it. The latter stood watching him, stiff and tall, an object of suspicion to the dog.

As he came to the end, the hand that held the paper went down to James's side. The silence in the room was unbroken for a space. When he turned, Callandar saw his powerful shoulders against the dusk and the jealous shadows of the beech-tree's mutilated arms.

"I can never thank you enough for bringing me this," said Logie. "My debt to you is immeasurable."

"I did it for him—not for you."

Callandar spoke coldly, almost with antagonism

"I can understand that," said James.

But something in his voice struck the other. Though he had moved as if to leave him, he stopped, and going over to the window, drew a playing-card from a pocket in his long coat.

"Look," he said, holding out the ace scrawled with the picture of the sentry.

James took it, and as he looked at it, his crooked lip was set stiffly, lest it should tremble.

"It was in his tent when I went back there—afterwards," said

Callandar.

He took the card back, and put it in his pocket.

"Then it was you——" began James.

"He was my prisoner, sir."

James walked away again and stood at the window.

Callandar waited, silent.

"I must wish you a good-day, Captain Logie," he said at last, "I have to leave Holland to-night."

James followed him down the staircase, and they parted at the outer door. Callandar went away along the street, and James came back slowly up the steep stairs, his hand on the railing of the carved banisters. He could scarcely see his way.

The yellow dog came to meet him when he entered his room, and as his master, still holding the letter, carried it again to the light, he followed. Half-way across the floor he turned to sniff at an old Kilmarnock bonnet that lay by the wainscot near the corner in which he slept.

He put his nose against it, and then looked at Logie. Trust was in his eyes and affection; but there was inquiry, too.

"My poor lad," said James, "we both remember."

THE END

NOTES

These notes draw on numerous sources. Among the works consulted most, and to which specific reference is made below, are the following:

William Ferguson, *Scotland 1689 to the Present* (Edinburgh: Oliver & Boyd, 1968); refs are to the pbk. ed., 1978.

James Holloway, *Patrons and Painters: Art in Scotland 1650-1760* (Edinburgh: Scottish National Portrait Gallery, 1989).

William Allen Illsley (ed.), *The Third Statistical Account of Scotland*: *The County of Angus* (Arbroath: Herald Press, 1977).

Violet Jacob, *The Lairds of Dun* (London: John Murray, 1931).

Bruce Lenman, *The Jacobite Risings in Britain 1689-1746* (London: Eyre Methuen, 1980).

Duncan Macmillan, *Painting in Scotland: The Golden Age* (Oxford: Phaidon Press, 1986).

Frank McLynn, *France and the Jacobite Rising of 1745* (Edinburgh: Edinburgh University Press, 1981).

Frank McLynn, *The Jacobites* (London: Routledge & Kegan Paul, 1985); refs are to pbk. ed., 1988.

Sir Charles Petrie, *The Jacobite Movement* (London: Eyre & Spottiswoode, 1959).

T.C. Smout, *A History of the Scottish People 1560-1830* (Glasgow: William Collins, 1969); refs. are to the pbk. ed., Fontana, 1979.

The New Statistical Account of Scotland vol XI: Forfar and Kincardineshire (Edinburgh & London: William Blackwood and Sons, 1845).

title Flemington The name of the central character and his family may have been suggested by the Castle of Flemington at Aberlemno in Angus, now a ruin but inhabited at the time the novel is set. According to the *Third Statistical Account*, the castle was a centre of Jacobite sympathy and was searched by government soldiers after the Forty-Five, but Jacobites sheltering there managed to escape.

page 3 Ardguys A note pencilled in the poet Helen Cruickshank's copy of the novel suggests that the house is modelled on Baldovie, near Kirkton of Kingoldrum, some 3 miles from Kirriemuir. The nearby burn would thus probably be the Cromie.

the Sidlaws Hills to the south of the Vale of Strathmore.

page 4 while the approaching middle of the [18th] century was bringing a marked improvement to country ministers as a class... 'Many ministers began to drop their primitive character of preachers and eager reprovers, and to adopt the *personae* of polite and unenthusiastic gentlemen, able to embellish God's word in an elegant address indicating to the poor the prime virtues of obedience and industry, and able to catch up the standard of Scottish culture to bear it proudly in the European Enlightenment' (Smout, p.214). It is also relevant, perhaps, that with the revival of patronage in 1712 ministers were more closely affiliated to the lairds and therefore shared their general outlook and aims (see Smout p.216).

page 5 the Court of James II of England at St Germain From 1689-1715 the deposed Stuart king, James II, his wife, Mary of Modena, and his successors, had residence at the château of St-Germain-en-Laye, outside Paris, as 'guests' of Louis XIV.

Mary Beatrice of Modena (1658-1718) was of Italian origin; her father was Alphonse IV, Duke of Modena. She was widowed when James II died in 1701.

page 6 the young Chevalier de St. George The title was conferred by Louis XIV on James Francis Edward Stuart (1688-1766), recognised by true Jacobites as King James VIII of Scotland and III of England, later known by supporters of the House of Hanover as 'the Old Pretender'.

smallpox had carried off her son This disease was quite common in the period, and carried off even members of royalty, including Princess Louise Mary Stuart, the fourth daughter of Mary of Modena, at St Germain in April 1712.

a rank Whig Originally a nickname for an adherent of the National Covenant of 1638 and thus of Presbyterianism in the 17th century, the name Whig later came to apply to Presbyterians in general; and at the time the novel is set, to supporters of the government, and of the royal House of Hanover.

She [Christian] was an Episcopalian This religous affiliation was typical of north-east Scotland at the time; Christian is atypical in having changed allegiance from the Stuarts to the House of Hanover.

page 7 himself and his community Mr Duthie is a minister of the Established Church of Scotland.

like a young David See Bible I.Sam.17. When no-one else would respond to the challenge of Goliath, the huge champion of the Philistines, David killed the giant with only his slingshot and some stones.

plunged deeper into the vernacular In this post-Union period, there was growing pressure in Scotland to speak 'standard' English, although as Violet Jacob notes in *The Lairds of Dun* 'the language of educated Scotsmen was still the language of their forbears' (p.244), i.e., Scots.

page 8 Venus goes stripped Venus, the Roman goddess of beauty and sensual love, is often depicted in art as a naked figure. The naked female figure also often denotes Truth. This links in with the novel's key engagement with questions of 'truth' and integrity.

The Pope of Rome Mr Duthie is a Presbyterian minister at a time when the Established church in Scotland was particularly austere and repressive (during the period approximately 1690-1720).

page 9 **His skin and his dark eyes hinted at his mother's French blood** It is notable that Archie is half-French. Besides reflecting the European, especially French, dimension of political conflict in this period (see Lenman, 1980), it emphasises his 'apartness' from the community and its narrow attitudes. Jacob was interested in 'outsider' figures of different kinds, as is suggested by her short fiction and some of her novels such as *The Interloper*. Archie's French blood may also suggest his passionate nature; as in some 19th-century Scottish and English fiction, many of Jacob's passionate figures have foreign blood. Violet Jacob herself lived in France for a short time as a child with her widowed mother, as an article by her, 'A Manor House in Brittany', in *Country Life*, 22 May 1920, pp.685–6, recounts.

Nemesis The Greek goddess of vengeance; personification of divine retribution.

page 12 **a square stone mansion** Almost certainly the prototype is the House of Dun, built between 1730 and 1742 for David Erskine, on an estate owned by the family since 1375, some half a mile north of the Montrose Basin (a semi-natural circular piece of water).

Lord Balnillo The estate of Balnillo is based on Dun; lands with the name of Balnillo were held by the Erskines in the past (see *The Lairds of Dun*, p.11).

David Logie based on David Erskine, Lord Dun, 13th Laird (1672-1758).

his wife Margaret The wife of the real-life David Erskine was Magdalene Riddell (d.1736). Her portrait, by Sir John de Medina, hangs in the house today, alongside that of her husband. David Erskine's portrait was painted by William Aikman (1682-1731).

page 13 **James Logie** Based on Captain James Erskine (b.1671), elder brother of David Erskine, who became a soldier serving in the 2nd Battalion of the Royal Regiment of Foot, and was gazetted to its 2nd Battalion as Ensign to Captain Peter MacIlvain at Breda in 1694. His regiment was in the Netherlands at the beginning of the War of the Spanish Succession. He fought with Marlborough at Blenheim (i.e. for the English against the French), and for the Jacobite cause in 1715. He died in his 70s, where and when exactly is unknown. The name 'Logie' appears in Violet Jacob's ancestry (John of Logy, the 7th Laird, d.1591). Logie is also a name attached to several places in the locality of Dun, such as the parish of Logie Pert.

the Scots Brigade in Holland The Scots Brigade had its origins in Dutch need of assistance against the Spanish Duke of Alva in the 1570s; three regiments of Scots were recruited and paid by the United Provinces, although swearing allegiance to the Scottish Crown. The Brigade tended to attract Whigs rather than Jacobites; indeed the Brigade had played a key role in the expulsion of James II. Like his prototype, James Logie is a soldier of Jacobite conviction; like James Erskine he is also presumably a professional mercenary soldier.

page 14 **an elder** Senior figure in the Presbyterian church and in Church of Scotland congregation.

the Den of Balnillo Again, suggested by 'the Den' to the west of the House of Dun.

page 15 Basin of Montrose...River Esk Still known as such, the Basin is a semi-natural 2000 acre tidal basin into which the river South Esk flows. It is now a local nature reserve.

page 17 his long chin Archie's appearance may have been suggested by the traditional Erskine family 'long chin', illustrated in family portraits at the House of Dun.

page 19 wore his own hair i.e., rather than a wig; this is significant, suggesting Archie's naturalness.

an agreeable ready-made figure from a selection brought forward by a painter Sir John de Medina (1659-1710), who painted David and James Erskine, came to Scotland to paint the family of Lord Leven, and 'some time either at the end of 1693 or the beginning of the following year Medina travelled north to paint the heads on his already completed bodies'; see James Holloway, *Patrons and Painters: Art in Scotland 1650-1760* p.38. De Medina was born in Brussels of a Spanish father, but lived first in England, then in Scotland, where he remained for nearly 20 years. His oval portraits of the Erskine brothers hang in the House of Dun.

Van Dyck Sir Anthony van Dyck (1599-1641), b. Antwerp, the great Flemish artist, court painter of Charles I, known especially for his portraits.

page 21 gean-trees Wild cherries. Compare Jacob's description of the House of Dun: 'Ancient gean trees in its eastern approach once held their twisted arms in fantastic angles against the winter skies till spring covered them with a sheet of white and they passed again through summer into the flaming red of their autumn leaf. But age and the gales have taken their glory now and left only a few battered trunks; and even the great beech trees are fast thinning in the storms of these later years' (*The Lairds of Dun*, p.3). There is also a poem, 'The Gean Trees', in Jacob's *Songs of Angus* (1915).

Montrose...like some Dutch town The Third Statistical Account comments that Montrose has many houses 'with their gable ends to the street, the entrance being down a close. No doubt they reflect the influence of the architecture of the Low Countries with which Montrose had in its heyday as a port much intercourse' (p.477).

page 22 whose acquaintance I had laid so many plots to compass Archie is a government spy. According to Frank McLynn, 'From the very first days of the small exiled court's existence at St Germain-en-Laye, espionage played an important part in the story of the Jacobites' (*The Jacobites*, p.171).

skirts...highlandman A reference to the wearing of the plaid or kilt by male Highlanders.

page 25 road...Brechin There is a modern road connecting Montrose with Brechin, a cathedral town in Angus of ancient origins (see also note to page 94).

page 26 Skirlin' Wattie This character's name makes reference to the 'skirling' or shrill sound of the bagpipes he plays.

page 27 the head of Falstaff, the shoulders of Hercules Sir John Falstaff, Shakespeare's celebrated comic character (*Henry IV* parts I and II, and *The Merry Wives of Windsor*), although a lusty and lying braggart, is nevertheless engaging. Hercules is the mythical Greek hero of fabulous strength.

Kilmarnock bonnet A broad flat coloured woollen bonnet, the traditional headwear of the Scottish peasantry. This becomes an emblem of Wattie himself.

pages 27-28 The Tod A song called 'The Tod' (fox) appears in David Herd's collection *Ancient and Modern Scottish Songs* (1776), but the version here is very different and appears in Violet Jacob's own volume of poetry *Songs of Angus* (1915). The fact that 'tod' can suggest a sly, cunning, untrustworthy person is significant in this context.

page 29 Logie Kirk This also appears in *Songs of Angus.* 'Logie Kirk' is probably the old church of Logie, close by the North Esk river in the parish of Logie Pert, near Dun.

Auld Nick Old Nick, the devil.

page 32 the curious mixture of awe and contempt accorded to charlatans and to those connected with the arts See also p.34, 'this womanish trade'. From the beginning of the novel, this is shown as a society hostile to the visual arts, which are criticised or sneered at by the minister, the soldier, and now the servants. Presbyterian Scotland is thought by many writers to have been especially antipathetic to creativity in all forms; in the early 18th century the influence of the Covenanters was still possibly felt, even in the Episcopalian north east. According to William Ferguson, 'They suppressed the "profane arts"...and their anti-art tradition took root' (p.100). Note, however, that music and dancing still flourish among the ordinary folk.

to ride the circuit The circuit is the journey made by a judge in a particular district to administer justice (there were three circuits in Scotland). 'The Scottish judges travelled their circuits in the saddle and even when road-making had so far improved as to permit of wheel traffic, the custom went on, it being thought a part of judicial dignity to "ride the circuit"' (*The Lairds of Dun,* p.246).

page 37 Charles Edward Stuart (1720-1788), son of James Francis Edward Stuart, grandson of James II; popularly known as 'Bonnie Prince Charlie', or, to his enemies, as 'the Young Pretender'.

the glamour of a manner 'glamour' here recalls the old Scots meaning of magic or enchantment.

he had extorted the wonder of an east-coast Scotsman by his comprehensive profanity Suggests that his oaths were impressive, the implication being that east-coast Scotsmen were not easily shocked.

page 38 the Pleiades, Taurus, Orion The Pleiades is the great cluster of stars in the constellation Taurus, particularly the seven larger ones, so called by the Greeks. Orion is the constellation pictured as a giant hunter with sword and belt, surrounded by his dogs and animals, named after the giant hunter of Greek mythology.

the North Port The old north entrance or gateway to the town.

stairhead The landing at the top of a flight of stairs, often that leading from one floor of a building to another.

page 39 Glenfinnan the Stuart standard was raised at Glenfinnan, at the north end of Loch Shiel, on 19 August 1745, over an army of some 1300 clansmen.

Cope Sir John Cope (? - 1760), the Government commander-in-chief in Scotland, defeated by the Jacobites at the battle of Prestonpans on 21 September 1745.

Lords Elcho, Balmerino, Kilmarnock, Pitsligo David Wemyss, Lord Elcho (1721-1787), Commander of Prince Charles' Life Guards; Arthur Elphinstone, Lord Balmerino (1688-1746); William Boyd, 4th Earl of Kilmarnock (1704-1746); Alexander Forbes, Lord Pitsligo (1678-1762). Pitsligo remained in hiding for many years; Balmerino and Kilmarnock were beheaded after the Act of Attainder was passed in June 1746.

Lord George Murray (1694-1760), Lieutenant-General of the Jacobite army.

page 40 the landing of those French supplies At this point the French were still supporting the Stuart cause, although their ships had difficulty in bringing the aid needed. See Frank McLynn, *France and the Jacobite Rising of 1745*, Chapter V, especially pp. 109–112.

David Ferrier 'Ferrier was a merchant of Brechin, who owned the farm of Unthank in the neighbourhood', according to *The Lairds of Dun* (p. 250); he was made Deputy-Governor of Brechin, and 'it is said that the Prince did this on the advice of James' (p.250), i.e. James Erskine, the model for James Logie.

Lord Ogilvie David, Lord Ogilvy, titular Earl of Airlie (1725–1803), a Jacobite who fought with Prince Charles at Derby, Falkirk and Culloden.

the village of Edzell Edzell is a parish in the north east of Angus, in which is situated the village, known for its castle. Beyond it lies Glen Esk.

page 41 The government sloop-of-war *Venture* Modelled on a vessel in reality called the *Hazard* which was, according to McLynn (1981), 'one of the very few maritime successes gained by the Prince's followers' (p.111). It was later renamed 'Le Prince Charles', for obvious reasons. For a full account of the events fictionally narrated here, see *The Lairds of Dun*, pp.249-257.

fishing village of Ferryden Now more developed.

page 42 the New Wynd...the Happy Land Real places in Montrose, the former still there in modern times. According to a review of *Flemington* in the *Montrose Standard and Angus and Mearns Register* 26 January 1912, p.12, 'There are local names and references that will strike strange chords in the hearts of the score of centenarians still surviving in Montrose, such, for example, as that famous residence in the New Wynd, so appropriately and satirically designated by our pious forefathers as "The Happy Land"'.

page 47 campaigning by the walls of Dantzig Probably with Field Marshall Lacy (see also note to page 62), who, commanding Russian troops in January 1734 in Danzig, besieged Stanislas, a contender for the Polish throne, on behalf of the claimant who later became Augustus III, after the death of Augustus II in 1733.

Inchbrayock Island The name of a real place, from the Gaelic *Inchbraoch*; more commonly known today as Rossie Island. A church or chapel formerly stood on this piece of land, which was also the parish burial ground.

page 50 'risp', or tirling pin A vertical serrated bar fixed on the door of a house, up and down which a ring is drawn with a grating noise, acting as a door-knocker or bell.

page 55 the parks The enclosed grounds of the estate; 'parks' can also denote 'fields' or 'farmlands'.

page 59 the unsuccessful rising of the '15 The Jacobite rising of 1715 which was a failure. The Earl of Mar, John Erskine (who drew up original plans for the

House of Dun) proved a vacillating and uncertain leader in Scotland, the Battle of Sheriffmuir was inconclusive, and the campaign in England was disastrous.

page 62 **Marshal Lacy...War of the Polish Succession** (see also note to p. 47) Peter Lacy (1678-1751), a Russian Field-Marshall. Born in Limerick, he had fought as an Irish Jacobite and in the French service, and entered the service of Czar Peter the Great of Russia around 1698/9. He commanded Russian troops in the War of the Polish Succession, already alluded to, which took place after the death of Augustus II in 1733. Augustus III was recognised in 1735-6.

bloody campaign against the Turks...and again in Finland The war of Russia and Austria against Turkey took place 1735–39; Russia acquired parts of Finland between 1721 and 1743.

page 63 **Holland with the Scots Brigade** See note to page 13.

the Dutchmen can paint them too An allusion to the Dutch skill at painting flowers and still-lifes.

page 64 **Diane...The Conte de Montdelys...Frenchman** It is interesting that Diane is French; apart from again reflecting the Scottish-French connection which figures in the novel generally, this may also illustrate a 19th-century association between romance/passion and 'the foreign', especially the French. The setting of the love and marriage of James and Diane in Holland echoes Stevenson, who sets the love interest in *Catriona* in that country.

page 65 **I was a Protestant** Somewhat unusual for a Jacobite.

a rich Spaniard Spain controlled parts of the Netherlands (now roughly Belgium and Luxembourg) 1579 to 1713.

Breda a town in Noordbrabant province, south west Netherlands.

page 66 **Bergen-op-Zoom** A town in Noordbrabant province, south west Netherlands. It was much fought over and came under the control of various powers from the 16th century onwards, including the French and Spanish.

page 73 **Muir of Pert** Old name for a tract of land in the area of Dun.

page 74 **Parental authority** See Smout: 'On such things it is always hard to generalise, but people later often referred with wonder to instances of domestic sternness in the early part of the century...' (p.269). Also: 'Marjorie Plant has produced a certain amount of evidence to show that child-rearing in the upper classses became less authoritarian in the course of the eighteenth century, but she believes it was still stricter in the first half of the century in Scotland than in England' (pp. 92–3).

feu sacré sacred fire (French).

page 81 **the Queen and her favourite, Lady Despard** Lady Despard seems to be a fictional creation of Violet Jacob's; she may be based on such historical figures as the Duchess of Powis who was 'among the most faithful of the Queen's ladies, and was greatly in her confidence. Burnet describes her a " a zealous managing Papist"' (Edwin and Marion Sharpe Grew *The English Court in Exile: James II at Saint-Germain* (London: Mills & Boon, 1911) p.270); she died, however, in 1691. Other possible models for this character are Lady Middleton and Lady Melfort, both Irish ladies at the Court of St Germain. Many Irish Jacobites did, in fact, flee to St Germain for refuge after the fall of Limerick.

page 82 Christian's affinity with savage creatures... This implies a view not unlike Stevenson's as suggested in, for instance, *Dr Jekyll and Mr Hyde*, of the closeness of the civilized and the 'savage'. The influence of Darwin may show here.

page 85 Magdalen Chapel A burial place at the eastern end of the parish of Brechin.

page 87 the tune of the East Neuk of Fife Popular Scottish dance tune named after the so-called 'East Neuk' of Fife; 'neuk' can mean either 'corner' or 'projecting point of land'.

page 88 the passion for dancing Dancing in this period was denounced by the General Assembly of the Church of Scotland, along with sabbath-breaking and merriment at weddings and funerals (see Smout, p.214). In Scott's *The Heart of Midlothian*, Effie Deans defies her father and the Cameronian community by taking pleasure in dancing. In many modern Scottish novels dancing appears to suggest, amongst other things, the enduring nature of traditional culture; see, for instance, Catherine Carswell *Open the Door!* (1920), Lewis Grassic Gibbon, *Sunset Song* (1932), Jessie Kesson *Another Time, Another Place* (1983) among others.

page 94 Brechin...its ancient round tower Brechin is one of the oldest towns and ecclesiastical centres in Scotland. The round tower stands at the south-west corner of the Cathedral; it is reputed to have been built in the late 10th-century, and is of Christian Irish origin.

page 95 'Dinna bring yon brute near me!' cried Wattie Wattie's fear of the horse is ironically significant given the nature of his fate (see pp.198-200).

page 96 Captain Hall According to *The Lairds of Dun*, the commander of the boat in the historical incident was one Captain Hill.

page 108 Dial Hill A real place mentioned by Jacob also in *The Lairds of Dun*, p.253.

page 122 a French frigate According to *The Lairds of Dun*, this was 'La Fère'.

page 124 Leith The port serving Edinburgh.

Aberbrothock An old name for the town of Arbroath; 'Aber' means 'at the mouth of', while 'Brothock' is the name of the river which enters the sea at this place.

page 127 Skirling Wattie...spirit of the national poetry of Scotland A figure akin to Wandering Willie in *Redgauntlet*, Madge Wildfire in *The Heart of Midlothian*, Edie Ochiltree in *The Antiquary*, and numerous other characters in Scott's novels.

page 134 Monrummon Moor Montreathmont Moor on the modern map, referred to here by the common local name.

page 145 Wattie Caird 'Caird' is a surname; it also means 'tinker, vagrant'.

page 146 Forfar Small market town in Angus, south west of Brechin, and in the eighteenth century a royal burgh of considerable antiquity. It was the capital of the county of Angus, which was also known as Forfarshire.

the muir o' Rossie Rossie Muir (or moor) is an area of land lying to the south west of Montrose Basin.

page 148 he might have sung 'The Tod' This song would have had more relevance to the situation, or at least appealed more to Madam Flemington, herself a schemer.

pages 149-150 My love stood at the loanin' side This appears with the title 'The Jacobite Lass' in Jacob's *Songs of Angus* (1915).

page 151 the Old Town of Edinburgh The area of the city stretching from the Castle down the Royal Mile to Holyrood Palace. Plans for the 'New Town' were already afoot in the first half of the 18th-century, but building did not begin until later in the century.

the Nor' Loch The North Loch, artificially created in 1460, was partly drained in 1763, and filled in, forming what is now Princes Street Gardens.

Lady Anne Maxwell...his kinswoman This character does not seem to be based on any particular individual in Violet Jacob's own family history, but may draw on other 18th-century figures.

lands Tenement buildings, often many storeys high.

page 152 Lord Grange James Erskine, Lord Grange (1679-1754), a kinsman of David Erskine of Dun, secretly intrigued with Jacobites though professing loyalty to the Hanoverian dynasty.

page 153 Lord John Drummond's troops Lord John Drummond (1715-47) was the brother of the Duke of Perth. He was sent by Louis XV to Scotland with his Scots Royal regiment and arrived on the east coast in early December 1745.

girls wore white roses The white rose was a Jacobite emblem.

page 157 Mrs Cockburn Possibly based on Alison Cockburn (1712?-1794), best known for the words of one version of the song 'The Flowers of the Forest'. Of the Rutherford family of Selkirkshire, she moved to Edinburgh and married an advocate, Patrick Cockburn. She was related to, and friendly with, Walter Scott, and counted other outstanding writers and thinkers among her circle. Described by Scott as having 'talents for conversation', she supported the Whig government in the 1745 Rebellion.

page 166 Hyndford's Close The name of a narrow passage giving entrance to a tenement at 34 High Street (south side), in Edinburgh. In 1742 the home of the Earl of Selkirk was here.

page 171 Culloden The Jacobites, led by Prince Charles Edward Stuart, were defeated disastrously in the Battle of Culloden at Drummossie Moor, on 16 April 1746, by government troops under the command of the Duke of Cumberland. According to Ferguson, 'Much more than Jacobitism died at Culloden. Thereafter the disintegration of the old Highland society, already advanced in some quarters, was accelerated' (p.154).

Cumberland's soldiers William Augustus, Duke of Cumberland (1721-65), third son of King George II, commander of the army which defeated the Jacobites at Culloden.

the country smelt of blood Atrocities were committed against many fleeing Jacobites and Highlanders after Culloden by both English and Scottish soldiers. There were also high-level reprisals, with many Jacobite leaders being executed. See Petrie, pp.392–401.

page 172 Kingston's Horse Cavalry regiment.

John Campbell of Mamore John Campbell, 4th Earl of Loudoun (1705-1782) supported George II in the Highlands, 1745-6. The Campbells as a clan were strong Whig supporters.

page 173 Ruthven, in Badenoch Those at Ruthven included Lord George Murray, the Duke of Perth and Lord John Drummond. See Petrie, pp.388-91.

page 175 Highland army's retreat to Scotland The shift of focus here to Christian Flemington is accompanied by a jump back in time to before Culloden: having reached Derby in December 1745, with the intention of conquering England, Prince Charles, the Jacobite leaders and their Highland army turned back, doubting support from English Jacobites and the French.

the Battle of Falkirk Having laid siege to Stirling Castle, a Jacobite army led by Prince Charles clashed with government troops under General Henry Hawley at Falkirk and defeated them.

the despatch of the Duke of Cumberland to the north After the Battle of Falkirk, Cumberland went north to take over from Hawley.

page 178 battle of Falkirk and the siege of Stirling Castle See note to p.175.

page 179 Glen Esk...Loch Lee Glen Esk lies in the large northern Angus parish of Lochlee, which derives its name from a loch in its western end. The area is Highland in character, surrounded by the Grampian mountains and 'Braes of Angus'.

No place had a darker record During the 1745 Glenesk was a Jacobite stronghold. The leading Jacobite Ferrier, based here, raised over 200 men in the surrounding glens; in response Cumberland sent a force of 300 men who were only just dissuaded from burning the Glen entirely. After Culloden, Government troops searched the area for Jacobite fugitives.

page 180 Ligonier's regiment Jean-Louis Ligonier, British government Field Marshal (1680-1770), born in France, went to Dublin 1697; fought many battles, including Blenheim (1704) under Marlborough.

page 182 Glen Clova from Braemar Glen Clova is another of the Angus glens. A pass leads over the hills from here to the town of Braemar in Deeside.

the little German general Cumberland, as 'this fat young third son of George II' (David Daiches *Charles Edward Stuart: The Life and Times of Bonnie Prince Charlie* (first publ. London: Thames & Hudson, 1973; ref. here to pbk. ed., Pan, 1975, p.185), came of the royal House of Hanover, and was thus of German origin.

page 184 Huntly Hill Name of an actual hill, so-called because Alexander Gordon, Early of Huntly, won a battle here in the 15th century.

page 191 King Geordie's business i.e., King George II (reigned 1727-1760).

page 194 dancin' wi' George, but he's takin' the tune frae Chairlie i.e., appearing to act for King George II, but working for Prince Charles Edward Stuart.

page 198 the beggar...his dislike and fear of horses Besides the obvious explanation for Wattie's fear, there is perhaps a symbolic dimension; the horse in Christian art is held to represent courage and generosity.

page 199 the dog the outcast of the East Violet Jacob had lived in India from 1895 to about 1900, and knew that dogs there and in some other countries were often scavengers of the streets who struggled for survival, but were held in contempt.

page 207 you mighty hunter before the lord Nimrod was so called; see Genesis 10. 9. The meaning seems to be 'a conqueror'.

page 212 Peterhead Fishing port on the east coast of Scotland, north of Aberdeen.

page 215 But you have not restrained your belongings Christian means Balnillo's family, ie. James.

page 221 the Duke of Cumberland See note to p.171.

Holyrood House At one time residence of Scottish royalty, in Edinburgh; subsequently the official Scottish residence of British royalty. Cumberland did, in fact, stay here at this time.

sick of Scotland On leaving his command in Scotland in July 1746, Cumberland expressed his feelings toward Scotland in a letter to the Duke of Newcastle:

> I am sorry to leave this country in the condition it is for all the good that we have done has been a bloodletting, which has only weakened the madness, but not at all used [it up] and I tremble for fear that this vile spot may still be the ruin of this island and of our family.

Quoted by Alexander Murdoch, *The People Above: Politics and Administration in Mid-Eighteenth Century Scotland* (Edinburgh: John Donald, 1980), p.35.

page 224 the mists of the Edinburgh smoke Edinburgh became known in the eighteenth century as 'Auld Reekie' (Old Smoky).

page 225 I hate old women According to Bruce Lenman in *The Jacobite Cause* (Glasgow: Richard Drew, 1986), 'Duncan Forbes of Culloden... had earned the epithet of "old woman" from Cumberland for urging that royal brute to show clemency in his hour of victory...' (p.116).

page 233 pollarded beech Beech tree that has been cropped, had its top cut off. The image recalls that of the maimed beech-tree at Balnillo near the beginning of the novel. In the second edition of 1915 this has been changed to a lime-tree; perhaps Jacob wants to emphasise the different location of Holland at the end.

the ace scrawled with the picture of the sentry The drawing has various kinds of significance. The playing card suggests the role of 'Chance'; the ace, of course, is usually a winning card, so that there is a sad irony here.

Glossary

The following lists words mainly in Scots; most lexical items and forms that might be unfamiliar have been explained, even at risk of obviousness. The primary works consulted are:

Mairi Robinson (ed.) *The Concise Scots Dictionary* (Aberdeen: Aberdeen University Press, 1985). Reference to the edition of 1987.

The Scottish National Dictionary 10 vols., eds. William Grant (1929-46) and David Murison (1946-76) (Edinburgh: The Scottish National Dictionary Association Ltd).

a in places denotes 'I'
a'body everybody
abune above
ae a certain; the same
aff off
agin against
ahint behind
aifter after
auld old
awa' away
aweel expression used to introduce a remark
ay yes
aye all; always
bairn child
bannock a round flat cake usually made of oatmeal, barleymeal or peasemeal, baked on a griddle (iron plate for baking over fire)
bawbee a coin
ben inside; in or towards the inner part of a house
bide remain, stay, await
billy close friend, comrade
billies fellows, lads
brae bank, hillside
braw fine, splendid
brocht brought
bubblyjock turkey-cock
burn stream
ca' pull
callant fellow
cankered ill-tempered
canna cannot
canny careful
cattle can denote birds and beasts in general as well as cows
chanter double-reeded pipe on which bagpipe melody is played
claes clothes
clortie dirty, muddy
close entry to a tenement; the passageway giving access to the common stair

clour blow
clout piece of cloth, a rag
coup (verb) to upset, overturn
couthy(ier) (more) agreeable; comfortable
cowp to fall over, capsize
crack talk, converse, gossip
cry on to call on (e.g. for help); summon
deave provoke, goad; annoy with noise or talk; perhaps also (p.147) 'drive'.
deef deaf
deevil devil
dicht wipe, rub clean
dinna don't
deuk duck
div do
doag dog
dod an interjection, exclamation
doited foolish, silly
doon down
dunt knock, blow
fa' fall
fash trouble, bother (oneself)
feared o' afraid of
feared for afraid for
fechtin fighting
fegs emphatic exclamation: 'indeed!'
fell fierce, ruthless, remarkable; extremely, very
feyther father
fine very, well
foo how
forbye besides; in addition
frae from
fut foot
gae(d) go (went)
gang(ing) go(ing)
gar to make (do something)
gear goods, possessions
gie(s) give(s)
gin if
gloamin' twilight
greet(in') cry(ing)
grat cried, wept
guidwife mistress of a house or place
hae exclamation; have
haud hold
haud awa' keep away
havering speaking nonsense; talking in a foolish way
havers nonsense
heed head
henches haunches
heuch exclamation
hoots exclamation expressing dissent, impatience etc
ilka every
in-by in (e.g., *come inby* to come from outside to inside)
I'se first person emphatic present form
ither other (*ither body* anybody else)
jalouse to suppose, suspect
kaipit met
keek glance, peep
ken/kent know, knew
kennel channel, street gutter
kyte stomach
lairn learn, teach
lands tenements
lang long (*lang-leggit* long-legged)
lauch laugh
lane (*eg. her lane)* alone
leddyship ladyship
leein' lying
liket liked
loonie young lad, fellow
loanin' part of farm ground or roadway; milking place, common ground; grassy track
losh interjection
loup leap, spring, hop about
lugs ears
mind remember
mirk darkness, twilight

mony many
mou' mouth
muckle big, great
muir(land) moor(land)
na no
naebody nobody
nane none
near doon nearly down
nor than
onything anything
oot out
noo now
oxter armpit
piece piece of food, snack, e.g., bread
poke bag, pouch
pouthered powdered
pow head
pruifs proofs
pucklie a small amount
puir poor
roof-tree main beam or ridge of a house; figuratively, house or home
roogit pulled
sabbin' sobbing
sair sore; hard
sang song
schule school
sconce screen
sic such
shelt shelty, pony
shieling roughly-made hut, hovel, small house
skelloch shriek, scream, cry
skirlin' (making a) shrill sound
sma' small
sodgers soldiers
soucht sought, looked for
soutars shoemakers, cobblers
speer(in') ask(ing)
stocks chaps, blokes
sweer unwilling, reluctant
swiggit go with a swinging motion, rock, jog
syne directly after, next, afterwards; since
tak take
tell't told
terrible terribly
thole suffer, endure, tolerate
tod fox
tolbooth town prison, jail
toon town
twa two
Tuts interjection suggesting expostulation or disapproval; 'nonsense!'
tynt lost
unchancy dangerous, threatening
vera very
wa' wall
wad would
waefu' woeful
wantin' lacking
waur (nor) worse (than)
weans children
weicht weight, amount
wha who
whatlike what sort of
whaur where
whiles sometimes
whisht be quiet! shut up!
wi' with
wiggie wig
wrang wrong
wumman woman
wynd narrow (often winding) street, lane
ye you
yer your
yersel yourself
yestreen yesterday
yon that or those (over there)

FLEMINGTON

VIOLET JACOB

Edited by Carol Anderson

TO EDZELL
(9KM NORTH OF BRE
HUNTLY
HILL
BRECHIN
RIVER SOUTH ESK
TO GLEN CLOVA
N
ABERLEMNO
A
KIRRIEMUIR
MONTHREATH
MOOR
FORFAR
5 K
5 MI
TO SIDLAW HILLS